PRAISE FOR THE NOVELS OF DONNA KAUFFMAN

The Big Bad Wolf Tells All

"Deftly spun . . . with a zippy style."
—*Kirkus Reviews*

"Humor and suspense . . . fans of Laura Zigman will enjoy this book."
—*Library Journal*

"All bets are off in this witty page-turner, just perfect for a day at the beach." —*Pages*

"Ms. Kauffman's exceptional talent makes her a versatile author whose venture into the Chick Lit genre will garner her a host of new fans to go along with those of us who have followed her career through many of the romance subgenres. Each new venture has become a rousing success and this one is no different."
—*Rendezvous*

"For a story that will touch your heart, tickle your funny bone and leave you begging for more, I highly recommend *The Big Bad Wolf Tells All.*"
—*Romance Reviews Today*

Featured Alternate Selection of the Doubleday Book Club, Literary Guild, Rhapsody Book Club, and Venus Book Club

Alternate Selection of the Book-of-the-Month Club

The Charm Stone

"I was totally charmed by *The Charm Stone*. Josie and Connal are delightful characters, sexy and fun to read. The touch of magic in the book seems to shine through every page, touching everything on the island. The secondary characters are original and interesting. Give me more." —Linda Howard

"From the fantastical to the erotic, this author never disappoints her readers with her spectacular repertoire of wonderful stories. *The Charm Stone*'s plot captivates while the endearing characters charm us. Combine this with sultry passion and this one becomes a keeper to be read over and over again." —*Rendezvous*

"The book's charm lies not only in the titular jewel but in its playful plot, lively Scottish island setting, appropriately funny writing style and eccentric cast of characters—which includes a gang of senior citizen surfers. With its well-balanced combination of humor and romance, this summer beach read is certain to make waves." —*Publishers Weekly*

"What a story it is! Donna Kauffman's talent knows no bounds. *The Charm Stone* is pure entertainment for the romantic at heart." —MyShelf.com

"Ghost sex rocks! Fun and sensuous."
—*Romance Reviews Today*

"Donna Kauffman outdoes herself in this tender, emotional and passionately intriguing tale."
—*Romance Fiction Forum*

The Royal Hunter

"Kauffman . . . anchors her readers with sensuality, humor and compassion." —*Publishers Weekly*

"I love Donna Kauffman. What a gift to create whole worlds, making them as real as the one we exist in now. This book is the perfect combination of romance, suspense and science fiction. If you're unsure about science fiction, cut your teeth on this one. You'll love it! I certainly did." —*Old Book Barn Gazette*

"Another winner . . . for masterful plotting, for suspense, for romance, for an intriguing visit to another time and place, for an all-round good read, I highly recommend *The Royal Hunter*."
—*Romance Reviews Today*—Jane Bowers

"Filled with magic, passion and danger, *The Royal Hunter* is a mind-pleasing read of high adventure and passionate romance. The characters are complex and fascinating. [It] is a complex, multilayered tale filled with sparkling dialogue, captivating narrative and some of the most wonderful characters you'll ever want to meet. If you're looking for a story to entertain you and take you to an enchanted time and place, far from the troubles of today, grab a copy of *The Royal Hunter*—it's guaranteed to please fans of all genres with its mix of fantasy, time travel, magic and romance."
—*Romance Reviews Today*—Terrie Figueroa

"A tremendous royal tale."
—*Midwest Book Review*

Your Wish Is My Command

"Whimsical and sexy!" —Jennifer Crusie

"This charming and magical romp takes genie folklore and twists it into three love matches. Just the right novel to lift up your spirit and bring a smile to your face."
—*Romantic Times*

"*Your Wish Is My Command* is a wonderful tale full of whimsy, unforgettable characters, and a delightful plot."
—*Rendezvous*

"A swashbuckling, sexy-as-sin pirate in modern-day New Orleans? That's enough to perk the interest of any romance reader; add a sensuous nature, a natural affinity for romance, and a wicked sense of humor and you have Sebastian Valentin. Sebastian is probably one of Kauffman's most delicious heroes to date. *Your Wish Is My Command* is a unique twist on the genie theme . . . [*Wish*] is filled with all the passion and emotion Ms. Kauffman's fans have come to expect. For a thoroughly enjoyable read, with a hero to die for, I recommend *Your Wish Is My Command!*"
—*Romance Reviews Today*

Legend of the Sorcerer

"Donna Kauffman has written a spellbinding romance that is so hot it near sizzles when the pages are turned . . . this is a really superb book to curl up with and get lost in." —*New Age Bookshelf*

"Ms. Kauffman's contemporary paranormal, with stirrings of romance and adventure dating back to the days of King Arthur, will tantalize your imagination . . . a truly multidimensional book, with real-life characters, this is a must-read for anyone who likes paranormals."
—*Old Book Barn Gazette*

"Donna Kauffman always knows how to set our hearts afire with passion and romance. Ms. Kauffman is fast becoming one of the top paranormal authors. Her fantastical tales always deliver simmering passion, sensual love scenes, an intriguing plot fraught with danger, adventure, and the unexpected which will leave readers anxiously awaiting the next enthralling tale from this immensely talented author. *Legend of the Sorcerer* deserves keeper status. Ms. Kauffman's originality knows no bounds, as she's proven time and again." —*Rendezvous*

"Ms. Kauffman is an amazing talent. Her strong plots are rivaled only by her strong and passionate characters. Readers are quickly brought into her stories and are held there captivated until the final pages."
—*Affaire de Coeur*

"Ms. Kauffman masterfully choreographs a wonderful love story with an intriguing plot." —*Romantic Times*

The Legend MacKinnon

"Adventure, passion, magic and betrayal are the bright threads Donna Kauffman weaves together to create the legend of three brave warriors out of their time."
—Nora Roberts

"Intricately woven together . . . This one kept me spellbound. A terrific read." —*Rendezvous*

"Sensuous love stories that will heat up the atmosphere wherever you are and some laughs to tickle your fancy. Excellent writing by an author who has mastered the craft of creating characters to die for. . . . *The Legend MacKinnon* is pure magic."
—*The Belles and Beaux of Romance*

Also by Donna Kauffman

The Cinderella Rules
The Charm Stone
The Royal Hunter
Your Wish Is My Command
Legend of the Sorcerer
The Legend MacKinnon

Yours 2 Keep
With Kay Hooper, Marilyn Pappano,
Jill Shalvis, and Michelle Martin

The Big Bad Wolf Tells All

Donna Kauffman

A Dell Book

THE BIG BAD WOLF TELLS ALL
A Dell Book

PUBLISHING HISTORY
Bantam trade paperback edition published June 2003
Dell mass market edition / May 2004

Published by Bantam Dell
A Division of Random House, Inc.
New York, New York

This is a work of fiction. Names, characters, places, and incidents either are the product of the author's imagination or are used fictitiously. Any resemblance to actual persons, living or dead, events, or locales is entirely coincidental.

Library of Congress Catalog Card Number: 2002034479

ISBN 0-553-58458-8

Manufactured in the United States of America
Published simultaneously in Canada

OPM 10 9 8 7 6 5 4 3 2 1

This book is dedicated to my sister Kathy,
who knows a thing or two about sheep and wolves.

A special thank-you to Karen Solem and Liz Scheier.
Your enthusiasm made all the difference.

The Big Bad Wolf Tells All

TANZY TELLS ALL

So I watched my best friend get married for the third time this weekend and I got to wondering ... does the wedding bouquet lose its matchmaking karma if the marriage doesn't last? Not that I want to be matched. Well, not for more than a few really good hours. A day or two, tops. In fact, they can keep the bouquet. Why risk it, you know?

I bring this up because it was at that moment that my life-altering epiphany occurred. It all happened when I attempted to dissolve into the crowd of bouquet-catcher wannabes ... and made the startling discovery that there was no crowd to dissolve into. In fact, upon further observation, I realized I was the only person at the crowded reception old enough to vote and not yet on social security who met the requirements for the Bridal Bouquet Rodeo.

How did this happen? How, at age twenty-nine, did I, Tanzy Harrington, officially become the Last Bridesmaid in a social circle filled with Till-Death-Do-Us-Parters?

Today's query ... is honeymoon sex really that fantastic? Or do the participants merely indulge in that fantasy as a way to deal with the dawning realization that this is the only kind of sex they will have ... ever again?

1

Tanzy waited in line, wondering for the umpteenth time how Sue had talked them into this. "A good cause," she muttered beneath her breath, thinking again that she could just as easily have written a check. And saved herself the embarrassment.

"What size?" the gentleman behind the counter asked her when it was finally her turn.

"Six-and-a-half, heel or sandal. Seven, flat or sneaker."

The guy merely looked at her. Apparently having a sense of humor was optional when being considered for a job at the Bay Area Bowl-O-Rama.

"Seven, please."

The man grabbed a pair of what had to be the most hideous shoes she'd ever seen and slid them across the counter. And she was going to pay him for the privilege of wearing those? She sent a silent apology to her feet. "I don't suppose you have something in a Jimmy Choo?" Again with the blank stare. "Never mind." She gingerly picked up the two-tone baby puke green and yellow leather lace-ups and scanned the lane monitors for her name. *Charity event or no charity event, Sue was going to owe them all big time for this little outing,* she thought as she settled in their team's alcove.

She watched as other people began filling up the lanes and waited for the rest of the gang to show up. Dreading it almost as much as she dreaded the thought of bowling for dollars. She glanced at her watch. She still had time to run for it.

Then Rina swept in. Rina never did anything as pedestrian as walk, or even stroll. She swept. Tanzy stood and waved to her, then promptly tripped over the mile-long shoelaces. Needless to say, Tanzy wasn't a born sweeper.

Rina stepped down into their little seating area and pulled her into the one-armed almost-hug that didn't muss hair or makeup. "I'm back," she announced with her typical élan. "The world can resume rotating on its axis now."

Tanzy breathed a dramatic sigh of relief. "Thank God, the wobble was getting to me." But she was glad Rina was home from her honeymoon. Of their group, Rina was her closest friend and confidant. Not to mention constant fodder for her biweekly column. Fortunately for Tanzy, and her readers, Rina found her occasional starring role amusing and flattering.

"What in the hell are those?" Rina was pointing to the baby puke leather rafts on Tanzy's feet.

"Schizophrenic shoes only a manic-depressive could love?"

Rina wrinkled her nose. "I'm getting depressed just looking at them."

"So, I assume the islands were fabulous," Tanzy asked, almost desperate to change the subject. It was bad enough she had to wear the shoes. She drew the line at talking about them. "Your tan is perfect." As were Rina's sleek dark hair, designer clothes, lean model's body, blah blah blah. Of course, Rina carried it off in a "Doesn't everyone look this fabulous?" kind of way that made her hard to hate. Despite her own unmanageable brown curls, the occasional freckle, and eyebrows that were a bitch to keep plucked right, Tanzy managed not to be jealous most of the time. Generally that was when she wasn't wearing baby puke shoes.

"It was utter paradise, Tanz," Rina responded, flashing a sly smile. "We even managed to leave the yacht to see some of them."

Rina's third husband was Garrison West, aka Old Money. Fifteen years her senior, he barely looked it. And thanks to a team of plastic surgeons and personal trainers he probably never would. Rina was convinced the third time was the charm. Tanzy hoped she was right. More likely it was the disposable investment capital that was the charm. Given how Rina loved to dispose of her husbands' capital, it just might be a match made in heaven.

Rina looked around the place. "How did we let her talk us into this again?"

"Beats the hell out of me. I'm thinking we just put a check on the little scorekeeper pedestal thing here and head to the lunch counter, whereupon we can stuff our faces while we watch other people make asses of themselves."

"You know how I feel about consuming grease. But . . ." She glanced at Tanzy's shoes and shuddered. "I'm thinking you have a plan."

Tanzy laughed. "Just be thankful you missed out on Mariel's 'lunch with the girls' last week." *She* shuddered just thinking about it.

"Please don't tell me she dragged you all to The Carousel. Again."

Tanzy nodded, expression grave. The Carousel was the latest place for new parents to take their vaunted offspring. Amongst other things, it featured booths carved out of actual carousel horses, and pipe organ music. "And you weren't even there to save me. I had circus nightmares for a week."

"Oh God," Rina whispered in mock horror. "Not creepy clown sex."

Tanzy nodded. "Sue and I were the only ones who made it. I have no idea what happened to Sloan. So it was really above and beyond the call."

Rina covered her hand. "I'll make it up to you. In fact, I'm planning a little dinner party and—"

Thankfully Tanzy was rescued from what she knew was coming next, the Special Dinner Invitation for Single Friends, when Mariel and Sue showed up.

Mariel was the other newlywed of the group, married seven months earlier. She was also in the middle of her third trimester and regarded her impending parenthood like a new religion.

"Let's hope she doesn't preach to the unbelievers today," Tanzy muttered to Rina, before stepping forward with a broad, teeth-clenched smile on her face. "Hi, guys. Sue, we need to talk."

"Now, Tanzy, you promised—"

Mariel ignored their little byplay, she was too busy waving something. "I have sonogram pictures!" she sang.

Rina caught Tanzy's eye and they shared a silent groan. "Great," Rina managed, then turned to Sue, who was still in her tennis club duds. "Oh, bowling alley shoes are totally going to make that outfit."

"Ha, ha. Come on, guys, it will be fun."

They all just looked at her, Mariel included, who had by now looked at the lanes, and Tanzy's feet, and was covering her belly protectively. Whether it was to shield her unborn child from the reverberating sounds of pins crashing against one another, or the horror of the shoes, Tanzy had no idea.

"How did the lesson go?" Mariel finally asked Sue, always the polite one.

Sue smiled, all flashy white teeth and those little crinkles at the corners of her eyes that only seemed to make her look perkier. Sunny Sue, as Tanzy always thought of her. Married to Perfect Paul. They were a disgustingly happy couple, the Barbie and Ken of Presidio Heights. "Well, let's just say I'm not going on the WTA tour anytime soon," Sue said with a laugh. "But I beat the snot out of Paul's sister, so that was a bonus."

So she was Barbie with an attitude. Which was why Tanzy hadn't slit her wrists when she discovered she'd been paired with the perennially Sunny Sue as dormmates, freshman year at UC Berkeley.

Tanzy clapped her hands together. "Whaddya say we write big checks to Sue's charity and go eat greasy fries while watching other people in bad footwear throw heavy things."

Sue didn't even try to put up a fight. She knew when she was outnumbered.

They all shuffled up to one of the booths and managed to wedge into their seats. Poor Mariel barely fit. But she didn't complain. Tanzy suspected she knew everyone wasn't exactly thrilled with her choice of lunch venues last week.

"Wonder where Sloan is," Mariel said.

"Probably ringing up some impossibly huge sale," Sue said. "She could sell sculpture to a homeless person."

"Or maybe she's home screwing Wolfie's brains out," Rina added with a sly grin. "She did say Wolfgang was being very apologetic and trying hard to please her. *Hard* being the operative word, I'm sure."

Sue smacked her hand. "You newlyweds, all you ever think about is sex, sex, sex."

"And you and Paul don't?" Rina shot back.

Sue sighed. "Not like we used to." She grinned easily. "But no complaints from me. After five years, you don't expect fireworks."

Tanzy tried not to blanch at the very thought. No fireworks? After only a couple of years? She wasn't as perkily optimistic as Sue, but she thought her friend should have at least a little problem with that scenario.

Sloan came in then, with her postmodern slinky body draped in her postmodern slinky black clothes, and her postmodern waif haircut framing undeniably flushed cheeks. It occurred to Tanzy that Sloan might be the only person who could actually pull off bowling alley shoes.

"Ding, ding, ding," Rina said, tapping her glass with her spoon and motioning to Sloan. "I think I picked the winning scenario." She leaned over and dropped her voice. "Of course, if I had a husband like Wolf trying to get back in my sexual good graces, do you think I'd be here given the choice?"

Tanzy just rolled her eyes. Despite the moniker, Sloan's husband, Wolfgang, was not exactly alpha material. At least, to look at him you wouldn't think so anyway. He was a soft-spoken artist from Austria; tall, thin, with wispy blond hair. His best features were his enigmatic blue eyes. Tanzy happened to know that was what drove Rina crazy. She had a thing about hooded eyes.

Of course, apparently so did most of the young female models Wolf used for his sculptures, as Sloan had recently found out the hard way. But they'd been trying to patch things up. Tanzy wondered if reconciliation sex was better than make-up sex.

"You have Garrison West III," Mariel said a bit plaintively to Rina, as if getting married made a woman oblivious to all other men. Which apparently was the case for Mariel. "Wealth, power, good looks. What could you possibly see in Wolfgang?"

Rina just gave her a look. "Honey, all the family money in the world can only compensate for so much."

Tanzy and Sue shared a look, then nodded sympathetically. Mariel simply looked perplexed.

"Never mind," Rina said. "And don't worry, I'm perfectly happy with Gar." She stood and gave Sloan the one-armed semihug as she found their table. "So, I guess you only need dessert now, huh?"

Sloan gave her a spare-me look, then quickly seated herself. "So," she motioned to the room at large, "we're not bowling for dollars?"

"We're writing checks and eating fries for charity," Tanzy said, enjoying the uncharacteristic flush on Sloan's otherwise pale face. At least someone was having great married sex. All hope wasn't lost.

When Tanzy first met Sloan, during her rebellious underground period in college, Sloan had been the sexiest unfeminine person Tanzy had ever seen. A retro beatnik who wore Doc Martens and black clothes, with a haircut so short it defied being called a style, sporting multiple body piercings way before it was a trend, Sloan still managed to exude a slinky sexy vibe.

She was still all those things, but falling in love with Wolfgang had softened something in her. Yet rather than ruining her edge, it had somehow only made it more complex and mysterious. Tanzy had been worried about her friend lately, though, so it was good to see her smiling again.

"You have to try new things, Tanz," Sloan said with a far more characteristic world-weary sigh. "Sometimes that means pulling yourself out of your comfort zone."

"Yes, well, her comfort zone apparently only extends to charity events where you can wear designer footwear," Sue said, and they all laughed.

Tanzy often thought about the odd dynamic of their little social circle, but she'd long since given up trying to figure out why it worked as well as it did and just accepted that it did. And thanked God for it. She didn't know what she'd do without them. In fact, it was worrying about her new role in that dynamic, as the last single woman of the group, that had dominated her thoughts in the two weeks since Rina's wedding.

She'd worried that everything would feel different today, with all of them finally together. That she'd feel somehow excluded sitting amongst her married friends.

"So, I take it things are . . . improving?" Rina pointedly asked Sloan. "Wolfie's keeping his clogs parked under your bed exclusively now?"

Leave it to Rina to not pull any punches, Tanzy thought. But she was surprised when, instead of looking happy and smug, or faintly irritated at having her marriage put up for dissection in a bowling alley diner, Sloan flushed with what looked more like embarrassment.

She managed to pull it together and lift a slim shoulder in an absent shrug as she slid the plastic-coated menu across the table. "We're working on it."

Rina shared a brief questioning look with Tanzy, but mercifully let the topic drop.

Mariel, never comfortable with any hint of social unrest, piped up. "Want to see my sono pictures? You can see his little penis!"

Tanzy almost swallowed the ice in her water glass. Rina burst out laughing, and snagged the picture from Sue, who, blue eyes twinkling, gestured with her fingers to demonstrate just how well hung unborn baby Benjamin was going to be.

Sloan kept looking at her menu. "No thanks, I've already seen enough tiny penises for one day."

Everyone fell silent, even Mariel. Sloan looked up at everyone's thinly veiled expressions of pity and sighed. "Sculptured. One of Wolf's current projects."

"Not a self-portrait, I hope," Rina said.

Sloan looked back to her menu. "Hardly." Then she snickered and ruined the whole unaffected artist vibe.

Rina raised her water glass. "A toast."

Everyone lifted their glasses. "To?" Tanzy asked.

"Baby penises, sculptured penises, and hot honeymoon sex regardless of penis size!"

Everyone laughed. Nobody cared that people were staring. When they were together, they were in their own little world.

Orders were placed, greasy french fries and burgers were dutifully delivered.

"I can't believe we're going to eat this. And we're not even throwing heavy things to dilute the guilt," Sue commented.

Sloan simply looked at her. "Think of food as art instead of fuel," she said in her snootiest art gallery tone, then leaned back and smiled. "Of course, I could definitely go for an impressionist milkshake to wash down these fries with. I'm starving."

Rina laughed. "Postorgasmic munchies, huh?" She gave a reminiscent sigh. "We had Gar's personal chef with us on the yacht. It was marvelous what that man could do with a white sauce."

Mariel grimaced. "That's not very romantic. Having other people all around on your honeymoon."

"Sweetie," Rina said, "it's not like the boat steered itself, either. Trust me, his staff is very well trained."

"I guess it has to be, considering," Sue murmured wickedly, making both Tanzy and Sloan snort.

Mariel shot a worried look at Rina, but she merely nodded and smiled knowingly. "Motion makes all the difference, trust me. And the boat rocking didn't hurt matters any."

Sue sighed. "Honeymoon sex. I remember every minute of ours. Seems a lot longer than five years ago."

Tanzy chewed thoughtfully, then waved her next fry. "It wasn't like you two hadn't, you know, already."

"Yeah," Sue said, "but there's something about being married, having just said your vows—"

"I know what you mean," Mariel chimed in dreamily. "Chuck was wonderful, the whole time we were in Paris." She giggled. "I don't even remember much about the city."

"I guess not," Rina said, "considering you're due almost exactly nine months from your wedding night."

"I already explained about that." Mariel rubbed her tummy, her eyes taking on that glazed born-again look. "But, you know, like I've already said, maybe the condom was supposed to break. I have to believe it was for a reason."

No one bothered to disabuse her of her fantasy. Once she'd gotten over the shock, she'd been deliriously happy.

"And Chuck is still wonderful," she chirped. "I mean, as hard as he works at the agency, he still manages to call me several times a day to see how the baby and I are doing. So what if sex isn't the same? That will come back at some point."

She didn't look as certain as she sounded, Tanzy thought, wondering how she really felt about it. It was bad enough to think about only having Chuck for the rest of her life, the least she should want is prime Chuck. And Rina, with Gar the Immeasurable. Sloan would only have Wandering Eye Wolfgang. And Sunny Sue and Perfect Paul's sex life had been reduced to missionary position twice a week, with the occasional Wild Sex Sunday—as Sue had termed it—when they got out of going to her mother's for dinner after church.

Tanzy tried not to shudder at the thought of having Designated Sex Days. Her friends seemed happy enough with their marriages, and that was all that mattered. As long as they didn't try to shove marital monogamy down her throat just because they'd opted for it.

Where other women might be feeling really inadequate and self-consciously available at this point, Tanzy's marital clock had yet to start ticking. Much less her biological one. Maybe they never would. And, even with thirty looming on the immediate horizon, she wasn't all that worried about it.

The thing was, while she was happy for her pals, she didn't envy them, didn't yearn to have a spouse of her own. She liked being single. Embraced it. She was one with her singlehood and wore it like the honorable badge of independence she liked to think it was. Only at that moment, with everyone around her sharing the knowing looks of the married, her beloved independence took on a whiff of something that smelled a lot like loneliness. Or would be as they continued to build on their experiences and she was slowly left outside the conjugal circle.

"Bullshit," she muttered under her breath, then braced that resounding proclamation with a fortifying sip of chocolate shake. She'd leave this restaurant and her stable of married friends and reenter her single-woman world with renewed gusto, relieved that she'd been the smart one, the one who'd escaped the surrender of all things wild and daring.

Otherwise known as settling.

Not just settling *down*, but settling period. Settling for the "right man," aka the "good provider."

She wasn't ready for the good provider yet. She was still busy enjoying the good weekender. Rina labeled the guys Tanzy dated as bad boys, renegades. Tanzy knew better. They were both of those things and more. Which was precisely what made them desirable. All about the moment and not about the future. And when *she* was their moment? Well, let's just say Hallmark doesn't make *that* card.

"Earth to Tanzy," Rina said, nudging her foot.

"She's working," Sue said. "I can always tell. She gets that vacant stare and forgets the rest of us exist." She waved her hand in front of Tanzy's face, then propped her elbows on the table. "Which is rude, considering without us she'd be out of a job."

"Yeah, then she'd just have to dip into that trust fund Millicent has all set up waiting for her," Mariel said. "Tanzy, I still think you're crazy for not taking your great-aunt's—"

"Please," Sue begged, "let's not go there again. She's explained until she's blue in the face why her stubborn independence is more important than fabulous wealth."

Rina ignored both of them. "Speaking of Millicent the Magnificent, how did your annual Thanksgiving dinner together go?"

Tanzy gladly latched on to Rina's lifeline. Mariel saw no reason why Tanzy shouldn't just set herself up in the ostentatious tradition of her Harrington forebears. Mariel, who couldn't wait to snag successful Chuck and begin nesting. Tanzy looked to Rina. "About as usual. She asked how work was going, conned me into doing some shopping with her—a terrifying experience, let me tell you—showed me the latest techno-wizard stuff she'd had installed in Big Harry, and that was pretty much it."

"Speaking of Big Harry," Sue interrupted, referring to Harrington House, the gated manse Tanzy's great-aunt lived in, "remind me to talk to you later."

Tanzy nodded, knowing what it was about. Mariel's baby shower. Sue was planning it and had decided to have it at her club, but she suspected Rina had mentioned something about having it at Harrington House, and rather than argue, Sue likely wanted to go with the flow.

Rina sipped her after-lunch coffee, then said, "So, any more notes from your 'Tanzy Tells All' soul mate?"

"Very funny," Tanzy said. "I should never have mentioned him. He's harmless. I just hit delete."

"So you've gotten more of them," Sue said, leaning forward. "Maybe you should send them to Martin."

"The delete button is pretty effective and a lot easier than listening to one of my editor's lectures on celebrity stalkers."

"A lecture you probably need to hear," Mariel said, looking worried.

"Martin's been distracted enough lately, he doesn't need me piling this on. Besides, I already got one from Millicent, thank you very much."

"You told Millicent?" Rina laughed. "I bet that went over well."

Tanzy knew her great-aunt admired her independence, but she could be rather controlling given an inch. "I was dazed from marathon shopping. It slipped out. Honestly, though, I think I'd know if it was a real threat. Can we drop this?"

Rina slid a considering glance Tanzy's way. "Sure, if you'll tell us what part of this discussion will show up in the next column."

"Yeah," Sue laughed, "baby penises or hot honeymoon sex?"

How to be happily single when all your friends are married, Tanzy thought, forcing a smile. What she said was, "I guess you'll have to read it and find out."

Does married sex always become routine?

Is it because Fun Single Guy is now Married Guy with a Mortgage? Is responsibility, not familiarity, the real culprit that kills exciting sex? Or is it more basic than that? Maybe a Fun Single Guy who marries is turning in his wolf badge for one stamped Sheep. He's become one with the herd. The herd being all the other Dependable, Responsible Guys with a Mortgage. And Sheep Sex, no matter how you position it, will never live up to Wolf Sex.

2

Killer column today, Tanz. I like the new tangent you're off on with this whole wolf/sheep thing."

Tanzy adjusted her phone headset and hit save. "Thanks, Martin. Let's just say I was inspired."

"Apparently. Who knew there were so many Last Bridesmaids out there?"

She snarled silently. "Yeah, I'm thinking of forming a club." It had been three weeks since her first column commenting on her wedding reception epiphany. Apparently she wasn't, in fact, the last bridesmaid on the planet. She'd heard from a whole slew of them in the past ten days. Hordes. Somehow, she didn't feel any less alone. "Listen, I'm getting Saturday's column in early. I've got that Single Santa radio thing this afternoon, then this month's stint on the *Barbara Bradley Show* is taping tomorrow morning. They're doing a Single at Christmas show, too." Hoo boy. She could hardly wait.

"Well, chat up this wolf/sheep thing you mentioned in today's column. I have a hunch it's going to play big with the serial solos out there."

She grinned. "Says the ultimate sheep."

He chuckled, not bothering to refute it. "Hey, at least I'm the herd leader." Martin was managing editor of *MainLine*, the hottest online magazine since *Salon* and home to the controversial, much-talked-about "Tanzy Tells All" column for the past four years. Despite being on the cutting edge of publishing technology, though, Martin was still a guy pushing fifty, with a wife of twenty-five years, two kids in college, and a nice house in Pacific Heights. He might as well have "good provider" stamped on his vanity plate.

"Yeah, you da Big Sheep, Marty."

"Hey, herd member I might be, but that doesn't mean I don't have a little howl left in me, you know. Did I tell you about the new ride?"

Tanzy rolled her eyes. What was it with middle-aged men and their toys? "Yes, Marty. Candy-apple red, leather interior, nice wheel package, and a whole herd of horses under the hood."

"Beats a herd of sheep," he shot back, and she heard the pride of toy ownership in his voice. Or maybe it was just sports car lust.

She did understand a little about that. But you were supposed to drive fast cars when you were young, right? Marty was a sedan guy. Marty had probably been born a sedan guy. Which is what made this whole toy car thing so weird. For him, anyway. Portly, balding, prescription glasses . . . nope, she couldn't picture him flying down the highway, top down, singing "Born to Be Wild." She gave a little shudder at the visual. Well, he'd just sent his last kid off to college this fall, so maybe that explained it. She'd heard empty nests made people do odd things. God only knew what Mrs. Marty thought about her husband's new fixation.

"Any time you want a test drive, you let me know, okay?"

She rolled her eyes. "Will do. I'll talk to you after I'm done taping Friday, let you know how it went." She clicked off and stared at her laptop screen, scanning back over what she'd already written, then began to type.

So, is that why we L.B.'s aren't willing to settle for sheep like the rest of our social circle? Sheep Sex aside, what's wrong with a man who puts family first, who maintains a steady job, has college funds set up for his kids, and builds that nest egg for his retirement? Member of the workaday herd, never straying.

Solid, dependable Sheep Guy.

Why can't I love Sheep Guy?

For me, it's all those wolves. They distract me from the sheep. Wolf Guy. Always on the prowl. Totally alpha. Not interested in being domesticated. Not only would he not turn himself in for a sheep badge, he's never even heard of it.

So, what is it about these men that makes my heart speed up in a way no sheep ever has or ever will? I don't want to tame them. I certainly don't want to take them home to Mama. No. I am the original self-sufficient, independent, and proud-of-it-dammit woman, and I want Wolf Guy to drag me back to his lair and have his way with me. Repeatedly. But that's all I want from him. That wild rush, that feeling of being taken over by something stronger and more powerful than I am.

Maybe that's it. I'm responsible for everything else in my life: my home, my career, my social circle. I don't have to ask permission to do anything, don't have to make any compromises unless I want to. I do what I want, when I want. And I like it that way. I intend to keep it that way.

I just need Wolf Guy to rip the reins from my hands from time to time and allow me to give up my grip for a little while. Let's face it, Sheep Guy will never do that. And until I don't need to have my reins ripped anymore, I can't imagine joining the herd on a permanent basis.

So where does that leave me? A serial solo, straying from the herd every time Wolf Guy comes sniffing around, that's where. And I'm sorry to all you permanent herders out there, but at the moment, I'm thinking that's fine by me.

"Take that, sheep lovers," she muttered, and saved. She logged on and zapped the column to Marty in an email before she could reconsider what she'd written. After all, it wasn't called "Tanzy Tells Some of the Things." Whatever she felt was what she wrote. No holding back, no worries about offending anyone. She was the universal bared soul of the single woman, put on display for all the world to read. Take it or leave it. Fortunately for her, a whole lot of people, both men and women, took it. They accepted it, rejected it, debated it, heatedly at times . . . and propelled the writer of it to a certain level of fame and fortune.

She scanned her email, a dry smile curving her lips as she skimmed down the potpourri already queuing up for today's entertainment. The fame part, even at her relatively insignificant level, had its pros and cons. She got date offers, marriage offers, offers to be saved by various clergy, offers to be fixed up with sons by various mothers, with brothers by an assortment of sisters, and with all-around good guys by well-meaning married matrons. And that was usually before ten A.M.

The flip side was that she also got the occasional Extreme Fan. Some aimed at messing with her person in a violent manner, some litigiously eyeing her bank account. Of course, the combination of being seen on television, heard on the radio, and accessible via the Internet was bound to bring out the less stable segment of society. She figured it went with the package and didn't take any of them seriously.

"Ah, there you are again." SoulM8, her latest Extreme Fan, had landed yet another missive in her inbox. Tanzy debated whether reading it would entertain or disconcert. This guy was particularly insistent, if not particularly original. His rap was that he was her savior, the one who would love her for all time, thereby relieving her of all her single-girl angst.

She smiled faintly as she skimmed past his most recent proclamation of eternal devotion. He didn't seem to understand that single-girl angst paid her rent. Besides, she wasn't really angsty. She was merely reflective. In a very public kind of way.

Forgetting about SoulM8, she clicked instead on an email titled "Howling 4 U." Her latest column, in which she'd only briefly debuted her "men can be put into two categories, wolves and sheep" theory, had been published on the *MainLine* site for less than an hour.

"And they're already crawling out of the woodwork," she murmured, a satisfied smile curving her lips as she picked up her second Coke of the morning. "It's going to be an interesting day." She read with great amusement the letter from a guy who professed he was an actual wolf. Of the werewolf variety. He was certain her column spoke directly to him and wanted to mate with her during the next full moon. Which—lucky her!—was the very next night. She hit delete and had just opened "Baaaahed Boy" when her phone rang.

"Tanzy dear, we need to talk," the caller said without preamble.

Tanzy almost choked when her soda went down the wrong way. "Aunt Millicent!" She quickly put the can down and pulled off her headset in favor of the old-fashioned phone. She found it was generally better to be gripping something substantial and, better yet, unbreakable, whenever her great-aunt deigned to call. "What a nice surprise."

"How nice of you to say, even if you don't mean it. I always wonder where you got that trait, since it certainly wasn't from your mother. Now stop gripping the phone like a drowning woman clinging to a lifeline. I've only got a few moments before the car arrives and we've got much to discuss."

"We do?" Tanzy found it best to merely go along with Millicent, as there was really no point believing she'd ever be in control when her somewhat eccentric great-aunt was involved. Okay, "somewhat" was her being nice again. And she hadn't gotten that trait from her mother. The only things she'd gotten from Penelope were green eyes and a distinct mistrust of long-term commitment.

"Yes, dear, we do. It seems my dear friend from Philadelphia, Frances Dalrymple, has suffered a decline in her health. She's asked me to come visit for what might become a rather extended stay. We went to Vassar together, as you might recall."

"Mmm," Tanzy said by way of reply, a sound she'd learned to use rather judiciously when conversing with Millicent.

"My, what a time we had. Young women in pursuit of higher learning were so rare in our time, you see. We were vital, so alive." She sighed wistfully.

"Real visionaries," Tanzy said, hoping Millicent didn't think she was being patronizing. She really did admire her great-aunt. In fact, Millicent had been a major force in how Tanzy had shaped her life, and what she didn't admire she was in awe of. But she really didn't need a replay of "Millicent Harrington: The Vassar Years." She knew them by heart. "I'm sure she'll enjoy having your company. Do you want me to stop by and water your plants or collect your mail?" This was merely a courtesy offer, as Millicent was loaded and had a houseful of people to look after every last detail of Big Harry. But she also knew her aunt enjoyed it when Tanzy played the doting grandniece.

Other than Tanzy's absent mother, Millicent was the only Harrington left. And although she wasn't exactly anyone's version of a cuddly, maternal figure, she also didn't pretend to be anything other than what she was: a woman who oversaw her inherited holdings, business interests, and God knew what other investments with a steely eye and a firm grip. At eighty-two she was a more intimidating figure than ever.

"Actually, in a manner of speaking, yes, I do require your assistance," Millicent was saying.

"I—I beg your pardon?" Tanzy had let her gaze wander back to her list of incoming email. "What did you say?"

"The holidays are fast approaching and my household staff has been given leave to be with their families. As I will likely be out of town through the beginning of the year, I didn't see any reason not to extend their vacation. My holiday gift to them for all their hard work."

Millicent might run her home and business interests like a general overseeing war maneuvers, but she was also generous to a fault with those she valued.

"That's really lovely of you, Aunt Millicent." No one called her Millie. Or they only did once. "But won't you need at least a skeleton staff to oversee business matters?" She asked this somewhat tremulously. As Millicent's only remaining heir—Penelope long since having been written off—Tanzy knew she should probably be more aware of exactly what might pass her way when Millicent cashed it in. Considering she'd never so much as dipped her pinky finger into the Harrington businesses and had less than no idea what sort of empire Millicent had truly amassed during her tenure, this would be no small undertaking.

But Millicent had never broached the subject with her, and cowardly or not, Tanzy had been happy to leave well enough alone. She hoped she'd luck out and her great-aunt's lengthy list of philanthropic and charitable endeavors would be the beneficiaries when the time came.

Millicent chuckled. It was a rather rusty, somewhat scary sound. "Actually, I do have someone staying on to handle certain business matters. I've given my regrets to the round of social events. My annual endowments have already been taken care of. I'd appreciate you cleaning up after yourself when you choose to cook, and I'm sorry, but you'll have to manage on your own with laundry and other such things. I'm certain you're well used to taking care of those matters on your own."

"Laundry? Cooking?" Tanzy was nonplussed. "If I'm just dropping by to check the house and water plants and such, I won't be needing to cook or wash, but I—"

"I'm sorry, I should have made myself clearer. With everyone gone but Riley, I would feel better if I knew someone was staying under the roof. Someone I could trust."

"But you travel all the time."

"For a week to ten days, yes. But this will probably be most of December and a good part, if not all, of January. And what with the winter weather on the East Coast, one never can entirely depend on airline travel."

Tanzy opened her mouth, but she had no idea what to say.

"I know this is asking a great deal of you. And I don't mean for you to spend every waking minute here. I realize you're a busy woman with quite the hectic schedule yourself. But you can bring whatever you need with you. I've had your rooms and private office all spruced up for the holidays, so writing your column here won't be a problem. Riley is fairly unobtrusive, but I've directed him to do whatever is necessary to make your stay comfortable."

"Riley? What happened to Margaret?" Margaret was her aunt's longtime personal secretary and valued confidant.

"You've not met him, but he's trustworthy. Still, I'll feel so much better knowing you're here as well. Margaret's about to become a great-grandmother, so I've given her extended leave, too. She's staying on with her son and his family in Ohio until the new year."

"That's wonderful, really. So who is this Riley and when did you—"

"Here's Wainwright with the car, darling. I've got to run."

"But Aunt Millicent, I—"

"I can't tell you how much this means to me, Tanzy dear. I'll contact you once I arrive in Philadelphia and see to my lodgings. I've no idea if Frances intends to put me up, but like as not I'll be staying at the Belleview as usual. If anything comes up, you can simply contact me there and leave a message. In the meantime, Riley can handle any other questions you might have. He's expecting you by dinnertime tonight. If that's not convenient, please let him know as soon as you can. Ta ta, darling."

Tanzy was left staring at the dead receiver. "Ta ta, my ass," she muttered as she hung up. She'd been hornswoggled by a master. "Nothing about this is convenient. Which you knew when you called me. Oh-so-cleverly on your way out the door." Tanzy had half a mind to call this Riley person and tell him he was on his own, and not just for dinner tonight.

And who was he anyway? Millicent was scrupulous about who she hired, but she still didn't trust new employees easily. Tanzy didn't remember her talking about him before, either. But to be honest, when her aunt started off on a tangent involving business matters, Tanzy's eyes tended to glaze over and her mind wandered. For all she knew, Riley had been in Millicent's employ for years.

She sighed and stared unseeing at her computer screen. Her aunt rarely asked anything of her. Actually, other than their annual Thanksgiving dinner together, she never did. Which made this whole thing even weirder. Millicent certainly didn't seem to be losing any of her faculties, mental or otherwise. But the fact was, she had asked, so it must be important to her. And despite her annoyance at being so expertly maneuvered, Tanzy owed her too much not to agree.

So, mentally rearranging her schedule, she picked up the phone again and dialed Big Harry.

Early holiday season query:

If you're doing a radio show with Santa and discover, after jokingly sitting on his lap, that the North Pole is more than a geographic location ... well, just how far down in hell will you go if you lay Santa? On the upside, he said I'd been a very good girl. On the downside, however, he only comes once a year.

3

"Helloo? Anybody home?" Tanzy's voice echoed down the central hallway and up the massive winding staircase as she let herself into Harrington House, a High Victorian Queen Anne with all the appropriate turrets, towers, and excessive ornamentation that was popular in the late eighteen hundreds, when the house was built.

Millicent was quite proud of Big Harry, as Tanzy called it when Millicent wasn't around. It was one of the few houses that had survived the great earthquake and fire after the turn of the twentieth century. Fitting, Tanzy thought with a smile, seeing as her great-aunt, a pillar of society, was somewhat of an architectural treasure herself, still sturdy and erect, facing a new century with nary a lapse in strength or conviction.

She quickly punched in the security code so the alarm wouldn't go off. Millicent treasured her heritage, but was also quite the techno-geek, enjoying all the latest gadgets. Tanzy sighed as she searched for the new pressure-sensitive light pad Millicent had raved about over Thanksgiving.

"Hello?"

Her own voice echoed back. So, where was this Riley person anyway? No one had answered her call earlier, so she'd simply planned on arriving around six and hoping for the best where dinner was concerned. Of course, it was closer to seven now, but her early morning Single Santa radio show had turned into a late afternooner with Single Santa. Single at Christmas she might be, but that didn't mean she had to jingle her own bells.

She sniffed the air, but no heavenly scents were wafting down the hall. Apparently she'd missed dinner. She tugged her cell phone out of her purse as she nudged her overnight bag with her toe, scooting it to the base of the stairs. She stroked her hand over the highly polished newel post. How many times had she slid down that banister, she wondered, still tempted every time she set foot in the place. It would be a little rough at the moment, what with the fresh pine garland woven with berries and other assorted stuff Tanzy had never learned the names of. It was barely December, but Millicent prided herself on her holiday décor. She always had a crew in the day after Thanksgiving, which had been the last time Tanzy had been here, bailing out early that morning as the first flotilla of vans and trucks had pulled up out front.

They'd done a masterful job as always, she noted, finally finding the pressure pad. Faux gas lamps sprang to life, softly illuminating the front parlor. She'd take her bags up later; first she wanted to see this year's pageant of excess. Humming "Jingle Bells" under her breath, she wandered the length of the room. Every year she assumed Millicent couldn't outdo herself. Why, she had no idea, as her aunt always accomplished what she set out to do.

Tanzy punched the speed dial code on her phone for Hunan Palace, then leaned down to inspect the intricate white iris ikebana arrangement on the sideboard. Each room, including the powder rooms, would have its own holiday theme, complete with coordinated color scheme and tastefully accessorized tree. It was enough to make Martha Stewart multiorgasmic.

Apparently the front parlor had been tagged Deluge of Doves or something, given the countless delicate little white birds flitting amongst the bows of the slender Douglas fir. The color scheme for this room was a blinding, yet ever-so-tasteful winter white. Even the rug and furniture had been replaced or re-covered. Millicent was nothing if not a slave to detail.

"Hunan Palace. May I take your order?"

Tanzy fingered one softly feathered dove and spoke without even having to think. "Kung Pao Chicken, as hot as you can make it, two spring rolls, extra rice. Delivered please." She gave directions, then tucked the phone away as she continued to wander the length of the front room. She made it to the center, then stopped dead and stared straight up, completely awed. The chandelier had been transformed, each crystal drop having been painstakingly replaced with hundreds of intricately cut crystal snowflakes.

"Well, damn. You da man, Aunt Millie," she declared reverently.

"I thought no one dared call her anything but Millicent," came a startlingly deep voice from the doorway. "That is, when they aren't addressing her as Ms. Harrington, or Madame H."

Tanzy spun around to find a tallish, somewhat lean man standing just inside the arched entrance to the room. *Rangy*, she thought, was a better term to describe him. Although somehow that didn't quite suit the rest of the image. *Rangy* indicated a certain edginess. This man was more ... generic. Generic charcoal-gray suit, made of generic cloth, styled in a generic cut, not ill-fitting, but not tailored, either. Nice enough black leather shoes, sturdy yet manly. Tanzy had always held that a man could be judged by the thickness of his soles. The thinner the soles, the thinner the character.

Average soles, she noted, with just a hint of thickness.

Interesting. Hair was styled in Generic Barbershop. Dark, not wavy, not overly straight, worn just a fraction too long. Somehow it looked more bookish than rakish on him. Although that might have been due to the thick, wire-rimmed glasses. All in all, not bad, really. For a sheep.

Well, except for that voice. Definite high wolf quotient on the voice. Maybe he should think about radio. Or phone sex.

She looked back up at the chandelier, hiding her amusement. "I'm Tanzy, Millicent's grandniece, and I only call her Millie when she's three thousand miles away." She glanced back at him, surprised to find he'd closed the distance between them. *Stealth quotient moderate to above average,* she thought. She'd have to remember that. She stuck her hand out. "I don't believe we've met. I assume you're the infamous Riley?"

He didn't react to the attribute, but simply delivered a perfunctory, somewhat cool-handed shake, barely grasping her fingers. Not the kind of grip that pinned a woman to the bed. Ah well.

"Riley Parrish," he said. "I'm sorry I wasn't able to greet you at the door."

He offered no other excuse and Tanzy didn't ask for one. She didn't need a watchdog, companion, or a hovering pseudo-host. Apparently he didn't aspire to be any of those things, either. Perfect. They should get along just fine. "I wasn't sure about dinner, so I ordered in Chinese. I'll be glad to share." She paused, gave him a not-so-innocent half smile. "That is, if you can handle the heat."

Not so much as a flicker of testosterone.

"Helen left several dishes prepared," he said. "I missed your message—"

"I didn't leave one."

He merely nodded. "So I thought I'd wait until your arrival to arrange dinner."

She wished she could see his eyes, but the reflection of the illuminated snowflakes danced across the lenses of his glasses, completely obliterating her view of what lay behind them. Not that she held out any remaining hope. She supposed she should be thankful for the ear candy he provided every time he spoke. "Don't go to any trouble. I'm happy with takeout. Besides, I sort of got behind schedule this afternoon. If you're not going to join me, I'll just take it upstairs and have a working dinner."

There was a small pause as he studied her from behind his shield of snowflakes. And if she wasn't mistaken, the tiniest spike of tension crept between them. Then he inclined his head slightly and said, "As you wish. I have work of my own to keep me occupied." He turned, escaping any further inspection on her part. "I'll leave a light on in the kitchens for you in case you need or want anything later. I'm seven on your phone pad if you need me, otherwise I'll bid you good night."

Bid you good night? Who said stuff like that? He was beyond the total sheep. He was the sheepmaster, the guy who taught other sheep how to embrace their inner sheepness. He was thirty, thirty-five max. *Couldn't you at least leave me something fun to play with for Christmas, Aunt Millie?* His aloofness wasn't even tempting.

"Have a good one, Riley," she called to his retreating generic form. She couldn't even make out his backside beneath the slack fit of his jacket. "I've got an early call in the morning, so I'll be quiet when I let myself out."

He paused beneath the archway. "Early call?" How anyone with a voice like that could make a question sound so completely lifeless was beyond her. Zero intensity with this guy.

"I've got to tape this thing for the *Barbara Bradley Show*. They screwed up the schedule again, so I'm on early. I've got a few other things after that, but I'll be back by dinner if you want to give one of Helen's mystery dishes a whirl." She had no earthly idea why she'd added that last part, but Millicent had asked her to be here and the least she could do was play nice.

"That would be fine. I'll have it ready by six."

"Six it is."

He nodded and left.

"Boy, can I get the hot dates or what?" she asked the doves clinging to a spray of what looked like sugarplums. The doves stared vacantly back at her. "Might as well get used to that look," she muttered, since she'd probably be seeing it across the table for the next couple of weeks.

Riley Parrish stood beneath the stinging spray of the shower and attempted to honestly assess his début performance. When Millicent had hired him for this detail, she'd been very specific about not falling under Tanzy's "spell." Apparently her grandniece attracted men like an open flower attracted bees. Or Santa attracted elves, he thought with a wry smile. Millicent had made it clear she wanted him to be vigilant, yet maintain a certain distance.

Riley hadn't really thought that would be a problem. He was a professional first and always. But Millicent had pressed, saying if push came to shove in this situation, she didn't want emotional issues clouding the waters. He'd been on the job for less than a week and he still wasn't convinced there even *was* a situation, but he'd already wasted his breath explaining that a few emails hardly constituted a serious threat. Millicent had paid the retainer plus expenses anyway.

So, in his professional capacity as both her personal protection and private investigator, he'd done some digging on one Tanzanita Harrington—and just what the hell kind of name was that anyway?—and learned that she was well educated, self-employed, had good business savvy, and confidence out the wazoo, was aggressive both professionally and personally, and was a minor media celebrity . . . and a man-eater, by all indications. More like a Venus Flytrap—emphasis on the word *flytrap*—than a flower. But he wasn't threatened by any of it. Intrigued maybe.

That latter part had been uppermost in his mind when he'd read her column this afternoon while parked at the end of the ninth-floor hallway at the Four Seasons. Killing time while she got her holly jolly ho ho's off. He had to admit that since beginning this job and reading archives of her columns, he had come to enjoy her biweekly diatribes on the single life. He found her brash, in-your-face style refreshingly candid. He admired people who didn't feel the need to apologize for their opinions. Even if he didn't completely agree with hers.

It was when he'd read her comment on the wolf versus sheep theory she was developing that he'd hit on a solution that would reassure Millicent . . . and make his job easier. Or at the very least, more entertaining. And he was a firm believer in enjoying his work.

Finnian Parrish, his father, business partner, and general pain in the ass, would think his idea was nuts. Which was expressly why he hadn't shared it with him. Riley had gotten them the job, hadn't he? How he ran it was his business. Not that Finn would ever even know. He was on another job, in Santa Rosa. Riley would likely have this wrapped up before Finn got back into town.

Besides, how better to go unnoticed on Tanzy's radar than to become a sheep? Of course, he hadn't really intended to do more than be wallpaper this evening. Unnoticed, background material, human white noise. Then she'd gone and flashed those expressive green eyes at him—which hadn't looked nearly so interesting on the tapes he'd viewed of her talk-show spots—and he'd found himself saying things like "bid you good night." Just to tweak her.

He flipped off the water, picturing that deflated look that had crossed her face when he'd limply shaken the tips of her fingers. *Not wolfish enough for you, sweetheart?* Grinning, he grabbed a towel and rubbed himself dry. Yeah, this assignment wasn't going to be particularly challenging, but it was likely to last a little while. At least until he could convince Millicent that her grandniece wasn't in any direct danger. So why not have a little harmless fun with it?

Besides, it would fill the Parrish coffers and get his dad off his back. Who was he kidding? He shook the water from his hair. Finn resided on his son's back, always had, ever since Riley had been named starting running back in junior high.

Riley limped a little as he strolled to the small office that was part of his suite of rooms—cushy assignment, but hey, it was the holidays, he deserved to treat himself, right?—and flipped on the laptop monitor. Between the damp Bay Area weather and all the recent surveillance, his knee was giving him fits. It was at times like this that he thought maybe his dad had the right idea after all about taking their business venture south, to warmer, more soothing climes, but he'd be the last to admit it.

After cashing in just about everything he owned to get his dad's business out of hock, Riley figured they'd do things his way for a while. And with this job coming on the heels of the Waterston job, they were finally getting somewhere. He figured Millicent would be good for at least a handful of referrals.

Still, the little daggers of pain reminded him to check online stats after he was done working. The Pioneers had a shot at the postseason this year, even though, in Riley's opinion, Coach Schilling had been nuts to take the draft pick over grabbing Harrison when he became a free agent.

But then, Riley was only a washed-up former player, so what the hell did he know? He'd been gone from the team as long as he'd been on it, having only four years in the pros before blowing out his knee in a collision on a punt return. Not enough to bank a serious nest egg, or get an on-air job announcing, much less a coaching position. Maybe at the college level, but his dad had needed him then and . . . well, here he still was.

A split screen popped up on the laptop monitor, showing views from all the security cameras and dragging his attention back to the matter at hand. Millicent had been nothing if not prompt in making the slight adjustments he'd recommended, things she should have done anyway, regardless of her grandniece being in residence. Actually, he'd been pleasantly surprised at how cutting edge her existing system had been.

He smiled, shaking his head once again at his luck. Who knew tailing Old Man Waterston's wife would lead to a recommendation for this job. Waterston was a frequent skybox guest of Pioneer owner Monk Williams and considered himself something of a football aficionado despite never having played the game himself. Riley had always thought him something of a blowhard, but hadn't exactly walked away when Waterston had called him up on business. A job was a job, after all.

He'd gotten some nice shots of Mitzi Waterston and her tennis instructor doing more than improving her topspin lob. It wasn't his fault that Mitzi had hired her own investigator and nailed her husband in a similar "educational" situation. Riley wasn't judge or jury, just the hired help. Thankfully, Howard agreed. Riley's work had kept Mitzi from taking the randy old coot for everything he had. They'd settled out of court, if not out of the papers. The media had had a field day with it.

But Riley had gotten paid. And a job rec. All in all, not a bad day's work.

In fact, he could get used to working for the *monde riche.* Sure they could be eccentric, self-important, demanding pains in the asses, but then he worked with his father, who was all of that and more. Besides, the rich not only paid well, even more important, they paid on time. Although, to be honest, he'd taken this job as much because he liked the grande dame as he had to keep Parrish Securities' income incoming.

He pictured Tanzy's amused expression when she'd discovered the snowflake chandelier. Apparently the grandniece thought Millicent was something else, too. A point in her favor, he thought as he scanned the monitor, seeing nothing out of order, indoors or out.

Comfortably naked, he sat at the desk, rubbing his knee as he flipped up another, smaller laptop. This was his own, personal unit. He typed in the code to unlock it, then logged on to his ISP. "Come on, Ernie, have something for me here, pal." A couple of clicks later, he was whistling appreciatively beneath his breath. "I owe you, man." But then, that wasn't surprising. Ernie always came through, and Riley didn't mind paying the going rate.

He was one of many connections Riley had made during his years with the Sacramento Pioneers. It was amazing what people did for a living, postfootball. In this case, Ernie was actually the father of the Pioneers' star place kicker, a retired agent who'd specialized in computer fraud, now in private consulting. Riley privately consulted him all the time.

"So," he said, highlighting the latest email, "let's see what SoulM8 is whining about tonight." He read the note, then added it to the file he'd already created. They'd started two weeks before Thanksgiving and had kept up a fairly regular pace of one after every column. Until today, when SoulM8 sent two. Still, despite the change-up, which was a flag of sorts, nothing he'd said was anything new. And not particularly threatening despite the somewhat obsessive tone.

Most celebrities got hit on by their fair share of whack-jobs. Millicent had only zoned in on this bozo because of an offhand comment by Tanzy, who apparently didn't normally share this part of her celebrity with her great-aunt. *Wonder what Millicent would think about Baaaahed Boy's rather sexually explicit note,* he thought with a grin.

But he'd explained all that, too. Ms. Harrington said she had "a feeling" about this one. Riley couldn't really fault the old dame. Tanzy was the only family she was close to, and, at her age, she was allowed to be overprotective. Though God strike him dead if his own father ever caught wind of that particular sentiment.

And if the time came when there was a distinct shift in more than just the email pattern, he'd zip the emails into a file and shoot them to another associate for analysis. Ernie was working on tracing the accounts of the sender, as he changed them often and always with bogus information, but they both agreed it was likely he worked for the service provider, which gave him greater access for spamming. Sort of like a sparky working for the fire department.

Yawning deeply, Riley decided against getting geared up over his old team and their current standings and signed off. He checked down the hall to the double-door entrance to Tanzy's rooms. No light beneath the door. All appeared quiet. Good. Time for one last round of the lower floors, then it was lights out for him. *In a bed designed by angels,* he thought with an appreciative sigh. He definitely had to consider taking on more work of this nature.

No more two A.M. surveillance crap in the dead of winter, waiting for some dumb bastard to leave his mistress's company-owned-and-paid-for shack-up because he thought his country club wife was too stupid to notice the smell of

White Orchid on his dry-cleaned shirts. No baby-sitting bratty local talent, sitting outside their thousand-dollar-a-night hotel suites, sucking down cold room-service coffee, while the spoiled inhabitants of said room were having wild, orgiastic groupie sex. Nope, he'd kiss that all good-bye in a heartbeat. Of course, working for high society wasn't always going to be like working for the Harringtons, or Howie Waterston, for that matter. But hell, just how bad could it be?

Of course, if his dad had his way, they'd be sitting in Scottsdale, Arizona, right now, preferably on the edge of some golf course. *Yeah,* Riley thought, pulling on a pair of sweats, *where I could be doing all the work and Dad could be perfecting his five iron.* He pushed away the edges of guilt that always threatened when he thought about what should have been his dad's golden retirement years . . . all financed by his only son's long and celebrated pro football career.

Finn shouldn't have banked on him, he told himself for the umpteenth time. And for the umpteenth time, it didn't make him feel any better.

Riley shoved the fake glasses on and pulled on the flannel robe he'd bought as part of his "sheep" look as well. He should have gone for the slippers, too, he thought, as his toes grew colder by the second on the marble flooring of the foyer.

He checked the lower rooms, still amazed, even though he'd been through them all already, at the very rich flights of fancy that filled them all. He even had a fully decorated tree in his bathroom, for Christ's sake.

He'd just pressed the lights off when he heard the scuff of slippers on the stairs. He could have stepped through the arched doorway and announced his presence, probably should have. It would have startled her, but there was no reason to remain hidden. And yet he did anyway. After all, he'd been tailing her all day, that's what he was paid to do. Just following orders.

He moved silently around the landing in time to see her duck down the hallway to the kitchens, in the rear of the house. However, when he didn't use this latest opportunity to step into the room on the pretext of getting a glass of warm milk—that's what sheep drank, right?—he supposed it might not entirely be Millicent's keep-your-distance instructions that held him back in the hallway shadows.

Tanzy stood in front of the massive WWE-size fridge he'd lusted after from the moment he saw it. The interior light silhouetted her jersey-clad frame. Niners, he noted, with a silent snort. Ever since Montana left, they'd been nothing but a bunch of benchwarming wannabes.

Oblivious to his mental trash talk, she studied the deep shelves, the contents of which probably rivaled Wolfgang Puck's personal fridge. Riley thought of his fridge and wondered, if he had a unit like this one, which did everything but deliver cold beer on tap from the door handle—and he wasn't too sure it didn't—would he still only have one half-empty box of Chinese carryout and two bottles of Miller inside it? Of course, if it did have the beer tap, who cared?

But right at the moment, his attention was more on what stood in front of it. Between his research and surveillance, he'd seen her dressed in everything from her fashionably hip daytime talk-show wardrobe to her young-heiress-social-set slinky stuff. So why in the hell the ratty old football jersey—team alliance notwithstanding—was the thing that got his attention, he had no idea. Probably because it was the only label he could identify on sight. Haute NFL.

She closed the door, empty-handed, and scuffed back out to the hallway. He sank farther into the shadows and slowed his breath as she passed within a foot of him. So, his covert mission had gained him a couple of new insights after all, he thought, letting his breath out in a quiet whoosh when she reached the staircase.

One: She was pretty damn picky about midnight snacks.

Two: She smelled pretty damn good.

And three: He bet she tasted better than anything inside that monster refrigerator.

He was still trying to erase that last one as he paused outside her door. One quick turn of the handle and he could talk her out of that jersey and show her all about his inner wolf.

"Be the sheep," he muttered as he slipped into his room and crawled into bed. He groaned as he sank deeply into the cloud masquerading as a mattress and reconsidered the value of gaining impossible wealth. Eighteenth-hole housing and golden retirement years aside, he'd be a happy man if he could only have this bed and the fridge downstairs.

Yet it wasn't feather down or the joys of beer on tap that chased after him into dreamland. "Baaahh. Humbug."

Why do married friends, who never meddled before saying their vows, have this genetic compulsion to fix up their perfectly happy single friends? Is it some sort of plot? There should be a law. No Special Dinners. Ever.

4

"Honestly, Rina, I can't." Tanzy pushed her sunglasses up and squinted through the blinding glare of the winter sun on her windshield. It had been a long morning already, beginning with this week's *Barbara Bradley Show* taping at the crack of dawn and ending with a screaming cell phone call from "Santa," whose girlfriend apparently hadn't been too happy when Tanzy had outed their little tryst in her column. Another downside of being the brains behind "Tanzy Tells All."

Men were afraid. Very afraid.

She smiled. Considering Santa hadn't exactly filled her stocking, his girlfriend was probably better off looking for her presents under another tree anyway. Still, she made a silent pact with herself. No more nooners. She wasn't really the nooner type anyway. That had been an aberration, the act of a lost lamb suddenly abandoned by her herd. Though she had to admit it had been amusing, checking into the Four Seasons with Santa for the afternoon.

"Come on," Rina wheedled. "It'll be fun."

Tanzy adjusted the headset of her cell phone, just before swerving around yet another car trying to squeeze in between the throngs already tucked bumper to bumper along Stockton. She liked shopping as much as the next guy, but not when every man, woman, and foreign national with diplomat tags was shopping with her. Shopping was something a person did on impulse. Preferably when handbags were on sale. Enforced holiday shopping, on the other hand, should be outlawed.

Taking a deep breath, she returned to the conversation. "Ri, you of all people know better."

"But, sweetheart, it's precisely because it *is* me of all people that you should say yes. You know I wouldn't steer you wrong."

"You've barely been married a month. What happened to my best friend? What, do you get some kind of special decoder ring when you get married? One that says 'Have Special Dinners. Make your last remaining single friend insane.' "

Rina laughed. "No, we get one that says 'So what if he never picks up his socks, he's rich, you can now afford a maaaaid.' "

Tanzy laughed. "Just don't do this to me, okay? And I'll pretend you never called."

"You haven't even heard who I lined up for you. I know all about your alpha needs. And, by the way, I'm loving the whole bridesmaid thing in your column, despite my terrible guilt at being the one to put you in that category."

"Yes, I can hear the pain in your voice. So leave me alone already. I'm perfectly happy. Haven't you read the whole column?"

She ignored that, as Tanzy knew she would. Rina was a woman on a mission. "So," she said, "is Marty loving this?"

"He's very much loving this. When he's not out in his new hot rod."

"And what is up with that anyway? Since when is he a sports car guy?"

Tanzy shrugged. "I don't know. Maybe he's having a midlife crisis and is trying to connect with his inner wolf."

"Do you think he actually has one?" They both laughed, then Rina said, "So I guess the reaction to your little wolf/sheep thing is still going strong?"

"The mail has been overwhelming." Tanzy thought of one particular email she'd inadvertently clicked on last night while eating the cold pizza she'd ordered the night before after once again bypassing dinner with Riley. She'd been a week at Big Harry, and so far she'd managed to avoid having even a single meal with him. Not that he seemed overly concerned.

Last night she'd skimmed Millicent's note informing her of a change in her suite number at the Belleview, smirking as she read the part about "hoping Riley isn't intrusive to your busy schedule." Was she kidding? The guy had the unobtrusive market cornered. The only one being intrusive was Aunt Millicent with her house-sitting detail. Then she'd heard the shower running and wasted a minute trying to picture Riley naked. But the only thing she could visualize was him standing there in suit and business frames, calmly sudsing his hair.

And she'd clicked past Millicent's note without paying attention ... and up popped SoulM8 again. She'd found herself reading it without meaning to.

I am the one you seek. Your words about desiring the wolves that prowl amongst the sheep will not divert me, my one and only. I will be the one that teaches you that you don't have to settle. What we will have together will be beyond all glory. Wolf... sheep. Those are merely labels. Look beyond the surface and you will know I am the one who will claim you as my own.

She'd shuddered then and, she couldn't help it, she shuddered now. Not that she took it any more seriously. Probably it had been the added effect of sitting in Big Harry, all alone, late at night. Well, save for Riley. But knowing he was sleeping somewhere nearby, likely in perma-press jammies, did little to reduce her spook-factor.

"So," Rina went on, "tomorrow night, eightish. I can count on you. You won't regret it, Tanz."

"But what about Riley?" So he wasn't a reassuring watchdog—she didn't want one of those anyway, right?—but he might as well come in handy for something.

"What about him? I thought you said he was the insular type. He probably won't even notice you're not there."

"I know, but I haven't been the most attentive cohabitant." It was a lame excuse and Rina surely knew it. But Tanzy was desperate. "I should probably have at least one dinner with him. For Millicent's sake."

"He can wait. I've got Prime A meat on the hoof, baby."

Tanzy snickered. "And you a married woman. Have you no shame?"

"Which is why I'm generously giving the hunky Brock Marshall to you. I'll live vicariously through your single-girl thrills and you'll get to listen to my lady-of-the-manor stories about trying to hire good help."

"And that's supposed to convince me? And Brock Marshall, why does that sound familiar? Wait a minute! Isn't that the guy from that television dating show? I thought he found his dream girl."

"Turns out she'd been having a secret fling with one of the camera guys. The wedding's off."

"Great, just what I need, a guy who was jilted on national television."

"Hey, it beats trolling the malls for hot Santa sex."

"That's so not funny. Remind me not to tell you anything."

"Me and your million readers."

Tanzy sighed. "I should have been an heiress and run respectable charitable foundations. What was I thinking, being a journalist?"

"You are an heiress. And Millicent already runs all the

foundations, there's none left. And you're not a journalist, you're a columnist."

"Yeah, yeah. And I'm not coming for dinner." She stuck her tongue out at the phone.

"I heard that."

"I've been tortured enough. I'm calling a moratorium on Special Dinners as of right now. Pass the word." Rina tried to break in, but Tanzy talked over her. "It was bad enough when Sue fixed me up with Tennis Instructor Guy."

"I thought Viktor was cute."

"How do you know Viktor?"

"From when Sue forced me to play doubles with her a few months ago. What was wrong with him? Didn't he want to play doubles off the court?"

"I don't know. I didn't want to know." Viktor was a towering, six-foot-five testament to why some men were destined to be alone despite being showered with all the genetic gifts. "Rina, honey, he's thirty-three and wore matching tennis gear with Mommy."

"Ew."

"Exactly. Sue thought he was precious. Sure, if you don't mind Mommy picking out your clothes, too."

"Well, I doubt Brock's mother had anything to do with his wardrobe."

"Thank God. Don't you remember her from episode six?" She and Rina shared a silent shudder.

"Okay, okay," Rina relented, "but you're not dating his mother. And didn't you tell me his animal magnetism is what made you watch the show? So, maybe you can be the one to tame him."

"What, I'm Gunther Gable Williams now?"

"Tanzy—"

"No. You don't get it. I don't want to tame them. In fact, it's precisely the untamable ones I do want. I'm not cut out for anything more complicated. It's genetic."

"So you say, but Sloan told me—"

"Don't get me started on Sloan. You were on your honeymoon during that travesty of a dinner party, so you have no idea."

"She said Alec was a total alpha."

Tanzy sighed. "Alpha, no. Neanderthal, yes. Rina, you should have seen this guy. He had more body hair than King Kong."

"Again I'm forced to say, Eww."

"Gave a whole new meaning to the phrase 'running my fingers through his hair.' "

Rina was laughing and gagging at the same time. "Okay, okay, I surrender."

"Thank you. I'm hanging up now."

"Don't forget to talk to Sue about the baby shower."

Tanzy agreed, then clicked off and tossed her headset on the passenger seat. *Thank God,* she thought with a heartfelt sigh. No more Special Dinners. No more dinners, no more nooners. Of course, all this was a great relief, but it didn't solve her dating dilemma.

The bar circuit was simply not happening. Even in her twenties she'd never been one to troll for ... well, other trolls. Which left the party circuit. The gang would still be hitting the seasonal social highlights, but it was different now. Instead of palling together to this charity event or that opening, they'd all be attending with their respective spouses. And she'd be arriving alone. How grossly pathetic. Mostly she loved being self-employed, but there were times when coworkers—namely single male coworkers—would have come in handy.

Someone pulled out right in front of her, but rather than swear and make rude hand gestures, Tanzy neatly dovetailed her little sports car onto Maiden Lane and into a newly vacated spot, smiled smugly, and strolled guiltlessly into the nearest store. Even the most dedicated shopper had to bolster her holiday buying stamina with a little self-gratification.

And if her only other gratification was going to be the kind that came with double A batteries, she certainly deserved a kick-ass Prada bag in the meantime, didn't she?

Riley groaned and circled Union Square. Damn, but what in the hell did she need to go shopping for? He'd already scoped out her closet—in the name of surveillance, of course—and for someone who was just visiting, she had a stunning number of designer clothes, all arranged in amazingly neat rows in the ample walk-in closet.

He did have to admit that his football jersey fantasy had taken a slightly twisted turn when he'd spied those ice-pick red heels tossed carelessly in the corner. Hey, it could work. And frankly, who cared if it didn't?

His cell phone buzzed just as he turned off on Maiden Lane and double-parked. He scooped it up, thankful for the distraction despite the phone number he spied on the display. "Hey, Pop. How's it going?"

"I got another two days on this detail in Santa Rosa. Mr. Shackelford wants me to stick with this a little longer."

"I thought you'd pretty much proved Mrs. Shackelford was on the straight and narrow."

He could picture the deep lines that bracketed his father's mouth sinking even deeper as he grinned. "They're paying, I'm staying."

Riley frowned. "They?"

His father cleared his throat and Riley's frown deepened.

"So, how goes it with the rich and famous?" Finn asked, before Riley could jump in with questions of his own.

"I can name every shoe store, crystal emporium, and lingerie department in San Francisco, but otherwise, fine."

"No action from Ernie on the perv?"

"We're pretty sure the guy works for the service provider the emails are being sent through, but tailing him beyond that is going to be almost impossible. One break is that it's a local outfit, so I'm hoping to get over there as soon as Ms. Harrington is otherwise occupied."

Finn chuckled. "According to her column, that shouldn't be a long wait."

It made no sense whatsoever, since Riley had just been thinking the same thing, but the comment jerked his chain. "She's not like that." When Finn snorted in disbelief, Riley added, "From what I've read about her, she's a lot of bark, but from what I've seen, she's not as much in the bite department."

"She's doing Santa. That's bite." He laughed again.

"Dad, really—"

"I'd love that detail you're on. Some of my best jobs involved—"

"Yes, I know. We really don't want to have that conversation." *Again,* Riley added silently.

"Fine," Finn said, in a tone that indicated it was anything but. "Have it your way. But you're missing out on some of the best perks of the job."

Riley bit back his retort. It wouldn't do any good anyway. "Trust me, I'm getting mine. I'm sleeping in feather down your dear ma would have cried for, and eating food fit for a professional wrestler."

"That's my boy. You still thinking you'll wrap this up by Christmas?"

"I hope so. I've got to phone in a report to Ms. Harrington Senior this evening."

"Fine, fine. You've got my number here if you need anything."

There was the sound of a woman's deep, throaty laugh in the background, then a rustling sound. Riley sighed.

"Listen," his dad said, suddenly in a hurry, "I've got to, you know, go take care of things."

"Please God, just tell me what you're taking care of isn't named Patsy Shackelford."

"Why, Riley James Parrish, I—"

"You're doing what you always do." When his father said nothing, Riley sighed again. More in weary resignation than any real disgust. "Just make sure you don't get into trouble." Finn started to splutter, but Riley talked over him. "I'm not jeopardizing this job—this well-paying job—by having to come and bail your ass out of jail. Or worse, the hospital." He clicked off before Finn could reply. Not that it would have mattered.

Riley scrubbed his face and sucked down the last of his cold coffee. Just when had he become the parent? Actually, he knew when, and the day had been long enough without reminiscing over that bit of painful history.

Tanzy saved him by popping out of the store just then.

"Jesus Christ," he muttered, spying not one, but three shopping bags dangling from her fingers. Good thing Millicent provided her only grandniece with a bottomless pit where money was concerned. All he cared about at the moment, however, was that she'd made as much of a dent in it today as she planned to.

He blessed the fates, the gods, and anyone else who might be listening, when she turned her little deathtrap of a roadster toward Presidio Heights. Now all he had to do was keep up with her and beat her home.

And he thought beating a three-on-one defense had been tricky.

Is it fear of gift giving that drives wolves into seclu- sion over the holidays? The inability to find that special gift that says, "I just want to have fun without worrying you'll start looking at minivans." Well, I'm going to do you wolves a favor.

All we want is to not be alone over the holidays. Not because we think being alone reflects poorly on our self-worth. But because the only thing worse than Special Dinners are Special Holiday Occasions.

If you really feel the need to give, an expensive bottle of champagne with dinner would be fine. Or a ski weekend at Taos for those who like the Grand (but commitment-free) Gesture. That will give you a place to wear that tasteful, yet totally nonintimate thick fleece pullover we'll be buying for you.

5

Good evening, dear."

Tanzy transferred the cell phone to her other ear as she juggled the handles of her shopping bags. The second major spree in the past week. Christmas shopping was hell, but someone had to do it. "Hi, Aunt Millicent," she said, bumping her hip against Big Harry's front door. "How is Frances?"

Riley appeared as she stumbled into the foyer, just as he had after the last foray. She smiled and mouthed "Thanks" as he helped unload the packages from her arms. Such a well-trained sheep. Leave it to Aunt Millicent. She wondered absently if he would do the actual shopping for her as well. Now, that was a worthy sheep perk.

"Not too well, dear," Millicent was saying. "That's why I'm calling."

Tanzy sank to the lower step of the grand staircase. "I'm so sorry to hear that." *Really sorry.* "Is there anything I can do?"

"As a matter of fact, there is. Before leaving, I was able to cancel all my engagements but one. I had arranged for Walter Sinclair to take my place and make the presentation, but—"

"Presentation?" Tanzy glanced over to see Riley lining

her packages up inside the tiny elevator tucked behind the staircase. He gave her a questioning look, but she just nodded and waved him on. "What presentation?"

"My annual scholarships at the Crystal Charity Ball." She sighed. "I do so dislike using that term, charity. Those children have had enough misfortune without being tagged as a charity."

Tanzy merely nodded as Millicent continued to wax rhapsodic about tapping into the energies of youth. It was truly wonderful what her great-aunt did for San Francisco's underprivileged, but she'd heard this speech many times. It was Millicent's version of the "I walked five miles uphill in the snow to school" speech that all elders felt genetically compelled to pass down.

Tanzy wondered absently what her speech would be. Or if there would ever be anyone to give it to. For some reason her gaze drifted to Riley as she forced her thoughts in a different direction. Namely coming up with substitutions for good old Walter Sinclair, who was cofounder of one of Millicent's many foundations. Because she knew where this was headed.

"I'm certain your calendar has been booked for months, but this is vitally important and I'd appreciate it if you'd clear your slate for this event."

Tanzy felt the tiniest flush darken her skin. In fact, she'd turned down several major seasonal events in the last week. She simply wasn't up to facing the whirl with her arm unadorned by a man. Not that she couldn't handle going solo. Under normal circumstances. But her conversation with Rina regarding Special Dinners last week hadn't done a lick of good. They'd merely moved on to Special Holiday Occasions and ambushed her there. And with her social circle all but dancing the Rite of Spring around her, the last thing she wanted was to broadcast in any way that she needed pairing up.

Usually in cases like this, she called on Carmine. He of the dashing manners and the tailor-made tux. Carmine was hands down the most gorgeous man she'd ever laid eyes on. He was also gay and deeply incloseto. But the Rite of Spring had apparently sprung him, too. The last she'd heard, his latest lover, Brice, was looking pretty serious. Tanzy privately bet Brice would have Carmine dancing out of the closet by Valentine's Day if not before.

Which left her with no backup. She'd meant to get around to that, but she wasn't up for faux fun with unavailable men this year anyway. Again her gaze strayed to Riley.

"I'll fax you the words I'd prepared for Walter. Of course, feel free to edit and revise, dear. You're the professional, and I'm sure you can say what I mean better than I can."

Tanzy opened her mouth to suggest any of three or four other perfectly suitable candidates, but what she said was, "I'd be honored to, Aunt Millicent." She smacked her forehead repeatedly with her palm.

"If you have no special suitor or beau, I'm certain Riley would be happy to escort you."

Tanzy clutched the phone a little tighter and tried to get as tight a grip on her control. Had it really come to this? Now even her eighty-two-year-old aunt was setting her up. A fate she'd thought she was eternally, blessedly immune to, considering Millicent's matchmaking history.

Millicent had never forgiven herself for being the one to pressure Penelope into dating Frank deLange, who came from the Right Family and had Good Prospects. Unlike the rough crowd that Penelope tended to run with under Millicent's brother's supervision.

Millicent's attempt at dragging Tanzy's mother into the realm of respectability had instead ended with Penelope knocked up and alone, while Frank flitted off to Europe to finish his education, only to wind up married to some French heiress instead.

Tanzy had met Frank, whom Penelope had always referred to as "the sperm donor," once. Which had been enough. It was one of the few times she'd agreed with her mother.

"I'll work something out," she assured Millicent. "Just send me your speech and the foundation contact and I'll set everything up. When is it?"

"This Sunday, dear."

Tanzy gaped at the phone. That was three days away.

"I'm sending Clarisse over with some dresses for you to look at. Consider it my holiday gift to you."

Tanzy gritted her teeth and said, "You're so thoughtful, but honestly, you don't have to do that." Please, dear God.

"Which is precisely why I am. Don't sound so horrified. I'm not sending over old-lady fuddy-duddy clothes. Clarisse is quite avant-garde. And we both know a woman can't have too many lovely things, so accept the gift gracefully, dear, and have a wonderful time. Oh, and she's been instructed to bring along a few things for Riley as well."

"Really, Aunt Millicent, that's not necessary. Besides, I hardly know him—"

"Well, that didn't seem to be a deterrent with Santa Claus, now, did it, dear?"

Millicent rang off, leaving Tanzy openmouthed and speechless. Would she forever be punished for that one indiscretion?

"I trust everything is going well with Madame Harrington?"

Tanzy snapped her mouth shut and stuck her phone back into her purse. "Oh, she's in fine form, all right." She stood and smoothed the wrinkles from her suede slacks. "Woman will likely outlive us all. God help us."

Riley raised his eyebrows behind his Coke-bottle lenses and nodded sagely. "I sent your bags up for you. Have you eaten?"

"Thanks, and no, I didn't. But I've got to answer some interview questions for an online thing and return some calls." Martin had beeped her three times today while she'd been out. Very un-Marty-like. She shook her head and said, "My editor has apparently decided to adopt me now that he's sent his youngest off to college." Riley didn't respond to that conversational gambit, so she sighed and said, "I think I'm just going to heat up one of Helen's dishes and take it upstairs with me if you don't mind." All of which was true. But it wouldn't have killed her to sit in the kitchen with him for one meal. She still hadn't done that, despite her excuses to Rina last week.

She wasn't exactly certain why. He seemed nice enough. Maybe it was because, while they were cohabitating fine, doing so from a distance seemed easier on both of them. At least that's what she was telling herself anyway.

"I hope that doesn't ruin anything you might have planned," she added, although she doubted it. He didn't seem too choked up about it. But then, how could she tell? He had one expression. Shuttered.

"No, not at all," he said smoothly, reinforcing her opinion. "I'll be in my rooms if you need me."

She was tempted, for just a brief moment, to ask him exactly what sort of needs he'd be willing to assuage. He was so uptight, the urge to tease him was almost overwhelming. *Play nice, Tanz.* She just wanted to see if she could make him blink. But she didn't think he'd appreciate the humor in it. A more dry, self-controlled individual she'd never met.

"Are you in for the evening, then?" When she looked surprised by the question, he added, "If so, I'll go ahead and secure the house now."

She wanted to ask him what century he was from, but she was forced to admit that with all the hectic shopping and generally crazed holiday atmosphere out there, his calm, if dated, demeanor, inside a house that had the same eccentric blend of old and new that he did, was somehow oddly reassuring.

"Actually, I'm expecting a guest a little later. Millicent is sending over a designer with some dresses I'm supposed to look at. I can handle it, though, so don't worry about anything. I'll lock up the fort when she's gone."

Riley held her gaze for a fraction of a second longer than was entirely necessary and Tanzy felt a surprising little spike of tension. Which made no sense whatsoever. Probably it was a trick of the light on those thick lenses of his.

"Fine, then," he said, his tone as even as always. "I'll leave you to your business. Have a pleasant evening."

Tanzy watched him disappear down the hall toward the kitchens and shook her head. She couldn't put her finger on it, but something about Riley niggled at her. She was almost tempted to follow him, nudge him a bit, see if she could push him, just to loosen him up a little, that was all, nothing more. Certainly nothing sexual. Just . . . because. Then she remembered that limp handshake, which led to images of what else would likely be limp. And she lost interest. Okay, so maybe the urge to provoke had been a teensy bit sexual. Apparently she was having Santa setbacks. It was that voice of his that prodded her, that was all.

She did smile a bit wickedly as she started up the stairs, unable to keep from wondering what it would be like to press his personal keypad number later and see if she could engage him in some hot phone sex.

"Yeah, so he could 'bid me to come' or something equally ridiculous," she murmured, then shook off the odd direction her thoughts seemed to take around him of late. She only had an hour or so before Clarisse showed up, which gave her an hour to get her work done and find herself a stand-in date for the ball.

* * *

Riley downed the rest of his beer in one long pull. He considered having another. Hell, he considered downing the entire six, but he closed the door to the monster fridge and leaned back against it. Tanzy Harrington was a piece of work. And then some. He'd run himself ragged tailing her all over town. Who knew buying Christmas presents could be a full-contact sport?

He had to admit she had pretty damn fine taste, though. Those suede pants she had on looked like the guy had tanned the leather right onto her body. He rolled the cold bottle across his forehead.

"She's getting to you," he muttered. No, no, she wasn't. Her leather pants were getting to him. And her slinky silky shirts, and those fuck-me-now heels she wore. And it wasn't her doing the begging, either. What was it about spike heels—on legs like hers—that made a normally aggressive alpha male want to be tied up and whipped just for grins?

"Jesus," he groaned, then pushed away from the cool steel doors. Just the mention of some dressmaker wrapping her up in God knew what kind of creation had made him take a moment to regroup. And it was a moment he couldn't afford. She was a very intent person. It would be a lot easier if she was just some rich, self-centered, spoiled brat whose thoughts were solely focused on "What can I have and where can I get it?" But he was discovering that was not Tanzy Harrington.

Oh, she was definitely rich—and with her own earnings, he'd learned. She didn't even need Millicent's millions to bankroll those shopping sprees he was learning were as crucial to her as water was to human survival. And yes, maybe she was a little bit spoiled. She was aggressively focused on what she wanted, and how she was going to get it, and more often than not, she succeeded. But there was nothing wrong with being hungry, motivated. Which was precisely what got to him. He identified with that drive, that hunger. It was what had gotten him to the NFL. And it was that same discipline, if not exactly a hunger, that got him through job after job with his dad.

The one thing Tanzy wasn't was self-centered. Quite the opposite. In fact, she missed nothing. Maybe that was what made her so interesting in print. She had an eye for details, paid attention to nuance. And all with a sense of humor so wry and sharp a man could bleed to death if he got too close.

Of course, there were other elements of her hunger that got to him, too. Just for a moment there, in the hall, he swore he felt her staring holes in his back. Big, hungry, Could-I-have-him-if-I-wanted-him? holes. It was the tiny flicker of disappointment he'd felt when she'd opted for the stairs that had driven him straight to a cold one. Or three.

He tugged the steel door back open, but opted for one of Tanzy's stash of Cokes this time and fixed himself a roast beef sandwich. Heading upstairs, he thought he might catch a bit of the Lakers game before digging into work and making his call to Millicent. Ernie was working on the employee listings from the service provider and he hoped something would pop from there. He was so deep in thought, he almost ran flat into Tanzy on the turn just before the third-floor landing. She stopped short, as if not quite prepared to see him, either. "Hi," she said after a momentary pause.

"Good evening," he replied, just barely remembering his persona in time. He moved to one side to let her pass. Praying like hell his stupid pleated sheep trousers were baggy enough to hide his half-aroused real wolf self. Suede pants should be outlawed, he thought, trying like hell not to look at them. Surely they endangered some form of wildlife.

Yeah, he thought, *men.*

He started to continue up the stairs, when she cleared her throat and said, "Um, Riley? Do you have a moment?"

He turned, opting to say nothing.

A moment passed, then another. "I, uh, well—"

How interesting, he thought, biting down on the urge to smile. What could make the normally word-savvy columnist so tongue-tied? And what in the hell did it have to do with him? His urge to smile faded. "Is there a problem?"

"Actually, sort of, yes." She smiled then and gave a little self-deprecating laugh.

And damn if he didn't understand exactly why men threw themselves willingly under those spike heels of hers.

"Millicent has asked me to attend a little function in her honor. One of her foundations awards scholarships every year and this time she can't be there to hand them out, so she asked me to do it. I don't suppose you'd be interested in being my escort for the evening, would you? It's this Sunday evening. Very last minute, I know, but she just sprung this on me."

And everyone she'd apparently spent the last fifteen minutes calling couldn't fill in, he thought, not sure why he was irritated to be her absolute last choice. Wasn't the end of the line exactly where he was supposed to be?

He should be happy she'd been forced to ask. He'd have had to tail her anyway. This would make things much easier on him. "I could work something out."

She smiled in surprised relief. "Thanks, I really appreciate it," she said, sounding sincere. "I don't know about you, but I just couldn't face doing the single thing at holiday time. What is it about this time of year anyway? Must be all that mistletoe." She paused, considering him, and for a split second, he wondered if she was thinking of finding some mistletoe and taking him for a test drive beneath it.

But before his libido could kick into full gear, she went on.

"Wait a minute. You *are* single, aren't you? I mean, don't feel that because you work for Millicent that you have to—"

Stupid. He was a mercy date. And, no matter that it was the best thing for both of them, he was really beginning to hate this whole sheep idea. "It will be fine."

She cocked her head and looked as if she was going to push—after all, it had been a nonanswer—but in the end she shrugged and favored him with another one of those morning-after smiles. God, how did she do that? Practice, most likely. Still, he was forced to shift ever so slightly. Shift and pray she didn't glance down.

"If you're worried about what to wear, don't," she added quickly, misinterpreting his frown. "The designer Millicent is sending over will take care of it." Just then the imperial gong Millicent favored as a doorbell resounded up the stairwell. "And there she is." She slipped past him, down the stairs. "I'll buzz your room when it's your turn. Thanks, Riley."

He stared down the empty stairwell. Buzz his room, would she? Millicent wasn't the only one who'd perfected the hit-and-run approach to getting her way. He swore under his breath the rest of the way up the stairs.

The Lakers were down by six and he hadn't even booted up his computer when the phone rang. "Great." He'd almost managed to forget about the fun and excitement in store for him this evening. *About as much fun as getting a tooth drilled.* He snatched up the phone on the third ring.

"We're ready for you, Riley."

Which wasn't the question at all, he thought. Was he ready for them? *That* was the question.

"The torture chamber is set up in one of the guest rooms

on the second floor," she said dryly, as if reading his mind. "You'll know it when you see it."

Despite wishing that he were anywhere else at the moment, he found himself smiling as he hung up.

But once inside said torture chamber, it took less than five minutes for Riley to realize there was going to be a problem. He could hardly stay in disguise if he had to strip down in front of Clarisse.

Fortunately, that problem was swiftly dealt with when she had summarily dismissed Tanzy from the room as Riley strode in. He'd enjoyed the brief look of surprise that had crossed her face, but his amusement had faded all too quickly once Madame Clarisse got busy.

She was a trim woman, barely five feet in her heels, with expertly coiffed strawberry blond hair framing a face that could only be described as manicured. She was anywhere from forty-five to sixty. Obviously not still sporting the facial structure she'd been born with, but wealthy enough, vain enough, or both, to afford to slow down the ravages of time without caricaturizing herself in the process. She was French, though he doubted she'd been born speaking the language, despite the cultured accent. And she hadn't a lick of modesty.

He winced, trying not to flinch as she measured his inseam with a quick zip of the tape measure, a tool she wielded as ruthlessly as a lion tamer wielded a whip. He'd rather face the lion.

"Your trousers." She made a tsking sound as she snapped the tape around her neck and straightened. "Is off the rack, no?" She waved a hand. "You have the frame to carry a double-breasted style, though I will insist you take off your jacket for the measurement.

"Your legs, they are long and lean enough," she went on. "Perfect for a single-pleated placket, seam pockets to keep the look clean." She shook her head as she ran her gaze over him once again. "Why do you wear such clothes? Surely Madame Harrington, she pays you enough to get your suits fitted?"

Which brought him back to the problem. How frank could he be with Clarisse? He should have contacted Millicent and discussed this, but he hadn't foreseen this particular problem. Nor had he mentioned his disguise to Millicent in their last several phone conversations. She'd approve, he was certain. But how to explain it to Dragon Lady here?

Maybe he could claim some horrible dermatological condition that precluded him from wearing properly fitted clothes. *Or maybe you could get over yourself.* Surely the nerd hair and Coke-bottle glasses were enough. It wasn't like he was a lady-killer in a tux anyway. Of course, he wasn't butt ugly, either. And maybe there was a tiny part of him that would enjoy strolling into the room, totally decked in full-tilt wolf attire, just for the pleasure of watching Tanzy's mouth drop open.

Of course, there was also the chance she wouldn't even blink.

He settled for saying, "I prefer my clothing to be roomy."

"Roomy? What is roomy?"

"Loose-fitting. I don't like to be constricted."

She slid her glasses down her nose and looked right . . . there, then nodded and said, "You have a point."

He was pretty sure well-traveled, thirty-two-year-old men didn't blush. But then he'd challenge any guy in the locker room to five minutes in a room alone with Clarisse and see if they didn't.

"I will take care of this for you."

Riley shook his head. "I don't mean to be rude and I'm sure you'd make me a tux that would rival Armani." She sniffed, and he quickly amended, "Put Armani to shame. But I have other . . . specifications. Why don't you take care of Tanzy's dress and I'll take care of finding something suitable to wear."

She shook her head. "Madame Harrington was very adamant."

That raised his eyebrows a fraction. So, Millicent had wanted him as the escort all along. He swallowed the little grin of satisfaction as he pictured Tanzy's frustration when her other choices hadn't panned out and she'd been forced to do Millicent's bidding. Again.

"You tell me these specifications you desire and we will see what can be done," she instructed.

"You will be discreet, I trust?" She looked so offended, he relaxed a little. He eyed the closed door, then sighed and slipped off his jacket.

"Oh my."

"Can you adjust the cut to hide this?"

She looked at his shoulder holster like one might look at a deadly snake, but quickly regained her professional bearing. He could see the multitude of questions in her eyes, but she asked none of them as she went about measuring his arms and back.

He relaxed completely. Or as completely as one could around Clarisse. He should have known Millicent would have seen to this detail as she'd seen to so many others.

"The jacket, it will not have as good a line here." She zipped her fingers down along his shoulder blades. "But you have broad enough shoulders to carry it off." She shook her head. "A shame really, to hide such a frame as this." She circled to the front of him, took his chin in her hand, and turned his head this way, then that. Another snort of disgust. "A waste." She turned then and began making notes on a small pad.

Riley stood there, but she didn't say anything else. Finally she turned and seemed surprised to find him still standing there. "You will have delivery Sunday by noon."

He shrugged back into his jacket. "Do you need help with this?" He gestured to the narrow rack that held a number of zippered garment bags.

"If you will wheel it to the elevator," she commanded dismissively.

He was tempted to salute, but he managed a nod. He rolled the rack to the elevator and out the front door to where a driver and car sat idling. He'd assumed Millicent had sent the ride, but the efficient way the driver dismantled the rack and carefully stowed the garment bags said otherwise. Clarisse came bustling out of the house a moment later. Riley thought she was going to blow right by him, but she paused at the last second and looked up at him.

"You are good at your job?" she asked quietly.

"It gets one hundred percent of my attention."

She peered in his eyes, then nodded. "I would not like anything bad to happen to these people." She jerked her pointed chin toward the house.

"Me, either." He slid his glasses off and gave her the grin he'd been hiding since he got here. "Bad for business."

Her eyes widened, then narrowed shrewdly. Her smile was equally sly. "You'll do," she said, without a hint of an accent, before sliding into the car and disappearing behind tinted glass.

Replacing his glasses, Riley gave her that salute, then watched the car ease away from the curb before glancing up to the turreted tower window in Tanzy's corner of the house.

She stood there, silhouetted by the lamplight. She didn't wave, nor did she move away. She simply stared down at him. Riley held her shadowed gaze for several long, very unwise moments, before finally heading back into the house.

Her door remained shut as he passed by. He let himself

into his own rooms, flicked off the game, and booted up his computer. And reminded himself that giving one hundred percent to the job was exactly why he was only allowed to look.

And never touch.

When did ballroom dancing cease to be a viable form of foreplay? Even a waltz, the most basic one-two-three one-two-three dance there is, when done with the right person, is more arousing than the naughtiest lambada. With the wrong person? About as stimulating as doing the wave.

6

Tanzy paused at the top of the final sweep of stairs. Riley waited for her below. He was no Carmine, but he didn't look half bad. He had a sort of Clark Kent in a tux thing going on.

"Is the car here?" she asked as she descended the remaining stairs. He looked up, exactly as she'd known he would. She tried to casually assess the impact her dress had on him. She had to admit that Millicent had done well by sending Clarisse. Strapless, form-fitting, with a definite movie star vibe to it. Not that she was all that glamorous, but if a dress could make the woman, then for a night she was Julia Roberts. Hell, she'd settle for Julie Andrews.

Riley, on the other hand . . . well, he was more Hugh Grant than Hugh Jackman—even Clarisse's talents could only do so much—but beta men did have their uses. Tonight being one of them.

However, if the flame-red sheath had any effect on him, he didn't let it show. She smiled as her inner Julia took his blank look square in the ego. *Honestly, Tanz, what did you expect? That he'd fling off his glasses, peel out of that tux, and take you right here on the stairs?*

And why did she think she wanted him to?

There might not be a big red S on his chest, but he was a

gentleman. And a genuinely nice guy for doing her this favor. She had to get over this unexplainable fixation she had with getting him to notice her.

She turned, presented her back—and the spine-baring rear cut of the dress—as he held up her wrap. "I hope Millicent didn't make you feel obligated about doing this," she said sincerely. He draped the silk-lined shawl around her shoulders and she couldn't help but notice he'd managed to do so without touching her once, not even a skimming brush of his fingertips. It was only the deflating sense of disappointment that revealed just how much she'd anticipated having his hands on her.

Remember the limp handshake, she thought, and still wished she'd had another moment for comparison.

"I just want you to know how much I appreciate you going through this, especially at the last minute."

"It's not a problem," he said, with no inflection indicating whether it truly was or not.

She resisted the urge to stamp her foot in frustration. Could a man really be so . . . so . . . vanilla?

Riley held the door for her as she strolled out in front of him. No noticeable aftershave or cologne, she noted. And yet, despite her mental talking-to, she still had this undeniable urge to pause next to him, lean in a little, push things. Just to see if she could get a reaction from him. Any reaction.

God, this whole last-bridesmaid thing was obviously getting to her. That, and the holidays, and the special dinners, and the whack emails, and the house-sitting. It was no wonder she felt so off balance. Any other time she'd have let him drift into the background and stay there, where he obviously wanted to be, without a second thought. Much less a third. Or a fourth.

She'd never been one of those women who needed the attentions of every man in her immediate orbit. In fact, she was often glad to be in the background. It was her business to be an observer of the ebb and flow of the serendipitous gender dance that swirled through people's lives. The little moments of awareness that could be enjoyed innocently and just as quickly forgotten . . . or acted upon and possibly end up as something memorable. She enjoyed watching it almost as much as she enjoyed the dance herself.

From the innocent flirtatious banter with the guy at the gas station pump, to the harmless ten-second fantasy about what she might do with the man in the elevator if they happened to suddenly get stuck, to the occasional double glances when brushing past a member of the opposite sex on the way into a bookstore. Everyone had them, it was all a matter of how aware you were of them—and what you did about them—that made them important.

Mostly she wrote about them. Amongst other things. And maybe that's what Riley was. Potential column fodder.

And then it clicked into place. That's exactly what he was, exactly why she was so intrigued by him. He was a prime opportunity to do a more in-depth study of her sheep theory. To discover what it was about the beta man that made women give up their independence for I Do's, honeymoon sex, and sonograms of baby penises. And after all, when was she ever going to get the chance again to actually observe one this up close and personal?

Excited by her little epiphany, she slid into the limo and Riley followed, sitting diagonally across from her. Clark Kent, she mused again. It was an apt comparison now that she thought about it, and found herself wondering how he'd stack up under closer observation. Of course, Clark Kent had been the ultimate wolf in sheep's clothing. Could that be the case with Riley? Could that be what her radar was detecting? Hmmm.

Observation Number One, she noted mentally. *He has long legs.* She'd never noticed before. Probably the relaxed cut of his clothes. But stretched out as they were now, right next to her, they were hard to ignore. That prompted a sole check. Hmm. Interesting. Medium to thick. He shifted his feet just then and she darted her gaze up to his, flashing a quick smile to brazen her way past being caught checking him out. But he was looking out the window.

Observation Number Two. Not a bad profile. Strong chin. Decent nose. Forehead not bulgy, hairline not receding. He still needed a decent stylist. The parted-on-the-side look definitely didn't work for him. Something short, natural, would define those cheekbones. Which led to the glasses. What would he look like without the Magoo lenses? *Why doesn't he go for contacts? Or laser surgery?*

The limp handshake came to mind again. Maybe all the laser surgery and fashion makeovers wouldn't help. Maybe there was no inner Superman here. Even in the tux, he was pretty much All Clark, All the Time.

"Have you been to events like this before?" she asked, expanding her unscientific little study beyond the physical to the personal. With what little she'd seen of him since moving in, she really knew next to nothing about him.

He glanced briefly in her direction, just enough to be polite. "Similar."

Tanzy nodded, smiled, but was privately sighing. Had she ever met such a nonstarter? Was he shy or merely retiring? "For the most part, you don't have to do anything but nod and shake hands with people. Oh, and I don't know if you're much of a dancer, but as Millicent is the key contributor, I should warn you that we'll probably be expected to at least make a showing on the dance floor. I should have mentioned it sooner." For heaven's sake, she was almost babbling, and why? It wasn't as if she was nervous. Riley would handle himself fine. She had a greater chance of being bored to tears tonight than anything else.

So the sudden spike in her pulse rate when his gaze

shifted to hers again took her totally off guard. It must be that tux. Clarisse was truly a wizard.

"It's not a problem," he said evenly, almost absently, but his gaze held hers steadily. Not remotely shy. Or retiring.

Again, her fingers twitched with the urge to do something rash. Grab him, shake his absolutely unshakable demeanor. Or maybe she was imagining this enigma factor. Had her new solo single status thrown her so badly for a loop that she'd become desperate for entertainment?

Then there was that moment the other night, when he'd glanced up at her window after seeing Clarisse off. It had been too dark to see his eyes, but as ridiculous as it sounded, she swore something had passed between them in that moment. *Yeah*, she thought, *jealousy*. She'd watched his easy camaraderie with Clarisse, their bent heads, his little salute as she drove off. There was nothing easy like that between them. In fact, there was nothing at all. And then he'd glanced up.

And she'd been thinking about him ever since.

The limo slid smoothly to the curb in front of the domed City Hall at the Civic Center, and the door was opened for them a moment later.

She wasted half a second hoping he'd slide out first, then reach in for her hand to draw her out. After all, those courtly manners of his should be good for something. But Wainwright, Millicent's longtime driver, was the one to reach in for her hand. Riley merely nodded and shifted his long legs to the side so she could slip out.

All the way through the grand marble lobby and up the wide sweep of stairs, she found herself wishing he'd put his hand on her lower back, even the lightest of touches, ever the polite escort. But he remained just a hair farther apart than polite society dictated. *And the hell with being polite,* she thought disgustedly.

She'd nodded hello to several of Millicent's acquaintances

she was familiar with, had even said a surprised hello to Martin and his wife, who she'd never met before. Giselle. Funny, she'd never thought of Marty as having a wife with an exotic-sounding name. She'd pictured a Betty or a Barbara. Someone with June Cleaver hair and a Doris Day smile. Giselle had neither. In fact, she didn't look all that thrilled to be here. Tanzy had forgotten her editor was one of the many supporters of the foundation. They'd both made polite introductions, but Martin had privately flashed her a surprised look at her choice of escort. Which only went to prove she was insane for thinking Riley could ever be more than he was. A sheep recognized his own kind.

Mr. and Mrs. Marty—which was how she'd think of them, regardless—moved on and Tanzy and Riley stepped into the crowded room. Pausing just inside the doors, Tanzy did the automatic single-girl visual scope of the place. Gorgeous marble floors and pillars gleamed, a perfect backdrop to the swirl of silks and diamonds floating about the floor. She didn't notice any of it. Tall, dark, and tuxed was what usually caught her eye. And it would be just her luck if every available gorgeous wolf on the prowl was here tonight. Carmine would have worked it out, as she would for him. Instead she got to be The Lady in Red for the one guy who wouldn't appreciate it, but would keep anyone else from appreciating it, either.

Observation Number Three: Nice guys ruin everything.

Jesus, she even made the soles of his feet sweat. What the hell had he been thinking to agree to something like this? Oh yeah, being her escort would be easier, sure. No one had bothered to tell him she'd be dressed like Santa Claus's personal sex elf. Hell, if sex with Santa turned her on, he'd don the jolly red suit right here and now. Beard and all.

His knuckles ached from keeping his fingers so tightly tucked against his palms. It was that or grab her and drag her back to the limo. See if that silky skin of hers tasted as good as he knew that silky dress would feel. He'd been doing a pretty damn good job with the aloof bit so far. She likely thought he was an asshole, if she thought about him at all. Probably not, seeing as she was looking everywhere but at him. Though he was damned if he didn't want to get her attention. The more she ignored, avoided, and sidestepped him, the more he perversely wanted to get in her way. Highly unprofessional, but there it was.

Maybe it was genetic after all. That was a hell of a thought. Though he'd rather be tortured before ever admitting even thinking it. To Finn, or himself.

Then she'd had to go and mention the dancing. Fancy shindig like this, he doubted it was the kind where partners didn't touch each other. He sent a private thank-you to his college coach, who'd insisted his players take a semester of dance to enhance their footwork. Only that had been a decade ago. He could only pray it was like riding a bike. Or sex.

He watched Tanzy shake hands and smile her way across the main room as they weaved to their table. The head table. *Jesus, what was he doing here?* He'd been lying through his teeth when he said he'd been to functions like this. Sure, he'd done fund-raisers with his teammates, for the organization and for charity, even some high-end stuff for the team owner. But the key word there had been *team*. Like awkward adolescents at homecoming, they could all hang together, grin a lot, and hope like hell no one asked them to dance. Those had been the times he'd been glad he wasn't a superstar, recognizable to all.

Still, it had been years since he'd even donned a tux. And, as it turned out, it wasn't like sex at all.

He made the best of it, nodded when introduced, tried

to look interested as everyone chattered on about how wonderful it was that Tanzy had come in Millicent's place, pasted on a smile when absolutely necessary . . . and scanned the place almost desperately for a glass of something other than fizzy sweet champagne. What was wrong with serving cold beer at fancy functions? he wanted to know.

He should be working the room himself. This place was a veritable smorgasbord of the rich and richer. He could probably muster up enough charm to bullshit his way into a dozen or so contacts and potential clients before the night was over. Unfortunately, he'd cast himself in this stupid sheep role, which precluded him from schmoozing the guests.

Or her.

Which only reminded him of what his father had been doing in Santa Rosa for the past couple of weeks. And not alone, most likely. When Riley agreed to partner up with his dad, he'd made it clear that if Finn wanted a retirement nest egg, then professionalism was key in turning Parrish Securities into a real player in the field. But his dad was a player of an entirely different kind. Not that Finn minded hard work, as long as hard play was incorporated on a regular basis. Which was all fine and well, except Finn incorporated his work directly into his pleasure. And he never seemed to understand why this was a problem.

The food was served, and the four-course meal kept them all thankfully busy. Afterward, Riley had to admit he enjoyed watching Tanzy up at the podium, handing out the scholarships. As much to watch her normally confident demeanor turn a bit flustered beneath the lights and attentions of a ballroom full of people as to watch the delighted expressions of the recipients.

He knew how much it meant, the chance for higher education. He owed his to his skills on the gridiron. He'd have never gone to college if he'd had to depend on Finn financially to get him there, but his father had certainly pushed him hard enough. Of course, Riley's degree was in physical education, and here he was, an investigative security specialist. Still, he could relate to the starry eyes and dreamy smiles of the young people as they gratefully accepted their endowments.

That didn't keep him from being intrigued by the dichotomy of Tanzy Harrington. Femme fatale with men, single-woman heroine to her readers, quick-witted in interviews, poised on her taped talk-show spots, and downright brazen on the radio ... but totally unaccustomed to the actual spotlight.

And then she was seated next to him again, a bit breathless, her cheeks flushed and her eyes a bit starry as well. "I can certainly see why Millicent gets off on this," she said, trying for that jaded wit she did so well. But Riley heard the honest excitement in her words, saw it on her face. "I felt like a total fraud up there, though," she went on. "My name might be the same as the foundation's, but I don't have a single thing to do with any of it. It's all Millicent's work. Hard work, too, from what everyone has told me tonight."

"So why don't you get involved?"

His quiet question startled her into silence. He hadn't meant to ask it, to cross even the most intangible line from professional into personal. But before he could retract it, she responded, and quite honestly if her expression was any gauge. And that was one thing he was learning about Tanzy—good or bad, she laid it out there for the world to see.

"Maybe I will. I've never wanted to before. In fact, I've done my best to run in the opposite direction where my ancestral obligations are concerned." She glanced at him, that clever, daunting smile curving her lips once more. One-on-one, she was definitely in her element. "Preferring to build my own heritage, as it were. Less to answer up to that way."

"You seem to have done all right for yourself. I'm sure your aunt is proud of you."

"I'm not entirely sure of that," she stated with her typical innate frankness. "Oh, she's happy enough for my successes. But I know she'd be happier still if I took an interest in the family end of things."

Riley managed to curb most of his instinctive smile, but not his tongue. "I don't know. I think your independent streak is part of your heritage as well. I'm not so sure Millicent would be all that fond of having another cook in the kitchen. As it were."

Tanzy laughed. "You have a point. My fervent wish has always been—and I'll hunt you down if you tell her this—that she will leave everything to her charitable foundations when the time comes. Although, like I said before, if anyone can outlive us all, Aunt Millie can."

He was trying like hell to remain restrained. But not responding to her natural vivacity and drive was like trying to resist taking his next breath. He was beginning to sympathize with all the poor saps she talked about in her column. Perhaps he should have taken Millicent's warnings about her grandniece's effect on the opposite sex a tad more seriously.

"I can be trusted to keep all confidences," he said, summoning whatever was left of his inner sheep.

Her lips curved. And he wanted badly to howl. Right after he tasted them, at length. Danger and genetics be damned.

"I don't suppose my aunt would have hired you otherwise," she said. "And when did Millicent hire you anyway? I don't really keep track, she has a hefty staff on retainer, but I think I'd have remembered you."

Which is precisely the kind of thing you don't want to hear her say. Time to rein it in, and rein it in hard. *Be the sheep.* "I've only been in her employ recently."

"And before that?"

He merely looked at her. "I was employed elsewhere."

Tanzy rolled her eyes. "Pretty mysterious for a personal assistant."

"Most of my employers prefer the low profile I provide." He'd meant to say it dismissively, but somehow it sounded ... suggestive. He made a mental note to never, under any circumstance, think role-playing was a fun way to beef up an assignment.

She propped her elbow on the table, rested her chin in her hand, her expression quizzical.

"What?" he asked, unable to help himself as her silent perusal continued.

She shook her head, and straightened in her seat. "You've strung together more words in the past ten minutes than I've heard you utter in the two weeks I've known you. Or is that all part of that low-profile thing?"

"We haven't spent much time together."

"Maybe we should work on that. And that low profile of yours."

Riley never thought he'd be so thankful to hear the orchestra play their introductory notes, but at that moment he could have kissed every one of them. Until it occurred to him that dancing was going to be even worse torture.

As the other foundation members at their table stood, then looked at them expectantly, Riley clamped his jaw and stood. He gestured silently to the dance floor with a polite nod.

Tanzy allowed him to pull her chair out for her. But as she stood, she sent him a private wink and whispered, "I'm sorry," as she passed him. Apparently he was as easy to read as she was. He'd have to work on that.

As the floor was rapidly crowding, he was forced to place

his hand on her back to guide her. Her excruciatingly beautiful and very naked back. She found a small spot and turned gracefully toward him, letting her hand easily come to rest on his shoulder as he took her other hand in his own.

Think limp, he schooled himself. And he wasn't just focusing on his hands.

Fortunately, the crowd made any real movement impossible, allowing him to basically just shift his feet to the music. Unfortunately, the crowd also pushed them together. Often. He did the best he could to move them apart as swiftly as possible after each contact, careful to send an apologetic look her way, but otherwise staring past her shoulder.

He knew he was being aloof bordering on rude, especially after their table conversation. He also knew she'd noticed, gauging from the tiny lines at the tightened corners of her mouth, despite her pasted-on smile. A smile he knew she only maintained because of the constant nods aimed in their direction as the throng ebbed and flowed around them. Which was all fine with him. If she thought him stiff-assed, maybe she'd lose the interest he'd unwittingly sparked. Okay, not so unwittingly. Uncontrollably maybe.

But as the music continued, he found his thoughts wandering, to the feel of her slender hand in his, the narrow waist his palm spanned, the rustle of her silk dress, the smooth flow of their movements as she matched her rhythm to his. And, despite never thinking himself much of a dancer, much less ever using the dance floor for seduction, he allowed himself several long moments of imagining what it would be like if he weren't here under false pretenses. Imagined smiling down into her direct and very knowing gaze as he guided her around the floor, the two of them so wrapped up in each other that the rest of the world faded away. It was just her, in his arms, following his lead . . . on the dance floor, then off.

And then he realized he was staring at her . . . and that she was very intently watching him stare at her.

"What?" she asked, although with the orchestra in full swing, he could only tell what she'd said by reading her lips. Lips painted as red as that siren song of a dress Clarisse was torturing him with. And then he was leaning, closer to those lips, closer to finally tasting what he so badly wanted to sample. Their bodies slowed almost to a stop as his mouth hovered just above hers.

Only at the last fraction of a second, when he felt rather than heard her indrawn breath, did he shift his mouth to her ear and say the first thing that came into his head. "My feet are killing me."

She paused, looking more than a little nonplussed, then pulled back and pasted that damnably fake smile on her face. Her laugh was forced. "Isn't that supposed to be my line?"

He didn't respond, as sorry he'd stopped as he was relieved he'd managed it. He focused on edging them closer to the side of the floor as they continued to dance, returning his attention to the blur beyond her shoulder. Her smooth, softly curved, and enticingly bare shoulder.

She bumped up against him again as other pairs of dancers weaved in and out of their path. Each time he carefully set her back, and just as carefully refused to look at her. *Just get the hell off the floor, where you can keep your hands to yourself,* he repeated silently.

Their table was mere yards away, yet it might as well have been miles, for all the people clogging their path. Again and again, she was pressed against him, her soft breasts pushing up against his chest, her knees rubbing against his, her breath fanning his throat. He fought the growing need to say the hell with it, clamp an arm around her waist, and pull her tight up against his quite aroused body. Let her know once and for all she wasn't dancing with a damn sheep.

And just as his fingers tensed on her waist, as his gaze shifted to hers, inexorably drawn there no matter what he willed, the music ended on a thrumming crescendo.

His mouth was descending toward hers anyway, beyond caring that the dancing had stopped, when she broke their locked gazes and stepped easily and all too quickly out of his arms, lightly applauding the orchestra with the rest of the dancers. He managed to clap as well, then balled his hands into fists to keep from reaching for her again.

His only thought was to get them off the floor before another number began. He turned . . . and walked right into the one problem he hadn't foreseen.

"Hey there," a portly tux-clad gentleman announced with a jovial shout, hand outstretched and a smile curving his fleshy lips.

But it was the look of recognition in his eyes that had Riley's brain doing a last-minute tango of its own.

"Aren't you—?"

Riley quickly turned to Tanzy and guided her a bit abruptly toward their table, which was only steps away. Then, leaving her staring confusedly, he turned back to the man, stepping forward so that both of them were absorbed into the edge of the crowd.

God save him from football fanatics. His name was known to dedicated fans of the Pioneers, but his face was not. Still, every once in a while, one crawled out of the woodwork that did more than read the stats on the Pioneer website. "Hello," Riley said, shaking the man's hand.

"Parrish," the man said, quite happy at his surprise find. "Saw you play that blowout against the Saints. Hell of a runback you made. A real shame about the knee."

Riley smiled, praying like hell Tanzy was still at the table. The NFL didn't breed too many sheep. "Thanks, appreciate it."

"What brings you here tonight? Saw you at the head table. You lending your name to the foundation?"

Riley would have laughed if it wasn't so pathetic a question. Why was it that everyone thought all football players were millionaires? "Actually, I'm just here as Miss Harrington's escort."

The man's grin turned a bit sly and he gave Riley a little *mano a mano* punch on the arm. "Nice work if you can get it, eh?"

Riley worked hard to keep his gritted teeth looking like a pleasant smile. Besides, who was he to get angry? Hadn't he been thinking exactly that about this job? "I'd better get back."

"Tell her hello from Sam Dupree. My daughters read her column. I'll bet she keeps you hopping," he added with another knowing little wink. "You athletes get all the hot ones."

Riley managed a tight nod and got the hell away before he said or did something he'd regret. Despite the years he'd spent in a very physical sport, he wasn't often driven to violence off the field. But there were always exceptions. He strode back to their table, wondering how often Tanzy had to put up with this kind of crap. Even though he'd been hip deep in the whacko side of her occupation for weeks now, he hadn't really thought about the social, one-on-one element she dealt with on a daily basis.

He smiled, thinking she probably handled it a hell of a lot better than he would. A clever little comeback, a witty rejoinder, a dry smile . . . and they were probably left drooling and kicking themselves for revealing themselves to be such shallow assholes.

His smile faded when he spied her, pale and stiff, staring

at a note she'd just unfolded. The rest of the table was back on the dance floor, leaving her sitting alone. *Jesus Christ,* Riley swore silently, covering the remaining distance between them in a blink. Leave her alone for one minute—He shut off that unproductive train of thought and pulled out the chair next to her. It was only at the last second he remembered to play his role.

With all of his other buttons having been pushed in the past hour, it took what little control he had left to rein it in. "Something the matter?"

She folded the paper quickly, awkwardly, as if her fingers weren't operating right. Her smile was smooth, but her eyes were overly bright when she turned to him. "No, no, just a note from a fan."

Riley went rigid, digging his fingers into his thigh to keep from snatching the note from her hand. "I suppose you get a lot of that out in public."

Carefully and as casually as he could, he settled himself back in his chair and scanned the room as he sipped some water. *SoulM8. You sick son of a bitch. Where the hell are you?* Every hair standing up on the back of his neck told him that was who the note was from.

"Sometimes," Tanzy said, also taking a sip, but in her case it was the champagne she reached for.

The liquid barely shimmied in the glass and he admired how swiftly she brought herself under control. He was also glad to see that the note, whatever it said, had rattled her. Millicent had made it clear that Tanzy was very stubborn when it came to acknowledging the potential downside of her growing recognition. The elder Harrington had been very concerned that Tanzy hadn't taken these kinds of threats seriously in the past.

When Tanzy had mentioned this one by name, Millicent had worried that perhaps there was more to it than there usually was. And when talking to Tanzy about it hadn't given her peace of mind, she'd had a private talk with Tanzy's editor, who, as it turned out, knew nothing of this latest "extreme fan." Rather than have Martin confront her, which would only make her backpedal even faster, knowing she'd refuse to believe she could ever really be a target, Millicent had taken matters into her own hands.

But after going over all the evidence, Riley had tended to agree with Tanzy's assessment. SoulM8's activities fit the general pattern of the harmless percentage of the lunatic fringe.

But now he'd made contact. And everything had changed.

Now it was personal.

Dependable and stalwart are attributes you look for in a dog, not a lover. And then things change, the world stops making sense, and suddenly dependable starts looking incredibly sexy.

7

She'd had her hands on him . . . and she still couldn't picture him naked.

At the moment, however, all thoughts of whatever wolf might be lying in wait beneath that double-breasted jacket of his—naked or otherwise—had vanished. Replaced by a few simple words.

You're beautiful. And soon, very soon, you will be mine. All mine.

How could a handful of words strike such terror in a person's heart? She forced a sip of champagne, determined not to give away how shaken she was. *Where was he? Was he still in this room?* She restrained the urge to wildly scan every face in the crowded ballroom. It was an impossible task anyway.

Leaving, however, was not.

She placed her long-stemmed glass overly carefully on the table, then folded her hands in her lap. On top of the folded note that had been waiting for her after her dance with Riley. Which she'd been deliciously anticipating analyzing even before the song had ended. Only now she couldn't remember a second of it. All she could see were those scrawled words, a black slash of ink on white paper. So innocent, yet so menacing. *Very soon.* She shivered.

What in the hell did that mean? Not the words of an obsessed fan willing to accept the limitations of easily deleted email. Instead they were words that put her stupid sheep/wolf theory, this dance, her fantasies about Riley, and even her column in relative perspective.

SoulM8 had just crossed the line from Extreme Fan . . . to stalker.

"Um," she began, then wet her lips and pulled herself together. With a bright, hopefully not too bright, smile, she leaned over and said, "I've got an early call in the morning, radio show. I think we've done our official duty. If it's okay with you, I'd like to say our good-byes and head home."

Riley nodded, looking vastly relieved, and instantly stood and moved behind her chair to assist her. Any other time she'd have felt that twin reaction that was becoming all the more typical when she was around him. Intrigued, even flattered, by his constant gentlemanly manners. And frustrated that there didn't seem to be any depth to his oh-so-still waters. One minute he appeared to be completely disinterested . . . and uninteresting. The next, she'd swear there was this spark arcing between them. Sexual spark. Any other time, she'd have been fighting the urge to reach up and tug those glasses off, look straight into his dark eyes, and see for herself, once and for all, what, if anything, lay beneath.

But at the moment, all she wanted to do was get the hell out of there with the least amount of notice.

She stood as Riley slid out her chair, and nodded to the guests who had filtered back to the table. She managed gracious good-byes to the organizer of the event and the few other board members she could easily locate, before mercifully heading to the nearest exit. She hoped Riley was keeping up with her, because nothing was going to stop her.

Then his hand came to the small of her back as they navigated the edges of the crowded dance floor. His chest, somehow broad and reassuring, was right at her back; his breath, warm and steady, fanned the curve of her neck. If she hadn't been so intent on getting the hell out of there, she might have wasted a moment or two wondering why he made her feel safer. Wasn't that an alpha trait? Of course, at the moment, any warm body at her back would probably make her feel somewhat safer.

Still, even knowing he was right there with her, her heart was pounding, and she wished desperately it were in anticipation of getting him inside the dark and intimate interior of their limo. Instead she was surreptitiously checking out every person they passed. Was that man smiling overly familiarly? Was there a psycho gleam in that waiter's eyes? Did the doorman stare at her too intently? She searched for a friendly face. Where was Marty when she needed him anyway? Not that she'd confide in him even if he did magically appear in front of her. He was here to enjoy himself. Even if his wife was not. No point in ruining what was left of his evening.

Besides, the last thing she needed right now was the celebrity safety lecture. He was overprotective enough as it was, even more so lately with all the attention her new column's tangent was getting. Another empty-nest kickback, most likely. But she could handle this herself. She just needed to get out of here and as far away from whoever put that note on her table as possible.

She all but gulped the night air as they finally pushed through the doors to the wide front steps. Limos lined the curb and Tanzy was tempted to leap into the first one.

The gentle but firm pressure of Riley's hand on her back steered her down the line instead, until Millicent's driver appeared like a savior.

"Wainwright, there you are." *Too breathless, calm down.* "I hope you can get us out of here with minimal trouble." She was still rushing her words, clenching her purse too tightly as he nodded and smoothly opened the door for her.

Finally they were both inside, with the door shutting them in . . . and shutting immediate danger out. She let out a long, unsteady breath.

"Are you all right?"

"Fine, fine," she said, knowing her skin was flushed and she likely looked anything but. Now that they were heading home, she was starting to feel a little silly for her headlong flight. Did she think she was starring in a James Bond movie? She'd had too much champagne and too little of the pasty chicken and rubber beans, was what it was. One little note, probably from some harmless sixteen-year-old or something, and she'd gone completely around the bend. "I'm not much for those kinds of functions."

"You'd never suspect it."

She looked at him now, surprised by the personal, non-Riley-like observation. But then, he'd been surprising her all night. She found him gazing out the window at the passing lights. Not looking at her. Again, the yin and yang of Riley. Attentive, yet aloof. It was maddening.

"Thank you," she said, still studying him. "You looked pretty relieved to be getting out of there yourself."

He glanced at her, a small smile hinting at his lips. "I'm not much for those functions, either."

"You'd never suspect it," she responded in kind, and just as sincerely. "I want to thank you again for doing this for me. I know it's not in your job description."

"I didn't mind." He shifted his gaze away again and she found herself wishing he hadn't.

They rode in silence for another couple of minutes. Her fingers began a restless tapping on her handbag and her thoughts returned again to what lay inside. *A joke,* she told herself. *Just a sick joke from someone with way too much time on his hands.* Probably had a good laugh over her white-faced reaction and was even now typing some message to a fan bulletin board somewhere, crowing about it. She wished like hell she could believe that was all it was.

The events that had led to her finding the note played through her mind. She remembered Riley looking like he wanted to kiss her—again—leaning toward her. It had taken all her will to step away, ending her own little fantasy before he could dump cold water on it by whispering some other totally mood-killing thing in her ear. *My feet are killing me.* Jesus, had she really been so deep into her little obsession with him that she'd misread the signals that badly? Twice?

They'd left the dance floor then, Tanzy thinking Riley's feet must really be killing him, as he all but dumped her into her chair. Then she'd looked over her shoulder, half tempted to make some pithy, smart-ass remark, only to see him disappear back into the throng, pumping the hand of some older, shorter man. Still trying to figure him out, she'd absently reached for her glass, and discovered the note propped against it, instantly forgetting all about Riley, their dance, and his newfound acquaintance.

Only now, on rethinking the sequence of events, she found herself wondering if the older man had purposely pulled Riley away. Did he have something to do with the prank? It had to be a prank. Sick, twisted, and totally unfunny, but people could be all those things and still not be dangerous.

Keeping that thought uppermost in her mind, she asked, "Did you run into someone you knew? At the dance?" At his blank look, she added, "I saw you talking to someone."

"Oh. Yes, I did."

"Who was he?"

"Just someone who recognized me from some previous work I've done."

"Oh," she said, relieved. It had nothing to do with her, then. Good.

"He said to tell you hello."

She stiffened, her thoughts scattering, and was only vaguely aware of the way Riley's attention sharpened. "That's . . . nice. What was his name?"

"Sam Dupree. Said his daughters read your column." His gaze grew more intent. "Do you know him?"

"No, no, I don't." Now she looked out the window. She finally had his focused attention, just when she wanted it the least. "Probably just another person who thinks they know me from reading my column."

"Sort of like the person who left you that note?"

She hoped her flinch wasn't too apparent. If it was a prank, it was a damn good one, as it had certainly done the job. Of course, the prankster couldn't know about the emails, about SoulM8. He'd just gotten lucky. "It happens," was all she said.

"Does it happen often?"

She shook her head. It was all she could manage without giving away her state of mind. Which was rapidly moving back to the James Bond scenario. Because things like this didn't happen all the time. Or any of the time, really. Sure, people acted overly familiar with her on occasion, feeling that they knew her because of the intimate details of her life she shared with them on a biweekly basis. But those people, while occasionally obnoxious, were harmless. Or had been, anyway.

"What does your editor think about things like that? Do they ever provide security for you when you're out and about?"

"Oh, believe me, if it were up to Martin, he'd be escorting me personally to every taping and radio show. Which is why I don't go to him with things like this. It was just an innocent little note from a fan. No sense in letting him make a big deal over it."

"Can I ask you what it said?"

She darted a look at him, suddenly suspicious. He was awfully interested in this, which was odd for a guy who, up till now, didn't seem interested in anything having to do with her. "Why do you ask?"

He shrugged. "No reason. I suppose I'm a bit starstruck. I don't meet too many celebrities."

Now she laughed. "Yeah, right. You? Starstruck?"

He looked offended. At least, she thought he did. Those damn glasses muted everything. And the dim glow of the tiny recessed running lights inside the limo did little to help.

"Is that so odd?" he asked, quietly sincere.

God, he was an enigma. Oh-so-formal-and-smooth, bordering on bland, and yet there would be these glimpses of . . . something else. "I guess not," she answered, though she wasn't really entirely sure. Of anything. "You just don't strike me as a guy who cares about that sort of thing."

"What makes you say that?"

Good question, she thought. She slid her purse to the seat beside her, thankful to put both literal and figurative distance between herself and the note. "You seem very . . . self-contained."

He seemed to think about that, then nodded. "That's a fair assessment. But that doesn't make me immune to the out-of-the-ordinary."

She grinned, on far more familiar ground now that he was responding to her, talking to her. Flirting she understood, even if she didn't understand the man she was flirting with. Yet. "Are you saying I'm unusual? I'm not sure if I should be flattered or not."

That smile flirted with those lips again. Chiseled, she thought, so unsheeplike. And that voice of his. Perfect for the intimate depths of a limo ride through the night. If she closed her eyes and just listened to him, she could imagine all sorts of carnal scenarios.

"You don't strike me as a woman who worries overly much about flattery."

Her eyes snapped open before the first wicked visual could take shape. Dammit. "What is that supposed to mean? Celebrity or not, I'm still human. I like flattery as much as the next person. As long as it's sincere, anyway."

"I didn't say you didn't. What I said was that you don't strike me as a woman who places undue value or importance on it."

"Meaning?"

"Meaning you don't define yourself by how others perceive you. Your columns make that clear enough."

She grinned. "You read my columns?"

She wasn't sure, due to the lighting, but she swore his cheeks flushed. "Surely I'm not the only one of my gender who finds what you have to say entertaining."

"You do read them!" She crossed her legs, folded her arms, feeling somehow smug, as if she'd proven something by snagging his attention. Even if it was her words, not her personally, that had done the job. It was still part of her. Maybe the most important part. Certainly the most revealing. "So, tell me what you think. Honest assessment. I can take it."

He didn't respond immediately, didn't look at her, either. She was thinking of something outrageous to say, to provoke him, when he shifted his gaze . . . and neatly pinned her to her seat with one thick-lensed glance.

"Honestly? I think you're either incredibly brave or incredibly foolish. Or both."

Tanzy was momentarily taken aback. She'd been equally lauded and panned in her brief career, so that wasn't it. It was that he'd summed up both sides of the argument so neatly. "I imagine you're right," she said, baldly honest. "I'm probably both." She laughed. "A brave fool."

That surprised a smile out of him. Or as much of one as he'd ever graced her with.

His lower lip in particular snagged her wayward attention. Sharply defined, yet not at all lean or thin. What would he do if she leaned forward and just pulled that lip between her teeth and tugged a little? If she slid her lips over his. Slid her tongue into his mouth and—

"We're here," he announced somewhat abruptly.

Ending her little fantasy. And just before the juicy parts, dammit.

He slid out first, not waiting for Wainwright, then leaned down and extended a hand.

She paused for a moment before taking it. Just a few hours ago, she'd hoped for just this opportunity. Since then, they'd danced together, talked, laughed. Well, she'd laughed anyway. He still needed a little work in that department. Her purse and the note forgotten, she took what he offered. And while he didn't drag her from the car, then press her up against it, his grip was anything but limp.

She slid from the car, keeping his hand in hers as she stepped out and straightened. It was as close to him as she'd been, other than on the dance floor. Only they weren't dancing now.

His gaze was steady, but completely nonthreatening, noninvasive. So why did she feel her stomach muscles flutter, why did she want to press her thighs together against the little twinge of need that sprung to life between them? It made absolutely no sense. There was no wolf beneath the kind manners and polite attentiveness.

And she found she didn't care. Her world, once so orderly and amusing, was no longer so clearly defined. Her circle of friends, though she loved them dearly and knew the feeling was reciprocated, had now formed a club to which she had no membership card and wasn't prepared to sign a lifetime contract to obtain one. Her great-aunt and the work she did suddenly called to something inside her, something she needed to explore, decide if she wanted to delve into . . . along with all the attendant family issues that would arise if she did. And now her work as a columnist, her one safe place, the thing she controlled above all else, her conduit to helping make sense of the things life threw at her, had thrown her way an obsessive person who might or might not mean her harm.

And then there was Riley. An amusing sidebar, column fodder, an intriguing diversion. She'd thought of him as a specimen to be analyzed. Only now she realized he'd come to represent the calm at the center of a storm. Dependable. Unflappable. Riley.

"Miss?"

Wainwright's understated voice penetrated her thoughts. He was holding her purse, but her gaze was quickly drawn back to Riley and her revelation.

Riley took it from him when Tanzy continued to stand there, staring at him.

"Thank you, Wainwright. I'll see her inside."

"Have a good evening, then." He tipped his head.

Tanzy nodded absently, might have lifted a hand, but her gaze was still rooted on Riley. Dependable, intriguing, mysterious Riley.

"Is something the matter?"

She shook her head. Nothing was the matter. In fact, staring at those murky dark eyes behind those lenses, everything finally started to make sense. "Maybe that's what it's all about."

"I beg your pardon?"

"The Sheep Attraction Factor."

His lips twitched, just a little. And she determined right

then and there that she'd get a laugh out of him if it killed her.

"Sheep Attraction Factor?"

She nodded. "You're more than a mortgage and Special Sex Sundays. You're the guys who help make sense out of everything when everything stops making sense."

And then it happened. He smiled. Full-fledged, white teeth gleaming and everything. Her stomach went from fluttering to a full-scale flip and dip. Without thinking, she reached up and slid the glasses from his face.

His smile faded, but she didn't regret it. He stilled, and for a moment she thought he was going to take them back, or turn away. But he didn't.

"You have beautiful eyes." And he did, but it was more than that. It was what she saw in them that pulled at her. Wariness, desire, frustration. A lot of emotions roiling around in there for a guy who rarely showed any.

She lifted a hand, wanting to touch him, just stroke his cheek, anything. But he stepped back then, and he might as well have put his glasses on, as his expression grew completely shuttered.

She sighed, unable to stem the disappointment. He surprised her by catching her hand and lifting it back up. Again she was taken by the gentleness of his touch. Not limp. Gentle. She understood the difference now. And with his eyes on hers, he bent over her hand and pressed a kiss to the back of it. His lips were warm, soft. How could something so reassuring, so courtly even, be so inherently sexual? But her heart raced ... and her thighs clenched hard against the insistent ache between them.

"Thank you for the evening out," he said quietly. Then he let her hand go, slipped his glasses back on, and motioned for her to lead the way to the front door.

She paused beside him, wishing she knew what to say, but for the first time in her life, words failed her.

She made her way to the door, her thoughts and emotions in a jumble. "Night," she murmured as she passed by him into the house, then made her way up the stairs to her room. She was so lost in trying to figure out what exactly had happened outside that she didn't feel his gaze at her back. Didn't know he slid his glasses off and watched her every curve and sway as she negotiated the stairs in her spiky heels and formfitting gown.

Didn't watch him finally turn away . . . and pull the note out of her purse and unfold it.

Is it really so hard to believe that men and women aren't all that different when it comes to sexual urges? Why is it okay for men to go on the hunt, enjoy sex when the opportunity presents itself, no harm, no foul? But let a woman go on the prowl and she's characterized as a man-eater, gold-digger, or worse. All I'm saying is, let us all prowl equally. And to the victor goes the climax.

8

You're beautiful. And soon, very soon, you will be mine. All mine.

Riley's gut knotted and he had to work to keep from crushing the note in his fist. He took the purse and the note upstairs to his room, pausing briefly as he passed her door. What in the hell had he been thinking tonight?

It was one thing to contemplate coming back to her when this was all over. And a shock to realize he actually had. Apparently the idea of revisiting the tension that had spiraled between them since the moment they'd stepped beneath that crystal snowflake chandelier had been too tantalizing to ignore.

He imagined what he'd say to her, how he'd explain who he really was, the surprise and shocked expression that would shift to that knowing, deliberate smile when she realized she'd found a fellow wolf to play with.

They'd burn hot and bright. He knew that for certain. Just the taste of her skin had been enough to set him off. They might last a night or a month of nights before they flamed out, but it would be well worth the singe marks.

She'd been saucy and sexy and so sure of herself tonight. She'd also been vulnerable, baldly honest, and willing to look at things in a whole new way. Willing to look at him, her resident sheep, in a whole new way.

His lips quirked despite the frustration gnawing at him. She did that to him, too. Amused and annoyed, most of the time simultaneously. Like with her Sheep Attraction Factor. "If she only knew," he muttered, his smile fading as he let himself into his rooms.

His body was still humming from the frustration of tasting her skin and knowing he couldn't do anything about it. But he couldn't dwell on that, not when there was a nameless, faceless threat out there. Watching. Waiting. He had no business encouraging her newfound attraction to sheep. Especially since he wasn't one of the herd. He'd been sent here to hunt. And his prey wasn't her.

He rolled on latex gloves and carefully unfolded the note again. He got out a small case, unzipping it and laying it flat before setting to work. Lifting prints was easy enough to do if you didn't mind the mess it made. But he knew she'd come looking for her purse and its contents in the morning, and he wasn't ready to tell her who he really was. Although after tonight, for more than one reason, he knew he was going to have to. Just not yet.

She was already going to be pissed at him, so the least he could do was supply a detailed course of action that would give her a sense of security. If she didn't have her aunt fire his sheep-posing ass first.

Swearing and muttering, he began the painstaking process, hoping to find more than his prints and hers. Would SoulM8 be careless? Had he risked exposure by propping that note on the table himself? Or had he sent someone to do it for him? He'd have had no idea that Riley was there as more than an escort, and yet the note had appeared the only time Riley had been more than a foot from her side. They'd been watched. If not by SoulM8, then by someone helping him out. But Riley would bet on SoulM8 operating on his own. Stalkers generally didn't work in pairs.

He snorted in self-disgust. All the lectures he'd given Finn, and what had he gone and done? The very thing he'd so passionately argued against. *Well, not everything,* he argued, his mind drifting back to that moment on the dance floor when he'd so badly wanted to kiss her. Thank God he'd had sense enough to pull back before he did anything too foolish. Though he'd gotten his mouth on her anyway, hadn't he? So what if it had only been the soft skin on the back of her hand? Tell that to his raging hard-on, which apparently hadn't known the difference.

He snapped up the phone as he lifted a third partial print from the corner of the note and punched in an East Coast number. He had some connections to a certain fed via a former running back's brother. If he was lucky, with the time difference Parnell would still be on shift. "Hey," he said abruptly when the call connected, "this is Parrish. I need you to run some prints for me. Partials, but they're pretty clean. Yeah, nationwide, but I'm betting he's a California boy." He grinned as he listened to Parnell bitch, then said, "I know, add it to my tab."

He hung up, then went about setting up his laptop and connecting the handheld scanner. Within minutes he was transmitting the images via email to Parnell's office. Hopefully he'd get an answer back by morning, before Parnell's shift ended. They'd worked together before and Parnell was good and, more important, thorough.

In the meantime, he'd check his email, see if Ernie had gotten him anything more. Then he'd check hers, something Ernie had made possible for him—computer-fraud consultants being some of the best hackers out there—and make sure SoulM8 hadn't followed up on his close encounter.

An hour later, he was scrubbing at his gritty eyes, contemplating coffee or a shower or both. Ernie's email had thrown a whole new perspective on the case. By itself, finding out that *MainLine* used FishNet for all their employee and business emails and Internet service access was no big thing. Except their account was a huge one, one of upstart FishNet's biggest. So they'd been given carte blanche with regard to the number of email accounts they could set up. And Tanzy's editor, Martin, was the guy in charge of doling them out.

Martin, the same guy Tanzy had mentioned was going through some kind of postparenting, midlife sort of thing. Acting out of character. Giving her dates odd looks, as Riley had noted earlier tonight. Then there was the comment that he was particularly interested in Tanzy's comings and goings recently. She'd chalked up his attentions as paternal. But what if in Martin's eyes there was nothing paternal about his feelings for his young, personable, sexy protégée?

One glance at the clock told Riley he was going to have to put any further analysis of this new trail off till tomorrow. He was cooked anyway. And Tanzy hadn't been bluffing about the radio program, which meant he had about two and a half hours before meeting her at the curb for her scheduled four-thirty A.M. pickup. No more following at a discreet distance. He went in the limo from now on.

He stripped out of his briefs—the tux long since having come off—and crawled into bed, setting his alarm for four. That would give him enough time to shower and check for any email from Parnell. If the prints didn't end up attached to someone with a criminal record, he'd have to look into getting her editor's prints and run a comparison. That should be fun.

Despite the frustrations of the evening, both professional and personal, he drifted off to sleep with a hint of a smile on his lips, imagining her reaction when she found him waiting for her in the morning.

* * *

Tanzy tried to keep her attention on the radio hosts and the mike in front of her . . . and off of Riley, who was presently standing on the other side of the glass separating the broadcast booth from the engineers, watching her intently. Not that there was much to watch.

She'd been a guest on this particular program before, which dealt mostly with the morning drive guys giving her a hard time, her giving it right back, then taking some questions from callers. She had to be on her toes with these two, but their audience was huge and *MainLine* milked her appearances for all the advertising dollars they could get.

Still, her answers weren't as snappy as she'd have liked this morning, which meant Billy Mac and JoJo were quickly getting the upper hand. Never a good thing. Her distraction was partly due to the note from the night before, but mostly due to Riley's unsettling and unwavering focus. How could a guy be so distant and yet so invasive at the same time?

She still couldn't get over the fact that he'd been curbside and chatting amiably with the station's driver at the crack of dawn this morning. She hadn't even had her first Coke of the day, so she'd somehow let him hornswoggle his way into the limo and into the broadcast booth. Something about wanting to see behind the scenes. It had all sounded reasonable to her sleep-addled brain. Plus, she recalled thinking, how much trouble could a guy like Riley get into?

She hadn't counted on being the one having the trouble.

"So, Tanzy, this sheep versus wolf theory of yours sure has got the Bay Area talking." Billy Mac grinned widely, which was always a warning.

Tanzy straightened and took a bracing sip of Coke. Her third. It was barely eight A.M. And it wasn't helping. "That's one of the things I hope my column does, Billy, get a dialogue going between the sexes."

Billy turned to his cohost—or cohort, as was more the case—and shared a chuckle that was probably being echoed in truck stops and frat houses all over town. If she looked close enough, she'd probably detect foaming around their mouths. But while they both had the voices for radio, their looks were far short of celebrity standards. Billy Mac reminded her of the rabid sports fan guy who paints his belly blue and yells obscenities at referees. And JoJo . . . well, imagine Dennis Rodman in full drag but without the muscles. Tanzy preferred not to look too closely at either of them. Or gnash her teeth that their salaries were likely triple hers.

"So," JoJo broke in, pulling his mouthpiece closer, "do you take any responsibility for the *dialogue* those women have been dishing on their sheepy other halves this past week? All those women who read your column, then looked up at their man and thought, 'Damn, but I wanna bag me another wolf.' "

Tanzy knew she had to fire back fast and sharp, but her reflexes were slowed by that one millisecond glance she sent toward her own sheep. It was a millisecond too long.

Billy Mac, ever nimble, had already pressed a button, filling the air with the horrific sounds of wrenching, screeching metal. "That was the sound of the marital discord erupting all over town this morning, folks," he taunted.

Tanzy's mouth was open, but JoJo had already pressed another button, and a wolf howl split the air. "And that, my friends, was for all those wolves out there, gearing up for some new action!"

Tanzy wanted to bury her head in her arms. Or go home and crawl back into bed. She never lost control like this. Martin was likely having a cow.

"You want to say something to those women you've stirred up, Tanzy?" Billy Mac tossed out.

"Or the wolves panting at their doors?" JoJo added with a cackle.

It was like watching a train wreck. Or trying to run hard in soft sand. She couldn't make it stop, couldn't seem to engage her tongue fast enough. She could only sit and stare. At Riley. Solid, dependable Riley.

Like he was going to do something to fix this?

And then the horror increased as Billy Mac zeroed in on the direction of her gaze. "Hey, maybe you want to tell us a little about this hunka hunka burning love you brought with you this morning." He pressed his lips to the mike, dropped his voice another octave, and added, "At the crack of dawn, I might add."

Tanzy's eyes widened. *No, no. Don't do this.*

"Who is he, Tanzy? Inquiring minds and single women everywhere want to know. Or . . . is he off the market?"

"He sure doesn't look like Santa's helper to me," JoJo added wickedly. He was already motioning for them to open the control door and send Riley in. Tanzy sent him an apologetic look . . . then frowned. Was that a smile playing at the corners of those lips of his? Lips she'd actually spent a decent portion of the night dreaming about?

"I believe this is the first time you've brought a guest, isn't it?" Billy Mac asked suggestively.

"Maybe he wasn't done howling when she had to come into work this morning," JoJo said with a sly wink.

Finally—thank God!—she found her voice. "He works for my aunt. He's just along for the ride, guys. No pun intended," she added quickly, cursing herself for giving them such an opening.

But it was too late. JoJo was sending the wolf howl over the airwaves again and someone was miking Riley. This wasn't a train wreck, it was a natural disaster.

"So, your name is?" JoJo asked.

And that was when Riley froze.

If Tanzy hadn't been so frantic, she'd have enjoyed that deer in headlights moment. Immensely. Not that it was Riley's fault he'd been dragged into this mess, but he hadn't exactly fought against being pulled into it. Of course, she couldn't actually imagine Riley getting physical or anything. But still, a few of those perfectly modulated words of his would certainly have calmed things down.

"I'd rather not comment on that," he finally managed.

"Hooee," JoJo crooned, "you got a voice on you, don't you, sugar?"

Riley looked at JoJo in a whole new way.

Now Tanzy did smile, and sent Riley a silent thank-you for taking the focus off of her for a moment and allowing her to regroup. He had saved the day after all. Her hero.

"Ah, thanks," Riley managed. "It's in the genes. Nothing special."

"Well, why don't you let me be the judge of that," JoJo murmured suggestively. "And we can discuss those jeans later, honey."

Apparently Riley didn't listen to the *Billy Mac and JoJo Show*—or he'd have known that they were the Will and Grace of morning drive time.

"So, you're just friends, you say?" Billy Mac stepped in, filling the dreaded dead air. "What do you think of Tanzy's latest theory? First off, would you categorize yourself as a wolf or a sheep?"

Riley's gaze went unerringly to hers. And in that moment, Tanzy found herself wondering just what his answer would be. Which was ridiculous. It was obvious to everyone but JoJo apparently, what he was. Except . . .

She tore her gaze away. As much as she'd like to leave Riley to the two radio wolves, rational thought must prevail. She depressed her mike switch and said, "I don't think he cares to share his livestock orientation any more than his name, guys. But I *can* share that many sheep in good standing have contacted me and are less than thrilled with my observations."

They both turned on her like vultures on fresh roadkill. Or Billy Mac did. JoJo was still sending lingering glances Riley's way. "So there *is* marital discord in response to your theory?" Billy Mac asked.

"Not the way you're thinking. It's more that men are surprised that their wives might occasionally fantasize about a quickie with some hot body, just like they do. Not that they really want to act on it, any more than their spouses do—"

She simply stared down Billy Mac's "Yeah, right" and dry chuckle.

"Most of them, anyway," she clarified. "But honestly, do you all really think we only care about getting our whites whiter and finding creative ways to cook leftovers? You think we don't notice the nice butt on the UPS man? You think we don't have a fantasy or two about doing the bicycle messenger right there in the elevator at work?" She smiled sweetly when Billy Mac almost swallowed his tongue. "We might not think about sex every two-point-three seconds, like men do, but I say we do pretty decently on a daily basis." She had to work not to look at Riley, for fear of losing what little momentum she'd built.

Billy Mac finally recovered. "And that's just the married women she's talking about, folks!" He turned to her. "So, what about the single women? Are you saying if it's available, they want it? Do women really have the hots for guys who just want a hit-and-run? Or do they want the hot sex, then secretly hope to tame the guy, dress him up nicely, and take him home to Mama?"

"I think some women want the thrill of satisfying sex without the attendant complications of a relationship, the same as guys." She waved a hand before JoJo could jump in.

"I know, I know, the safe-sex thing." She leaned closer to her mike. "I am not, repeat not, advocating unsafe, unprotected random sex acts." She grinned, then got snagged in Riley's attentive gaze as she hit the stride that had eluded her all morning. When it worked right, it could be a real rush. And somehow, rather than distracting her, having him watch her now made it all the more stimulating. She didn't question it, not right then. *When you're on a roll, you go with it and count casualties later.*

"I am, however, advocating that with proper protection and precautions taken, women should get their satisfaction the same way men do," she continued. "Whenever, wherever. And with the same lack of stigma that men enjoy, and have since the dawn of time."

"So you're saying wolves come in both genders," JoJo said.

Tanzy shifted her attention to him, surprised. "You know what? I hadn't thought about it like that, but you're exactly right. Prowling isn't the exclusive right of men."

The station manager signaled that time was up and after one last wolf howl and a quick thanks for stopping by, Billy Mac switched to a series of taped commercial spots. "Entertaining as always," he told Tanzy. "Thanks for letting us have some fun." He looked to Riley. "Hope you didn't mind, man."

Riley merely shook his head and allowed one of the techs to retrieve his mike.

"You want to stick around a while?" Billy Mac asked Tanzy. "We didn't get any call-in time and the board is lighting up like Christmas."

Tanzy was glad she'd salvaged the worst of it and wanted nothing more than to get the hell out of there. But she also wanted to be invited back and knew Martin was hoping for that as well. Still . . .

"You have another appointment to get to, don't you?" Riley quietly interjected.

Actually, she'd been planning on calling Rina and Susan to discuss shower plans over lunch, but Riley didn't know that. She caught his gaze then, and realized he was giving her a speedy exit if she wanted one. *Thanks again,* she signaled with a brief nod, then turned a bright smile toward the disc jockeys. "He's right. I'd completely forgotten. Good thing you tagged along," she told Riley. "Maybe I should get my own personal assistant."

"I was thinking the same thing, honey," JoJo added dreamily, and Tanzy and Billy Mac laughed.

"Well then, until next time," Billy Mac told her, shaking her hand, then Riley's. "I'll schedule more time for call-ins the next go-around. Maybe we'll do an entire call-in show, whaddya think?"

"That could be interesting," Tanzy said, but what she was thinking was, *Not in this lifetime.* It was tough enough dealing with these two. She knew she'd dodged another bullet this morning by not having to take callers. You never knew who was going to be on the other end on a live program, and sometimes that delay button just wasn't enough.

Not to mention there was a certain individual she didn't need to provide that kind of opportunity to.

Shoving thoughts of the note and SoulM8 out of her mind, she gathered her bag, and with a quick grin snagged a Dr Pepper from Billy's minifridge, then followed Riley out of the station.

There was a small crowd gathered outside, which wasn't all that unusual during the morning drive show. It was a bright, sunny mid-December morning, but it wouldn't have mattered if it was foggy and dank. People always seemed to show up. Some were students from the nearby campus, some were commuters, some just passersby. Most were hoping Billy Mac or JoJo would send someone outside with a mike to give them their fifteen seconds of fame and let them ask a question or just gush.

Most of the time, Tanzy didn't mind. Depending on the mood of the crowd, she'd occasionally respond to shouted comments, even sign an autograph or two. Today she just wanted to get in the car and get home. She should have been happy. The show hadn't been a total disaster, she'd gotten the return invite. Martin would be happy, the sales reps in advertising would be happy. Why wasn't she happy?

Because there was something about looking at a crowd of nameless people that made her edgy in a way she never had been before. She couldn't help but eye them suspiciously, and hated that she felt that way.

Two women pushed through the small throng, making her jump slightly. Riley immediately pulled her back against him and was in the process of putting himself between her and the intruders when the women both smiled and shouted, "You tell it, Tanzy! You go, girl!"

More disconcerted by Riley's immediate reaction to the perceived threat than by her uncustomary jumpiness, or by the women themselves, she managed a nod and thumbs-up before pushing on. Riley's hand was planted on her lower back and he was steadily moving her toward the limo. But when she glanced back at him, his face was the same calm, imperturbable mask. *Steady as she goes,* Tanzy thought.

Someone in the crowd, probably a fraternity inhabitant, cut loose with a wolf howl. The call of the wild was quickly adopted by the other dozen or so campus denizens in the group. Several of the women joined in, pointedly showing the men that they could be wolves, too.

Riley bent down close to her ear even as he continued propelling her forward. "See what you've started?"

His deep voice gave her a hot little buzz, but it was overruled by her need to get out of the crowd and into the car. Sort of like the creepy feeling you got when you climbed the basement steps in the dark. Any other time she would have enjoyed the little buzz, milked it even, maybe shot him a wiseass grin and suggestive comment. But not at the moment. At the moment she was wishing she was some anonymous office-worker drone who'd never gotten the idea to share her every last thought with the public at large.

Then someone yelled, "Who's the dude? Tell us your name!" The rest of the crowd chimed in.

Someone called out, "Take off the glasses! He's hot, Tanzy!"

Another shouted, "Is he the next wolf on your list?"

Then the howls started again.

She heard someone chuckling close behind her, but didn't dare a glance. The limo was so close . . .

"Is it always like this?" Riley asked, pressing closer as the crowd shifted inward.

"Sometimes," she called back.

"You usually do this gauntlet alone? Maybe your editor has a point about getting some protection when you're out on appearances."

"The driver helps me out when necessary, or someone from the station accompanies me out. It's harmless fun. They're just fans." Now if only she could shake the feeling that there might be one fan in particular out there, possibly in that very crowd, who wasn't so harmless.

The limo was right in front of them, the driver was opening the door, when something sailed overhead from the rear of the crowd. Someone shouted, "Look out!"

The next thing Tanzy knew, her head was being pushed down and she was being body-planted onto the backseat of the limo. She straightened in time to see the driver already behind the wheel, even as Riley pulled the door shut behind himself. Which meant Riley had been the one to shove her in the car.

"Drive," Riley barked at the driver, in a tone she'd never heard him use before.

They immediately pulled away from the curb and into the growing crowd. The driver did this for a living, Tanzy told herself as the crowd reluctantly shuffled away from the moving car. He'd moved far bigger celebrities through far bigger throngs than this. Thankfully the station and the mob quickly faded from view. A view Riley steadily watched until it was no longer visible. Only then did he turn to Tanzy.

Who was looking at him like she'd never seen him before. And maybe she hadn't. "What the hell happened back there?"

"I don't know and I didn't think you wanted to stick around and find out."

"It was a paper airplane, sir," the driver informed them after hooking his radio back in its holder. "Everything's okay."

"Thank you," Riley told him, then settled back in his seat as if everything really was okay.

She continued to stare at him, until he finally looked at her again. "Is something else the matter?"

Yes, she wanted to shout. *Everything was the matter.* "You didn't answer me. What went on back there?"

"I think the driver explained that—"

"That's not what I'm talking about and don't pretend you don't understand what I'm asking."

He stared at her in silence for a long moment.

"Answer me, Riley. And take those damn glasses off."

That had him raising his eyebrows, but nothing more. And the glasses stayed put. She folded her arms and stubbornly held his gaze. Finally he said, "I just wanted to make sure you weren't hurt. I'm sorry if I got a little rough."

"That's just it, you don't get rough. Ever. And you don't

bark commands. It's not in you. Or not in the you I thought you were."

He simply looked at her and, in that damnably calm voice of his, said, "But then, you don't really know me all that well, do you?"

"No," she said just as reasonably, though her thoughts were anything but. "You're right. Apparently I don't."

But I'm going to.

Friends know you better than anyone else.

Which can be really annoying. Especially when they point things out to you that you already know ... and would sincerely like to pretend you didn't.

9

I'm telling you, Rina, I don't know what to think." Tanzy pushed back her hair as she leaned down to sip her milkshake.

"How can you drink those things?" Rina asked, sipping at her own chilled mango cooler.

"Milk's good for you."

"You're forgetting the ice cream and chocolate."

"No I'm not." Tanzy took a long drink, then sighed with gusto. "What's not to love?"

Rina just shuddered. "The only thing I like milky is my complexion, thank you very much." She leaned forward and peered toward the dining room doorway, then glanced back to Tanzy. "So, what is it exactly that you think he's hiding? And where is he hiding anyway?"

"He's in Millicent's offices on the second floor, on some conference call." She picked at the chicken and arugula salad Rina had brought for lunch.

"You're wishing those were fries and a burger, aren't you?" Rina said, crunching on a walnut.

"It's what any self-respecting person has with a milkshake."

"I brought the food. You could have been sharing my mango juice."

"Shoot me now," Tanzy said with a shudder. "And can I help it if milkshakes are the one thing I know how to cook? Besides, Millicent has this killer blender that—".

Rina laughed and held up her hand. "Spare me, please. How you keep that figure, I have no idea."

"Easy. There's more of it to keep all the time," Tanzy joked, slapping at her thighs.

"I hear you."

Tanzy just snorted. "Right. When you live on arugula, it's such a struggle."

"Actually, Garrison has this personal trainer, Rod, who is amazing. I could send him over here if you're interested."

"His name is Rod? For real? Just exactly what kind of workout does he give?" Tanzy asked, wiggling her eyebrows.

"Not that kind, Ms. Sex-on-the-brain."

"Oh, and not you? Wasn't that you, just a week or so ago, lusting after Wolfgang? And really, what is it about him anyway? He is the last guy you'd look at and think, 'Now, there's a guy who must have women piling up at his feet.' "

"It's those eyes, I tell you," Rina said with a dreamy sigh.

"Yeah, and it doesn't hurt that the women he works with are butt-naked half the time."

"I always wondered what it would be like. Modeling for an artist," Rina pondered. "Those hooded, soulful blue eyes staring at you while he brushed you onto his canvas. Feeling each brush stroke as if it were—"

"Enough. You're turning *me* on. And Wolf does nothing for me."

Rina laughed. "Well, sex is fun and fun to talk about, but you do know there is more to life and love than sex."

"I have a life. And sex is a nice benefit of it."

"What about love? You want to grow old alone?"

"Does anyone actually *plan* to do that? It's just the thought of living under one roof, under one blanket, with the same man ... forever ..." She shook her head. "Can't picture it. Not yet, anyway."

Rina propped her elbows on the table and gave Tanzy a considering look. "You're already living under the same roof with a man. So why isn't he under the same blanket already?"

"Riley?" Tanzy snorted a laugh, but it sounded forced, even to her own ears. "No thanks. I'm not ready to enter the sheep derby just yet."

"But didn't you just get done telling me about this macho stunt he pulled at the station today?"

Tanzy chewed on the end of her straw. "I know."

"Aha! So you are thinking of going over to the baa-aad side."

Tanzy groaned. "Oh please. Don't you think I get enough of that in the emails? I'm beginning to wish I'd never mentioned my stupid theory. Or at least picked a different representative species. It's bad enough having to listen to Martin's corny sheep jokes all day."

"He's still being a bit clingy?"

"Yeah. And here I thought it was the mom who got all weirded out when the last baby bird flew the nest. But Martin ... well, whatever. I'm sure it will pass."

"Does he talk about it a lot? Maybe he's having trouble at home."

"I operate strictly under the don't-ask-don't-tell theory regarding mixing personal information with my business life."

"Which can get tricky, considering your personal information is your business life."

"All the more reason not to chat about it with my boss." She sighed under Rina's stare. "Martin is really wonderful, and he's done more for me than anyone. I love the guy. But I don't want to be buddies. And I definitely don't want to get in the middle of whatever personal crisis he's got going on at home. That's what he's got a wife for. Let Betty Barbara handle that."

"Betty Barbara? Her name is actually—"

Tanzy waved her hand. "Actually, it's something French. Not at all what I'd have imagined for him. Small, nice figure, with that vaguely bored Gallic thing going on. We ran into them at the foundation ball."

"And you call her Betty Barbara because . . . ?"

"It's not important. The important thing is, she exists. And if Martin needs help, he's got her to get it from. I'm not an advice columnist. He keeps his personal life to himself. And I'll keep my personal life . . ." She stumbled, made the bad mistake of looking toward the hallway, but finished defiantly when Rina grinned at her. "To myself. Thank you very much."

"Speaking of that personal life, when do I get to meet him? I'm dying to size him up." She sent a salacious glance Tanzy's way. At her eye-roll of disgust, Rina merely smiled and added, "I might not be in the market to make a purchase, but I can window-shop to my heart's content."

Tanzy laughed. "I wish I'd thought of that one this morning. I could have used it. I may still."

Rina nodded graciously. "Be my guest. And speaking of guests, I'm having a few people over—Now hear me out," she said when Tanzy began her automatic protest. "He's a doctor—"

"Rina, you know that's not exactly a selling point with me."

"Just because he has an MD and a six-figure income doesn't mean he can't be a bad boy. You know how surgeons can be so alpha."

"Arrogant isn't necessarily the same as alpha. Look at Wolfgang. Prime example."

A troubled look crossed her friend's face.

"What? Sure, he's bounced on his share of models.

Models with the collective IQ of belly button lint. They wouldn't know the difference between alpha and beta if their emaciated bodies depended on it. My point is, he's screwing these bimbos right in his own studio. In their own house. *That's* what I call arrogant. If you want to call it alpha, well, it's a genus of wolf I can do without, thanks."

"That's not it." Rina paused, then sighed and said, "Remember when Sloan showed up at the bowling alley looking all flushed the other day? We all assumed she was having reconciliation sex with Wolf? Well . . . now I'm not so sure."

"Meaning?"

"Remember she was a bit evasive when I first said something about it?"

"I just remember the way she tucked into that steak and cheese sub. Very un-Sloan-like."

"Her whole attitude that day was."

Tanzy shrugged. "She's going through a tough time. Cut her some slack."

"I actually didn't think about it after that day. Until . . ."

Now Tanzy frowned. "What happened? What's up?" When Rina hedged, she gave her a look. "You brought it up. Now spill."

"Okay, okay." She blew out a breath. "I was supposed to meet Garrison at the Huntington yesterday afternoon, for early cocktails with a client of his. Well, I saw Sloan coming out of the elevator."

"So, she could have been there for any number of reasons."

"Yeah, and one of them was about six-two, blond, and built like Adonis."

The straw popped out of Tanzy's mouth when her jaw dropped. "No way!"

"Yes way."

"But—" She blinked, trying to picture Sloan having a

nooner. She couldn't manage it. "I thought they were working things out."

"So did I."

The gong sounded just then. "That must be Sue." Tanzy pushed her chair back, then paused. "Does anyone else know?"

Rina shook her head. "Not from me. I debated on even telling you. I mean, maybe it was something innocent. I just . . . well, I'm worried about her."

"Yeah," Tanzy said, leading the way to the foyer. "We'll talk about it more later." She paused at the base of the stairs. "Let's hope it's not what you thought it was. I don't think they could survive another infidelity, even if it is hers this time."

Rina smiled, but it was a little sad. "Well, look at it this way, you wouldn't be the only single one anymore."

Tanzy merely gave Rina a look, then shouted, "I got it," up the stairs when the gong sounded again.

"Spoilsport," Rina muttered, casting a look up the stairs.

"You and Sue are here to check out the house for the shower. Not my aunt's personal assistant. No getting distracted."

"Sounds like you're the one who's distracted," Rina mused.

But Sue was bustling into the foyer just then, arms overflowing with fabric, and bags full of God knew what else, depriving Tanzy of a good comeback. If she'd had one. Because, dammit, Rina was right. She was distracted, and the frenzy over her recent columns, along with the whole SoulM8 thing, was only part of it.

"Hey, what's all this?" she asked as Sue literally spilled packages into Tanzy's arms.

"Swatches. Theme ideas."

"Um, Sue? It's a shower, not *Designer Showcase*."

Sue and Rina shared a look of pity, then shook their heads in sad agreement.

"What?" Tanzy shifted the bundles in her arms. "Millicent has this place decorated to the teeth for the holidays. What more could you possibly do?"

"It's a baby shower, not a Christmas party," Sue said, as if explaining the obvious.

"Fine, but they're still perfectly good, if excessive, decorations. There's even cherubs. Somewhere. So why do you need to go to the trouble of—"

"When it's your turn for a shower, you'll understand."

"Another reason to stay single and childless," Tanzy told Rina.

Rina and Sue shared another look, another sad shaking of heads.

Tanzy waved a hand. "Fine, fine. Have at it."

"You know Mariel will appreciate the effort."

Tanzy couldn't argue that point. Mariel's wedding cake alone was a testament to what could be done with cake, icing, and a degree in engineering. "Where do we start? Never mind, I don't want to know." She headed toward the front parlor.

Sue sidestepped her and blocked her way, then smiled brightly. Too brightly. "I was hoping you'd consent to letting us use the formal sitting room. It has that great wall hanging with the angels and the ceiling mural and—"

"Do you think Millicent would mind?" Rina cut in, sensing Tanzy was already rapidly reaching her shower-planning saturation point. One of the many reasons Tanzy loved her.

"I'm sure she wouldn't." Tanzy led them back through the foyer and sent a short, wistful glance up the stairs. She'd love nothing more than to be in her office just now, working, thinking, whatever. Alone.

Only when she glanced up the stairs, it wasn't her office she imagined herself in. Nor did she picture herself alone.

And the first thought she had of how she'd while away the afternoon had absolutely nothing to do with typing . . . or creative thinking.

Rina bent her head and whispered, "Baaa," in Tanzy's ear.

"Very funny," she murmured, then smiled as Sue turned back with a questioning look on her face.

"What's going on?"

"Nothing," Tanzy said, shooting Rina the Silent Look of Death.

Which, buzzed from the mango cooler, no doubt, Rina blithely ignored. "Tanzy's got the hots for Millicent's secretary."

Sue's eyes popped wide even as Tanzy groaned. "You mean—What's his name again? Randy?" She snickered. "How appropriate."

"It's Riley. And he's a personal assistant, not a secretary. Please, can't we just go into the parlor and swathe and drape things?"

Sue obviously forgot all about swathing. "I thought you said he was the quintessential beta man. Not your type at all."

"That was before he saved her life today," Rina added with a smirk.

"What?" Sue's wide-eyed gaze shifted from Rina to Tanzy.

Tanzy skipped the Look of Death and pantomimed wringing Rina's neck instead. "It was nothing," she told Sue, talking over Rina's overly dramatic explanation. "He just overreacted to the crowd, that was all. He wasn't used to that sort of thing."

"Funny how he knew exactly how to put you in the limo, though," Sue said, sending a thoughtful look up the grand staircase. "And you say he tried to block you when those women burst through the crowd." She smiled slyly at Rina. "How very . . . alpha of him."

Tanzy couldn't have agreed with her more, which was why she shepherded both of them through the anteroom on the opposite side of the foyer, to the formal sitting room just beyond it.

But even as Sue deposited her remaining armful of fabrics and whatnot, her thoughts were obviously still spinning on Riley and the radio station. "So, you panicked because someone threw a paper airplane?"

"I didn't panic. Exactly. And we didn't know it was a paper airplane until after. I was just a little edgy from the show—"

"And why was Riley with you anyway?" Sue wanted to know.

"I'm still not sure, really. He was waiting by the limo this morning and asked if he could tag along. At the foundation thing last night he said—"

"Whoa. Wait a minute. Riley was your date for the Crystal Charity Ball?" Rina asked. "You didn't tell us about that. Why didn't you tell me about that? What about Carmine?"

"Carmine is unavailable. Probably permanently."

Rina sighed. "I'm sure he's going to make some guy a really wonderful husband. What a shame."

Tanzy and Sue laughed, but nodded. "Riley was nice enough to step in," Tanzy explained. "I'm sure he felt obligated because of Millicent, though I told him he certainly wasn't expected to—"

"Yeah, yeah, yeah," Sue cut in, "get to the good stuff. Did he dance with you? Is that what started all this?"

"We danced, but honestly, it wasn't anything special."

Rina tipped Tanzy's chin up with one long, lacquered nail, and peered into her eyes. "Liar. Something happened."

Tanzy opened her mouth to say . . . something, anything,

to get them off this subject. She was regretting bringing it up at all. But the last twenty or so hours had been more than a little disconcerting. She sighed and plopped down on the Queen Anne settee, letting her bags slide to the floor. "I thought he was going to kiss me, okay? But I was wrong. It was just, I don't know, the music going to my head, or the champagne."

"So . . . you wanted him to kiss you." Rina made it a statement. "Then what?"

"What do you mean? Then nothing. He bent down, I thought . . . what I thought, and instead of locking lips, he told me his feet were killing him."

Sue spluttered a laugh, then covered her mouth. "I'm sorry, honey, but honestly, you have to admit that's funny. So then what?"

"Nothing."

"Liar," Rina said again. "Something else happened. Something else that has you still thinking about that dance and almost kiss."

"It wasn't an almost anything."

"It was. You're experienced enough to know what a man is thinking before he does."

"Thanks, I think," Tanzy said with a sideways glance. "And I can't tell anything with that man. Those damn glasses he wears murk everything up. And his eyes are pretty damn se—" She stopped short, but it was too late.

Rina and Sue were grinning.

"So," Sue said consideringly, "you've seen the eyes, have you? What else do you want to uncover about our Riley?"

Tanzy folded her arms. "I refuse to answer that on the grounds that you two will make me crazy if I do."

"Aha!" Sue crowed. "So then what? What happened on the limo ride home? I bet that was fraught with all sorts of sexual tension."

Something in her expression must have given her away,

which she could have kicked herself for and would later, repeatedly.

"Something else did happen, didn't it?" Rina asked, her smile fading. "And it wasn't about kissing Riley."

Tanzy thought about trying to backpedal her way out of it, but in the end she relented. And, she had to admit, it was a relief. Maybe she should have leaned on a shoulder sooner. "I got another note."

"What?" they both asked in a hushed whisper.

Then Rina straightened. "Wait a minute. I thought he emailed the notes. Are you saying—" She let out a shocked gasp as Tanzy nodded.

"He was there," Tanzy confirmed. "At the dance."

"He who?" Sue asked.

"SoulM8," Rina said, and Tanzy nodded.

Sue gasped then, and moved to sit down across from her, pushing piles of fabric and her legal pad of notes out of her way. "Your cyber stalker? He's made personal contact now?"

Rina sat next to her and tugged Tanzy's hand between her cool, smooth palms. "Why didn't you tell us? This has gotten serious. Are you sure it was him?"

"Who else professes his undying love to me on a biweekly basis? Unless the loonies are just crawling out of the woodwork." She shuddered at that possibility. "But I'm pretty sure it was him. The tone was the same. Sort of."

"What do you mean, 'sort of'?" Sue demanded.

Tanzy shrugged, very uncomfortable now. "Well," she began, before finally looking away from their worried expressions. "This time he was more . . . specific."

Now Sue shuddered. "Oh, Tanzy, how creepy. Did you alert security?"

She shook her head. "No, we just left."

"Well, it's no wonder Riley was on alert for you, then. What did he say about it?" Rina asked. "The note, I mean."

"He didn't read it. I told him it was just a fan letter."

"What? And he believed you?"

Tanzy didn't answer right away. She'd thought he had. "We'd talked about being a celebrity and he told me he could understand being starstruck. It was why he wanted to come to the station with me this morning. To see behind the scenes."

Sue sucked in her breath and Tanzy and Rina both looked at her.

"What?" Tanzy asked.

"You said he was starstruck, and then he wanted to follow you this morning. You don't think he's—?"

Rina and Tanzy shook their heads at the same time.

"Why bother with emails and notes," Rina pointed out. "He's right under the same roof."

They all gave a collective little shiver.

"It's not Riley," Tanzy stated flatly. "Besides, we were on the dance floor when someone left it on our table."

"What did it say? Exactly."

Tanzy looked at them both. She really didn't want to put it into words. She'd just spent the better part of the night trying to make herself believe that she was being overly dramatic. Then the stupid hoopla at the station this morning had rattled her again. It was all getting ridiculous. "I don't want to pull you guys into this, you've got enough—"

"Tanzy," Rina broke in quietly. "What did it say?"

She shifted her gaze to her best friend, then sighed. "It said, 'You're beautiful. And soon, very soon, you will be mine. All mine.' "

"Any other time I'd have loved to get a note like that," Sue said, rubbing her arms. "You have called the cops or something by now, right?"

Rina nodded in agreement. "This is definitely not the garden-variety obsessed fan. He's threatened you now,

Tanzy. What did the cops say? Is there anything they can do? Anything you can do?"

"I didn't call them." Tanzy lifted a hand when they both started in on her. "They can't do anything. He hasn't done anything illegal. He's emailed me and left a note on a table at a public function. And I don't think what he said was threatening. You could interpret that note a million different ways."

"I don't know. It sounds like he's planning something," Rina said. "You should at least make them aware you're being stalked."

Even though she'd thought the word in her head, hearing Rina say it out loud was ten times spookier. She finally nodded, feeling vaguely queasy as reality finally forced its way in. "You're right. I'll call them."

"Does Martin know, at least?" Sue asked. "Is he offering protection?"

"No. I will tell him, though," she added quickly when they both looked at her. "I have to get my next column in tomorrow. I'll tell him during our phone conference after I send it in." She sighed. "Just what I don't need. Giving him any reason to hover over me more than he already does." Just thinking about that conversation made her head throb.

"Maybe you need hovering over," Rina said pointedly.

"Yeah, but you know how he's been lately. He's going to go way over the top about this and demand all kinds of whack things." Not the least of which was probably a bodyguard.

"At least you're staying in Big Harry," Sue said. "Millicent has all kinds of security, right?"

Tanzy nodded. "The latest and greatest." It was the first thing either of them had said that actually made her feel better.

"So, wait," Sue said suddenly, still putting it all together.

"You thought the stalker was in the crowd at the radio station, then? And Riley knew about him by then, right? So it's no wonder he was edgy. Maybe that's the real reason he went with you in the first place. He was worried about you."

Tanzy sat there. Sue had just unwittingly nailed the thing that had been bugging her about this morning since it happened. "That's just it. I never did tell him."

Sue and Rina exchanged glances again. Tanzy sighed in disgust. "You know, I never thought I'd hear myself say this, but can we talk about the baby shower now?"

She had to stare them down, but they both finally nodded. Reluctantly. She knew it would come up again, and soon. Not that it would make any difference. Now that Sue had zeroed in on it, Tanzy would likely think of little else until she had it figured out.

After one last lingering look and a little sigh, Sue summoned her trademark sunny smile and turned her attention to the bags she'd dropped on the floor by her feet. She dug around in one of them and came up with a frilly yellow umbrella and a floppy stuffed bird. "Okay, first order of business. Themes, ladies. Showers, storks, or both?"

"I feel simply terrible. I should have never asked her to substitute for me." Millicent sighed. "Who would have ever thought someone would approach her at a function like that?"

"You couldn't have known," Riley said, reassuring her again. "Even I didn't predict he'd make personal contact. As I explained before, most obsessed fans—"

"Hogwash, let's call the little bastard what he is, a stalker."

"Well," Riley reluctantly conceded, "he qualifies for that description now, I'm afraid."

"Oh dear," Millicent said, for once sounding every one of

her eighty-plus years. "I know I made a big to-do about keeping your identity under wraps, but now I think it's imperative she knows what's going on. I'll warn you, she won't like it one bit."

"No kidding," Riley muttered under his breath.

"I beg your pardon?"

He cleared his throat. "There is something I need to explain first. I've, uh—"

"Speak clearly, Mr. Parrish. I didn't hire you because you were the most likely to suck up. Sycophants I don't need."

"Yes, ma'am," Riley said. "It's just that, well, you made it clear that I was to keep my distance and keep my identity secret. So when I read your grandniece's recent columns as part of my research, I thought it might be wise to take on a certain . . . demeanor along with my supposed job as your personal assistant."

"Explain."

Riley sighed silently. "Do you read her columns, ma'am?"

"Yes, when I can."

"Then you're aware of this new theory of hers."

"You mean this thing she's going on about with the wolves and whatnot? Of course, but I believe I explained about her personal—"

"I know. And I can certainly understand the caution." *Boy, do I,* he silently added. "So I thought it . . . prudent to maintaining my focus that I adopt a rather, well, unwolflike attitude around her." There was complete silence, and Riley kissed the rest of his retainer good-bye. "It seemed like a good idea at the time and, well—" He stopped when Millicent began to laugh. "Ma'am?"

She slowed and took a moment to catch her breath. "Oh, my. That's the most amusing thing I've heard in absolute ages." She chuckled again. "You *are* the clever one."

"Well, not so clever now that I have to fess up."

Millicent merely made another amused sound. "I think you'll do fine."

"She might well be on the phone ten seconds later, demanding my head on a platter."

"She very well might, though I daresay I doubt it will be your head she'll be interested in removing."

Riley flinched and instinctively covered his crotch.

"But she didn't hire you," Millicent stated flatly. "I did. And so far I've been quite happy with your services."

Riley thought she'd feel different if she knew of the very unsheeplike feelings he was developing for her grandniece. "I was hoping to gather a bit more information before approaching her. I'd feel better if I could detail a course of action regarding this increase in contact."

"Did you get the results of the fingerprint search?"

"Yes, and there are no matches."

"Which means whoever left the note has no prior arrests, correct?"

Or simply hasn't been caught, Riley thought, but kept it to himself. "Yes, ma'am."

"Well, that's good news, then, isn't it? Dovetails with your interpretation that he is unlikely to cause physical harm?"

"Yes, well—"

"I still want the sneaky little bastard caught, mind you. Threat or no threat, I won't tolerate this kind of emotional sabotage."

Riley agreed, one hundred percent. He hedged a moment before bringing up the next question, but he was working for her, and she deserved to know any and all directions the case might be taking. "Let me ask you something, Ms. Harrington. What all do you know about Tanzy's editor, Martin Stanton?"

"Excuse me? Tanzy's edi—what on earth are you focusing on him for? Aside from the fact that it was his foresight in recruiting Tanzy directly from the column she wrote for that campus paper that she is where she is today, I've also spoken to him personally about this. Before I decided to hire you."

"You told me that, but you said you only asked him if he was aware of Tanzy receiving any threats from anyone."

"Which he denied any knowledge of."

"Perhaps he wasn't aware you meant the SoulM8 notes. If he's sending them, he might think of them as flattering. A sort of secret admirer."

"To a woman half his age? An employee? Someone he thinks of as a protégée?"

"You're the one who warned me about her allure with men." An area he really didn't want to get into.

"Yes, but I certainly didn't mean—" She broke off with a huffing sigh. "What possible set of circumstances have led you to suspect him of this?"

"It very well might be a dead end, but there are several things adding up here that individually look harmless, but when put together paint a different picture. And I understand the ramifications if it is her boss."

"None of them good," she said, her tone a clear warning for him to tread carefully.

"However," he pressed on, undaunted, "I'm paid to be thorough. Sometimes it's the person directly in front of us that we least suspect."

"Well," she said with some resignation, "I appreciate your diligence, but I believe you are, as they say, barking up the wrong tree."

"She hasn't mentioned his unusual behavior? Marital problems? Midlife-crisis conversations?"

"Heavens, no. But we don't spend a great deal of time discussing that sort of thing. I'm hardly a gossip, Mr. Parrish."

Riley found himself suppressing a smile. He'd bet money

she had more dirt on more people than anyone suspected. She was simply more discreet than most.

"I want him caught," she stated flatly. "And I don't want you spending all your time chasing dead ends."

"I can assure you I'm not. We're still following the leads on the FishNet employees. That remains the higher percentage chance here. I'm just trying to cover all the bases. You don't want your niece left vulnerable and—"

"Do you honestly think there is a real chance he's the one perpetrating this—this abuse?" she asked, doubt beginning to creep into her voice.

"I don't know enough at this point. I'm still tracking down evidence. Part of which is asking you these kinds of questions."

She sighed. "I know. And I'm sorry I was so quick to defend. It's just the very idea that it might be someone close to her—" She broke off.

Riley felt bad for putting a scare into the older woman, but it didn't pay to stick your head in the sand. And Millicent Harrington was hardly the type to duck reality. "If it is him, you do realize there might be an innocent angle to this. He might be under the impression that she'd see this as notes from a secret admirer. It might be a secret little thrill for him, a game. Something to make him feel young and desirable, without having to confront her and face rejection or ridicule."

Millicent was silent for a long moment, then finally sighed heavily. "I can see your point. But we must tread very carefully here. You cannot simply confront the man with your suspicions. The ramifications against Tanzy and her career could be quite damaging."

"Understood."

"You'll contact me when you know more?"

"Yes, ma'am."

"Ultimately, I want proof and I want a name. Leave the rest up to me."

Riley frowned. "Ms. Harrington, we can contact—"

"Yes, well, I have my own contacts. Money and power can do more than fund charities, Mr. Parrish. You get a name and leave the rest to me."

"Ms. Harrington, I really must caution you—"

"I'm eighty-two. Caution doesn't have as much to recommend it when you reach my age. Contact me again when you hear anything more."

"Yes, ma'am," Riley said.

There was a pause, then she said, "And may I say you need not worry I'll find you a suck-up."

She was gone before he could react. He scrubbed a hand over his face, then he picked up the phone again and called FishNet, the service provider SoulM8 used and likely worked for. If they fingerprinted their employees, it was possible he'd have a name shortly, putting an end to the more uncomfortable speculation about Martin Stanton.

Then he got to go downstairs and confess.

Oh joy.

Why is it we think we must handle everything alone?

For men, I'm guessing it's the fear-of-vulnerability thing. But what's up with us women? Just who are we trying to impress? We presumably have friends and/or family to lean on in times of need. So why is it so hard to do?

Or is it just me?

10

Tanzy stared at her monitor for several long seconds, then hit save. Was this sending a potentially dangerous message to SoulM8? Admitting she was in a "time of need"? She silently argued that need came in many forms, and made the decision to let it stand.

Leaning back, she chewed on the straw in her second chocolate milkshake of the day—no sense in letting a perfectly good, state-of-the-art blender sit idle—and let her thoughts wander. She was lucky. She might not have the traditional family, but she did have friends. And solo single or not, they *were* her family and she knew they'd always be there for her.

So what if their group conversations occasionally shifted to topics she had nothing to contribute to? She supposed Mariel would feel the same way when she was the only one with a baby.

Of course, it wouldn't be too much longer before that didn't hold true, either. Sue and Paul had been making nesting noises for the past year. And just watching Sue rhapsodize over gender-neutral nursery color schemes pretty much guaranteed the baby-making process was going to start any minute now.

Tanzy couldn't picture Rina, or for that matter Sloan,

doing the mommy thing, but stranger things had been known to happen. She tried to picture Wolfie Jr.'s probable nursery décor and decided it might give her nightmares. Poor Wolfie Jr. Of course, given what Rina had told her, it was unlikely there was ever going to be a Wolfie Jr. She sighed, remembering when Sloan had first found out about Wolfgang's extracurricular activity—and clueless, self-absorbed idiot that he was, he had actually talked about starting a family as a way to reunify their marriage. *Yeah, a squalling newborn would be just the thing to put the romance back in their relationship.*

Which made her wonder for the umpteenth time what in the hell Sloan had been doing at the Huntington with Blond Adonis Man. Of course, Wolfgang didn't have the market cornered on self-absorption in that relationship; Sloan was very intensely dedicated to her art gallery. But, as far as Tanzy knew, he had been the only adulterous one.

She made a mental note to call Sloan in the morning, pin her down to sharing a drink or quick cup of coffee. Even if it meant cornering her in the gallery. That's what friends did, right? Provided a shoulder, even when one wasn't requested? Or maybe even desired?

Which brought her full circle back to the friendship thing and the concern Rina and Sue had shown today. She honestly hadn't planned to talk about it, but their reaction had only proven that she was officially beyond being able to rationalize the situation out of existence. She had to deal with it now. Somehow.

She logged on so she could send her column to Martin. She'd have to tell him now, about the emails, the note, all of it. And she would. Tomorrow, when he called to discuss the column. Then she supposed she needed to call the local authorities, too, alert them to what was going on. She punched send, trying to figure out just how to broach the whole subject with her editor. Her instinct, of course, was to downplay the whole thing, reassure him it was probably nothing, and hope like hell he agreed.

Then she opened her incoming email file and felt her stomach pitch and squeeze as she scrolled down through the list of sender names. Just the thought that another note might be waiting for her every time she signed on made her feel ill. And she knew she was going to have to admit to Martin that it wasn't nothing and she wasn't fine. She needed help.

And she hated that more than anything.

She was the anchor, the person who was traditionally The Shoulder the rest of them leaned on. After all, Tanzy Tells All was the one with all the answers, right? "Ha!" she groused, snatching up her milkshake again. *Not feeling too damn clever at the moment, are ya?*

And could anyone blame her? Nothing was making sense anymore. Rina had given up on love, deciding marrying for money was a more stable option, no matter what she claimed. Mariel had married for love, but Tanzy wasn't sure if it was love for Chuck or love of being a wife and mommy. And Sloan had apparently decided if you couldn't beat the wolves, join them. Leaving Sue and Paul, who had somehow defied the odds and were rapidly becoming responsible, contented adults despite it all. Before too long they'd probably take off to spend their time with the rest of the grown-ups and leave their neurotic, dysfunctional friends behind.

"God, Tanz. You want some cheese to go with that whine?" She wasn't usually this pathetic. But then, she wasn't used to feeling vulnerable. The one thing her unstable, untraditional childhood had done for her was to make her the invincible, self-reliant one. So finding herself on the needy end of a shoulder for the first time at age twenty-nine sucked.

And that was when she realized just whose shoulder she'd feel the most comfortable turning to.

Riley's.

And not because of the strong, tall, and silent thing. She did have a habit of turning to men in times of need, but those needs were generally physical, not emotional. And while she was past the point of ignoring that she might have a few urges of the physical variety where Riley was concerned, that wasn't why his name had popped into her mind.

She couldn't help but wonder how nice it would be to know his calm, rational, ever-steady presence would always be available to her. She wasted another moment wondering at the concept of having a guy for a buddy, then laughed. "Yeah, that could happen."

For someone else maybe. Hell, he was a sheep and she still had the hots for him. She was apparently missing the platonic gene. If she tried to pursue the friendship thing with him, she knew damn well that at some point she'd give in to her inner wolf and seduce him into taking her to bed . . . or up against the wall . . . or . . . whatever.

She had a delicious little shiver of awareness at the thought of him putting his hands on her, taking her as confidently as he'd put her into that limo . . . hell, taking her *in* the limo. She shook her head with a dry smile and sadly came back to reality. Of course, it wouldn't be like that, all hot and sweaty and demanding. With Riley it would probably be gentle and caring and maybe wonderful even, in its own way. But as novel as the idea of gentle, caring sex was, or the surprising realization that she might actually enjoy it—once, anyway—at some point it wouldn't be enough. She'd want more. Harder, faster, stronger. She'd want what it wasn't in him to give.

Then she'd be in the awkward position of wishing he was just her friend again and, well, bottom-lining it, she'd end up ruining everything.

But none of that changed the fact that he was the one she

wanted to talk to now. He was the only one she could discuss all of this with and know that instead of panic and overreaction, he'd calmly sort it out and come up with some cool, logical solution. And she would trust his judgment. He would make her feel safe.

There, she'd gone from ridiculous to insane. She better than most knew it was the height of foolishness to depend on a man like that. Or anyone, for that matter. Look where that had gotten her mother. Where it still had her mother. Traipsing around the globe after the next shoulder to lean on.

Annoyed with herself for letting those thoughts surface, Tanzy finished off her now watery milkshake and shut her computer down. She wasn't up to facing emails tonight. She would take a warm shower and climb into bed, maybe dig into a book or flip through a magazine.

What she wouldn't do was wander out into the hall and see if the light was still on under Riley's door.

Because she'd be knocking on it a moment later. And which Riley would she want to open the door? Friend? Or potential lover?

"Neither," she told herself sternly. "Employee. That's all he is." *All he'll ever be. The only reason he's even in your life at all.*

She made a mental note to never agree to anything Millicent suggested ever again. Surely if she was home in her little Russian Hill row house right now she'd have a much better grip on all this.

One thing was for sure. If she *were* at home, she wouldn't be thinking about Riley. Certainly wouldn't be thinking she needed him. Emotionally or physically. Definitely wouldn't be thinking about those lips of his, how surprisingly much she'd wanted—ached, even—to have them on her. Wanted his hands on her, too. Wanted—

A knock sounded on her bedroom door and she jumped.

Then flushed hotly when she heard his voice on the other side of her door.

"Tanzy?"

Annoyed at her guilty reaction—What did she have to feel guilty about? She hadn't gone to him, had she?—she looked up at the ceiling. "What is this, a test?" A ring of fat, sassy cherubs were smirking back at her. "Yeah, yeah, yeah," she muttered. "Very funny."

He tapped again. "Tanzy? It's Riley."

And who else would it be? she grumbled silently. And why did hearing him say her name in that rumbly deep voice of his make that buzzy little hum scoot down her spine again? Surely he'd said her name before.

Thinking about it, though, she decided maybe he hadn't. Hmm. Why now? And why did he want to talk to her at—she glanced at the clock—almost midnight? He'd never come to her room before. Shoot, she barely saw him in the rest of the house. She'd spent more time with him in the past twenty-four hours than in the entire couple of weeks she'd been here combined. But they *had* spent a lot of time together since last night. And last night he had kissed her hand. And now he was at her door. At midnight.

As a friend? Or potential lover?

"Don't forget door number three," she reminded herself pointedly as her pulse sped up. *Employee.* She left her office and crossed to her bedroom door.

"Yes?" she asked, keeping the door closed between them. Partly because she was wearing her usual late-night working attire: a well-worn Niners football jersey, ancient slippers, no makeup, and a hairstyle that could only kindly be described as bedhead chic. Cameron Diaz might be able to pull it off, but on Tanzy Harrington . . . not even a Dolce & Gabbana gown would save her with this 'do.

But her shabby-chic fashion sense notwithstanding, mostly she kept the door shut because she wanted so badly to open it. To do exactly what she'd just convinced herself she could never do. To push this tension between them that she knew damn well was becoming increasingly sexual.

"What do you want?" she asked, her hand clenched in an indecisive death grip on the doorknob.

"I need to talk to you."

That made her pause. For all that he didn't sound alarmed, he didn't sound like her Riley, either. Her Riley.

That was hardly the case.

Hadn't he pointed out, very clearly in fact, just this morning, that she really didn't know anything about him?

Well, you could change that. Just open the door.

"It's late," she hedged, hand clenching and unclenching the knob. *And I'm right on the verge of opening this door and dragging you in here by the lapels of your perfectly pressed jammies.*

She heard him clear his throat.

Which meant what? Was he nervous about something? Was that why his outrageously sexy voice sounded so uncharacteristically edgy and therefore even more multiorgasmic? Was he standing there, not two inches from her right this very second, wanting what she wanted?

Why else would he be at her door at this time of night?

She was turning the knob before she could come up with all the arguments for why she should be locking it instead.

Then he said, "If it's not too much trouble, could you meet me downstairs?"

And her hand fell away from the knob as she stood there, stunned. Would she ever read this man correctly? First his feet were killing him, now he wanted to chat in the kitchen. Probably over warm milk. "So, it was door number three after all," she muttered, then to him she said, "Is it that important?" She sounded a bit pissy now and she didn't care. So what if he'd simply asked to speak to her and she'd been the one running off on some wild sexual-fantasy scenario? "Can't this wait until morning? I was just going to bed." Alone. Again. Dammit.

"Yes. Yes, it can."

She paused again, surprised by the annoyance in his tone. Why on earth was he annoyed at her?

"Good night," he said abruptly, sounding frustrated and somewhat, well, angry.

"Hey!" she called out defensively, "I didn't ask you to come banging on my door in the middle of the night." She flung said door wide open and stepped—okay, stomped—into the hall. "So why in hell are you irritated with *me*?"

He stopped, turned, but said nothing. And neither did she. It was impossible, what with her tongue lodged in her throat and all.

Because Riley—her Riley, anyway—was *not* the Riley currently standing in the hall outside her door. This Riley . . . well, she must still be in sexual fantasyland.

She gawked. She couldn't help it. But since she was obviously hallucinating, what did it matter, right? First off, he had a five o'clock shadow. It did amazing things to his jawline. And his hair. It wasn't parted on the side and ruthlessly combed into place. It was . . . tousled. Wavy, sexy, wolfish even. But what really struck her was the combination of the hair and the bristle with the fact that he'd left his glasses in his room.

Dear God, the man was a hunk.

She *was* hallucinating!

Then she realized that he was staring at her just as intently as she was staring at him. She was still so caught up in his transformation that she forgot what she was wearing, or that she should be mortified. But this was her fantasy, so who cared how *she* looked?

Then he raked a hand through his hair and swore beneath his breath. "You're right. I'm sorry. We'll talk in the morning."

It was such a frustrated, totally un-Riley-like gesture that she snapped out of her hormonal daze and stepped toward him. "Wait a minute."

He paused, but didn't turn this time.

That's when she realized he was wearing sweats. Sweatpants. Riley. It simply didn't compute. Like picturing him naked in the shower.

And damn if they didn't look good on him. Then there was the faded blue muscle T-shirt . . . and damn if the man didn't have a chest under those suits, as well. And shoulders. And—dear God have mercy—triceps. She was a sucker for well-defined arms, and his were so nice they'd tempt even a good girl to want to run her tongue right along the lovely indentation, right beneath those—

"What?"

She blinked, trying like hell to remember what it was she'd said. Jesus, she felt like she'd been ambushed. Did he always look like this during his off hours? "Uh. Why, um . . ." She had to pause, claw her libido from her throat. It took a great deal of willpower to stay where she was. Normally, with the tension arcing like this—and honestly, had tension ever arced like this?—she'd have upped her advantage considerably by closing in on his personal space. She wouldn't have even thought about it. It was instinctive prowling behavior.

She gripped the doorframe. "Is there an emergency of some kind?" *Like, you simply had to come give me multiple orgasms or die with wanting?*

"No," he said after what felt like an eternity. His voice was as rough and raspy as his jaw. And it abraded her senses just like his whiskers would abrade her neck. Or stomach. Or inner thighs . . .

She clenched her teeth against the little moan threatening to slip out. And clenched her thighs together for good measure. *Just go into your room and close the door. This is simply a late-night aberration.* She'd never forgive herself if she acted on impulses that would go away with a good night's sleep.

Her libido just snorted. She would have, too. But Riley was turning to face her. And every muscle in her body tightened in anticipation.

"It's about the fan letter," he said.

Every muscle went slack. And the breath she'd been holding came out in a whoosh of disappointment and disgust. The latter self-directed. Mostly. "Well, at least you didn't say your feet were killing you," she muttered.

"What?"

"Nothing." Which was exactly what was ever going to happen between them. Nothing. And she'd be smart, not to mention a damn sight less sexually frustrated, if she could just get that one simple message through her thick, hormonally fogged brain.

"We need to talk about it," he reiterated, frowning now.

"I don't think you need to worry about that. It's not really your concern," she said, blunt to the point of rudeness. No matter that she'd just been thinking about discussing that very thing with him. It had obviously been a rationalization for giving herself a shot at seducing him. Which was never going to happen. Ever. God only knew what ego-mortifying thing he'd blurt out then. And she'd be damned if she'd give him another chance.

"Actually," he said, surprising her with the challenging tone. "We do need to discuss it, and we will. Just not tonight. I'm sorry I bothered you. Good night." He turned and walked down the hallway toward his room.

Well, that snapped it. She was after him before she knew what she was doing. Her hand was on his arm, stopping him, turning him around, before she could question her judgment. Or lack thereof. "Just who in the hell do you think you are?" she demanded, and realized once she had just how badly she wanted an answer to that. Because it was clear he'd been very right. She had no idea who he really was.

He carefully took her hand from his arm, almost too carefully. A glance from his hand on her wrist to his face revealed the tic of a pulse at his temple, the tightened skin at the corner of his jaw.

"We're going to talk about that, too," he said calmly. Only this controlled calm was nothing like the smooth, emotionally removed tone she'd heard from him before.

"But we're not going to do it here, and we're not going to do it now." He took a step back and it was like a shield dropped over him. "I'm sorry I bothered you with it tonight. It will wait until morning."

But no matter that it was the old Riley talking, it wasn't the old Riley standing in front of her. When he turned, she moved to block his exit. "You just expect me to waltz back in my room and go to bed like a good little girl? After this . . . this little display?" She waved her hand, gesturing toward his hair, clothes, the whole thing. "I don't think so."

He shocked her by moving deeply into her personal space, so deeply she had to tip her head back to look up into his face. Had he always been this tall? Or maybe it was just that she'd never faced him down in bunny slippers.

"If we both know what's good for us," he said quietly, "we'll go back to our separate rooms. And stay there until morning. Because we both know you're not a good little girl." He stepped back. "And though you might not believe it, I was never all that good of a little boy."

His door shut moments later with a quiet little click, leaving Tanzy standing in the hall, mouth hanging, wondering what in the hell she was going to do about it.

Is there such a thing as a wolf/sheep hybrid? Or only wolves in sheep clothing? Or more interesting still . . . is it possible for a sheep to doff the fleece for a fur coat? Even temporarily? I guess what I'm really asking is, can a sheep get his inner wolf on? And, while he's at it, get me off?

11

Riley flipped his bacon and scraped at the scramble of eggs frying on the massive stainless-steel griddle. Any other time he'd have been drooling over what amounted to a three-foot-square frying pan.

But it wasn't any other time. It was morning. The morning after, to be more specific. The morning after he almost blew the best chance Parrish Securities had to climb permanently out of debt and start to become the successful company he'd been telling his father it always should have been.

Not that Finn seemed overly concerned one way or the other. Riley sighed and scraped the eggs in the other direction. At what point, he wondered, had everything stopped making sense?

He'd always thought it was the moment his knee had connected with John Rockingham's helmet, ending everything his life had been focused on since he first picked up a football at age seven. Then he'd come home, teamed up with his dad, and convinced himself that maybe things happened for a reason. That maybe the two of them would find a deeper satisfaction building something together, both professionally and personally. But, while he knew his dad loved him, Finn didn't seem as interested in building something as he did in getting a little something-something.

"And, apparently, you're not much better," he muttered disgustedly, flipping the bacon, then swearing when hot grease spattered his arm. He'd had no business going to her room last night. His rationale had been that she'd be more open to listening to him at the end of what had been a long day. Tired, exhausted from party planning, anxious over the note, over what had happened at the station. He'd somehow convinced himself that it was best to deal with it, with her, right then, straight out.

Then she'd opened the door. And what in the hell was it about that faded old jersey and those damn ridiculous bunny slippers anyway? He might have had no earthly clue, but his body sure had. In fact, it had stood right up and saluted the whole ensemble. Of course, it had probably been at half mast before he'd left his room. A good indicator he'd had no business going anywhere near her, no matter the rationale.

"Something smells good."

It took willpower not to look at her. It took even more not to swear when the grease spattered him again. "There's enough for two, if you'd like."

God, he sounded like Sheepman Riley even when he didn't mean to. Maybe it was a defense mechanism.

Then she moved in behind him and his entire body tightened. And he realized that not even the best offense in the NFL could get him out of this one unscathed.

"Looks that way," she said, observing the mound of eggs and raft of bacon sizzling in front of him.

So maybe he had gotten a little too enthusiastic about the griddle. Better he was too carried away with eggs and bacon than with her.

"That is, unless you've got a football team coming over to help you out," she added dryly.

Football team. There was an opening if ever there was one.

Then she darted a hand past him and snatched up a piece of bacon. He reached instinctively to block her. "Watch it. That's hot!"

She just smiled and crunched down on her pilfered slice—hard enough and with just enough gleam in her eyes to make him think about switching to defense.

Green eyes still glittering, she added, "And here I seem to recall you making it clear that, in your opinion, hot things don't bother me overly much."

"That's not what I said." He knew. He'd spent a sleepless night trying to forget the stupid things he had said.

She ignored him. "You also mentioned something to the effect that you weren't impervious to the occasional . . . hot element yourself. Or you implied as much." She snapped another chunk of bacon between white shiny teeth.

He turned his attention back to the griddle, deciding retreat might be the best strategy at the moment. She was in rare form this morning and he wasn't prepared for this yet. Any of it. He'd hoped for a nice, hearty breakfast, followed with a rejuvenating shower and shave, by which time he'd have miraculously figured out exactly how he was going to handle this whole thing. He hadn't even gotten to the hearty breakfast part yet.

Time for a draw play. Divert and conquer. "I thought you slept in on Tuesdays."

"Really. And you would know this how?"

He paused, then turned off the heat before carefully placing the spatula on the counter. It was too handy a weapon. He turned to face her, arms folded. "You know, I was going to handle this calmly, rationally, with great finesse and charm," he said evenly.

"That would be predictable," she said. "Except for the charm part."

"Very funny."

"Thank you, I try. But you have to admit you take calm and cool to a whole new level." She looked at him consideringly. It made him edgy. "Until last night, anyway."

"I believe I apologized for that."

She threw her hands up. "Okay, I give. Which guy are you? The calm, polished professional, or the sweats-wearing dude who looked at me last night like he wanted scrambled eggs with me on the side instead of bacon."

Riley just stared at her. It was a good question. He thought he'd been playing a role. But somewhere along the way the sheep Riley and the real Riley had intersected, until he had no clue which part was what. He shrugged and decided to run the ball straight up the middle. He looked her dead in the eye and said, "Maybe I'm a little of both."

That shut her up.

Which was great, as it gave him a whole split second to huddle up and draw his next play.

She still snapped the ball early. "So you didn't come to my room just to talk last night?"

"Yes. I mean, no. Dammit." He pinched the bridge of his nose and wondered when he'd lost total control of the ball. *Pretty much every time she comes within three feet of you.* Great. He took a deep, calming breath. "I wanted to talk. I knew I wasn't going to sleep until I explained everything. I should have waited."

Now she folded her arms. " 'Everything' being what exactly?"

He ground his teeth. "If you'd give me half a chance, I'd tell you."

She nodded at the grill. "Well then, why don't you serve us both up a plate and I'll get some drinks, then you can explain to your heart's content."

"Fine." With barely restrained, very unsheeplike violence, he snatched another plate from the cupboard and slapped it smartly on the counter, muttering under his breath as he heard her open up the Mighty Fridge. "Try to explain things and you can't because they won't let you, then they get all pissy because you don't explain things."

"I heard that," she said.

And she was going to hear a lot more before he was done, too. He scraped eggs and flipped several pieces of bacon onto each plate, wishing he felt more confident about that.

"And I wasn't pissy," she went on, talking over the sound of ice grinding out of the icemaker in the Mighty's door. "In fact, I think I'm being pretty perky, all things considered. And if you really knew me like you seem to think you do, you'd know what great lengths I'm going to to embody said perkiness prior to my first injection of carbonated caffeine." This statement was followed by the unmistakable hiss of two pop-tops being flipped open.

He turned to find her pouring Coke into two glasses filled with ice.

"What are you doing?" he asked, heavily laden plates in hand.

"Getting us something to drink."

"I heard ice hitting glass, so I was thinking orange juice. Tomato juice, maybe."

"Hey, I can only maintain this front for so long. I need caffeine."

"What's wrong with coffee?"

She sniffed the air. "I don't do coffee. Roasted beans." She shuddered. "And if you know I sleep in on Tuesdays, which I only do when I turn in my Tuesday column Monday night, by the way, then you'd think you'd have noticed my morning beverage of choice. Come to think of it, it's my midday and nighttime choice, as well."

"I thought you just didn't have time to make coffee."

"Well, I would have poured you some, but I didn't smell any being brewed and just assumed—"

"That I drink Coke with my eggs?"

"Gotta get the caffeine from somewhere and this"—she raised the famous red and silver can—"is as valid a source as any." She eyed him when he scowled. "I thought you could use the energy boost. The fizz will perk you right up if the caffeine doesn't."

When he merely continued to look at her like she was speaking in foreign tongues, she sighed. "There's juice in the fridge if you insist."

"On what, having something healthy and good for you?"

"You mean like bacon?" she countered sweetly.

Again he was reduced to muttering under his breath.

"My hearing is really quite acute, you know. Comes from eavesdropping on other people's conversations in public."

And to think he'd admired her forthrightness.

"What, you didn't think all my column observations were from personal experience, did you?"

He put both plates on the table and ran a glass of water for himself before taking a seat.

"Taking the fifth, are we?"

He just picked up his fork and nodded at her plate. "Sit. Your eggs are getting cold."

She eyed him, but sat without comment. They'd consumed about half of the eggs when she finally said, "I'm not sure I like this Riley better than the old one."

"Tough," he said, wishing like hell he had a newspaper to read. A cereal box, even. Anything to give him an excuse to look anywhere other than across the table at her.

"So, what's this big explanation? Will it explain this whole split personality thing?"

"Finish your eggs, then we'll talk."

She raised both eyebrows. "Wow, quite the autocrat, aren't we?"

An autocrat who is saving your personal bacon, he wanted to retort, but didn't. This whole thing was already way off on the wrong foot. Best to just keep his trap shut until they were done eating and out of this room. It felt too intimate in here, which was ridiculous, considering the cavernous size of the kitchens. Maybe it was eating together at the same table. Too ... domesticated for his peace of mind. Which was a joke. Tanzy was about as undomesticated as they came. In every sense of the word.

Still, he'd feel better when they moved to one of the more formal rooms in the house. Maybe then he'd have a chance in hell of remembering that he was an employee.

And not a man who had no other right to sit across a breakfast table from her.

Tanzy grabbed another Coke and waited for Riley to scrape the plates off and put them in the sink. It was like being with an entirely different man. She snapped her fingers. "Wait a minute! You're Riley's identical twin, right?" She looked around. "Am I on *Candid Camera* or something? Did Marty put you up to this?"

He just scowled and moved past her.

A scowling, unshaven, grouchy, and amazingly hunky Riley. Who could ever have imagined? "So, I take that as a no." She shifted, barely, out of his way as he headed out of the kitchen and down the hall, toward the front parlor. What would he have done, she wondered, if at the last second she'd shifted and let him come up smack against her?

Okay, so maybe she was wondering what *she'd* have done. She'd been wondering about that, in fact, since he'd left her gaping in the hallway last night. She'd finally pinpointed the limo ride home from the dance as being the real moment where everything had changed. But she'd be damned if she could figure out what had triggered it.

She scuffed down the hall after him, bunny slippers sliding across the polished oak flooring. He'd hardly looked twice at her this morning. In fact, he seemed to have gone out of his way not to notice her. And although it appeared as if she'd just thrown on sweats and the first T-shirt in her drawer for that totally-unconcerned-with-my-appearance look, the pile of clothes on her bed upstairs was proof of her preoccupation with exactly what sort of persona she should project this morning. For all the good it was doing.

Of course, she'd noticed every detail about him. Unable to tear her gaze away from him as he stood at the stove. The way his navy blue sweats hung low on his hips. The way the gray and blue Pioneers T-shirt snugged up tight around those triceps and draped across shoulders whose breadth and definition still defied explanation. Was there really tailoring so bad that it would hide a body like his? And if so, why?

She watched him now as he strode down the hall, totally at a loss to explain any of this amazing transformation, even after a night of no sleep. He even walked differently.

One conclusion she had come to, and it had been somewhat of a relief, she realized now what her hormones had been reacting to. Obviously they'd sniffed out the wolf beneath those sheep suits. She hadn't really been aching for the quiet, calm Riley to put his hands on her. This man striding down the hall in front of her ... now, that made much more sense. And yet, she'd continued to toss and turn.

Even now, in the light of a new day, she couldn't entirely erase the vague sense of disappointment. That while it was possible she might have gained a formidable opponent to play bed tag with, she'd lost something special. That shoulder, maybe? The calm, rational center in the eye of the storm?

She was still ruminating when she flap-flapped into the

front parlor, to find Riley pacing beneath the snowflake chandelier. She wandered over to stand beneath it herself. "It seems like a lifetime ago that we stood right here." She looked at him. "I was going to say that you were a completely different person then. But, somehow, with everything that's happened lately, I feel like I was, too." She lowered her can, all taunting and provoking aside now. "What's going on?"

He stopped pacing, looked at her, then let out a deep sigh and gestured to the small grouping of furniture behind her. "Why don't you sit down."

She lifted a brow at his tone. "Sounds ominous."

"It is. In a way."

That gave her pause. "Okay," she murmured, thinking she'd rather stand for whatever this was about, always the one to hold her ground. But looking into his eyes—so dark and mysterious without all that wavy glass hiding them—she found her knees bending and her butt hitting the hard, floral surface of the nearest settee. "Shoot."

He paced to the mantel, then turned and leaned against it. "I was hired by your great-aunt."

"I believe that's old news."

He merely gave her a look. "I was not hired as her personal assistant."

Oh. Well. This was unexpected. Not that she'd known what *to* expect. "Exactly what were you hired as, then?"

"She contracted my services, the services of my company." To his credit, he held her gaze directly. "Parrish Securities."

"Aunt Millicent hired a—" Tanzy stopped, trying to process what this meant. "I'm sorry, you'll have to explain. Do you mean securities as in stocks and bonds? Or—"

"As in private protection and investigation. I was hired to watch out for you and look into the threatening notes you've been receiving."

If he'd told her he was the Easter Bunny, she couldn't have been more shocked. She took a moment to let the news filter through the shock. Regrouping quickly, she replayed the events of the last couple of days, the last two weeks, in fact, and it all fell rather slickly into place. She was so stunned, she didn't know exactly how she felt. Angry? Betrayed? Embarrassed? A tiny bit relieved? She was all of those things and more.

Striving for a calm she definitely *didn't* feel, she clutched her Coke and said, "What, exactly, have your, uh, duties been?"

He stayed by the mantel, several yards away. Smart man. "I spent some time researching you, your background, your work. Millicent aided me in that, but I used my own sources as well. I've been following the contact being made, assessing the threat to you."

Her mind was spinning, so she opted to stay focused on the specific matter at hand. The rest she could deal with—and be mortified by—later. "But the contact being made was in email. You couldn't have been reading—" One look at his face told her that, in fact, he could have been. And was.

"I was only interested in notes from SoulM8."

"Thanks. I feel so much less violated now." Then she thought about the other contact SoulM8 had made. The note, the dance, and her mouth fell open again. "Millicent made sure you accompanied me to the dance. Not as my escort, but as my bodyguard." And after the note popped up that night on their table, he'd accompanied her whenever she'd gone out in public. The radio station. His reaction to the paper missile and the crowd . . . putting her into the limo. "Oh my God."

Now he crossed the room, but before he could sit next to her she was springing up and putting as much distance as she could between them.

She paced the length of the room, then swung back around. "So you've been my bodyguard for how long?"

"A little over two weeks."

She stopped abruptly. "But you've only been my shadow since Sunday night. So how, exactly, were you providing protection before the dance?"

"You were under observation when you were away from the house."

Under observation. "You followed me?" She rapidly tried to recall every place she'd been since moving in here. Only one leaped out in her mind. The Four Seasons. Her face colored despite her wishing desperately that it hadn't. "Oh no."

He nodded. And damn if there wasn't that hint of a smile playing at the corners of his mouth. "I was under orders."

She crossed to the couch and sank onto it.

"If it makes you feel any better, sitting at the end of the hall on the ninth floor of the Four Seasons was a much better detail than hauling ass after you while you did your Christmas shopping. It's like an Olympic event with you or something."

She merely glared at him. He merely shrugged.

"What else?" she demanded, unable to think clearly. Her brain was a red haze at this point. "I want to know everything. From day one."

"I followed you as part of the protection Millicent thought you should have. I didn't eavesdrop, I didn't watch, I didn't do anything other than make sure you weren't approached or contacted by anyone unusual."

His reassurances didn't make her feel even remotely better.

"And the investigation part? I only told Millicent about the emails, I never showed them to her. How did you get a look at them?"

He shifted on the settee to face her more squarely, resting his arms on his knees. "This is where my contacts come into play. Trade secret. And I told you, I didn't look at anything else."

She huffed. "Fine. And what did you do after reading them?"

"I have someone tracking them back to their source, trying to identify him that way. I took some prints off the note he left. We ran those and—"

"Wait a minute. How did you get—?" Then she remembered. She'd been sidetracked by him, in the limo, by the new side of him that was emerging. Only now she realized it was because SoulM8 had made direct contact, on his watch. She'd left her purse in the car. It had been on the table at the foot of the stairs the next morning. She hadn't thought a thing about it, too sidetracked by the note inside.

"Nothing popped on him, so he has no priors. We're trying to see if his employer has prints on file for their employees. If so, we should have a name shortly."

"Employer? You know who he works for?"

"We think we do. The service provider for your Internet account, FishNet. It's why he's been so hard for us to track. He uses the same screen name, but the account information continues to change. Normally when you close an account, your screen name is canceled for a period of time, usually six months. Only he's been able to open up new accounts with the same service, using the same screen name. So we believe he's an employee."

"Who is 'we'?"

"I work with my father, but we have contacts in other fields that we use from time to time."

She slumped back, beyond anger and embarrassment now. All this talk, such serious talk, about SoulM8 and all the work being done behind the scenes for her benefit left her feeling numb more than anything.

"We have . . . we have one other lead."

The clear discomfort in his tone got her attention. "Who?"

"Let me give you the details first. And I will say your aunt was quite adamant in not believing this one, but a trail is a trail. Even if the facts are seemingly coincidence and nothing more, I—"

"Oh, for heaven's sake, who is the other suspect?"

"Martin Stanton."

Her mouth dropped open in shock, then she laughed. Hard. He was scowling at her by the time she got her act back together. "You can't be serious," she said, shaking her head. But the expression on his face made it clear he was. "What did he do to warrant your suspicion?"

Riley explained about the email accounts, the fact that he was present at the charity ball, and his recent changes in behavior.

"What do you know about that?" she asked.

"Just what little you've commented on. As I said, taken separately, they might mean nothing, but together . . ." He shrugged. "You've got to be prepared to look at anyone and everyone."

"Meaning you've looked into all my friends and acquaintances."

He nodded. She blanched. He held up his hand. "I can assure you I've been discreet. They don't realize a thing. And I agree with your aunt that extreme caution must be used in our suspicion of Martin. I don't want to jeopardize your career."

She sat there, numb again. He was serious. "You really think someone who is that close to me would terrorize me this way? What possible reason would he have for doing that? What's the motive?"

"Could be a number of things. You mentioned he seemed to be in some sort of midlife crisis. Maybe, from his perspective, he thinks he's merely being flattering. An anonymous affair of the heart. He's a good deal older than you, so this way he can indulge in the fantasy without fear of rejection."

"Do you honestly think he'd assume I'd be flattered? That I'd see these notes as being from some secret admirer and enjoy the thrill of it?"

"It's possible. As I said, it's only one path we're following. But you needed to be made aware of it. If I could get his fingerprints on something, that would help. We could match it to the latent prints I pulled from the note."

"And if it's not a match, you stop suspecting him?"

Riley just looked at her.

She held his gaze for a long moment, then said, "You weren't kidding when you said I didn't know you."

She'd said it kind of hollowly, not really intending to elicit a response. So she was surprised when his face colored slightly.

"Yeah. About that."

She sat up a little straighter, glad to be off the subject of her stalker, her very real stalker, whoever the hell he was. Martin? No way. She simply couldn't—wouldn't—believe that. "About what?"

"My, uh, split personality."

She'd been so caught up in the revelations, she hadn't really thought about that part. "I assumed you were just maintaining some sort of professional distance or something."

"Partly, yes. But I took it a little further than my job actually dictated." He paused, shifted his weight, then shifted it again.

Tanzy didn't exactly smile, but she suddenly felt a little better. Something about not being the only uncomfortable one in the room. "In what way?"

He blew out a sigh, might have even sworn a little beneath

his breath. Which made her think about his behavior in the hall last night, in the kitchen this morning. This was the real Riley. All the rest had been an act. At the dance, in the limo . . . all of it. The calm, rational center of the storm didn't really exist. At least not in the way she knew it.

Somehow, rather than anger her all over again, it left a rather hollow, achy spot inside her chest. Like she'd lost a friend. She glanced over at him. A friend she'd never really had.

"Why?" she asked quietly.

He looked up, directly into her eyes, and she knew he understood what she was asking. "You know," he said, his tone just as quiet, "one of the things I admire about you is how direct and forthright you are. And you're as honest about yourself as you are in dealing with others." He straightened then, held her gaze. "So you deserve at least that much from me now. When Millicent hired me, I looked at the information available, and my recommendation at the time was that this was not a serious threat. That you weren't in any immediate danger. In fact, up until the dance the other night, I still felt that way. I was going to do my best to come up with a name, something to give the authorities, so that we'd at least have gone on record with our concerns about this guy, but that was all I thought this would amount to. A nice, cushy job over the holidays."

"Go on."

"Part of my research was reading your columns. I enjoyed them. More than I thought I would. You're sharp, witty, but the jabs you take, while meant to be amusing, are usually dead-on, with a kind of insight that forces a person to look at things in a new way. I don't always agree with your conclusions, but I respect the way you present your case."

She could only nod, stunned again, as much by his well-thought-out opinion as the obvious sincerity behind it.

"In the meantime," he went on, looking a bit uncomfortable again, "your aunt had given me explicit instructions. She knew that if you were aware she'd hired me, you'd hightail it out of here."

"Wait a minute." She hadn't put this part together, though she would have as soon as it had all sunk in. "Millicent set me up to stay here, didn't she? With you."

He nodded. "It was the easiest way to keep an eye on you while we dug into the situation. Don't be angry at her, she was—"

Tanzy just laughed, though there wasn't much warmth in it. "Oh no, this is Aunt Millicent at her manipulating best." She sighed, her smile fading. "I'm not happy about it, but I know she only did it because she was worried."

"There's more."

"More?"

He nodded. "Yeah. She warned me to steer clear of you."

Now Tanzy laughed for real. "Oh? So much for me being worried about her meddling in my social life. I guess I should be glad she only sets me up with guys she's paid to go out with me."

Riley didn't laugh. Or smile. "She didn't want me getting tangled up with you, didn't want me to compromise my ability to maintain my objectivity."

Tanzy's laughter faded. The expression on his face . . . the way he was looking at her . . . She thought again about their dance, the moment when she knew—*knew, dammit*—that he'd been going to kiss her. And last night, in the hall . . . he had wanted her, had come to her room . . . to tell her this. But the way he'd looked at her, before shutting the door between them . . .

"I thought it was going to be a short assignment," he went on, "so when I read your column about the wolves and the sheep . . ." He didn't finish, merely lifted a shoulder, his expression apologetic. "It seemed like an amusing idea at the time. I didn't intend it as an insult or anything, but . . ."

Her mouth dropped open as his meaning became clear. Then she burst out laughing.

"What's so funny?" he demanded, obviously feeling as if he'd exposed his soft white underbelly, only to have her laugh at him. Well, he deserved at least that much.

"Nothing, it's just that if the situation had been reversed and it had been me, I might have done the same thing." She snorted again. "You know, I was researching you, too."

"What?" Now he looked confused.

Good. She ought to get some pleasure out of this whole fiasco. "You were my Sheep Research Project. Here I am, alone, with all my friends married off and planning families. And I'm trying to figure out what the attraction is to the guy you take home to Mama. Do they marry him because they just think it's time? Or because he will make a steady, stable mate? Or is there some underlying attraction?" She looked at him. "I had an underlying attraction to you," she said with a half laugh. "So I decided to try to figure out why."

The sudden change in his expression had her realizing that perhaps she'd just revealed too much. And now the advantage was shifting again.

"But now I realize why," she hurried on to say. "You were just a wolf in sheep's clothing. That's what some part of me was reacting to."

He got up off the settee and she started talking faster, and somehow, a lump had crept into her throat.

"You're not a settling down kind of guy at all. You're just like me. Another wolf on the prowl."

He was crossing the room toward her.

She kept up, almost babbling, even as her throat started to close up. "You're not the stable, dependable, calm, rational eye of my storm. Not my shoulder to rely on, not the friend I needed, the one I'd turn to—"

And then he was pulling her up off the couch. And to her absolute horror she realized she was crying.

"Come here."

"Riley, don't. You aren't—You can't—"

"No, you're right," he murmured, pulling her into his arms anyway.

He didn't kiss her. That she could have understood, dealt with. Instead he tugged her close and tucked her against his chest, so that his heart thudded beneath her cheek. Steady, and strong.

And there she was, being held tight inside the calm center of her storm anyway.

And she was confused all over again.

She felt him press his lips against her hair, heard him say, "I can't be all those things. But I'll be damned if you don't make me want to be."

So they're all wolves. In some way, shape, or form. Maybe that's the key element I've been missing. Even herd animals have their alpha males, right? Problem is, some wolves are just plain wolves. I don't think there are too many willing to embrace their inner sheep. Not for the long term. And maybe I fall into that category. Because, frankly, I'd still rather howl at the moon with a wolf than have a baaah-ed time with a good guy.

12

She felt too damn good. Better than too damn good. And she was in his arms. The very last place she should be . . . and the only place Riley wanted her.

He tightened his arms around her and felt her fold her body into his. His heart thudded. Might have even stumbled a little when her fingers dug into his back as he heard a muffled sniffle.

I can't be all those things. But I'll be damned if you don't make me want to be.

What the hell was that about anyway? Where had that come from? He just wanted to get into her pants, right? That's what the sleepless nights were about. The cold showers. Bottom line, that's what he wanted, what all Parrish men apparently wanted. Good—make that great, mind-altering even—sweaty, headboard-banging sex. Nothing more, nothing less.

Okay, nothing less, definitely. But he seemed to be having a little problem with that "nothing more" part.

Maybe he could blame it on an instinctive male reaction to tears. Say anything to make them stop. Although, from the look on her face moments ago, he wasn't sure who had been more momentarily horrified by those glassy eyes. She didn't strike him as the sort to indulge in crying jags.

And even now hers were silent tears, if she was still crying at all.

There is one way to find out, his little voice helpfully suggested. All he had to do was touch her face, look into those eyes again. *Yeah, there's a brilliant idea. Dance even closer to the edge.*

And yet there went his hand, touching her chin, tipping it up. What he found there was like a punch to the gut.

Huge and glassy, her eyes were completely un-Tanzy-like. And suddenly there was no edge to dance on. He was free-falling.

"I am sorry," he said, his voice gruff with sincerity. "About all of this."

She merely held his gaze, lips pressed tightly together as she visibly tried to gather her control.

He cleared his throat, struggling mightily to land on his feet, regain some control of his own. But God almighty, he wanted to taste that mouth of hers. Wanted to do something, anything, to make them both okay.

His fingers tensed with the desire to pull her closer, drop his mouth to hers, to finally take what he'd been wanting since the last time she was in his arms. All those lectures he'd given his dad nudged at his conscience. And helped him relax his hold on her. But he was beginning to understand at least a part of his dad's side of the argument. That, at times, being purely professional sucked.

He let his hands skim down her arms, but lingered, unable to break contact altogether. He might never have the opportunity to touch her again. "I can promise you that I'm doing all I can to find this guy," he vowed.

She sniffed, then hiccuped, which brought her dry smile back to life, albeit a watery one. Another hiccup followed. But instead of embarrassment, she laughed. "God." *Hiccup.* "Real smooth."

His smile came naturally then as well. For all that her innate frankness appealed to him, her steady sense of humor, especially when it was self-directed, drew him in even more. "If I said you were cute when you hiccuped, would you whack me?"

"No." Another hiccup. "But I'd seriously question your sanity." Wiping the tear tracks from her cheeks and taking several slow, deep breaths, she moved from his grasp and stepped away.

He recalled his half-formed fantasy of how this moment would play out, of telling her who he really was. That fantasy had ended with them devouring each other. He supposed he should be happy he'd come to his senses in time.

She put more distance between them as she collected herself, took several more deep breaths, and held them, trying to get rid of the last of the hiccups. It worked, but she stayed on the other side of the room from him.

He decided he wasn't all that happy.

But the alternative was to quit. Then he could pursue her free of any other conflict of interest. Which, of course, he wouldn't do. For business and personal reasons. No way was he walking away from this, or her, until he had SoulM8 locked down or strung up. Besides which, ending their professional relationship might mean ending the only relationship he could hope to have with her. It was pathetic, settling for what he could have instead of going for what he wanted. But there it was. And hadn't he been doing exactly that since the day his knee blew out?

"Is there anything we can do?" she asked, her voice still a bit rough. "I mean, I thought about telling the authorities after I got the note. Actually, I didn't think about it, but my friends suggested it."

His attention snapped back—mercifully—to the real matter at hand. "You told your girlfriends about this?"

She looked surprised by his sudden sharp tone. "I'm sorry," she said when he merely looked at her expectantly.

"I'm still not used to the other you. You keep switching back and forth. It's confusing."

"The other—?" He swore silently, wishing he'd never heard of her stupid sheep/wolf theory, much less adopted it. "Never mind that. How much did you tell them?"

"Not much, really. We were actually talking about you."

He refused to ask, despite the teasing spark that returned to her far too expressive green eyes. She seemed quite willing to shift the tension away from her problems, and onto his problems.

She didn't move closer, but her steady regard seemed to shrink the space between them nonetheless. "Don't you want to know *why* I was talking to my friends about my great-aunt's assistant? Don't you want to know how I characterized our date?"

"It wasn't a date."

Her smile faltered and he hated that, but, like Millicent, she was a formidable opponent. He didn't think there was an edge she wouldn't dance too close to.

"Right," she said. "I forgot. For you it was surveillance. I guess you were relieved when I was forced to take you along as my escort. Beats skulking around in the halls, right?"

Talk about a loaded question. "I was just glad to help out." He shrugged at her wide-eyed snort of disbelief. "Okay, yes, it helped me watch out for you. But I'd have done it anyway." *Great, just hand her the edge, why don't you?*

Still, she only managed a dry smile. "Thanks. Your loyalty is impressive."

He could have told her it had nothing to do with professional loyalty and everything to do with getting to touch her while she was wearing that nothing of a dress Clarisse had no doubt gleefully chosen to torture him with. But he wasn't that suicidal.

"Well, since you dragged it out of me," she said, sitting down.

Did her legs really just go on forever, or what? he caught himself thinking as she crossed her legs and tucked the toe of her slipper behind her calf. Even dressed like an unmade bed she made him sweat.

"I was actually telling them about how you took control of the situation at the radio station and how at odds it was with the man I knew you to be." She laughed then, but there was a sharp edge to it. "Boy, you really weren't kidding when you said I didn't know you."

He sighed and muttered beneath his breath.

"What was that?"

He looked over at her, hands on his hips. "It was a stupid idea, okay? The whole sheep thing. But if it makes you feel any better, I'm sure I suffered more trying to pull it off than you did having to deal with an overly polite, anal-retentive employee."

"Rather than what?" She folded her arms. "What are you really like, then, Riley?"

She was infuriating. He threw up his hands. "This." He gestured to his T-shirt and sweatpants. "I normally dress a little better, but this is pretty much what you get." *A broken-down athlete trying his damnedest to make his father's lifelong business pay off so they could both move on to doing something they really enjoyed.* Which stopped him dead in his tracks. Had he really been marking time with all this? He knew he'd been doing it for Finn, to make enough so the old man could retire. He managed not to snort. Retire from something Finn had only ever worked at hard enough to make ends meet. But it was all Finn knew. That and women.

Standing where he was at the moment, Riley wasn't sure he knew anything about either. And now was certainly not the time to ask what in the hell he really *did* want to do with his life. Because, the thing was, he thought he'd already done it. He'd made the pros. Now he was doing this. Because this was what there was to do.

"Riley?"

He snapped his gaze to hers. "I'm just doing the best I can, Tanzy. Your aunt wanted me to stay behind the scenes as much as possible. The rest . . . well, I take full responsibility for that." He sighed and let his hands drop to his sides. "Maybe we should just step past this and focus on what's important." He let himself take one last long look at her, then reluctantly let go of every fantasy he'd had regarding her. "You said you told your friends about the note. Did you tell anyone else? Did you say anything to Martin?"

She stared at him for another eternally long, very disconcerting moment. His control wavered, as it was wont to do around her and probably always would. He thought if it went on another second, he'd snap and just cross the room and drag her off the couch and plant one on her. He'd either get kneed in the balls . . . or her naked on the carpet. At the moment, he was almost willing to risk it.

Then she sighed, and her gaze dipped to her hands, which she folded tightly on her knees. He wasn't sure if she was wrestling with the same urges he was, or if she'd been thinking about the case the entire time. He was really going to have to stop lecturing Finn about women, he decided. It was quite obvious to him now that he'd been talking out of his ass.

"I haven't told Martin yet. I was planning to today."

"Well, I think maybe it's best you don't. For now, anyway. Is there some way you can meet him in person?"

"You think he's my stalker and you want me to invite him over for tea?" All teasing and sparks were gone now.

"He may be leaving you strange notes, but that doesn't mean he's dangerous. Just—"

"Deluded?" Now she snorted. "Come on, I know what you told me, but I still can't imagine it. It's just not in him."

"Well then, invite him over so I can get a print off a water glass or something. I'll be right here the whole time, so you won't be in any danger."

"Didn't you just say he probably thinks this is some sort of fantasy romance or something?" She didn't wait for him to respond, she just shook her head. "I'm sorry, but I just can't believe this."

"Fine, then help me get his prints and eliminate him from the short list without ever having to let him know you suspected him in the first place."

She shot him a look. "*I* don't suspect him."

"Okay, fine. You let me do the suspecting."

She didn't react to that, instead she switched gears. "My friends think I should take this to the police. But I just don't see how that will make a difference. He's not doing anything illegal and he hasn't tried to harm me, or threatened me with harm. Could they do anything?"

"Not much at this point. I explained that to Millicent when she hired me. However, she felt then, and we both feel now, that it's important to keep pursuing this, at least to identify him. Whoever he is," he added.

"And if it's not Martin—and it won't be—what will that give us?"

"With a name, we can do some digging, maybe determine his character, get a better handle on what he's capable of. See if he's done anything like this in the past, has any assumed names, that sort of thing. We can also monitor his movements and so on."

"You mean tail him?"

"That's one way. There are others."

She looked at him, but apparently decided she didn't want to know just what that involved. "For how long? Until he latches on to someone else?"

"As long as we think necessary."

She sat back, folded her arms again. "Or as long as Millicent pays you."

"Tanzy—"

She shook her head. "No, I'm sorry. I understand what she was trying to do. It's just frustrating to have her go behind my back." She gave a humorless little laugh. "Although why that surprises me, I have no idea."

"Would you have listened to her?"

Tanzy just looked at him. "That's not the point. I didn't think he was a problem. I should have never have mentioned him to her. I hate it that I've worried her with all this."

"She just wants to know that you're safe. She loves you very much."

Tanzy sighed and Riley found himself wondering again what was going on in her mind. He knew for a fact how much Millicent cared about her only grandniece, and looking at Tanzy now, he felt that love was most definitely reciprocated. But he'd only dug as far back as her college years, mostly to establish how she'd come to be close to her current crop of friends, to rule out the possibility that they had any hand in this.

Still, he knew very little about Tanzy's distant past and wished he'd dug back a bit further. Although there was nothing professional about his curiosity now. He did know the general story, that her mother hadn't been around much and had stuck her only child in boarding schools while she jetted around the globe. He was surprised, knowing Tanzy and her great-aunt a bit better now, that Millicent had put up with Penelope treating her only child so callously. But then, he wasn't privy to all the skeletons in their closets.

"I'm going to have to call her," Tanzy said, more to herself than to him. "Tell me something, is Frances really ill? And for that matter, is Millicent really in Philly?"

"I couldn't say about her friend. I know Ms. Harrington is visiting her."

Tanzy blew out a breath and raked a hand through her hair. "Okay." She stood and walked over to him.

He stood, too, when she stuck out her hand.

"Don't be so suspicious," she said with a wry smile when he regarded her hand warily. "It's not like I'm secretly a black belt or something. I just wanted to thank you."

He could tell her that having her in his arms, even briefly, had almost been payment enough. Fortunately he was able to keep his mouth shut. For a change. He took her hand. "Thank your great-aunt, for caring," he said.

"Oh, I will."

Her tone had him raising an eyebrow. "She really was only trying to protect you, you know."

"I know." Tanzy turned away then and abruptly walked to the door.

"Where are you going?" He assumed she'd have more questions for him.

She looked back at him as if surprised by the question. Like it wasn't any of his business. He didn't at all like how that made him feel. Problem was, that reaction was far more personal than professional.

"I'm going to pack."

"For what?"

"I do appreciate that she's worried about me. But I don't see the need to stay here any longer. I realize your employment is up to my aunt. But my residence here is not."

"It makes a lot more sense to stay here," he said, surprised by this sudden turn of events. "Security is established, everything is monitored."

She was moving to the door again. "I appreciate that but—" Then she stopped, turned. "Just how much of 'everything'?"

Riley shot her a look. She wasn't the only one who could do that. "I'm not a pervert, okay? I don't have your rooms directly monitored."

"There's a relief," she said dryly.

Continuing to give her the same look, he went on. "But most of the rest of the house is. The entries, exits, exteriors, interior halls, that sort of thing. I doubt you have anything set up like that at your place, so—"

"Oh, you're not coming to my place. I'll talk to Millicent about your retainer. I'd feel better knowing who this guy is, too, if for no other reason than to prove you wrong about my editor. But it's only right that I foot the bill. However, I don't need a watchdog."

"Excuse me, but have you forgotten the note you received?"

"No. But your presence hardly thwarted that little maneuver, now did it?"

Riley gritted his back teeth. "We didn't think he'd make contact. Which is just my point. Until we do get a better handle on him, you should stick with the established program. It's not perfect, but it beats the hell out of being an open target."

He saw her try to hide the little shudder. She wasn't very good at it. But then, she wasn't very good at hiding much of anything. Another reason he needed to stay on top of her.

He tried not to groan at the unintentional visual that brought up.

"You keep saying 'we.' You're in business with your father, right? So is he in on this somewhere? Have we met and I don't know it?" Her eyes lit up. "Was he the older man at the dance?"

"No."

"Ah. Well then, who was that guy anyway? Another client?"

"My father is on another assignment," he said, deciding he'd revealed enough. If she wanted to find out about his past, she could do it on her own time. "As for the 'we' part," he doggedly continued, "I told you, I use outside resources."

"Which you get how?"

"The same way any business does, through connections made doing business." So what if, in his case, the business had been football? Sporting events had long been a venue for making outside business connections. So his had been done on Astroturf instead of a putting green, it wasn't all that different, was it?

"How did my aunt come across Parrish Securities?"

Riley propped his hands on his hips. "What is it, exactly, that gives you such a low opinion of me, huh? I explained about the dance and the note—"

"It's not that. It's just that she usually goes for big and centuries-old, not independent mom-and-pop. Or son-and-pop, as the case may be."

"Nice to know your opinion of small businesses is equally flattering."

"I didn't mean it as a slam."

His expression told her what he thought of that. "We got the referral from a friend of hers that we did some work for a few months back. Mr. Waterston."

Tanzy's eyes widened. "The guy that just got hammered in a headline-making divorce?" She smiled. "Nice work."

Riley glared at her. "You don't know all the details. Nor will I be telling them to you."

Folding her arms, her smile widened. "Now you're sounding more like the prissy Riley I've come to know and—"

"Prissy?" He was spluttering, he couldn't help it. "I wasn't prissy. I was—"

"Punctilious? Sententious?"

"Remind me never to argue with a writer. I was just trying to blend in with the background. Fly under the radar."

"You mean my man-eating radar." She laughed, but there was no humor in it. "Nice to know my own flesh and blood has as high an opinion of me as the media does." She held up a hand to stall whatever response he would have made. He was still wishing he'd shut up long enough to hear what she was going to tack onto "the Riley I've come to know and" *blank*.

"I know what you're thinking. And God only knows what you've read about me in your"—she crooked her fingers in a quotation mark gesture—"research."

"Tanzy—"

"Sure," she interrupted, "I date. Sometimes more often than others." She eyed him directly. "But Santa notwithstanding, I don't sleep around. I mean, men have their definite uses and all—"

He couldn't help it. He rolled his eyes.

She pounced on it. "What? It's only okay for you guys to be sexist when you refer to women?"

"Have you ever heard me refer to a woman like that?"

"I haven't been around the real you long enough to know how you refer to women. Besides, I was generalizing."

"You do that a lot."

"It goes with the job. And I thought you said you read my column. Surely you'd know, then, that we are just as shallow and obsessed with sex as you men are."

Now he smiled. "I respect that you believe that. But I highly doubt it."

"Which was my point exactly, I believe."

"Oh, we may think about sex most of the time, but we like to fool ourselves into believing you need us for more than just that."

"Oh, but we do."

He lifted a brow, thinking she looked too damn sexy, sharply decimating his entire sex while wearing bunny slippers.

And just when in the hell had he developed this fetish with animal footwear, he had no idea. But he suspected it coincided with the first time he'd seen her in them.

"So," he asked, "you do realize we can be witty companions, good providers, and defenders of home and hearth?"

She shrugged. "That, too, I suppose. I was thinking of the important stuff."

"Which is?"

"The ruling triumvirate of genetic male abilities. Bug squashing, tire changing, and moving heavy things."

He couldn't help it, he laughed. He'd never figure out how it was that she could simultaneously annoy and arouse him. But she did all the time, and made it look effortless.

"But getting back to my original point, I'm just saying that I don't necessarily deserve the tag that's been hung on me." At his questioning look, she gritted her teeth and clarified, "Man-eater."

"I never said you did."

"You don't have to when the rest of the world does it for you." She lifted a hand to stall his argument. "I'm not even complaining. About the rest of the world, that is. I accept that as part and parcel of revealing things of a personal nature to a readership of over a hundred thousand people. I guess I just thought, when it came to Millicent, that she knew me better than that."

"I suspect she does. Maybe you should take it as a compliment. That she thinks so highly of your appeal to the opposite sex as to warn me about it."

She snorted. "Highly overrated, trust me."

"I might have agreed. At first."

Her mouth dropped open, and he just grinned.

He had to hand it to her, caught bare-faced, she ended up smiling and rolling her eyes. "Nothing wrong with my ego, apparently."

"I said, 'at first.' "

Now that gleam came into her eyes, that carnal one he'd dreamed about. He took a mental if not physical step back when she stepped more fully into the room.

"So, what changed your mind? Was it my sterling wit? Or, being a man, likely it was Clarisse's wizardry with a needle?"

"Honestly?" he said, though he had no idea why. She was teasing, expecting him to dish the nonsense right back at her. But apparently her say-what's-on-your-mind-at-all-times attitude was catching. "It was a lot of the former and admittedly a little of the latter. But you got my attention way before that."

"Oh?" She looked a little more unbalanced by his revelation than she sounded. "Do tell. A woman needs to know these things. For future reference, of course."

She'd pulled it together admirably, but he was still smiling, knowing he'd snagged the edge away from her, even if only momentarily. Holding her gaze, enjoying his grasp, and not really thinking about possible future fallout, he said, "It was the first time I saw you in those things." He pointed to her feet. "That and the Niners jersey. Which is something else we really have to talk about. San Francisco? Just because you live here—"

But she wasn't interested in talking football. "What do you mean, *the first time?*"

Oops. Oh well, it had been fun having the upper hand while it lasted.

"The only time you've seen me in that jersey was last night." Her eyes widened as his cheeks probably colored just a touch. "You said you didn't have voyeuristic tendencies."

"No, I said I wasn't a pervert. No red-blooded male can claim to have no voyeuristic tendencies. We picture all women undressing. It's genetic."

She shook her head, smiling despite herself. "The more I get to know the real you, the more amazed I am you pulled off the sheep act."

He wasn't sure, but he thought his feelings might be a little hurt. "I'm not all that bad a guy."

She simply looked at him, reserving judgment.

"Well, if it helps improve your opinion of me, and I see where it can only go up, I never actually watched you undress."

"Meaning you have imagined it."

She just shook her head when he shrugged and smiled shamelessly. "Like I said, it's—"

"Genetic," she finished with him. "Yeah, yeah. Go on."

"Fine. It's really not that big a deal. I happened to be down here that first night when you came down to raid the fridge. I was closing up the house and watched you scuff down the hall. Where did you get those things anyway?" He pointed at the ragged pink ears that drooped to the floor.

"My friend Sue. She has an odd sense of humor. But they happen to be really comfortable."

"I can see that."

Her gaze narrowed even as she smiled sweetly. "I can have her get you a pair if you'd like."

"Gee, thanks."

"So, why didn't you say anything?" she asked. "That night, I mean. Instead of ogling my bunnies?"

"I was being stealthy. I can do that when I'm not being punctilious and sententious."

She finally broke down and flashed a genuine Tanzy smile. "Is this the witty companion part on display?"

"So I'm no Cary Grant, but at least I make the occasional effort to tamp down my inner troglodyte."

She hooted. "Oh, please say you'll let me use that in a column."

"You mean you haven't already?" He'd been teasing, but the slight hint of color that bloomed in her cheeks was very interesting. He wondered just how much Riley the Sheep had influenced recent "Tanzy Tells All" musings.

"Only because I hadn't thought of it." Her smile caught his, she hesitated, looked into his eyes, then abruptly turned to leave. She paused in the doorway, her smile no longer there, but that irrepressible gleam still twinkled. "I do appreciate what you're doing, Riley. I know Millicent can be mighty convincing in getting things done her own way. And as for my opinion of you, professionally that is, if she hired you and trusted you under the same roof with me, then that's quite a testimonial."

"For a son-and-pop operation, you mean?"

She just made a face at him, which made him smile. "For any operation. Will you report what you find out to me directly?"

"I have to tell Millicent—"

"No, I understand that. But I'd like to hear whatever else you come up with directly from you, rather than via my great-aunt. I'll discuss your fee with her. As I said before, considering it's my ass you're trying to save, I should be footing the bill. Or whatever part of it she'll let me pay. Perhaps we can work together on that?"

At that moment Riley really hated that he was the hired help. He wanted to tell her he'd take care of this as a friend. But though he'd blubbered on about wanting to be all those things she'd listed when she'd fallen apart, he knew that had just been the stress talking. And he'd been a convenient outlet. They were both back in control now, and they knew their actual boundaries. He was fooling himself to think they were anything more.

Yeah, he was definitely having trouble with that "nothing more" part. "We'll work something out," he told her. He didn't add that no matter what part of his bill she was going to pay, it was highly likely, given what he was going to report to Millicent, that she'd request he continue the protection services as well. It was just going to get a hell of a lot more uncomfortable for him to do so. Camping out in cars instead of comfort. His knee twinged just thinking about it. "What about that fingerprint? I don't want you meeting him without me knowing about it."

"We'll work something out," she tossed back at him.

He sighed. He should have known working for the rich wasn't going to be any different. Just then his pager went off. He tugged it out of his sweats pocket and looked down at the number. Ernie.

"I'll let you get that," she said, slipping out of the room before he could stop her.

"Don't think we're done yet," he muttered, then scowled as he went to find a phone.

Is *love* a four-letter word? It's certainly more com-plicated than sex. But while sex without love is easily understandable, and at times quite preferable, why would anyone desire the reverse? I suppose I should just be thankful there are only three letters in sex.

13

He was out there again. Watching her.

Tanzy sighed, letting the drapes flicker shut. She leaned back in her office chair and tried to focus on the column she was supposed to be writing. But it was hard to concentrate, knowing he was down there.

She looked around the office of her cozy two-bedroom Russian Hill writer's nest. It was good to be home again. In her own space. Her own perfectly broken-in office chair, her own framed Trevor Southey prints. Her own mini-fridge, stocked with the staples of a writer's life: Coke and a bag of miniature Snickers.

And then there were her newest additions. Not that she hadn't enjoyed the sassy little sugarplum fairies Millicent had chosen for her rooms in Big Harry. But she was forming a definite attachment to the growing herd of sheep figurines crowding the bookshelves that lined the wall next to her.

Readers, apparently filled with the holiday shopping bug, had sent them to the magazine's post-office box. It all began with a stuffed sheep, sent by a male herd member, that came with the sign that read, "Join the Herd, the Grass Is Greener." She'd joked about it during a *Barbara Bradley* taping, and it had snowballed from there. They ranged in size and shape; some were glass, some stone or plaster, all of them hilarious. Someone had even found one wearing a wedding dress, the ultimate last bridesmaid.

Her personal favorite, however, was the Wile E. Coyote Martin had given her to put in the midst of the herd. Not exactly a wolf, but it made her laugh every time she looked at it. Or it had. Now she looked at it and hated herself for wondering.

No way SoulM8 was Martin. But she was forced to admit she'd been uncomfortable enough by what Riley had said to blow off their phone session the other day and opted to do their usual postcolumn analysis via email. Martin questioned her evasiveness and she'd chalked it up to the holiday crush overwhelming her. He'd been nice about it, understanding. Too nice? Too understanding?

"Stop it already." He'd been analyzing her column and she'd been analyzing every word he typed, looking for some deeper meaning. Mostly to reassure herself there wasn't any. But if she was so sure of herself, why hadn't she set up the face-to-face meeting Riley requested? She looked at the Wile E. Coyote again, frowning. Then she suddenly sat up straighter. Martin had surely picked up the figurine, had to have handled it when he sent it. Maybe she could just give the figurine to Riley and be done with this whole thing.

Feeling better—and less like a louse for suspecting, even for a heartbeat, her friend and mentor—she turned back to her computer. Her phone rang, and she froze, then shook herself. It's not like SoulM8 was going to call her. He hadn't so much as emailed since the night of the dance. Maybe he'd given up. Moved on. *She should be so lucky.* She checked her Caller ID anyway, then clicked the receiver on. "Hey, stranger. It's about time you returned my call."

"I know," Sloan said, sounding harried. "It's been crazy around here with the show coming up. I'm going to need a holiday after the holidays."

"I don't want to wait that long. Can we squeeze in a lunch? A drink, even? We need a break from the insanity. Rina and Sue are planning this shower like they're on a mission from God. Or Martha Stewart. Which might be redundant. And Mariel is filling a photo album with images of her child's penis. You're all I've got left." *And I'm worried about you,* she wanted to add, but left it unsaid. Tanzy was the group shoulder, but Sloan rarely took advantage of her time-share portion of it.

"I'd love to," Sloan said, sounding sincere. "But as it is, I'm going to have to do my best to be there for the baby shower."

Tanzy chewed on her lip, then decided this phone call might be her only shot. "So, uh, how are things? With you and Wolfgang, I mean. Still okay?"

There was a pause, then Sloan said, "We're fine. Doing fine."

It was dismissive to the point of being hurtful. And, messy marital tension be damned, Tanzy called her on it. "I thought we were closer than that."

Another pause, then, "We are. I just . . . it's not a good time to talk right now, okay?"

At least she hadn't pretended she wasn't dodging. "Okay. But I'm here, anytime. Have you talked to Rina or Sue?" Maybe they'd gotten more out of her.

"And get the full lecture on my lack of commitment to my social life and blah blah blah? No thanks."

"Gee, I guess I should be honored you returned my call."

Sloan laughed dryly. "Yes, well, you always know when to back off."

"Thanks. I think."

"Listen, I have to run, but you can tell the gang that I'm officially RSVPing the shower invite. But you're coming to opening night, right?"

Sloan was showcasing a new artist, hoping her gallery

patrons' pre-holiday shopping sprees would extend themselves to include buying artwork. And if anyone could get people to pay attention to art only days before Christmas, it was Sloan.

"I'll—uh, do my best." Tanzy hated to admit she'd planned to curtail attendance at all public functions until this SoulM8 thing was wrapped up, even to herself.

"Why don't you bring along that guy you dragged to that charity thing?"

"You said you hadn't talked to Rina or Sue."

"I haven't. Rina emails me daily. She swears if it weren't for her updates, I'd have long since lost touch with reality."

Tanzy wondered if Rina had mentioned the note, then decided she hadn't, or Sloan would have contacted her sooner. Busy or not, she was still a friend. Rina had probably decided, correctly, that Sloan had enough on her shoulders. "Yes, I know. I rely on her extensively for shoe sale information."

"So, you'll bring him?"

"I'll do my best to get there. I'm not committing to anything else," she said, then quickly changed the subject. "Will Wolfgang be attending?" She knew Wolf could be a bit sulky when Sloan introduced new talent. She supposed it was an artist thing. But that constant need for reassurance would drive her crazy. Apparently it had driven Sloan into the arms of another man.

"I'm not sure." She laughed without humor. "I'm not sure I care."

"Uh-oh. You want to talk about it?"

Sloan sighed, obviously wishing she hadn't slipped. "Don't read too much into that. You know how he can be. I meant what I said earlier, Tanz. Wolf and I *are* moving along. It's just . . . it's complicated."

"Meaning us single gals wouldn't understand?"

"Partly."

Tanzy winced, but she'd asked for it. "Okay, then talk to Rina, or Sue."

"No thank you. I don't need that lecture, either."

"Rina can hardly lecture you about marriage, but she'd listen. And Sue is as levelheaded as they get."

"Sunny Sue and Perfect Paul?" Sloan snorted. "Right. No thanks. And don't even suggest Mariel. Newlywed wisdom I can do without."

Tanzy laughed. "Then I guess you're stuck with unenlightened me. Sure you can't spare time for a drink? You know you won't have time to do more than wave at the opening, if that. I promise to be nonjudgmental."

"Can I get that in writing? Listen, I promise, once we get past the holidays and things die down a little, we'll get together."

"Face-to-face. So I can make you spill your guts. I have my vays, you know."

"Why do you think I phoned this in? But if I'm the one getting grilled, we're having more than drinks. I pick the place, you pay the tab."

"Sounds fair."

"Great. One thing checked off my guilt list." Then just when Tanzy thought she was going to ring off, she blurted, "Thanks, Tanzy, for ... just thanks. It *is* complicated, but I'm glad you called. In the meantime, don't worry. Things are ... good. For me. Okay? And when you report in to Rina right after hanging up, tell her to tell the rest of the gang to stop worrying, too. I'm going to be fine." Then her voice warmed up and Tanzy's interest shifted from concern to out-and-out curiosity. "Really fine," she finished. "Gotta run."

The dial tone hummed in her ear before Tanzy had a chance to ask if the reason Sloan felt "really fine" had anything to do with a certain blond Adonis. She was sorely tempted to call her right back and demand details. Or march down to the gallery. Oh, the torture! But that's what she got for tangling with Sloan during business hours. Of course, all of Sloan's hours were business hours, it seemed.

And she should have been insulted by the crack about reporting in to Rina, except that was exactly what she was going to do. She clicked her speed dial. She didn't even announce herself when Rina picked up. "I talked to Sloan. I think you were right."

"About the affair?"

"Yeah. She sounded exhausted. I think it's more than the usual work-related stress. When I asked her about Wolfgang, she got all evasive. But then she ended by making a point of saying things were going fine for her personally. Really fine," she added, putting the same intensity on the words Sloan had.

"Fine for her . . . but I'm guessing not for Wolf?"

Tanzy snorted. "*I'm* guessing whatever this is about, he probably deserves it. She definitely sounded like a woman getting laid on a regular basis. And we both know Wolf's too caught up in his art for that. For that matter, Sloan isn't home often enough anyway."

"Aren't hotel rooms convenient that way?" Rina stated with a sardonic little laugh. "And speaking of being home, how's that going? Is Riley still dogging your every step?"

Tanzy leaned forward and flicked the blinds apart, looking down two stories to where Riley's midnight blue SUV sat parked across the street. With Riley in it.

Watching her.

She smiled and waved. He didn't wave back. It was too hard to tell with all that tinted glass, but she'd bet he wasn't smiling, either. "Yep."

"You said you were only paying for him to investigate this thing."

"I am. Millicent apparently has other ideas. I knew

things were too easy when she relented on my taking over paying his tab without a fight."

"It's been what, three days now? And you're still making him sit out there in that car?"

"It's an SUV, massive, almost mobile-home-size. Leather interior. All the bells and whistles."

"And you know this how?"

"He's not the only one with telephoto capabilities."

Rina just laughed. "You two are a pair. For all your professed nonchalance, when you found out who he really was, I'd have bet you'd have him between the sheets a heartbeat later."

Tanzy had thought about that. A lot. "You know, I'm really getting tired of this man-eater rap. I know my column rep gets a little out there, but you guys should know better."

Rina stayed tellingly silent.

"Geez. Harsh. I seem to recall you being the one doing the yacht circuit for the past several years."

"Just until I hooked the big one," Rina said with a cheeky laugh. "And I seem to recall a raft of jet set jokes from you, missy. But trust me, for most of that time it was more business than pleasure."

"Yeah, okay," Tanzy snorted. "But it's not like I have a boy toy of the week, either."

"You could, however, put out an annual calendar."

Tanzy paused, did a mental count, then sighed disgustedly. "Okay. But really, that's basically saying I only get laid twelve times in an entire year. When you look at it that way, it's almost pathetic. Am I right?"

"You're counting weekend marathon sex as one time, then?"

"Ha, ha, very funny. We wish there was such a thing as marathon sex. I'm convinced it's an urban myth."

"Quantity versus quality aside, you know I love you—"

Tanzy groaned. "But, I hear a distinct but. Resist the

urge, Rina. I'm begging you." But she knew resistance was futile where this particular lecture was concerned, and resigned herself to hearing it. Again.

"But," Rina stated, undaunted as predicted, "as your closest friend, I feel honor bound to point out that you'll never find Mr. Forever if you keep recycling Mr. Right Now after one use. You don't even get to know a guy."

"I know what I need to know," Tanzy grumbled. "Besides, I'm not interested in Mr. Forever." She realized she'd flicked open the blinds, was staring down at Riley. "I'm perfectly happy with Mr. Saturday Night. Or Mr. Monday Afternoon." She grinned at Rina's snort of disgust. "I may be shallow, but at least I'm flexible."

"So I've heard," Rina said with a sly laugh.

"Oh, har har har. But, since you pointed it out, you'd be right about that, too," she said smugly. "So put that in your yacht and sail it."

"And you call yourself a writer? With lines like that? But if you think to distract me with your oh-so-clever wit, you're wrong."

"What is up with the sudden need to see me shackled?" Again Tanzy flicked open the blinds. Again she realized she was staring at Riley, and flicked them shut. "I have simple needs. My most complex problem is whether to buy the shoes now or wait for a sale so I won't feel so guilty for spending that much money on heels I'll likely wear only a handful of times. And that's the way I like it. I don't want to get married. Men are great, but they're hell on a girl's shoe budget."

"Well, I can see why marriage is out of the question," Rina responded dryly. "But you shouldn't be too worried. For that to happen you'd actually have to have a relationship with someone." Tanzy opened her mouth to respond, but Rina plowed ahead. "I'm not even advocating marriage. I'm just suggesting you might consider wading into an actual relationship. And here's a novel concept—you might consider getting to know him *before* you get between the sheets. Or on the living room floor, as the case may be."

"See, and I view that as a total waste of time wherein I could be indulging in serious foreplay. The guys I date would agree with that view. At least, I get no arguments from them, at any rate."

"Exactly. You don't even know them well enough to *have* an argument."

"Exactly *my* point. Who wants to waste time arguing when there are climaxes waiting to be reached?"

"Yeah, I guess if you knew him well enough to disagree about more than what kind of chocolate sauce is best for food sex, then that would mean you might, God forbid, have developed actual feelings for the man. And—oh no!—that would ruin everything. Next thing you know, he might want to use the L word, and that makes dumping him a hell of a lot messier, doesn't it?"

Tanzy sat back in her chair with a thump. "Ouch?"

Rina let out a breath. "I'm sorry, that was a little over the top, even for me. But I know you. Better than anyone. At some point you're going to wish you'd let someone into your head, maybe even your heart, instead of just into your—"

"I get it already," Tanzy interrupted.

"Yeah, well, maybe you've gotten so good at getting it without giving anything of your real self, you don't even know how to anymore."

Tanzy found her gaze skating to the window again. Scowling, she promptly spun her chair so she faced her office door. Then she did what she always did when confronted with her own faults. She went on offense. "You're one to talk. Where did letting people in get you besides divorced?"

"Okay. I deserved that, I suppose. And I know you think

I married Garrison for the money and that rubs you the wrong way. Which is hilarious coming from the alpha wolf of our little pack. I would have thought you of all people would approve of taking what you need and damn the rest."

"Jesus, Rina, do you really think so little of me?" She wasn't sure she wanted an answer to that, so she kept on talking. "I don't hurt people, or treat them callously. Everyone knows up front what's what. And do you really think I think so little of you? I don't."

"But you don't approve," Rina said, then let out a little laugh. "You think people should only get married if they're in love. Who'd have thought you'd be the closet romantic of the bunch, huh? If the world only knew. But just because I bombed out on finding my soul mate doesn't mean you shouldn't even try. I still believe in marrying for love, just as much as you do."

"Except you keep conveniently forgetting I don't plan on actually doing it. For love or money. You know my reasons. It's not in my genes to dream of white picket fences."

"And you're old enough to stop hiding behind the choices made by your mom and the sperm donor. You're smart enough to know you can make your own choices when it comes to love and marriage. And men, for that matter."

"I do make my own choices about men. I choose to enjoy them and leave the messy relationship part to someone else to deal with. Besides, Millicent never got married. She seems perfectly happy to me. Maybe she's my role model."

"Okay, fine, I give up. And you're right. I'm not one to talk, with two exes to my credit. Except to say that I'm happy now. Happier than I've ever been, in fact. You think I settled. I think I gave up expecting the impossible, only to end up miserable when all my expectations weren't met. Garrison and I might not burn up the sheets, but I do care deeply for him. Him, not his bank account. He loves me,

Tanz. More important, he's nice to me. Respects me. And he makes me laugh. Like I said before, there's more to life and love than sex. I'm still learning just how much more. Everyone's needs are different. Believe it or not, Garrison fulfills more of mine than I ever thought possible." Her voice softened. "I just wish you'd think about letting someone fulfill yours for more than a few hours at a time."

For the second time in one morning, Tanzy was left listening to a dial tone. She sat there for long moments, Rina's words echoing through her mind, growing more uncomfortable by the second. Introspection was fine when it was indulged in for the entertainment of her readers. It sucked when it was purely for her own personal enlightenment.

Frowning, she abruptly spun her chair back around to face her desk. "What does she know anyway?" she demanded of the row of sheep. They stared silently back at her, looking more accusing than amusing. "Oh, sure, easy for you to be judgmental. You're sheep." She turned to face her blinking cursor. She hated to admit it, but maybe Rina had a better handle on all this than she did. Or ever hoped to, if you listened to her tell it.

She blew out a long breath, then resolutely shoved the whole thing from her mind. She leaned forward in her chair, placed her fingers on the keys. Work. She had a column to write.

Not much of an escape at the moment, is it?

She could confront her feelings, think deep thoughts. If she had to. It's what she did. And she was good at it. But she really didn't want to think about the tangled love lives of her friends, much less her own family. It had been almost three years since she'd last heard from her mother. A brief birthday call placed from some yacht in the Greek Isles. There had been so much noise and raucous laughter in the background, Tanzy had barely been able to hear her. She had heard the invitation, though. Contact might be few and far between, but Penelope always assuaged whatever guilty-mother pangs she might be feeling by asking her only daughter to come and join her.

Tanzy had made the mistake of saying yes precisely one time. It had been just after her twenty-second birthday and, freshly delivered college degree in hand, she thought it was time to conquer that other bastion of antiquated ideals. Her relationship—if you could call it that—with her mother.

She'd lasted forty-eight hours. As it turned out, and it shouldn't have been a great surprise, her mother wanted a girlfriend, a playmate. Not a daughter. When Tanzy had refused to call her by her first name, thereby spoiling her youthful fantasy, Penelope had pouted and said some rather nasty things. It was when she'd tried to make it up to Tanzy by introducing her daughter to her latest lover, then blithely offered him to her when she was through with him, that Tanzy had booked a flight home.

She sighed and propped her chin on her hands. Was that what she was destined to become? Had she really avoided being around her mother because somewhere deep down inside she was afraid she was looking at her own future? No, she'd never be so desperate, would she? She'd certainly never start banking her self-worth on whether there was a man in her life. Young or otherwise.

She prided herself on her personal strength and her self-sufficiency. She didn't need anyone to make her whole. Sure, Millicent was there to fulfill her familial needs. Her friends were there to fulfill her day-to-day needs. And yes, there was the occasional man to, well, fulfill those other needs. Honestly, what wasn't to like about that setup?

And when she got older? Well, she'd just face that when the time came. But not the way her mother had, by trying to entice younger and younger men into her bed as a means of proving something.

She slumped back in her chair and harrumphed. Why in the hell had Rina dredged all this up now? Didn't Tanzy have enough on her plate? Of course, when she thought about it, there was no sense in blaming Rina for this sudden wave of self-doubt and discontent. She had to put the blame where it really belonged.

Squarely on the surprisingly broad shoulders of Riley Parrish.

It had really started with him. Rina's wedding, which had left her as the last single in the group, was just part of it. Sure, it had thrown her for a loop. But she'd rebounded, turned it into something positive with her recent column success. Then Riley had come along. And he'd done the unforgivable really. He'd gotten under her skin instead of into her pants.

And try as she might to blame her little emotional breakdown the other day on outside stresses, it really boiled down to one thing: She wanted Riley. In bed . . . and out of it.

There. She'd admitted it.

She wanted a man. For more than sex.

"Fat lot of good that's going to do you." Especially considering that instead of being all cozy back in Big Harry, he was presently sitting in a cold drizzle inside his SUV. She was imagining him in her bed . . . and he was probably trying to devise the fastest way out of this assignment.

Sure, she could move back to Millicent's. Or invite him in here. She wasn't certain which prospect disturbed her more. Millicent had come back home once all was revealed, and while she loved her great-aunt dearly, living with her for more than a long holiday weekend was simply out of the question. And this place was too small to house both her and Riley. She had precisely one bed. And, amazingly enough, she didn't want him in it.

Okay, that was a total lie. Of course she wanted him in it. Had dreamed about it. Hot, sweaty dreams, in fact. And yeah, there'd been a little of that urban-myth action in there as well. She shifted in her seat. Just thinking about it made her twitchy. But, fantasy marathon sex notwithstanding, for the first time in her whole life she realized that going to bed with a man would actually make the situation worse, not better.

And why is that? her inner voice pestered.

She ignored the little pain in the ass. It wasn't because she was afraid she'd never want to let him out again. Although that scenario did have a little something going for it.

It was that, for once, maybe she didn't want to skip directly past Go. If she did, she had this feeling she'd miss out on the best part. Which meant that Rina might actually have a point. Tanzy just might want to explore having a relationship outside of sex with him, and if she jumped into bed with him right off, it was likely the rest would be over before it could go any further. That's the way she operated. Because the continued intimacy of sex carried all sorts of other complications along with it. Like expectations.

And there was no going back, pretending they didn't have carnal knowledge of each other. Which meant if she wanted Riley as a friend, she had to keep him out of her bed.

Of course, given that he was proving to be as frank with his opinions as she was with hers, it was highly probable they'd want to kill each other inside ten minutes anyway. And all this mental tap dancing ignored the simple fact that she might not be able to get him into bed, even if she wanted to. A revelation that did not give her as much comfort as she'd hoped.

He'd wanted her. Of that she could be certain. At least for the odd moment here and there. Some of them very odd. She thought back to his very disconcerting and totally unwolflike revelation that what did it for him was her in a faded Niners jersey and worn-out bunny slippers.

She refused to be endeared to him because of that.

But ultimately his professionalism would have probably precluded him from doing anything horizontal, or vertical for that matter, that involved removal of clothing.

All of which left her up here in her office, trying to do her job, while he sat down there, trying to do his.

With a huff of resignation, she sat forward, fingers on the keys, and resolutely faced the blank monitor. What to Do About Riley would have to wait. She had a deadline to meet.

"Thank you, God," she whispered in relief.

Friends and lovers. It seems such a simple concept and yet it's one I've never been able to master. Not with the same person, anyway. Admittedly, I've never been all that interested in trying. I have friends. I have the occasional lover. Mixing the two always seemed to be borrowing trouble. So much better to keep them separate, then everyone understands what's expected of them. No muss, no fuss. And you always know who to call for what.

14

Have you closed this one yet?" Finn asked via cell phone.

"Still working on it, Dad."

"Well, stretch it out, boyo. Might as well live the high life for a bit longer, eh?"

Riley watched the raindrops track down the windows of his truck. "Yeah, right." He hadn't told his father about the recent change in his assignment. He didn't feel particularly compelled to, either. His father didn't care how the job got done as long as it got done and the checks came in. "What about you? Things wrapping up there?"

"Well, that's why I called." He hesitated, then asked, "You need me to come in and help out?"

Riley shook his head, didn't bother to sigh. "No, I've got it under control. You staying in Santa Rosa, then?"

"For a bit longer, I'm thinking."

Considering everything, he should just keep his mouth shut. Apparently he was incapable. "Dad, do you really think this is wise? I mean, the assignment was to—"

"I'm quite clear on my assignment. I don't need any lectures from you, boyo. You just leave me to mind my own."

Riley could have pointed out that leaving him to mind his own was exactly what had driven him to the brink of losing everything. And continued to be an obstacle to their finding continued success. His father should have been born with a trust fund. Unfortunately, he'd trusted in his son's pro career instead. But there was no point in trying to get his father to be fiscally responsible. It was always going to be up to Riley. One way or the other. "Did you send the package in on the Gordon case? Silverman also called asking for specifics about what the two of you set up."

"I'm on top of it, don't you worry. You take care of yours. Speaking of which," Finn added, the defensive posturing disappearing in a wink, as it always did, replaced by the charming Irish rogue that saved his father's bacon on a regular basis. "How is she going? Made any headway?"

Normally Riley would shake his head in weary disgust at his father's sly innuendo. This time, however, he felt the heat creep up the back of his neck. His father couldn't have any clue about the internal battles Riley had been waging with himself . . . and his wandering libido, but that didn't make him feel any less guilty for having them. Still, he responded as he always did, by pretending the question was strictly about business. "We were hoping to match up a latent print, but the suspect's employer doesn't keep them on file. They do keep photo IDs, though. I'm getting copies along with the complete employee list. We'll at least get some faces to work with. We have a second suspect as well. The man she works for. I'm working on getting a print from him to see if it's a match."

"Good, good," Finn replied assuredly, though Riley knew he couldn't care in the least. It wasn't his case, after all. "What about the skirt?" Finn pressed with a chuckle. "Gotten a peek at what's beneath it yet, eh?"

Now the disgust came honestly. Riley might be wrestling with "like father, like son" issues regarding his growing attraction to a client, but hearing his father reduce that attraction to the same kind of tawdry liaison he'd indulge in himself only served to piss him off.

It also clarified better than Riley could have on his own the distinct and permanent difference between the two men and their approach to the opposite sex. It was a defining moment, bordering on profound. He didn't, however, thank his father for his unwitting paternal assistance.

"Listen, Dad, I have a call coming in. Just let me know when you'll be getting back in town."

Finn sighed, clearly disappointed. "You behave like it's a sin to indulge in a little of what God put us on this green earth to enjoy. We have things hard enough, no? Don't be so high and mighty. It hurts a lot more when you fall." He merely chuckled when his bit of wisdom was met with stony silence. "You always were a tough one. Like your ma that way, you are, God rest her soul."

Not for the first time Riley wondered if Finn's focus would have remained on hearth and home, not to mention business, if Mary Theresa Parrish had lived past Riley's first year in high school. Riley had buried his grief on the gridiron. Finn had buried his between the legs of other women. He wondered if that was still his dad's excuse now, but had no interest in finding out.

"I'll call when I'm back in town," Finn went on. "But don't expect me until after the holidays."

Finn rang off, leaving Riley as he usually did, feeling frustrated and somewhat helpless. "Merry Christmas to you, too, Dad," Riley muttered. For the millionth time he found himself wishing he was more impervious to his father's regard for him. But no matter how old he was, no matter how well categorized his father's failings, no matter that his road was the better one to take, he knew Finn could still plink him with the parental-guilt thing, and far too easily.

Tamping down the urge to smack something, Riley punched a number into his cell phone instead. "Hey, J.B.," he said when the young man answered.

"Coach. Long time, no see. What, you can't talk to us now that we're out of contention?"

Riley grinned, quite relieved to put his conversation with Finn behind him. "I've been busy. Sorry to hear you guys got knocked out of postseason. Figured you might like to put your newly acquired free time to some use, earn a little Christmas money." Riley had a few players from SFSU he kept on call for occasional assistance with cases. Some knew of him from when he played, some didn't, but like all aspiring jocks, they liked being around someone who'd achieved the ultimate dream; an alumnus who'd made it to the pros. Didn't matter to them that here he was, a few years later, his knee shot and struggling to earn a living. He'd played with the big boys, and they were sure if they ever got the chance, they'd make it last a lifetime.

For his part, he enjoyed the connection with them, seeing that hunger and drive. Helped him keep a healthier perspective on his achievements, not focus on what he'd lost. Or so he told himself anyway.

"We missed you at the gym the past couple of weeks. What hot case you on? Who you protecting, someone famous?"

Riley smiled. Everything seemed so much bigger and more dramatic when you were twenty. "I should be back after the holidays. Just in time to whip your sorry postseason-lacking asses back into shape."

"That's just harsh, man," J.B. said, but the affection was clear in his tone.

"Hey, I'm simply trying to prepare you. You think life is tough playing college ball, you don't know shit." He could just see J.B. rolling his eyes. That was the other thing about being twenty, you thought you knew every last thing. Riley's smile grew as he realized he was thankful to be reminded that being thirty-two and still not knowing shit wasn't that bad after all. "Listen, I need you to pick up and deliver a package for me." He told him where to pick it up, then gave him the address of the corner nearest to where he was presently sitting. "Sometime in the next hour if you can do it."

"I'm on it, Coach."

Riley hung up, shaking his head. The moniker had begun as an "old guy" joke, but as more guys began to look to him as a kind of mentor, at least in the weight room and during the occasional pickup game, it had stuck. Grinning, he stretched, then winced and swore when his knee protested painfully. "Oh yeah, being thirty-two is sooo much better."

He glanced up at Tanzy's office window. She wasn't peeking out at the moment, trying to be cute with the little grins and the occasional wave. Sitting in the chilly rain, knee cramping, he hadn't been in the mood to respond in kind. Now he thought about simply storming the fortress. She hadn't offered, but he'd bet she wouldn't refuse.

And the reason she'd let him in was exactly the reason he was still sitting in his truck.

After another look up at her window, he glanced at his watch, figured he had enough time to boot up before meeting J.B. Ernie should have something for him by now.

Angling his body so he could keep an eye on her row house, he connected his computer to his Palm Pilot and logged on to get his email. It would have been a hell of a lot easier if FishNet had digitized their photo file. Then they could have just emailed it to him. Or he could have had Ernie hack it for him so he wouldn't have had to deal with the FishNet CEO at all. He shuddered thinking about that call.

Lori Sack was her name, and boy did she have a major chip on her shoulder. He had no idea why she was taking it out on him, but it didn't take long to figure out his Y chromosome played a large role in the matter.

He'd hoped to bypass her as they had up to this point. Ernie had been flying below their radar, extracting the information he needed so they wouldn't have to announce their involvement. If SoulM8 was a FishNet employee, Riley didn't want to risk giving him any indication that they were tracking him. The fact that the perv kept changing his account info, always with a false name and address, told him the guy was either paranoid or had a pretty good clue that Tanzy wasn't going to take his devoted act lying down—figuratively or literally—and would hire someone to look into it.

They'd managed to continue behind the scenes with the fingerprinting issue by contacting FishNet's personnel director. Riley had made the anonymous call, asking about their employment and hiring procedures and if they printed or drug-tested their employees. He didn't really care about the drug question, but knew it would divert the personnel manager from the fingerprint info he really wanted. As planned, she assumed he was some guy looking for a job where he didn't have to give a sample at the office. Disgusted, she'd curtly informed him they ran a complete criminal and drug history on all new hires and therefore didn't need to fingerprint them if they passed.

So, with the print comparison a bust, Riley's second choice was a list of employees and, hopefully, photo IDs. But Ernie couldn't extract what wasn't there. Not that it was all that surprising FishNet didn't store stuff like that on their mainframe. Many firms, especially those directly involved with Internet service, went out of their way to hackproof company information. Riley shook his head. Hack all you wanted into their clients' information—what did they care?—but God forbid you tiptoe through their personnel or business files.

Which had forced the call directly to Ms. Sack. He made her aware of what he suspected and asked for her cooperation so they wouldn't have to involve the police. Usually just the mention of the cops was enough to get assistance. No one wanted that hassle if they could avoid it. Ms. Sack, however, wasn't afraid of a little hassle. In fact, she demanded to know why he was the one pursuing this instead of the police. Her position was that if they didn't take the case seriously, why should she?

After patiently explaining how stalking cases worked and how little the police, by law, could actually do about it, he'd pushed hard on the issue of a woman's right to protect herself—which, given her tone, was a subject she felt strongly about—and made it clear that if anything happened to his client, he'd be more than happy to point the finger at her, ringleader of the She-Woman Man-Haters Club. So, okay, he didn't use exactly that term, but it had put a chink in her self-righteous armor.

She'd grudgingly agreed to give up a list of names, but had held steadfast on the pictures and address and phone number info. He didn't care about the latter. With a name, Ernie could get him the personal info. But the pictures were crucial to the rest of his plan. Fortunately Ernie had also done some digging on Ms. Lori Sack. Background information that at the time had seemed useless. But given her rather open hostility toward the opposite sex, Riley didn't think she'd want it to get out that she'd once applied to be a contestant on *The Bachelor*. Like she had a chance in hell, he thought, having seen her publicity photo on the FishNet website. Now, *Survivor* he could see her on. And winning the million. Hands down. But a dating show?

He still hadn't figured that one out, but now that she'd set herself up in this new business venture, going brass to balls with the big boys, she wasn't all that keen on having that information broadcasted, either. She did subject him to a blistering tirade on men's continued subjugation of women—which he privately began to think was exactly what she really wanted, complete with leather bondage gear and a riding crop—but she gave him what he wanted.

Not his best day. But he'd gotten the job done. He also knew he'd burned that bridge, so whatever he got from this information was pretty much going to be his last shot at proving a direct link between SoulM8 and FishNet. Which would shift the focus entirely back to Martin. Martin, whose fingerprints Tanzy kept promising, but not delivering on.

He was working up an alternate plan for obtaining them himself, but had been busy working with Ernie on collecting additional information on possible fresh leads. Millicent had been able to give him a guest list to the charity ball. Ernie was working on getting a list of the wait staff, doormen, and valets who had worked during the event. If they were very lucky, when they cross-referenced those names with the employee list from FishNet they would get a hit. Hopefully SoulM8 was arrogant enough to think no one would make that particular connection. Riley was banking on it.

He glanced up at Tanzy's building as his Palm Pilot connected, only to see her dash out of her front door and across the street. She ran around the back of his SUV and tapped on the passenger window. Juggling two Cokes, a couple of sandwiches, and what looked like a Road Runner figurine in a plastic bag, she motioned him to unlock the door.

He spent a moment considering the wisdom of that move, and maybe enjoying keeping her in the rain a fraction longer as well. After all, if she'd just been a little less stubborn about all this, they could be dining on real food back in Millicent's roomy kitchen.

Her teasing smile shifted to what he'd come to think of as "that look." She was very good at it, which still didn't explain why it turned him on. Fighting a grin despite being annoyed with her—so what else was new?—he popped the lock.

She slid in and snapped the door shut behind her. "I thought you might like some company for lunch."

As if she wasn't the reason he was dining alone. In his truck.

She dangled the bag, immune to his glare. "And I brought you a fingerprint sample."

"Wile E. Coyote?"

"A gift from Martin."

Riley frowned and took the bag. "When?"

"When what? Oh, when did he give it to me? Just after the wolf/sheep thing hit big. Readers have been sending me sheep figurines. It was the closest he could come to a wolf." She glared at him. "I know what you're thinking, but it wasn't some kind of hidden message of his sudden and profound obsession with me. More an example of his sweet but dorky sense of humor."

Riley withheld comment on that and inspected the figurine through the plastic. "Who else has handled this? Has it been dusted?"

"I believe that's your field."

"I meant as in housecleaning dusting."

"I've handled it, but no, no dusting."

He regarded the figurine dubiously. "The uneven surface will make it difficult. You couldn't get a meeting with him?"

She sighed. "Try to cooperate and all I get is a bunch of complaints."

"Meaning you could get a meeting, but you didn't."

She held up the sandwiches. "Ham and Swiss, or tuna?" She put them on the padded console between them and went about popping the tops on the soda cans and putting them in the console holders. "I'm more the tuna type, if it helps you in the decision-making process."

"Tanzy, listen, we really have to discuss—"

"Listen, I came out here, being nice, bearing food and fingerprints, because I'm getting tired of seeing you sit out here in the rain. You won't even wave."

He gave her the look. Judging from the little flash of response in her eyes, he was pretty good at it, too. "I'm working."

"Come on, Riley, I know Millicent is worried, but you're handling this, right? So there's no need for her to—"

"Yes, she is worried. And yes, she'd rather us both be under her roof."

"I told you I couldn't live with her. Just as I told you—and her—that I didn't think it was necessary for you to watch over me like this. So don't blame me for your having to sit out here like this. There's no need for her to pay you to—"

"Your aunt isn't paying me for this detail."

That shut her up. For a moment, anyway. "Did something go wrong between you?"

"No. You demanded taking over the bill payment and she accepted it."

"But I made it explicitly clear that *I* didn't want a bodyguard, I—"

"Yes, I know." He scowled, though how he'd hoped to avoid this particular discussion, he had no idea. "You're not being billed for this, either, okay?"

Nonplussed, she sat back and stared at him. "Why?" she asked finally.

He didn't pretend to misunderstand. "Because once I start something, I see it through to the end." Whether it was his pro career, rebuilding his father's life, finishing cases . . . "Just because you don't think you warrant protection doesn't mean I agree. And as long as I'm working this case, where and how I choose to work it is up to me. And I choose to work it where I can also keep my eye on you."

She stared at him for a long moment, opened her mouth, then shut it again.

He couldn't help it, he smiled. "What do you know. It can be done, and I don't even think hell had to freeze over."

Now he got the look again, and felt better for it.

"I've been known to remain speechless for entire minutes at a time," she informed him frostily. Then the dry smile surfaced, followed by a resigned sigh as she flopped back in the seat and watched the rain splatter against the window. "I appreciate what you're doing." She glanced over at him. "Really, I do. But SoulM8, whoever he is," she added with a warning glance, "hasn't contacted me in days. Not since the dance. I've had two columns out since then and no email after either one. Martin hasn't done or said anything remotely suspicious to me in our emails."

"I know."

She just looked at him. "Great. Thanks. So, did it ever occur to you that maybe it's over and he's moved on to some other unfortunate recipient of his twisted lust? I mean, at what point do we stop all this?"

"It doesn't make sense that he's just given up. Whatever drew him to you in the first place hasn't changed. If anything, it's magnified. The focus and attention on your column is white-hot and gaining. You've got more media exposure with that piece in last Sunday's paper, and now the appearance on *Good Morning Bay Area* next week."

"Maybe that's it, maybe he's shying away from the spotlight. Or maybe he made you. You haven't exactly been hiding yourself." She snagged the tuna sandwich from the bag and unwrapped it. "I mean, I go to the grocery store and you're right there in the frozen-food aisle. I stop to meet Sue for lunch, and you're two tables away. I get in my car, you're right behind me. It's silly."

"It's one more shield than you'd have without me."

She paused midbite, then lowered the sandwich altogether. "You really think he's going to come directly at me? You said most stalkers lacked self-esteem, that they kept their distance in order to keep their dreamworld intact. That contact was too risky, because rejection of their twisted reality would burst their fantasy bubble."

"And that is statistically true. But after the note at the dance, it's a chance I'm not willing to take. And neither should you."

The sandwich completely forgotten now, she stared past him out the window. Riley had no idea what she was thinking this time. "Do you really think it could be Martin?" she said finally, breaking the rain-pattered silence. "I mean, he has plenty of other means of letting me know if he has . . . feelings for me." She rubbed her arms. "I'm sorry. I can't buy that."

"I'm not just looking at Martin. He's only a possible. We're still looking at the stalker being an employee for FishNet."

She fell silent again, then very quietly said, "I get this shuddering, creepy-crawly feeling every time I open my email file. I hate knowing he has access to me, even that way. And as much as I hate even considering it's someone I actually know, I think I hate even more the idea that it's just some stranger, with a face I wouldn't recognize, out there somewhere, watching me. I want to believe he's moved on, gotten over it. I *really* do." She was absently shredding the crust of her sandwich into little pieces.

"I know," he said, just as quietly. "And maybe he has."

She looked at him. "But you don't think so."

Riley just shook his head, wishing he could tell her otherwise.

"So when do we give up? How long do we pursue this if he stops making contact?"

"Until we at least have a face or a name. Otherwise, he's

still out there, knowing who you are, knowing things about you, with you knowing that at one point at least, he developed a highly unstable crush on you. And it leaves you here, knowing nothing at all about him." He clicked his laptop and Palm Pilot closed, email forgotten, turning to face her fully. "Information is power, and right now he's holding too much of it to suit my peace of mind. And yours, from what you've just told me. So that's how long we stay on."

"What is the chance he'll become an actual threat to me? Your professional opinion," she added.

Did she suspect the monumental struggle he was waging keeping the personal out of this? "I don't know. I have someone running an updated profile, taking this latest contact into consideration. I should get it back later today. I can try to lift something from the figurine. Even a partial would be enough to give us an indication. But until we find out a name at least—a face would be even better—I stick close to you."

Her dry smile flickered to life. "Whether I want you to or not?"

"Unless you want to hire someone else, someone who will only play by your rules."

She immediately shook her head. "No."

Riley tried to tell himself the immense relief he felt was because of the paycheck. And knew it was a lie before the thought had completed itself. Just as he knew he'd see this through whether she was paying him to or not.

"I do trust that you know what you're doing. I—I just guess I hate admitting how much I need you to do it, is all."

Riley hated the defeated look on her face. One of the things he admired most about her was her chin-first attitude. And right now he wanted to reach out, stroke that chin, turn it toward him, lean over, and—

"I guess we need to discuss the current situation here, then."

The current situation, he wanted to tell her, was that he was achingly hard and dying to taste her. He could tell himself his professional judgment wasn't clouded, but the fact was, he was in a fog so thick and sensually charged, he was completely incapable of discussing anything.

She sighed, apparently oblivious to the fact that he had to curl his fingers into his palms to keep from reaching for her. She looked small somehow, when she'd always been larger than life to him, and he hated that defenselessness about her. He wanted her to be mad, like he was, furious that someone dared to mess with her head like this guy was.

"I agree that I need to at least know who this guy is. For my own peace of mind. And . . . although it pains me to admit it"—she flicked a hint of her special dry smile his way—"I've slept better knowing you're out here watching me. Only I can't let you go on doing this. Sitting in your truck, I mean. Christmas Eve's less than a week away, for God's sake. I feel like Scrooge."

"Afraid you'll be visited by some ghosts in your sleep, are you?"

She laughed then and he was glad to see her regroup. "I have plenty of ghosts, trust me. But that's not what's motivating me."

"Then what is?"

The quiet seriousness in his tone had her turning toward him. She started to toss off some smart remark, he could see it in her eyes. Then she stopped, and her expression grew as serious as his. "I like you."

Riley couldn't help it. He laughed. "Is that so bad a thing to have to admit? Are you still mad because of how I handled—"

"No, it's not that. It's just that, to be quite honest, I don't have many men I consider friends." She looked at him directly. "And so, I like you. I like knowing I can talk to you. And while I'm making a fool of myself here, I'll admit that I like thinking I could talk to you about things unrelated to the case." She raised a hand to fend off his response. "I know you think that sheep thing was all an act, but I have to tell you, Riley, you've got more sheep in you than you think."

Whatever he'd been about to say dissolved in an open-mouthed snort. "You've got to be kidding me."

"Oh, don't get all offended on me."

He could have told her he wasn't in the least offended. In fact, it was probably the most flattering thing she'd ever said to him. "Go on."

"I guess I feel like if I had something that was bothering me, you'd listen. I mean, really listen, and rather than over-react like some of my girlfriends would do, you'd think about it and offer some kind of sound, rational advice. That's your inner sheep." She folded her arms. "Go ahead and laugh now."

He didn't. He was too confused. "Why is my being a supposed nice guy and all-around good listener a problem?"

Her eyes widened in disbelief. "Because. I can't live with Millicent. A weekend is one thing, but you don't know what it's like. I simply can't do it for the long haul. I'll be running foundations and making speeches at luncheons before I know it."

"Would that be so bad?"

She merely glared at him.

"I meant, you said something at the charity ball about getting more involved."

"Involved, yes. But on my own terms. Under the same roof with Millicent, nothing is on my own terms. So I can't live with Millicent, ergo I'm living at home. I can't stand you living in your truck, ergo—" She motioned toward her row house.

"You're offering your place?"

"I'm not getting us adjoining hotel rooms."

Riley settled back against his door, quite happy to discover that apparently he wasn't, in fact, the only one having sleepless nights. Nights that SoulM8 hardly factored into. "And I appreciate that. And the offer to bunk in. But I still don't understand the problem."

She swore under her breath, and damn if it didn't make him even harder. How she did that would always be a mystery to him.

"Fine, then, might as well just sacrifice what's left of my ego here." She shifted her body so that she faced him, pulling one knee up on the leather seat. "I like you, okay? But I also want you. And all the mixing business with pleasure stuff aside, I generally don't do well with keeping men around very long after we—after I—"

"Have your way with them?"

"Oh, you're really enjoying this, aren't you?"

"So, let me get this straight. Mixing business with pleasure aside, you want to be friends, but you also want to . . . have your way with me?"

"Must I completely abase myself here?" At his amused but very direct look, she swore again. "Fine, maybe this is what I deserve after all. My friends certainly seem to think so." She held his gaze directly. "Yes. Okay? Happy now? But, more important, I want to be your friend. I want to know you'd be there for me. And not because I'm paying you to be."

"I would be," he said, all kidding gone. "Will be."

"I—" She swallowed, surprised by the solemnly stated vow. "Thank you. I'd . . ." She let out a little laugh. "God, you threw me, there. I, uh, I want to be there for you, too. If you ever needed anything, that is. I know we don't know each other that well, but—"

"So what is the problem, Tanzy?"

"If you move in with me—professionally speaking—it's

going to be hard for me to, well, only want to be your friend."

"And you don't think I can resist such a temptation?" He'd been teasing, fully expecting her to take a shot right back. So he hadn't expected the little flicker of hurt in her eyes. Which is when all the teasing, the torturing, and the worrying about inherited sins and professional distance flew right out the window. "I'm not sure I could," he said, then reached over and ran his fingertips along the side of her face. They both shuddered at the contact. "Would that really be so bad if I didn't?"

She lifted a wary gaze to his. "It's been my experience that," she said, her voice wavering as he continued to stroke her face, play with her hair, "while a whole hell of a lot of fun, sex generally ruins everything."

"I don't have sex with clients," he said, already leaning over the console, tugging her closer, wishing like hell they were somewhere other than in his damn truck.

"Well, then," she said, already sighing and letting her eyes drift shut. "I guess that's one problem solved."

"Yeah," he murmured, "so fire me already."

"You're totally fired."

"Thank God. Because I'm not going anywhere anyway." He pushed his hands into her hair, rubbed his thumbs along her cheekbones. "And no one is going to get close enough to touch you." He stole one taste, and that was all it took to put him over the edge. He tugged her bodily across the console, across his legs and chest and into his arms, sending computer, food, and God knew what else skidding everywhere. He could care less. She was finally right where he so badly wanted her to be.

"Except me." And then he crushed his mouth to hers.

You can give your heart to your family.

You can give your heart to your friends. And you do so, with relative ease, because they've earned it, because they feel the same, or simply because you want to. And despite the inherent risk of having that gift mishandled or even broken, you still do it. Even feel pretty secure in your ability to maintain your end of things; the love, the dedication necessary to back it up.

So why is it, then, that giving your heart to a lover is so downright terrifying?

15

He tasted perfect. Who would have ever thought her sheep would turn out to be such a damn fine wolf?

She could hardly believe he'd just reached out and taken what he wanted—her—and damn the consequences. And there were going to be consequences. Nothing this amazing came for free.

But she couldn't worry about that now. His mouth was on hers, his tongue insistently penetrating her mouth, making everything inside her clench with a need so deep she literally ached with it. He commanded this kiss, nothing tentative about the way he tasted, touched, took.

Consumed.

Which is exactly how it felt . . . and she liked it. A lot.

No one is going to get close enough to touch you. Except me.

Damn if those roughly spoken words hadn't done her in. That voice, like velvet; the strength behind it, like steel. She wanted his hands on her in the same insistent way his mouth was.

More room, she desperately wished they had more room. Room to move, to take as well as give, because her hunger was just as insatiable. She skimmed fingers over sinewy shoulders and along his neck, corded and tight as he continued his assault. His hair, thick and warm, slid through her fingers. His muffled moan as she raked her nails along his scalp vibrated all the way through her body. She wanted to touch all of him, make him moan like that for hours. She knew he could easily return the favor.

But she wasn't willing to end this delicious, pulse-spiking kiss, not even to move the short distance to her bedroom. Or living room floor, for that matter. God, at the moment, any flat surface would do.

His mouth left hers, traveled along her jaw to her neck. Now the moan was hers as he ran his tongue down the line of her neck. "Better," he managed, then pulled her earlobe between his teeth. "Incredibly better."

She swore hotly at the sharp spike of desire his hoarse whisper sent through her. "Than what?" she gasped, leaning back, limp and breathless when he finally lifted his head.

Dear God, his lips were wet, his skin taut and flushed, and those dark eyes of his were gleaming. It was all she could do not to grab his head and drag him to her. It was a toss-up which body part she'd drag him to first.

"Than anything," he said, drawing in a steadying breath. "I've wanted a taste of you, Tanzy. For what feels like my entire life."

It was a good thing she was crammed into such a small space, or she'd have slithered to the floor in a puddle of need. "The things you say," she said on a shivery little sigh.

Which got her flashed by that smile, that broad, teeth-baring, predatory grin that made her nipples stand up hard.

"Nothing you haven't heard before, I'm sure," he said.

It was like tossing a cup of cold water on her heated parts. Okay, so that would have taken several cups at the moment. "You might be surprised about that."

"I'm nothing special, Tanzy. That's all I was trying to say."

Without even thinking, she reached out and stroked his face. She wasn't sure who was surprised more by the gentle touch. "We're all special, Riley."

She'd never meant anything more, and yet she saw him write off the sentiment with barely a blink. It made her wonder just what went on behind that enigmatic face of his. Who was he, this man who'd vowed to protect her?

"I want you," he said, and so directly, so honestly, it riled her parts up all over again. It touched her in other places as well, places she wasn't used to feeling.

"And I can't be the first man to feel the way I do about you. I don't want to disappoint you."

She laughed. "You couldn't possibly be worried that—"

"Shh," he said, quite serious as he pressed a finger against her lips. "I don't mean in bed. I wasn't referring to not being the first man to want your body. We're men, we all want that."

Her lips quirked. "I've been saying that for years."

"But of the select few whose wildest dreams you chose to make come true . . . how many of them were still around a year later? A month even?"

How was it he could be so damn gentlemanly about her amorous past, and at the same time make her feel so defensive? "Do you really need an exact figure, or would a rough estimate do?"

Now he smiled, damn him. "I'm just telling you it's a statistic I don't care to be a part of."

"If you're worried that I'll dissect us in print—"

"You wouldn't do that." He didn't say it in fear, or as a threat. He was stating simple fact. Which actually was scarier, since it proved just how well he'd come to know her. How had he done that, when he was still such an enigma to her? Wasn't she the one who paid attention to detail, to nuance?

"You're right," she said. "I wouldn't. Not directly anyway."

What they did together would stay between them. Which was another revelation. For the first time she actually had a private life she wanted to keep private. "But I can't make any promises about the rest." He started to speak and she pressed her finger against his lips, then found she couldn't help tracing the sensitive pad of skin along those sexy contours. She sighed when his expression turned fierce at her touch. "How in the hell did you do it?"

"Do what?"

"Baaaa," was all she said.

"Was it really so big a leap?"

"Sometimes it seems so. Other times . . . Besides, didn't you just get done telling me that you didn't consider yourself the sensitive-male type?"

"Well, I wouldn't go that far, but I'm not exactly a—"

She shushed him now. As much to have an excuse to continue touching his lips as anything else. Damn but they were so soft, yet she knew how firm they could be when they were on her. How they would take her, touch her, drive her right up the—

He leaned in then, took her face, kissed her lips fast and hard until her heart threatened to pound right out of her chest, then just as abruptly he let her go and swore beneath his breath.

She laughed a little self-consciously. "What was that for?"

He shook his head, then his frown turned to a little laugh of his own. "You have this habit of making me crazy, and for some reason beyond all comprehension, it makes me really want you at the same time. I can't tell you how many times I had to dig my nails into my palms to keep from reaching for you."

"I don't think I've ever actually annoyed someone into desiring me before," she said with a wry smile. "But I wasn't even saying anything just now."

He shook his head. "I know. Sometimes it's just this look you get, like you want to—" He broke off, looked out the window.

She laughed, totally intrigued. "Oh come on, you say these incredibly direct, tantalizing things to me. Don't get all quiet and controlled on me now."

He turned his gaze back to her and made her throat go dry. Everything else it made wet.

"You look like you want to consume me. It's incredibly . . ." He gave a brief laugh. "It makes me crazy in a whole different way. This time I did something about it."

"Speaking of which . . . what are we going to do about this?"

"Which part of this? You fired me, remember?"

"It's a moment I don't think I'll forget anytime soon." She'd never forget the sound of his voice, vowing to protect her. It was ridiculous how that made her feel, the woman who had sworn to always protect herself.

And yet, she looked at him and felt . . . well, certainly not weak. But not entirely strong, either. The threat of needing him for more than the occasional multiple orgasm was petrifying enough. The idea that he might need her back, in the same way, was almost paralyzing. What if she let him down?

He tapped her temple, then traced a finger along her hairline. "Tell me what's going on up here." He smiled and it was so perfectly wicked she couldn't help but smile back, despite the fact that she was in emotional free-fall.

"Or?" she asked.

"Or I'll be forced to drag it out of you."

Her smile grew. "It's amazing how silent I can be."

"And here I pegged you for the type to make some serious noise." When her mouth dropped open, he took full advantage. Key word being *full*. His mouth closed over hers, his tongue sliding, taunting, teasing. His hand slid from her hair down her neck, until his fingers brushed along the curve of her breast, just missing the nipple, now throbbing for attention. The moan, when it came, was guttural and needy. And she didn't care.

To his credit, he didn't look smug as he lifted his head.

"I'll get mine," she said, surprised by how rough her voice was. Damn but the man could kiss.

"I'm counting on that."

She couldn't help it, she laughed. She liked his hint of arrogance, liked the way he teased her so confidently. She liked the way he could seem annoyed even as his eyes screamed "Don't make me take you." She wanted to make him. And she wanted him to taunt her into doing it right back. God, this emotional involvement stuff was more complicated than she'd ever realized.

His finger slid beneath her chin, lifting her gaze back to his. "The wheels are spinning so fast I'm surprised there isn't smoke curling out of your ears."

She shot him a cheeky grin. "Don't worry, I wasn't plotting my next column."

"You weren't working."

His continued display of how intimately he was aware of her was as stimulating as it was disconcerting. No one had ever paid such close attention to her. "So sure of yourself, are you?"

"You get a very specific look on your face when you're working."

"And you know this how? When have you seen me work?" Her mouth dropped open. "You said my rooms at Millicent's weren't bugged."

Was that a slight flush coloring his cheeks? "You didn't always work in your rooms," he muttered.

"And you watched me?" Somehow the indignation she should feel, the sense of violation of her personal space, didn't happen. Instead, dammit, she was actually a little turned on by the idea. She laughed, surprising them both. "God, watching me type. Talk about boring assignments."

"I've had worse."

"And I suppose it goes without saying you've had better. Jobs where you actually got to be yourself, even."

Instead of smiling, or tossing it right back at her, he frowned. She wondered if she'd ever be able to read him as well as he apparently read her. She wanted to, she realized. *Getting more complicated by the minute, Tanz.*

"I've had all kinds of jobs, but I don't do this," he stated flatly. "I want you to know that."

"This?"

"I've never met anyone who made me want to compromise my—" He broke off, swore. "Just ask my father. He thinks nothing of mixing business with pleasure."

She turned his face to hers. "Riley, I don't want you to beat yourself up about this. I didn't mean for this to happen any more than you did."

"I'm not. I just needed you to know. I'm not sorry, I'm not second-guessing. We're in it now and I don't want to be anywhere else."

He just blew her away when he did that, up and said things, so flat out and direct. "If you want me to talk to your dad, explain—" His look of horror had her torn between laughing and wanting to console him. "That bad, huh?"

"No, it's not that. Finn is ... well, he's quite the lad, always has been. Very charming rogue, or so the ladies seem to think. It's, well, it's a little tricky because I have a history of haranguing him about this very thing and—"

"And then you go and get tangled up with me."

He eyed her steadily. "We're getting tangled up in each other. And I'll handle my father."

"Well, if you're worried about telling him about the job, don't be. There is no way I'm hiring anyone else. I want you to do it."

"Oh, I plan to," he said, his tone unequivocal.

"Then you will be paid for services rendered," she stated just as evenly. When he looked at her sharply, she sent it right back. "Please tell me your opinion of me is not so low that you actually thought I meant to include sex—"

"If I had a low opinion of you, we wouldn't be sitting in my truck, in the rain, discussing, well, anything. As for the other, you will not retain any of my services for pay. I'll not be doing this as a job, but because I have a personal stake in wanting to see you safe. Unlike my da, I do not get involved with clients. And I won't start now. We may not be flush, but we won't lose the business, such as it is, without your account."

She simply stared at him, thoroughly enjoying the heated tirade, almost as much as the tiniest hint of brogue that had crept in once he'd gotten rolling. "Is Finn first generation, or were you born there as well?"

"What?"

She smiled, enjoying flustering him. "Ireland. Were you born there?"

"Here. My parents were born there. Came here as children. Met at a church social."

"Born in Ireland, but met a continent away." She sighed. "How poetic."

He just looked at her. "A romantic, are you?"

She narrowed her gaze. "Why does that always shock people? You know, I'm beginning to think baring my soul to millions has seriously warped my image." She smiled impishly. "Can't imagine how that happened." He did it again. Just kissed her. Only this time he didn't let her go so quickly. This kiss was gentler, sweeter, and therefore far more dangerous.

"What you do to me, Tanzy," he murmured, his eyes searching hers.

It left her feeling needy, achy, mixed up, and confused. She didn't mind the first two. But the latter two she'd spent a lifetime avoiding. For God's sake, she'd made a profession out of keeping every thought, emotion, and reaction to said emotion explained, categorized, and compartmentalized. Why go and screw all that up now?

She looked right back into Riley's face, a face she didn't think she'd ever tire of looking at, and realized why. Because she was already screwed.

"The rest of the world might have a warped view of the real you, but I could give a flat damn," Riley said, almost fiercely. "I like the person you are, and I respect you even more than I want you," he said, then pulled her more tightly into his lap. "You can't possibly know how amazing that is, especially at this moment."

She felt him, so hard, nudging at her. "Oh, I—" She had to stop, wet her lips, swallow, or try to. "I think I have an idea."

"Do you, Tanzy? Do you have any idea how difficult this is? I don't do this. If you want the God's honest truth, we're a lot alike, you and me. I enjoy my life, my friends, the occasional romp. But I don't get involved. With clients, with anyone. It's just . . . easier. So I've never . . . fallen. And so damn hard, so fast." He said the latter more to himself than to her, even shook his head as if still trying to wrap his mind around what was happening to him.

She could have told him they had that in common, too. If she could have found her voice through the lump in her throat, that is.

"Am I scaring the hell out of you?" He laughed a little. "Because I'm scaring the hell out of me."

She nodded.

"But we are involved, you and I," he went on. "I don't see anyone else, think of anyone else."

"Me, either." And it surprised her, how truthful a statement that was. And it had nothing to do with her solitary singleness. "Not even when I thought you were a sheep."

He sighed. "Haven't we figured out by now that we're a little of each? Both of us?"

She opened her mouth, then closed it again. "I didn't—I never meant it as an insult. I just . . ." She took a breath. God, this was hard. But he'd certainly laid it all out there. It was only fair that she do the same. "It's easier for me. To separate things out."

"Easier how? To avoid feeling anything?"

Stung, she shifted away from him, but his arms came around her, kept her close. One thing she was learning very quickly about Riley, he didn't allow retreat. And while she wanted to resent it, she also found she admired it. And refused to back down from the challenge of it. "You said yourself you don't get involved because it's easier. But that doesn't mean I close myself off entirely. I'll bet you don't, either. I feel a great many things, deep things, for a great many people."

"Just not men."

"Men, as in lovers?" she said, refusing to shrink from this. "You're right about that. I haven't seen the point in opening myself up to that kind of pain."

"Because you got hurt?"

"In a roundabout way, I suppose you could say that. I prefer to think of it as learning from others' mistakes."

"The others being?"

"My parents, although just the term credits them with far more than they deserve."

She didn't know what kind of reaction she'd expected, but she wasn't prepared for the thoughtful silence that followed. It was almost as tantalizing as the things he said to her, this insatiable curiosity he'd roused in her. Curiosity to know his every thought, to understand why he believed this or that, to involve herself in who he was. To let him matter.

"I understand," he said finally. And she believed, without any further explanation necessary, that he did. "Maybe more than I'm comfortable admitting."

"I don't think we're merely a product of those who gave birth to us," she said into the suddenly serious silence. "I believe we all have choices to make, some control over our lives and how we live them."

"I've always felt the same." He rolled his eyes. "And yet, here I am, living a life not of my choosing."

Her gaze narrowed in surprise. "What life would you choose instead?"

He didn't answer. Instead he asked a question of his own. "Why me?"

"What?"

"This," he said, motioning with his chin to the clinch they were presently in. "Us. The two who don't get involved, getting involved. Why me? We've determined this isn't going to be just about sex."

She grinned. "It's going to be a little bit about sex."

He grinned back, but it faded as he traced a finger down the side of her face. "But it's going to be about a whole lot more. If you'll let it."

"I'd like it to be," she said, her voice suddenly gone shaky.

"So?" he asked. "Why me?"

How did she answer that? "I'm usually pretty self-sufficient," she began. "And when I need help, I have people to turn to. Yet, I kept finding myself wanting to turn to you. Your quiet confidence called to me. You listen, you think things through, you don't leap before you look. I guess somehow, when I wasn't looking, I began to trust you, lean on you." She shook her head, laughed a little at herself. "And even in those awful suits and Mr. Magoo glasses, your voice made me totally hot."

He grinned even as he flushed. She loved it that she

could make this man who seemed so sure of himself be self-conscious, even for a moment.

"Okay, your turn." She took a breath. "Why me?"

He answered instantly. "Because no one else could wear wet, soggy bunny slippers and make me want them as much as I want you."

Surprised, to say the least, she glanced down at her feet, hadn't even thought about what was on them when she'd given up trying to pretend he wasn't out here and dashed into the rain. "And I've been wasting all that money on Jimmy Choo and Prada. Who knew the secret to a man's heart was soggy bunnies?"

"Come here," he said, and pulled her closer still, lowered his lips to hers. "I don't want to screw this up," he said against her mouth.

She smiled, feeling her heart pitch forward and take that final free-fall. "As long as I've got my trusty footwear, I think we'll be fine."

He smiled as he kissed her, then looked back into her eyes. "The real reason it's you is because you're the last person who looks like she needs rescuing. And yet when I look at you, I can't help but want to save you."

"I've never needed saving."

He nodded, smiled. "I know that. But I don't know how else to explain it. I can't help the feeling. And I'm actually arrogant enough to think I'm the man to do it, to be there for you, and at the same time pretty much terrified that I'm not."

"Oh, Riley—"

He shook his head. "But here's the tricky part. I never thought I needed to be rescued, either." He tipped her chin up, dipped his head, brushed his lips against hers. "So explain to me, then, why, when I look at you, when you kiss me, something inside of me feels saved."

Then he kissed her again, and again, and Tanzy mercifully let her need for him take over. She better than anyone understood the power of words . . . and yet his had stunned her, robbed her of the ability to analyze, rationalize, compartmentalize.

She shifted, wanting to be closer, and was surprised when he flinched in pain. She pulled back, intending to find out what was wrong. But instead she screamed.

Because just on the other side of the window stood a young black man of monolithic proportions, a wide smile beaming from his surprisingly cherubic face.

Obligations.

What do we really owe the people we love? Do we owe them labor we would not otherwise choose to commit to? After all, if they truly loved us, would they honestly expect us to do something we didn't want to do?

Would they feel right, benefiting from those labors? Would we feel better doing it if it had been our idea in the first place? If so, then who are we really doing it for? The good of the family? Self-gratification? Maybe a little of both isn't so bad. But it would be much easier to figure out if guilt could be taken out of the mix. Too often guilt blurs the line separating what does get done from what should be done.

16

Riley swore while Tanzy scrambled from his lap back across the center console, certain she'd crippled him for life. "It's okay," he bit out, groping for the window switch.

"You know him?" Her eyes were wide, her skin pale. And it hit him that she'd thought J.B. might be SoulM8. *Oh sure, getting involved won't cloud your judgment.* Jesus, they'd been sitting in a car, making out like teenagers, free targets for anyone.

"Yeah," he said, stabbing the window button. "I know him."

"Dear God, he's huge," she whispered. "Is he harmless?"

"Only off the field." The window skimmed down and he turned to face J.B. "What the hell are you doing?"

J.B.'s smile wavered. He lifted a large padded mailer. "Special delivery, Coach."

Tanzy perked up, her color rushing back, right along with her inborn curiosity. "Coach?"

"I waited at the corner," J.B. said, "but you didn't show. I saw your truck, so . . ." He leaned down so he could wave at Tanzy. "Sorry I interrupted."

Riley snatched the package from J.B. and fished his wallet out of his pants. He passed him some bills. "Thanks. Appreciate it."

Naturally J.B. didn't get the hint. Not because he was the stereotypical dumb jock. He just wasn't ready to leave. And at six-five, three-forty, nobody usually made J.B. do anything he wasn't ready to do. There were some exceptions, however. Riley was one of them.

"Don't you have classes to study for?"

"I'm up to speed, Coach."

"Coach?" Tanzy repeated. "You coach this guy? In what?"

Riley didn't know whether to be affronted at her apparent surprise that he was capable of such a thing, or just annoyed at the topic in general. "He should be so lucky," Riley said, but J.B. was leaning down again, smiling over at Tanzy.

"You don't know who the man is?" he asked incredulously. Obviously assuming that a woman who had just moments ago been sprawled in a compromising position with "the man" in the cab of a truck would know who she'd been sprawling with.

Tanzy shook her head, her gaze darting to Riley, then back to J.B. again. "Apparently I don't. Why don't you enlighten me."

Riley just groaned. If he thought there was a chance it would knock any sense into him, he'd have thumped his forehead on the steering wheel.

J.B. was beaming. "Back in the day, our man Riley here—"

At Riley's glare, he quickly corrected himself. "Coach Parrish was a cornerback for the Pioneers. Known as R.P., number twenty-one. They used to call him Rocket Power." J.B. smiled proudly. "He put the special in special teams."

Tanzy swung a surprised look at Riley, then grinned. "Really."

Riley noted it took about five seconds longer for the grin

to waver as the rest of it clicked in. No one would ever accuse Tanzy Harrington of being slow.

"So, the guy at the dance? From another job? He recognized you, didn't he?"

Riley just sighed and nodded.

Her eyes widened farther as the wheels continued to spin. "And the radio show, when you wouldn't give your name? Afraid someone would call in and spill the beans?" She shook her head and sighed. "And here I thought you were being endearingly shy."

"Hey. I can be as endearing as the next guy," Riley shot back, affronted. J.B. just snorted behind him, but quickly wiped the smirk off his face when Riley swiveled around to glare at him.

"Totally endearing," J.B. agreed solemnly.

"So, Rocket Power, how famous were you?" Tanzy asked, but when he shifted the look to her, she quickly amended it to, "*Are* you?"

"It was a long time ago, and for a very short time. No one remembers me, I'm sure. Now can we please—"

"Blew out the knee," J.B. said, with a sad shake of his head. "A sorry day for the NFL. Pioneers haven't gone the distance since."

Now Riley rolled his eyes. "I was a punt returner, J.B., not the quarterback."

J.B.'s grin returned. "And faster than Darryl Green, slicker than Deion Sanders."

Riley gave up and simply punched the button to put the window up. Tanzy was faster, hitting the button on her side and lowering it right back down again. "How do *you* know Riley, J.B.? He was probably before your time." She shot Riley a fast grin when he scowled.

"He's an alumnus of SFSU," J.B. said. "Helps us out from time to time." As if finally remembering his manners, he leaned past Riley and stuck out his hand. "Jamal Brown. Folks just call me J.B."

Tanzy leaned across the console and shook his hand, which totally swallowed hers. Riley frowned. Nothing against J.B., but he wanted those smooth, slim hands on him. Time to end this little tête-à-tête.

"Tanzy Harrington," she said. "Folks just call me—"

"Ms. Harrington," Riley interjected.

She rolled her eyes. "Make me sound ancient, why don't you?"

"Isn't he a little before your time?" Riley mimicked, then rolled his eyes right back at her. Which only made her laugh.

But J.B.'s eyes had bugged out and he blurted, "You're *the* Tanzy Harrington? With the column? On the Internet?"

Surprised, as her audience tended to skew a bit older . . . and decidedly female, she nodded. "That's me. You've read my column?"

He shook his head. "I've caught you on the *Billy Mac and JoJo Show,* though. You're off the hook." The "for an old chick" was implied.

"I assume being 'off the hook' is a good thing?" she murmured to Riley.

"Oh, definitely," Riley said. "The cat's meow, even."

J.B. was oblivious. "My older sister reads your stuff, lectures me on how to treat the ladies." He grinned then, and not for the first time Riley thought it was amazing how young and innocent a three-hundred-pound man could look. "Wait till I tell her I met you."

Riley put a hand on J.B.'s forearm. "I don't think Ms. Harrington would appreciate details—"

J.B. merely shook his head, looking sadly disappointed. "I'm not about that, Coach. I can be subtle."

"Yeah, right. Be discreet, too, while you're at it. And the *b* in subtle is silent," Riley added. "Just like you're going to be about this little meeting. You dig?"

Tanzy was obviously struggling not to laugh out loud at J.B.'s comical facial expressions. Riley didn't look at her, or he'd have ended up laughing, too. Totally blow his badass rep with the guys. What little of one he had left. "You're a bad influence," he muttered out of the side of his mouth.

"And don't you forget it," she shot back.

J.B. shook his head, opened his mouth, shut it again, then laughed. "I can't even say it. Don't be such a fossil, Coach. 'You dig,' " he repeated, then giggled, making his entire midsection rumble. It looked like an earthquake inside a football jersey.

"He's really cute," Tanzy said.

"Yeah, like a baby rhino." Riley tapped the window button again. "Time to roll, J.B. Thanks for the delivery."

"Yeah, no problem." He smacked the top of the roof, making Riley wince. J.B. had hands like hams. Riley was surprised the roof didn't buckle in. "When are you going to trade this thing up, anyway?" J.B. asked. "Have you checked out the new Escalade?" He hummed. "They are tight."

"We're tight enough, thanks," Riley said, then glared at J.B. when he started to explain. "I was kidding. I know what it means. Now beat it." Sometimes you had to hit him over the head. Or crush his fingers in the window. Whatever worked.

J.B. sighed. "Always dissing me, man. It's a good thing you pay well." He patted his pockets, then bent down and looked over to Tanzy one last time. The smile came out again, in full cherubic force. "It was a pleasure to make your acquaintance, Ms. Harrington," he said ever-so-formally as he tipped his chin in a little bow. Then ended by shooting a smug little "See?" smirk at Riley. "Subtle. Hunh." He sauntered away, still smiling.

"He's something else," Tanzy said, laughing. "Glad I

don't have to feed him, though. I'd need a government grant."

Riley couldn't help it, he grinned. No matter how irritated, frustrated, you name it, he got, she made him smile. "I was thinking of that WWE-size fridge at Millicent's." He chuckled. "It would be a minibar for J.B."

Tanzy nodded, watching J.B. as he disappeared around the corner. "How many others are there? That you help out, I mean."

Riley shrugged. "A couple." It was more like most of the offensive linemen and special teams players, but it wasn't important. "They help me out, too. It's an even trade."

"I'm not so sure," she said. And then she got that look on her face.

"Oh no, don't do that."

"What?" she said, eyes wide.

He didn't buy the innocent tone. "You know what. Analyze me. I don't fit into any neat compartment, trust me."

"Oh, that I know. But as for analyzing, fair is fair. You've got me pretty well pegged, it seems."

Riley snorted. "Fifty years and I'll never have you even half pegged, trust me."

"Is that a sexist remark?"

"Hardly. Give yourself some credit."

"Hmm." She leaned back, folded her arms, lips curved in a satisfied smile. "I rather like thinking I'm bold and mysterious."

Riley couldn't help it. He reached for her. It was automatic, like breathing. And it amazed him, now that he'd given in to it, how natural a response it was. And how far away she suddenly seemed, how empty his arms. He'd never thought anything like that before.

"I'm not hauling my butt over that console again," she warned him, leaning back. "It was only sexy once."

"It was sexy?" He grinned, rather liking that she thought that. "I thought it was more my usual bull-in-a-china-shop kind of maneuver, but I wasn't really thinking finesse at that moment."

"Me, either." She smiled, then tucked her slippered feet beneath her legs and leaned over to buss him loudly on the cheek. "You make a sexy bull."

He snorted. "I've known you less than a month and already I'm representing half the animal kingdom. A fact they can't be happy about, by the way."

She sat back, laughing, then nodded at the envelope still clutched in his hands. "What's in the pouch? Is it about my case?"

He'd forgotten all about it. Just as he'd forgotten for the entire time she was wedged in his lap that there was someone out there, somewhere, stalking her. Clouded judgment, loss of perspective. The exact things he railed against with his father. "You know, I think we should bring someone else in on this. I know some people—"

She shook her head resolutely. "Just you."

He started to argue, then figured he'd just handle it on his own, make some calls. What she didn't know, she couldn't bitch at him about, right? "We'll see" was all he said. He stretched reflexively and his knee locked. He swore a small streak before he could stop himself. "Sorry," he ground out, rubbing his knee until he could bend it again. "You'd think I'd be used to it by now."

"That's okay. I might borrow a few of those words the next time I stub my toe on the foot of my bed, though, if you don't mind." She looked at his knee, reached out as if she wanted to soothe him somehow, then pulled her hand back again, as if she wasn't sure of herself. "Will the pain ever go completely away?"

It made his body tighten, just the thought of her touching him. Reaching for him without thought, the way he wanted to with her. He could have told her that no amount of soothing would make the pain go away, but that her touching him would at least make him forget about it for a while.

He shook his head. "Not totally. It's a lifetime memento from the NFL. It's usually not this bad. The rain makes it worse." That and sitting holed up in his SUV for hours on end.

"So," she asked quietly, "when you said earlier about not doing what you'd planned to be doing, football is the career you would have chosen?"

"Yeah. I worked toward that one goal from the day I first picked up a ball." He shrugged. "But it's a crapshoot. We all know it from the day we're signed. I was fortunate enough just to make it to the big time." He held up a hand to stall the myriad questions he could all but see bubbling inside her. "Mind if we head inside? I need to go over what's in the package. And we need to talk about what's next."

"About the case? Or about us?"

He merely looked at her. "Yes."

Tanzy opened the front door to her three-story row house and waved Riley through. She nodded toward the small front room that flanked the tiny foyer. The room had a huge bay window that made the room seem bright, even on a rainy day.

Her décor ran toward comfort rather than style. A puffy black futon couch, an oversize red armchair and ottoman, perfect for curling up with her laptop when she needed a break from her office. A cluster of pillows on both in no particular color or pattern scheme, throw rugs on the floor. A big chunky coffee table with a scatter of magazines, bills, and books all over it. At least they covered the rings left by her Coke cans. She kept meaning to buy some plants, but had somehow never gotten around to it. Fortunately Sloan had contributed to her empty walls. And one of Wolfgang's sculptures graced the corner. She absently wondered now if he'd screwed the woman who'd modeled for it.

"Just sit wherever is most comfortable. I'll get some ice and Advil."

"That's not—"

"Stop being a tough guy. I'm not J.B. You don't have to impress me with your manly fortitude."

He grinned. "Good thing."

She impulsively lifted up on tiptoes and bussed his cheek. "You'll always be manly to me." Feeling silly when he merely studied her, she gestured again to the front room. He was tall, but she'd never thought of him as being a particularly large man—J.B., now that was a large man—but he filled her foyer. Or maybe it was the tension screaming between them that filled the foyer. Whatever it was, she could barely breathe because of it.

But he was in pain. And that was partly her fault for not inviting him in sooner. They had a case to discuss, business to take care of. The screaming tension would have to wait.

She started to turn away, but he took her wrist, stopping her. When she looked back at him, he simply tugged her the rest of the way around, pulled her wrist up, and turned her hand so he could kiss her palm. "Thanks."

Now it was her turn to study him. That and feel her knees go a bit wonky at the look in his eyes. "For?"

"The spontaneous kiss. Touching me. I like it. A lot. Please feel free to do it often."

She tried to respond but her throat had gone dry, so she merely nodded. Then smiled a bit wickedly and reached up to kiss him again, this time on the lips.

He tucked her wrist behind her back and levered her up against his body as his head came down, his eyes half closing. He groaned with satisfaction as her lips skated across his. She loved the feel of his chest, hard, solid. Her free hand slid up his arm, all sinew and muscle, and tucked around his neck as she lifted herself more fully into his body. With a grunt he let his weight fall back against the foyer wall, yanking her up against him as he dropped her wrist and wrapped his arms around her.

Now she was the one moaning. Damn but he felt wonderful. She loved the way they fit together, the natural give and take of their kisses. No one led, no one followed. It was the most perfect of kisses. But when she slid both hands into his hair and moved her hips against his, he shifted his weight to accommodate her . . . and his knee gave way, almost taking both of them down to the floor.

He swore, she winced, they both looked at each other and half laughed, regretful for a moment lost. She helped him limp into the front room, angle his body onto the futon couch. She shoved a stack of papers over so he could prop his foot up on the coffee table.

She straightened and put her hands on her hips. "We aren't behaving too responsibly here, are we," she asked with mock seriousness. "What would J.B. and the boys think if they knew their coach was—"

"Oh, I think J.B. saw enough out in the truck, thank you very much." Riley shifted and she flinched at the audible popping sound his knee made. "Don't worry. It hurts like a son of a bitch when it does that, but it will start to feel better now." He sighed and leaned back. "And I'm not their coach."

"I think they feel differently. Have you ever thought about that? Coaching professionally, I mean?"

She noticed he looked away, down at his foot, his knee, anywhere but at her. Hmm.

"Briefly. But my dad needed me." He shrugged. "And though the family business wasn't my first choice, for all his faults Finn is good at what he does. We make a pretty decent team."

He didn't have to add "when he chooses to do his part," but Tanzy heard it all the same.

He looked at her now. "He trained me well, I took some additional courses with an eye to expanding the business, got my license."

She leaned against the doorway. "But it's not what makes you happy." She didn't make it a question.

He shrugged. "I've fulfilled more of a dream than most people ever get to. So it didn't end like I'd planned. And no, I didn't plan on bailing my father out. But it's what came next, so I'm giving it my best. It's what you do."

Tanzy thought about that, about obligations to family. It didn't make her think about her mother. Any obligation she might have felt there had been blasted away a long time ago. However, to Millicent she owed a great deal. Most recently for caring enough to do something to ensure her safety, regardless of whether Tanzy felt it was warranted or not. She loved Millicent all the more for loving her enough to want to watch out for her. "I guess you have a point. But does your father know? That given a choice you might choose something else? Does he care about that, or don't you talk about it?"

Again, Riley half lifted a shoulder as he continued to massage his knee. "He was counting on me."

Tanzy's eyes widened. "Counting on you turning pro and taking care of him for the rest of his life?"

Now Riley looked defensive. "Yeah. He gave up a good chunk of his life for me, for my mom. She died of cancer when I was in high school. He knew I was good enough. I knew it. Hell, everyone did. I wanted it, for myself. And yes, I was fully prepared to take care of him for the rest of his days. I owed him. He's my father. He's all I have."

Tanzy respected the love and admired the devotion, but

she wasn't too sure about owing anyone anything. His father had made his choices, banked on hitting the NFL lotto, and it hadn't paid off. It didn't mean Riley should be his indentured servant for the rest of his life. She thought about saying what was on her mind, even liked the fact that under normal circumstances she could be this open with him. This direct. It made her realize how much different a role he already played in her life than anyone she'd known. But then, Rina had been right. She'd never really let anyone in.

And yet, here was Riley. Already in, planted in her life as firmly as he was presently planted on her futon. In pain. Which was why she didn't badger him about his dad and perceived obligations, and left to get him some pain relievers and some ice.

She was one to talk about obligations anyway, she thought as she stepped into the small bathroom off the hallway and rummaged through the medicine cabinet. She made a silent promise then and there to sit down with Millicent and talk over what kind of role she could take on with the various foundations. She'd have to make it clear she had no intention of running anything, but it was high time she started to give something back to the woman who had all but raised her. The fact that Millicent would never expect her to, as Riley's father apparently had, made her want to do it all the more.

Snagging the Advil, she grabbed a couple of sodas from her kitchen, thinking she'd pop back out to his SUV and retrieve the sandwiches, if they weren't hopelessly crushed, anyway. They could eat while they went over the contents of the envelope.

She balanced the sodas in one arm and scooped the envelope off the foyer floor where it had fallen during their passionate embrace. She sighed, wondering how long it would take to go through whatever it was they had to look over. About as long as it would take for the pain relievers to kick in, probably. Work . . . then play, she thought. Sounded like a good plan to her.

A plan that would have to be put on hold, she realized with regret as she paused in the doorway to her front room.

Riley's head was tipped back, eyes shut, mouth slack. She felt another pang of guilt for making him sleep in his SUV. Between the chilling rain and his bum knee, it couldn't have been easy. She grabbed the crocheted throw that Mariel had made her in her learn-something-maternal early-pregnancy phase, and tucked it around him.

"Out for the count, big guy," she murmured, then leaned down and kissed him. He smiled in his sleep. Pretty damn cute, if she thought so herself. And she did.

She settled into the oversize, overstuffed chair that sat in the pushed-out bay-window part of the room, kicked off her soggy bunnies, and tucked her feet up. She polished off her Coke while doing nothing more than watching him sleep. And thinking how it would be, having him around. It was a pleasant daydream, then she laughed at herself. At best she could only hope it didn't end in some painful emotional blowout. That was the more realistic view.

And speaking of reality . . . She drank his Coke while going over the contents of the envelope.

Independence. Self-reliance.
These are things to be proud of, things that make you a stronger, more confident person. Not to mention they're good for your general mental health.

But can you take self-reliance too far? I'm beginning to think so. And the signs are when independence stops looking like freedom, and starts feeling a whole lot like isolation. I'm not advocating total dependence, or even partial dependence really. I think I'm talking about teaming up. Joining forces. Realizing when you can't do it alone, and not being afraid to reach out for a little assistance. Sure, all the trust issues rise up. Along with fears of losing that oh-so-valued independence. But is it really such a bad thing to follow on occasion, instead of always having to lead? And, most important, is it okay not to feel guilty when, rather than feeling threatened by letting someone else handle a tough spot, you simply feel relief?

17

"Damn." Riley continued to swear as he flipped through the pages. He didn't even bother to look at the photos. It was bad enough that he'd crashed on Tanzy's couch for four straight hours. Although he had to admit he felt better than he had in days. Some of it due to sleep, some due to the fact that he could look over at Tanzy and know he'd be tasting that mouth, hearing her laugh ... Until she kicked him out on his sorry, unhelpful ass, anyway.

His sense of well-being was rapidly dwindling as he slapped the FishNet employment list onto the coffee table. He really wanted this lead to pan out. He really didn't want SoulM8 to be Martin. "All women." He scrubbed a hand over his face, then sighed. "I guess I should have known after my run-in with Ms. Sack."

Tanzy scooped up the stack. "An all-women Internet firm." She ruffled through the pictures, pausing to look at this one or that. "Hence the name FishNet, I suppose. After the stocking?"

Riley shuddered at the mental image of Lori Sack in fishnet anything. "I suppose," he said.

"Interesting concept," Tanzy mused. "Although I'm not exactly sure what her message is. Girls Can Be Geeks, Too?" She straightened the stack he'd slapped down and began looking through the names and dates hired. "This doesn't necessarily mean he isn't connected to them somehow, does it? Isn't it possible that he has a gal pal and she's the one setting up the false accounts for him?"

Riley shook his head. "Wouldn't fit the profile."

"A sister, then? Cousin?"

Riley sighed and shoved his fingers through his hair. "A long shot there, too. Most of these types don't have great relationships with women. Family or otherwise. Except for the fantasy ones in their heads, anyway."

"Well, doesn't that rule out Martin, then? He has good relationships with women."

"His profile is a bit different. He's been married all his adult life to one woman. We don't know how close they are, but from the looks of things at the charity ball, I'm guessing now that the nest is empty, they're discovering they don't have all that much in common anymore. He's not a big socializer, wasn't all that popular in high school and college."

Tanzy's mouth dropped open. "You've done a background check on him?"

Riley looked at her. "It's my job. He's none the wiser and we're informed. It's the only way," he added when she looked as if she was going to protest. "And now he's having some kind of midlife crisis. Goes and buys a fancy sports car. Maybe starts developing an attachment to his protégée. Starts sending notes. You know, there's a reason Martin is in a computer-oriented field. He communicates better via the written word. Nonconfrontational. Removed from face-to-face situations with other people. Starting to sound familiar?"

Tanzy stared him down for ten full seconds, then finally, stubbornly, looked back at the photos. "I don't recognize any of them. Or these names. Dammit."

Clearly she was not going to discuss the Martin angle.

And Riley was more than happy to let it go. For now. He had the coyote figurine to work with. Hopefully that would put an end to their speculation. One way or the other.

She put both piles on the table. "I know you explained this already, but why isn't it possible that this guy is just hacking into their site and setting up these accounts?" She smiled. "I'm a failed girl geek, so indulge me."

Despite his frustration, his lips quirked. "Ernie tracked that. As best as he could, anyway. The way their system is set up, it would be hard to hack in that often and not get caught. On the inside, he'd have a much easier time covering his tracks. Besides, if he had that kind of technological ability, he could hack into any provider. No sense in sticking with the same one and risking getting nailed. FishNet does have some pretty tight shields in place, plus they don't keep any of their company files stored online. It's all backed up, and managed off-site." He sighed. "I know you don't want to hear this, but it is one of the main reasons Martin stays on the radar. Because of the size of the account with *MainLine*, he has carte blanche with FishNet on setting up email accounts. We've tried tracing them, but they set up dummy accounts all the time for vendors and such. He's got a pretty good background in computers."

"As good as your pal Ernie?"

"Good enough," he told her. "But I'll be honest, I really thought we had SoulM8 pegged as a FishNet employee. I still thought that was the stronger lead by far." And the one he wanted to be true, for her sake, even if it meant more work for him.

She sat silently for a while and he wasn't sure what was going through her mind, but when she finally spoke up, it was about the FishNet angle. "Maybe we should stick with the family angle. Maybe a female relative or friend that looks more like one of the guys?" She nodded to the photographs, and dryly added, "Not that that description would narrow things down much."

Sad, but true, he thought. "It's a possible. I do wonder why Ms. Sack never mentioned the company's gender slant when we had our little talk."

"Maybe she assumed you knew."

"More likely she's sitting somewhere, right this minute, cackling over my disappointment and frustration."

Tanzy shot him a wry smile. "Internet Feminists: one. Stupid Arrogant Males: zero."

"Hey," he said in mock affront. "I'm not stupid."

He finally got an honest laugh out of her. "So, now what do we do? What other leads do we have?" She shot him a look that made it clear she wasn't referring to the Martin angle, only the FishNet angle.

Riley felt like he'd beat on her enough with that anyway for one day. He didn't enjoy the idea that it was someone she trusted doing this to her, innocent flirtation or not, any more than she did. "I'm compiling a list of people who attended and worked the foundation benefit the night of the Crystal Ball. My original plan was to cross-check them with this list and see if any of the names popped. It still wouldn't hurt to look. Using the sister or relative theory, maybe we'll at least get a last-name match."

"And if we don't?"

Riley sighed and stared directly at her. They both knew where he was going to focus his attention if this didn't pan out. "We keep looking," he said. "We have one other thing we're working on, but it's taking some time to perfect. Ernie is working on a virus—"

"Creating one, you mean? Can you do that? Legally?"

"Ernie is working on a virus," he began again, purposely not answering her, "to put in your machine that will automatically attach itself to your outgoing emails."

"And that works how?"

"It's called a Trojan Horse. It will email everyone in your address book and when they open it and download the attached file, it's like a worm. It will slide into the recipient's computer and set up shop, allowing us to go anywhere we want in his machine."

"Wow. I hear stories, but I always thought they smacked of paranoia. You can really do that? And if so, I don't want to infect everyone I know." She smiled. "Although there are a few people it might be fun to—" At his warning glare, she smoothed her mouth into a straight line, lips shut.

"We won't infect anyone else. We'll set up a duplicate email account on your laptop, with only one name in the address book."

"Ah. But for this to work, he has to open the attached file, right?"

"Assuming the guy is a stranger, and this is his first contact from you directly, do you really think he'd be able to resist?"

Tanzy shuddered. "True. But what will the note say? And won't it just encourage him?"

"It will be a standard promotional thing. We'll make it look like it's something your magazine is having you send out. The file will be a list of your upcoming appearances."

"But won't that encourage him to—"

"Yes, and we hope he does show up. He can access that information from the magazine site anyway, but not in a list like this. They only announce things as they come up. He'll see this as a personal invitation. After all, you've never sent him anything before, right? He'll take the bait, trust me."

Tanzy rubbed her arms. "Bait. Not giving me the warm fuzzies, here."

"I'll get some help and we'll cover the audience at your upcoming talk-show appearance and also watch whoever hangs outside the radio stations, and so on. We'll record everyone, then scan the films to see if we notice a recurring face pop up."

"Why haven't we done that already? I mean, even if the virus doesn't work, should we send him the email anyway, to spark him into action? Should we wait until he contacts me again?"

"No, we don't wait. And I've already started recording things."

"Since when?"

"Since the day after the dance."

"Because we didn't take him seriously until then," she said, nodding in understanding. She lifted a hand when he started to speak. "No, I don't blame you. Hell, I didn't take it seriously, either. And I've been doing some online research about stalkers, too. You were just following standard protocol with these guys. Not usually a threat, only considered potentially dangerous when the pattern changes." She looked at him and he hated the vulnerability he saw there. "And now the pattern has changed. First the note at the dance. And now no emails after my columns come out."

"I don't have anything from the radio show, but I do have film from your last *Barbara Bradley* taping. So we don't have anything to compare it with yet. But we're going to ask the television station to give us a copy of whatever film was taken of the audience during your last handful of tapings. If we don't get a name pop on the list comparisons from the charity ball, we'll hopefully recognize a recurring face in the crowd."

"Okay," she said, but he could see that it wasn't. That although she was taking a very hands-on, direct approach to helping herself be safe, the reality of how vulnerable she was, and had been for some time, was just sinking in.

The eyes she lifted to his made his chest tighten. There

were no tears, which he hadn't expected anyway. But there was a sort of haunted look. Or perhaps *hunted* was a better word.

"I really want this to be over," she whispered fiercely. She rubbed her arms again and looked away. "One way or the other."

He got up and went to her, pulled her from the chair and into his arms. "We'll get him, Tanzy. We'll ID him."

"I wanted to think the cease-fire meant he'd moved on," she said, still sounding somewhat hollow. She looked up at him. "But it's just another change in the pattern, isn't it?"

He looked steadily into her eyes. She was having a momentary lapse, but he knew her. She'd rebound quickly, and likely hate it that she'd let the bastard get to her, even for this brief moment. So she wouldn't appreciate him sugarcoating anything. It would be the same as telling her he thought she couldn't handle it. "Yeah," he said quietly. "It looks that way. But it doesn't mean he'll do anything, or that he hasn't given up. Pattern breaks are signals, but they don't always mean something dangerous is going to happen." He stroked her face, rubbed his thumbs over her cheeks. "But we'd be foolish not to prepare for any possibility. And that includes—"

She pressed her fingers across his lips. "Don't. Just . . . don't. I can't think about that any more today. About it being—you know. I just can't, okay?"

"Yeah," he said quietly. "Okay." He tipped her chin up. "But you need to know that I'm not giving up. We're not giving up. Not until we nail the little bastard down."

"Yeah," she said, then pressed her cheek against his chest and slid her arms around his waist. "Bastard-nailing sounds good."

The circumstances sucked, but he couldn't help but think how right it felt to hold her like this. She had such a huge personality, and it was still rather stunning to realize how small she felt in his arms.

He rubbed his hands up and down her back, then tucked her even more tightly against his body. He only wished he could make her feel this safe, this protected, twenty-four/seven.

She sighed deeply. "You know what I really hate?" she asked, her voice muffled against his shirt.

He leaned back. "What?"

"That I have him to thank for meeting you. I hate giving him even that much." She slid one hand around the back of his neck and along his jaw. "But I'm glad it was you."

"Thank your great-aunt for any introductions and leave it at that." He took her hand from his face, turned it, and kissed her palm, then curled her fingers inward. It was a silent promise, one he hoped to hell he could keep.

A light flared to life in her eyes as he pressed his lips to her closed hand, then covered it with his own. It wasn't the flare of fear, or vulnerability, or even hope. It was a flare of desire.

He had a brief thought of how dangerous situations could make two people feel things, want things, do things they'd never ordinarily do. He knew that wasn't the case with his own feelings, but he didn't want Tanzy to regret anything that might happen between them.

She ran a finger down the side of his face. "You're still worrying about the whole mixing business with pleasure thing, aren't you?"

He should be. Considering all he'd gone through with Finn. And his father would be the first to hoot with laughter if Riley dared to say that this was different, different because it was Tanzy, because what he felt wasn't just lust. That, at the very least, it was the beginning of something that could be a whole lot more than simple sexual chemistry. In fact, he could already say that.

"I want us to do this because we want it," he said finally. "Not because we've been thrown together in a sort of surreal situation."

"Is that how you feel?"

He shook his head. "And because of that, I might as well tell you something else now. I'm going to make some calls. Bring some other people in on this. We need more eyes and ears."

Instead of balking, she merely said, "Well then, they'd better be billing me for it. I know you're worried about me and it's more than professional concern, but I won't accept you doing that out of pocket. It's only fair—"

He kissed her. When he managed to lift his head, he said, "My perspective with you is shot. I need help with this. And, frankly, yes, I'll feel better when I know there are other people watching out for you." He gently gripped her face between his palms. "But I won't—can't—step completely out of the way."

"I believe I specifically asked you not to."

His lips quirked. And he loved that no matter the intensity of the moment, humor and amusement were always lurking just below the surface between them. It made this alliance he felt they shared seem all the more solid. "Ordered would be the more appropriate description, I believe."

She shrugged, unconcerned, and wrapped her arms around his waist. "As long as you don't let me out of your sight, I'll be perfectly fine with whatever solution you feel best serves the situation."

Now his body was the one doing all the flaring. She nestled closer to him, her body warm and pliant. Okay, maybe not *all* the flaring was exclusive to him. "Round-the-clock attention," he promised, his voice growing a bit rough as she continued to stroke his face, his chin, his lips.

She smiled and he didn't mind the hint of satisfaction. Not one bit. "Could give the term *bodyguard* a whole new slant."

"Could." It was all he managed to get out before taking those sly lips with his own.

He tasted sweet from the milkshake she'd made him and something else that was a flavor all his own. He took his time with her, kissed her slowly, like a man who planned to stay awhile. She relaxed against him, worry and fear receding as he continued his lazy seduction. She could get used to him staying awhile if it meant a lot more time spent doing this.

His hands skimmed down her back, then tucked her hips snugly into his. He was so hard, it took her by surprise. A man with such an urgent need was usually a bit more . . . impatient. And yet though his fingertips gripped her hips, it wasn't with barely leashed passion, but with gentle confidence. As if he knew they had all day—and night—to see where this could lead.

Normally *she'd* be impatient with this kind of pace. And it hit her, as his mouth left hers and traced a slow, wet path along her jaw, that she'd always been the one to push it, never allowing either party to take more than a second to think of anything other than slaking lust. She tipped her head back, a soft moan escaping her lips as he had his way with the tender curve of her neck. What on earth had she been afraid of?

She knew exactly what. She trailed her hands up his back, lifted her head, and kissed him gently, sweetly, on the lips. His eyes opened and she thrilled a little to see how deep the desire ran. "Thank you," she whispered.

His eyes widened a fraction. But his hands were moving

now, trailing along her spine, toying lazily with her hair. "For?"

"Taking your time." She smiled briefly. "Making me take my time. Making me want to take my time."

"I'm just doing what feels right. With you."

Her lips curved deeply. It was the perfect description of how she felt. She so hadn't expected this slow, smooth glide into want. Although if Tanzy was honest, she'd admit she'd long since gone past want, to pure, unadulterated need. But with all the banked heat, the zing of tension that was such a constant thing between them, she'd expected some sort of cataclysmic explosion when they finally came together. Not this sweet, aching tenderness.

And while a part of her wanted to pull away, automatically protect what little of her she could from such a vulnerable sort of intimacy, she realized it was too late for that. The real intimacy was all the things that had happened leading them to this moment. And it was that, her wanting this man as a whole, that made this tender moment more emotionally explosive than the wildest sex ever could.

"You have good instincts," she told him finally, then slid her fingers into his hair and tugged his mouth back to hers.

Riley's heart teetered on the brink. He really hadn't begun this interlude with any sense of calculation. She'd needed him, needed to know she wasn't facing this alone. He needed her to know she'd never have to face anything alone. The words hadn't been there, so he'd kissed her, held her, stroked her.

Had he planned their first time, he'd have assumed she'd want the full wolf treatment. And, frankly, he was pretty damn sure he could accommodate her on that score. If they stayed together long enough, he would. Or die trying. But not this time.

Her tongue was warm and ice-cream sweet as it slid into his mouth. He wondered if he'd ever tire of tasting her, dueling with her. His appetite for her exploded and he was tempted to simply take over, dominate, go for all that he suddenly was so desperate to have. Only the exquisite torture of keeping it slow, exploring rather than conquering, was all the more tantalizing, each little sigh all the more rewarding.

"I have to tell you," he said roughly when she began the slow exploration of his jawline and neck, "I've dreamed of having you." He felt the shiver run through her and his body tightened further. "It wasn't slow. It was always hard, and fast. Nothing like this."

She ran her tongue along his neck . . . and now it was his turn to shiver. With pleasure.

"No," she agreed, dropping small kisses beneath his ear, "it was nothing like this."

It gave him a little jolt, knowing she'd fantasized about him, too.

As if she'd read his mind, and he was beginning to think she could, she looked at him, lips curved in that wry tilt. "What, you think men are the only ones who think about stuff like that?"

"It wasn't about women fantasizing in general," he said, his own lips curving. He toyed with the hem of her sweatshirt. "It was very specifically the idea of you fantasizing about me that got to me."

"That surprises you? You do realize you're total fantasy material, do you not?" She ran her hands down his chest, then up over his shoulders and down his arms. "Totally." Then she grinned at him. "But, and here's the real shock, I was dreaming of doing this . . ." She slid his shirt up, rubbing her palms flat along his chest as she did, until it was bunched up under his arms. "Uncovering this," she went on, no longer looking into his eyes, but staring at his chest. "Doing this." She leaned in and ran her tongue around one nipple, then the other, making his entire body jerk in surprised response. "Even when it was covered by those awful shapeless suits and I hadn't a clue such a magnificent chest was hidden beneath it."

He simply stared at her, his entire body humming. "Did you, now?"

She nodded, the playful, almost smug smile faltering only slightly when he pulled his shirt completely off, then very deliberately placed his hands on her waist. "Well," he said, enjoying her little intake of breath when he nudged her baggy sweatshirt up, revealing a scant inch of bare abdomen. "I always knew what sort of body lurked beneath your clothes." He nudged the shirt an inch higher, pleased that she gripped his biceps, as if needing the support. "I almost blew my sheep cover, literally, that night on the stairs when you had on those suede pants that looked like they'd been tanned directly onto every inch of those legs of yours."

"Yeah?" she said, but her voice was shaky, ruining whatever edge she might have hoped to gain with that cocky smile.

"Yeah," he said, stroking his thumbs up underneath the edge of her sweatshirt, which was now just below where her bra should be . . . but wasn't. Damn, but she kept him a little off balance, too. He stroked a little higher, nudging the thick cotton up until the round fullness of her breasts dipped below the ribbed hem. "But when I closed my eyes at night, it wasn't suede pants or couture ballgowns that had me hot and hard."

He saw her throat work, felt his own go a bit dry as he skated his fingertips beneath the soft material . . . and found something entirely softer. The softest skin in the world.

"No?" she managed, the word more like a croak.

He just shook his head, dying to dip down, taste the hard budded nipples he was stroking. Dear God he was hard for her, every inch of her. "I—" He had to stop, clear his throat, wet his lips.

Her pupils shot wide at the unconscious action and he almost lost his last scrap of control right then and there. "I fantasized," he said, covering her breasts entirely with his hands, making her moan . . . smoothing his palms gently over her now distended nipples, making them both suck in a little breath, "about that damn football jersey." He slid his hands around her back, sliding the sweatshirt up and over her head, then finally, mercifully, pulling her against him, so bare skin could finally kiss bare skin. "About tearing it off of you . . . and making love with you wearing nothing more than those goddamn slippers."

She'd already been reaching for him, pushing fingers into his hair, tugging his head closer, when his words registered, and she stilled . . . then burst out laughing.

He grinned. "Smooth, aren't I?"

"The best kind of smooth," she said, her smile pure, her eyes so bright, so filled with an emotion he was too afraid to put a name to. Mostly because he wanted to so badly.

Then she tugged him close, put her mouth on his, and murmured, "I'm sure that can be arranged."

He kissed her, hard and fast, then slow, and excruciatingly slower still. "I've never felt the need to make the sweeping romantic gesture," he murmured as he lifted his mouth from hers. "But I'd love nothing more than to carry you up those stairs to bed. Only we'd more than likely end up a broken, twisted heap at the bottom." He was thoroughly enjoying the roller-coaster pace of this moment, the slow, tortuous ascent, the screaming plummet, only to climb once again.

"There's a romantic image," she agreed. "But the sentiment

is appreciated." She abruptly slid from his arms, took his hand, and completely unself-conscious of her half nudity, turned and tugged him along. "However entirely unnecessary it is." She tossed a grin over her shoulder as she pulled him up the stairs behind her. "We can play follow the leader instead."

And though he wanted nothing more than her naked, in a soft bed, with him driving deeply into her, it was almost as enjoyable keeping her off stride. She'd had entirely too much experience in calling all the shots. If nothing else, he'd be the one to show her that following was sometimes more fun than leading.

They reached the landing on the second floor and she turned to hike them up another flight, when he suddenly swung her around and expertly trapped her against the wall. Her eyes were wide with surprise, but filled with delight as well.

Oh yeah, definitely going to enjoy the battle of their particular wills.

He braced his hands on either side of her head, leaned his body into hers, almost but not quite touching. "What rooms are on this floor?"

She lifted her hands to run them up his chest, the playful gleam swiftly returning to her gaze. He turned the tables easily, snagging both hands before they could brush his chest and pinning them back to the wall.

Now her pupils all but exploded, her mouth dropping open even, before she reined it in.

"What rooms?" he asked, almost conversationally, an easy smile on his face.

"I, uh . . ."

His grin widened. Speechless. This was even better.

"Rooms, Tanzy," he whispered, leaning down and nipping her shoulder, then running a quick tongue up along her neck. "Name them," he murmured against her ear.

She tensed under his erotic assault, but tellingly didn't fight back. "Office. Bathroom."

She gasped when he cut her off with a deep tongue kiss. "And?" he asked, as if he hadn't just made her knees buckle. Again.

"Closet."

Damn. The bathroom could be fun . . . but he wanted her on a flat surface. First. Preferably one with cushioning. "Third floor?" he asked, dipping his head down to run a wet ring around her nipple with the tip of his tongue.

She gasped, then moaned when he gave the other one the same treatment. Or maybe that was him.

"I have no idea," she said, then half laughed. "Damn, what you do to me."

He lifted his head, grinned. "I do expect paybacks, you know."

She tipped her head forward, managed to open her desire-blurred eyes. "Yeah?"

"Oh yeah."

Her eyes began to clear, that smile began to form. A worthy opponent. They were going to have fun with each other.

He pulled her arms over his shoulders, then lifted her backside away from the wall. "Put your legs around me," he instructed.

"But—"

"Wrap 'em, Tanzy," he commanded. "Tight."

She did, and he turned for the last set of stairs.

"Your knee—"

"Is a minor inconvenience compared to other, more centralized aches." He smiled. "Piggybacks aren't as dashing as sweeping you into my arms and racing up the stairs two at a time, but—"

She wiggled a little against him. "Piggyfronts definitely have their bonus attributes."

She had him there.

And it was precisely because he couldn't wait another moment for her to have him—and if there was a God, again after that—that he did take the stairs two at a time.

And he didn't care in the least that he'd have to ice his knee for a week.

Play sex.

We've all had it, right? And I think we'll all agree (those of us bold enough to admit it) that while it's fun during the moment, afterward, well, it's sort of like the fast food of lovemaking, isn't it? And there's another word I've been thinking about. *Lovemaking.* Different from sex completely, really. It's scary to contemplate all those attendant expectations that come along when the L word is introduced into the bedroom. (Or wherever.) Because, when it's love you're making, there's a whole lot more than sex being shared.

Intimacy on an entirely different level. Totally terrifying. But wonderful, too. Because the amazing thing is, when it's love you're making, even play sex is fulfilling.

18

They fell across her bed, his hands all over her. Gone was the measured pace he'd instigated downstairs, and the confident swagger of the man who'd pinned her to the wall on the second-floor landing. Now it was all hunger and heat. Need that somehow seemed to border on desperation.

And when he tugged her beneath him, helped her claw her way out of her clothes just as rapidly as she helped him out of his, Tanzy knew this need, this sense of desperation, was shared equally.

If she'd had the presence of mind to think about what that meant, she'd probably have leaped off the bed and run screaming from the room. A last-ditch effort to protect the coveted independence she'd spent her whole life nurturing and fortifying. Not to mention protecting. Because she'd have known then that once she let him into her body, there would be no shutting off the avalanche of emotions that would come barreling along right behind it. There would be no losing herself in physical pleasure, no way to avoid admitting that she'd already long since let him into places inside her far more intimate, far more sacred.

And yet, even in their rush to claim the other they still had that ultimate connection, one that wasn't remotely physical. The gasping and panting, clawing and grunting didn't keep them from laughing, even while their bodies were throbbing for release.

"Condoms," he croaked as she slid her hands, for the first time, down his fully naked torso, cupping his backside and smoothing her palms along those oh-so-sweet indentations on the sides.

"Unless you're feeling particularly infectious," she gasped, "we don't need them. I'm on the pill."

He lifted his head from where he'd been doing incredibly carnal and erotic things with her earlobe and looked at her. "Infectious?"

"What, you find that word offensive? Are you telling me that you aren't a member in good standing of the Guys Who Think Bodily Noises Are Funny Club? But *infectious* is an eww?" She watched him try to frown, but she'd caught him off guard and the snicker was out before he could stop it. "Aha!" she crowed. "Busted."

"Still," he managed, trying to scrape his dignity together, "*infectious* was a little too—"

"Descriptive?"

He just gave her a look. "Mood killing."

He was lying on top of her, the rigidly hard length of him prodding her, so close to where she absolutely had to have it . . . and she was delaying nirvana so she could tease him? But it was so much fun. He was so much fun.

She lifted her hips slightly, pushing him just between her thighs, and made him moan involuntarily. "Oh yeah, you're totally not in the mood anymore."

He growled, then nudged a bit higher, and it was her turn to gasp. On a quite wicked grin, he said, "What can I say, something about you is . . ." He pushed a bit more. "Infectious."

She laughed, sliding her fingertips back down along his spine, along those perfectly tight butt cheeks, making him shudder now and loving it. "I can be very descriptive about a lot of things, you know."

"Can you, now?" His eyes were glittering, fierce, his body so intent as he continued to nudge at her, making the muscles between her thighs almost cramp with pleasure. And yet he was still smiling. Willing to play. Despite the desperation they both felt. Like, just maybe, they had time.

All the time in the world.

And there it was, the elusive promise of a future. Just moments in time, but when strung together, they could add up to something. Something lasting. So tantalizing a prospect, so stunning that she wanted it. All she had to do—

He leaned down and whispered in her ear, "If you don't stop this torture and let me inside you, I'm going to have to take desperate measures."

"Oh?" A wicked smile of her own curving her lips. "You aren't interested in my descriptive powers when it comes to, say, explaining just how I intend to bring you to a screaming climax? In minute detail?"

His eyes flashed, but so did his white teeth. "Why waste time talking about it?" And to punctuate his point, he pushed her wrists to the bed, beside her head, then traced his tongue along her lower lip. A quick kiss, then he moved before she could pull him in. "When we could be doing it."

With a teasing glint in his eyes, he traced his tongue lightly over her chin, then dipped below, leaving her to press her head back against the sheets as he drew a damp line down her neck. He slid his body down a bit, making her whimper when the sweet, hard length of him no longer pressed between her thighs.

He looked up at her. "You did say minute details?"

She managed to nod, but couldn't lift her head. It was difficult, as he took her nipple in his mouth just then, making her arch off the bed with a gasp of pure delight.

"I can do minute details," he murmured, then shifted his attention to the other nipple. "Very sweet," he said. "Perfect." Then he let her wrists go, covered her breasts with his palms . . . and slid his tongue lower.

"Dear. God." She was a writer of some reputed talent, and that was the absolute best she could come up with. She heard him chuckle, felt it, squirmed beneath it . . . and found herself grinning right along with him.

And when he plunged his tongue right into the spot that most needed plunging, she screamed in pure delight as the climax ripped through her with stunning speed and strength. "More," she managed, breathless from both gasping and laughing. "More details."

"Greedy," he said, already climbing up her body.

She pouted.

He pushed inside her in one smooth, deep stroke.

She quit pouting. She was too busy arching beneath him, wrapping herself around him, both inside her body and out.

He paused, she pushed. He shook his head, gathered his breath. "Wait."

"Why?" she demanded, still needy.

He lifted his head, smiling, eyes telling her there was so much more going on here. Between them. "Because I don't want this to be over yet."

And just like that, tears sprang to the back of her eyes. Emotional tears, good tears, scary tears.

"Not yet. Not—"

But it was too late. Her muscles had needs of their own and clenched convulsively around him, making him growl as he thrust deeply and repeatedly inside her, all control gone. She met each stroke eagerly, shifting so the humming sensation of her climax continued to buzz even as she coaxed him over the edge.

He pressed his face into her neck when he came, groaning

long, deep, and sounding so satisfied it made her smile. "Not ever," she whispered.

His heart pounded so hard, she could feel it inside her own chest. He started to move off of her, but she wrapped her arms and legs tightly around him, keeping him there, keeping his heart there, right on top of hers. "You know what?"

He lifted his head, hair damp from exertion, skin flushed. "What?"

That velvet voice, all rough and hoarse, made her shiver. Her body thrummed to life, needy despite the fact that she'd never felt such bone-deep satiation. Soul deep. She knew it for sure when his eyes met hers, looking directly at her, into her, knowing her, alert to every detail about her, and only her. This wasn't the postcoital, pleasure-hazed, self-involved, and already-halfway-home look she usually saw. The one she usually gave.

"You do have an eye for details," she murmured.

He grinned. It was lazy and sexy, contented. And somehow still oh-so-predatory. "Minute details," he corrected.

She smiled as she sighed, stretching her legs beneath his, then rolling them so she was sprawled half on top of him. "Well, J.B. was right about one thing."

His eyebrow quirked in surprise. "What?"

Her sleepy smile spread to a grin. "You do put the special in special teams, Rocket Power."

He groaned, then pulled her reluctantly from the bed.

"What are you doing? Why—where are we going?" Her body was a limp, way past al dente, very satisfied noodle.

"Shower. Together," he said, and tugged her along, scuffing barefoot and naked behind him.

As it turned out, it was *his* behind that had her coming around. *Such a nice, firm tush,* she thought with a sigh. And was apparently unconcerned with showing it off. Double bonus points. All that time spent in locker rooms, no doubt.

Well, as far as she was concerned, flagrant nudity was absolutely, one hundred percent fine with her. Encouraged, even. Especially when it was his.

And just imagine how those buns of steel are going to feel, all hard and slick with soap . . .

He stopped, looked back, caught her ogling. "You coming?"

She sighed, smiling. *Not yet.* "You scrub first, detail man."

Riley limped down the stairs and made his way to Tanzy's kitchen for some ice. His knee had survived the piggyfront and the romp in the bed fairly well. He had paid dearly for taking her up against the wall in her tiled shower. But he wasn't swearing at the hot dagger of pain being shoved inside his knee with every step.

Hard to swear convincingly with a stupid, lovesick grin plastered all over your face, he thought . . . still grinning.

God, he hadn't had an afternoon like this in . . . well, never, actually. And he was already plotting strategy, planning for that postcoital distance he'd bet she'd try to put between them once the haze of lovemaking and multiple—dear God, they'd been multiple—shower orgasms wore off. Hell, he already wanted her again. And not just in bed. Or the shower, for that matter. They'd gasped and moaned, shrieked and growled their way through some fairly spectacular sex. And yet, the images that came first to mind were the grins, the laughter, the fun.

And that's what he didn't want to lose. All the in-between stuff. All the things that made Tanzy . . . Tanzy.

He thought he'd be more hung up on the guilt part, questioning himself endlessly on having breached the very rules he'd so adamantly set for himself, tried to instill in his hopeless rogue of a father.

But he wasn't. Not really. He already knew this wasn't a fling. He had no clue how he was going to manage it, but she wasn't putting him out. Not anytime soon. Stalker or no stalker.

He was so lost in his thoughts as he levered his bad knee off the last riser, he almost missed the slender cream envelope lying beneath the mail slot of her door. A mail slot he'd tried to convince her to seal shut, at least temporarily. A suggestion that had met with the same stony refusal his request to install a motion detector and outside security measures had.

Not that she didn't take the threat seriously now. She did. In the way that anyone as self-sufficient as Tanzy could believe, she really was in danger, anyway. Ultimately, she just placed too much trust in his ability to personally keep her safe. Which was another argument they'd had. One that he had a sick, angry feeling he was about to discover he'd been right about, too.

Heedless of his state of dress, he immediately flipped the locks and hopped outside, scanning the street. But it was merely rainswept, empty of any cars or people. Swearing, he stepped back inside and locked the door once again, before crouching down as best as he could next to the note. He flicked over the sealed envelope with the edge of a fingernail, careful not to put any prints on it, or smear ones already there. There was no name, address, or stamp on the outside. Which wasn't a surprise, as Tanzy had stopped getting regular mail delivery at her home years before, when her column first started heating up. She had diverted all mail to her post-office box, hence her belief that her mail slot wasn't really an issue.

Apparently SoulM8 didn't agree.

On the back, in a jerky scrawl Riley recognized from the note left at the dance, were the words *For You.*

It made his skin crawl, made his hands clench into fists

so tight he thought his knuckles would pop through the skin. He wasn't a violent man off the playing field, but if he could have gotten his hands on the little prick right at that specific moment—

He shut that avenue of thought down, forcing himself to stay on track, stay focused. She was depending on him and the last thing she needed was for him to go off half-cocked and pissed as hell. Despite the fact he could have easily done it at that moment.

He looked around for something to slide beneath it. He went into the front room and got several papers from the employee list, slid them under the letter, then transported the whole stack to the coffee table, where the rest of the papers still lay. He had to sit down, his knee was throbbing. He flicked the envelope over, but there was nothing else written on it.

He didn't tear it open, despite how badly he wanted to. Burning it would give him even more satisfaction. But he didn't even touch it. He had to go out to his truck and get his kit, see if they could get more prints. Make sure they matched the ones left on the first note. At least they might be able to ascertain if SoulM8 had delivered one or both of the notes himself. Or used the same delivery person, anyway. He still didn't think this guy—whoever the hell he was—played well with others. He'd bet money the bastard had been at the dance, just like he'd bet money he'd been just outside Tanzy's front door.

And Martin had been at the dance. Just as he damn well had Tanzy's private address.

Acid pitched hard against his stomach lining. He didn't want it to be her boss. But things were looking worse all the time. They were going to have to confront him, one way or the other. Ernie had been trying to track down handwriting samples, as all Martin's work with Tanzy was done online. But Ernie'd been all caught up in tracking the charity ball information and setting up the virus and hadn't gotten to that yet.

And maybe, just maybe, Riley hadn't pushed as hard as he should have on the Martin angle, because he'd really wanted it to be some anonymous asshole instead. Then he remembered the figurine. He hadn't run prints on it, had forgotten about it after his little nap and their foray into the FishNet employment lists. Well, he could run both the note and the coyote at the same time. First he had to get some damn clothes on.

He turned to leave the front room, and the doorbell rang.

"I'll get it," Tanzy called from right outside the front-room door. She must have just come down the stairs, only she was yelling down the hall toward the kitchen, assuming he was getting ice.

He instinctively lunged from his seat on the futon toward the door to stop her, but his knee locked up, sending him staggering. His warning shout ended up a grunted curse as he hopped on his good foot, catching his weight with a hand on the wall to keep from falling to the floor.

"Aunt Millicent!" Tanzy said, obviously surprised.

"No more than me," Riley muttered. Looking upward, he mouthed *Why me?*, wishing he *had* been in the kitchen getting ice. At least there he'd have a place to hide. As it was, he was trapped in the front room, wrapped in nothing more than a towel and a grimace. Not exactly how he'd have hoped to let Millicent know about the shift in his relationship with her only and beloved grandniece.

He did have the presence of mind to shift a stack of papers carefully on top of the envelope. He put a hefty coffee table–size book on art on top of that for good measure. He didn't want to talk to either of them about the envelope, or the breach of personal space made by SoulM8, until he'd had a chance to examine the note more closely. In the meantime, he had to get them the hell out of the open doorway.

"Tanzy," he called out. "In here."

She stepped back and leaned into the sitting room doorway. Fortunately she was wearing shorts with her Niners jersey. "Riley? I thought you were—"

"Oh, Riley, how wonderful," Aunt Millicent trilled, stepping around Tanzy before either of them could do anything to stop her. "Why, it's about time Tanzy let you in out of the—Oh my."

And the three words he'd hoped never to utter came all too easily to his lips. "I can explain."

Millicent had dropped the little monocle she was fond of using, but quickly retrieved it. After a silent and unnerving head-to-toe appraisal of his towel-clad body, she turned to Tanzy and said, "Got caught in the rain, did he?"

"No, ma'am," Riley said, stepping forward, biting down on the wince when his knee protested the movement. "As much as I'd like to take that out you so nicely provided, I think it's better to stick with the truth."

Her monocled gaze swung his way again. If she'd had a British accent she'd have put Maggie Smith to shame. "Which is?"

"I'm no longer working for your grandniece."

"I fired him," Tanzy said, finally finding her voice.

Riley glanced at Tanzy, expecting her to be mortified, at the very least. He should have known better. A slightly amused tilt to her lips, a twinkle in her eye. She was having no problems with this little ménage à trois. Of course, she wasn't the one in the towel.

"You did what?" Millicent looked to them both. "Did something happen?"

"You might say that," Tanzy murmured with a suppressed snicker. "Several times."

Riley shot her a glare. "We haven't gotten him yet—"

"But you've ID'd the little perp?"

Tanzy folded her arms. "My great-aunt, the armchair detective."

Millicent shot her a look that would have made a grown man quail. To her credit, Tanzy's smile wobbled only slightly. Riley actually found himself stifling a smile. At least he knew she'd come by her moxie honestly.

"Dame Agatha Christie might have been a clever octogenarian, but she had nothing on a Harrington," Millicent stated, then turned to Riley, brow raised as she waited for an explanation.

"I'm not working for Tanzy any longer, but I am working with her. I'm going to have some other associates help me out in a paid capacity and I promise you we will see this thing finished." He cleared his throat under Millicent's steady gaze, his respect for Tanzy growing by the second.

"And you're taking this backseat role because . . . ?"

Tanzy stepped in. "Because we're having an aff—a relationship," she corrected, with a little smile. "As of about an hour or two ago. And Riley doesn't think he has the proper perspective to be in charge of this any longer." She waved her hand, oblivious to his soft groan. "I didn't agree with him, but it's a compromise I can live with."

"Ms. Harrington, please—" Riley began, but was waved silent, this time by Millicent.

"You are no longer in my employ, Mr. Parrish, so, in that regard, what you do with your time and who you do it with aren't any of my concern. Professionally speaking." She held her hand up again when he went to speak. He bit down hard and shot a look at Tanzy, who appeared far too satisfied for his peace of mind. *Having fun, was she?* Well, they'd see about that later, wouldn't they.

"I admire that you're still handling the case in a manner that will best protect my grandniece. As for the rest, well,

I've never presumed to interfere in her love life and I won't start now."

It wasn't exactly a blessing, but it beat the hell out of whatever else he might have had coming. Riley nodded, sincerely grateful. "You have my word that I'll do my best to see her safe." He looked to Tanzy. "Speaking of which, I believe we talked about opening the front door."

"I could see her through the doorpanes."

Riley merely ground his teeth, surprised he had any left. "Still, until this is over, I'd appreciate it if you'd do things as I ask."

Tanzy's hands went right to her hips, knee cocked, obviously ready to let fly with all the reasons why she could take perfectly good care of her own self. So it was a surprise when she only snapped her mouth shut again, then sighed, and finally nodded. "Yeah. Okay."

Riley wasn't sure who was more shocked, him or Millicent.

"Well then," Millicent said, her quite clear-eyed gaze shifting from Tanzy to Riley, her tone shifting to something more . . . considering.

Just what she was considering, Riley wasn't sure he wanted to know.

"Why don't you go make yourself presentable and we'll make some tea," Millicent said, quite pleasantly. Almost too pleasantly.

"That sounds great, Aunt Millicent," Tanzy said, "but Riley really needs to ice his knee. He—"

Riley did manage to cut her off with a glare before she blurted out any additional details. Minute or otherwise. He'd been mortified quite enough for one afternoon, thanks. "Old injury," he cut in. "Rain makes it flare up." He glanced through the front bay window and spied Millicent's driver resting his hip against her car as he skimmed the afternoon paper. Riley relaxed a little then. It was doubtful anyone would approach the house with a block-long limo idling by the curb. And Wainwright might have had a career in the NFL himself had he been so inclined, he had the size for it.

"I'll let you two talk and be back down in a while if that's okay," he said, edging to the door, careful of his knee . . . and his towel.

"Can you get upstairs all right?" Tanzy asked. "If you can manage that, I'll bring up the ice while the tea is brewing."

Riley nodded, eternally grateful. "That would be great. You don't have to save me a cup. I'll make some coffee later."

Millicent raised her hand as he limped to the door. "Before you go, *have* there been any new developments in the case?"

It took considerable will not to look at the table and the stack of papers presently beneath the art book. "We'll hopefully have something more to tell you soon," he said, deciding it was close enough to the truth. Now he just had to hope like hell they left the coffee table untouched during teatime.

He was levering himself up the first riser when he heard Millicent make a *tsk*ing noise. Thinking she was going to lecture Tanzy privately about their relationship, he turned back, ready to defend her.

Just in time to hear Millicent say, "Such a pity about his knee. If I'd had a gun, I think I'd have shot Hendrick myself for not using double coverage in his last game. I don't know why Monk allowed Schilling to hire such an ineffectual ass as special teams coach anyway." She sighed. "He really should have listened to us when we explained that Farber was the better man for the job." Another *tsk*. "Men. Invite you to the owner's box, but don't want to listen to a thing you have to say."

Riley blinked. He might have gaped. He must have made

some noise as well, because Millicent looked over and saw him standing in the open doorway.

"What, you don't think I hire a person strictly based on a recommendation, do you? Besides, Howard Waterston can be a real nitwit. Especially when it comes to keeping his pants zipped. But then, I suppose you know all about that."

Riley's face reddened until he realized she was referring to his knowledge of Waterston, not him personally. "Yes, ma'am." What else was there to say?

"Howard's recommendation brought your current line of work to my attention, but that wasn't the sole reason for your employment. You had a hell of a college career. A shame what happened with Sacramento."

Completely nonplussed, Riley said, "You saw me play college ball?"

She nodded sharply. "I thought you might have been the start of something good for the Pioneers."

"I don't know about that, but thank you for the vote of confidence. I didn't know you were a fan of the game."

Tanzy snorted. "Are you kidding? My great-aunt is the Yogi Berra of her peer group."

"Yogi played baseball," Millicent and Riley said simultaneously.

"Whatever," Tanzy said with an unconcerned shrug. "I'm a total cliché. I just look at the uniforms."

Riley's gaze narrowed. "So, you're telling me you don't wear that old jersey because you're a diehard Niners fan?"

Tanzy squared her shoulders. "I'm a fan of tight pants and thigh pads. I'm not too particular which team wears them." She fingered her shirt. "I borrowed this from Sue's brother when I stayed with her one summer, between sophomore and junior year in college. I never got around to giving it back." She hugged her waist. "It's comfy."

"So, let me get this straight," he said, quite seriously, "you don't watch the game at all."

Millicent sighed. "She wouldn't know a field goal from a three-point jumper."

Riley swiveled back to Millicent, his expression lighting up even as Tanzy groaned. "You watch a little roundball, too?"

Millicent sniffed, cleaned her monocle with a lace hanky she had tucked in the sleeve of her beautifully tailored floral dress. "I wish I could say the Lakers were overrated, but the fact is, as long as Mr. Bryant and Mr. O'Neal continue to play on the same team, I'm afraid the rest of the teams might as well take the season off. Play golf." She sniffed. "Never did develop a liking for that particular sport. Too tedious."

Riley hooted. "My father gets Lakers tickets occasionally. From, uh, a friend of his." Riley didn't elaborate on who the friend was, or that she'd been a client once. A very thankful client. And not for Finn's professional skills.

Another snort. "Are you kidding? She's got season tickets, fifty-yard line."

She didn't even pause when Riley and Millicent both shook their heads pityingly and said, "Center court."

"Right behind Jack Nicholson," Tanzy finished, then smiled smugly. "I know that much."

"If our schedules permit, perhaps we can take in a game someday," Millicent offered graciously. But there was a definite twinkle in her eye. "However, I must have your solemn vow that we leave this one at home." She nodded toward Tanzy, who put her hands up, palms out.

"Trust me, you won't hurt my feelings."

"I tried, honestly I did," Millicent said with a resigned sigh. "But she's beyond all hope."

Riley just grinned. He'd get her to a game. Or three. She was too competitive not to enjoy sports. He'd start her with hoops first. It was faster-paced. But they'd get to football. Eventually.

"Thank you," he told Millicent, almost reverent with sincerity. "I'd very much enjoy it." And he realized he would, as much for the company as the courtside seats.

He finally managed to leave the room, only to have Tanzy lean back into the hall and whisper, "And don't think I didn't see that gleam in your eye back there. Bigger men than you have tried to force me to understand sports, Mr. Rocket Power. All failed. Miserably."

Riley winced as he climbed the first few steps, but he was grinning, all the same. He looked back down to Tanzy. "Bigger, maybe. But not better."

Riley watched her struggle valiantly not to laugh. Her lips quirked anyway. "We'll see, ball boy. We'll see."

How is it we grow up and think we know everything about our loved ones, and then are shocked to discover they have secrets? Just like the rest of us. I used to think life would be easier if families came complete with how-to manuals. But I suppose that would spoil the fun. Besides, no way would I want every detail in mine! I guess we learn things when we're meant to, when we can put them to use. Or not.

19

Millicent stepped out into the foyer as Tanzy watched Riley limp up the stairs.

Millicent lifted her monocle and followed Tanzy's gaze. "He does fill out a towel quite nicely, doesn't he, dear?"

When Tanzy's eyebrows rose, Millicent merely sniffed. "The casing might be a bit worn out, but the engine still hums along just fine."

Tanzy decided this fell into the TMI category. Too Much Information. Certainly it produced a visual she could have done without. "Let me run some ice up to him and I'll fix us some tea. You can just make yourself comfortable in the—"

"Nonsense," Millicent interrupted. "I can certainly get a pot of tea going while you take care of your man."

Tanzy paused. "He's not my man."

Millicent smiled indulgently. "Whatever you say, dear."

Tanzy planted her hands on her hips. "I would think you of all people would find being patronizing most unbecoming behavior."

"So is fooling yourself and hiding behind old truths."

Tanzy's hands fell to her sides at the same time her mouth dropped open. "Old truths?"

Millicent gently took her arm and turned her toward the kitchen. "We can discuss this after you've tended to—"

"Riley," Tanzy interjected stubbornly.

"Yes, dear."

She scowled but didn't bother continuing the conversation. She took the stairs two at a time with the ice, expecting Riley to be sleeping with his leg propped up. Instead she found him on the second floor, in her office. At her computer. She cleared her throat from the doorway.

He didn't jump, nor did he turn around. "Hope you don't mind. I needed to check on something."

She wanted to be at least a little miffed at the invasion of her most personal space. But he looked so damn good with his damp hair curling at his neck and her melon-colored bath towel barely hanging on around his waist, she found it hard to be surly. Horny, now that she could manage. With hardly any effort, as it turned out. She wondered absently how long that would last. His ability to run her pulse straight up by doing nothing more than, well, breathing.

"You've been snooping around in my computer for weeks now, why should I mind?" She moved into the room, shifting the bag of ice as the chill began to sting her palm. "At least now you can take the direct route. I brought your ice."

"Thanks."

The fact that he hadn't so much as glanced in her direction did manage to miff her, however. Men might have to compete for her attention when it came to her and her computer, but she'd be damned if she'd have to compete with it. She smiled as she walked up behind him, bent down, and pressed a warm kiss at the base of his neck.

"Mmmm," he murmured. "Nice."

"Uh-huh." Then she planted the ice pack where her lips had just been, making him yelp and jump.

"What was that for?" he said, grabbing the ice bag.

She smiled sweetly. "You're looking at me now, so it worked, didn't it?"

He gave her a calm, steady look. "Must you always be the center of attention?"

She rolled his chair out and spun him slowly so he faced her, then very gently placed the ice on his knee. "Just with you."

He hissed at the contact, but clamped his hand on hers to keep her from taking it away again. "It takes a moment or two to get used to it."

She slid her hand free, all desire to tease him gone. "Is it really bad? You should have said something. We really didn't need to—"

He looked up at her. "Yes, we needed to. And we just might need to again. Later."

Now she found a smile. "I think we can be inventive enough to spare the knee, but not . . . well, anything else. Don't you?"

His lips quirked and he reached out and snagged her, pulling her across his lap before she could dodge him.

"Your knee!"

"Is numb. Now hush." He made sure she did by planting his mouth on hers. He was grinning when he lifted his head.

"What?" she asked warily.

"I think I like having you fuss over me."

"I don't fuss."

He kissed the tip of her nose. "You do. And you're damn cute at it, too."

She merely rolled her eyes. But at the same time felt inordinately pleased by the compliment. Not that she was about to let him know.

He stroked her face, her hair, the teasing light leaving his eyes. "We need to talk. When Millicent is gone."

She frowned. "Has something happened? Did Ernie email the list from the charity ball?"

"Yeah, but I haven't cross-checked it yet."

She felt her skin go clammy. "He sent another email, didn't he?" She couldn't help it, she shuddered.

He tugged her closer, smoothed his hands down her arms. "Not exactly. But there has been contact."

"What? How?"

He sighed. "I'm working on it. You go visit with your aunt. But if the phone rings, or anyone comes to the door, I don't care who it is, just let me handle it. Promise me." She must have looked as spooked as she felt, because he leaned closer and kissed her. This time it was gentle and reassuring. And still made her pulse race. "You really have to start taking this more seriously, okay?"

"I am," she insisted, but at his look, she sighed and said, "Okay. I promise. And I'm sorry. About opening the door, about worrying you. It's just—" She paused, looked down at where his hand was stroking along her arm, and covered his hand with hers. "It's going to take some getting used to. Having someone else worrying about me." She smiled a little. "Fussing over me."

He touched her chin so she looked at him. "Get used to it. And I promise to do the same. Deal?"

She smiled, ridiculously pleased at his proprietary tone. She could lie and say it was just because there was a threat against her, someone stalking her, and it felt good to have a big, strong body by her side.

But it was more than that. And for the first time she realized she was afraid. Not of SoulM8, but of what would happen once there was no longer a threat. Would Riley stick around then, or would they drift apart when he inevitably moved on to another job? One that might consume as much of his time as this one had. She wished there was a guarantee, some absolute thing she could do to ensure that this wouldn't end until she was ready for it to end.

Which made her sound rather cold and calculating, didn't it? Had she always been so controlling? She didn't think so. Mostly because she was never with anyone long enough to worry about it.

Riley blew next to her ear, startling her from her thoughts.

"I was just blowing the smoke away," he explained, then tapped her forehead. "From all those gears grinding up there." His smile faded. "I shouldn't have said anything until Millicent was gone. Please, go have some tea, enjoy her company. I take it she doesn't usually stop by."

It was cowardly, but Tanzy took the out anyway. Besides, she wasn't ready yet to lay her heart at his feet and risk having it trampled on. "No, no she doesn't."

"Christmas is around the corner, maybe she wants to make plans."

"I didn't even think she'd be here for Christmas, remember? Besides, we spend Thanksgiving together. That's our holiday. She spends Christmas making the rounds. Friends, charities, a few parties. I usually do the same. Maybe I'll ask her if I can help out this year, test the waters, so to speak." She looked at him. "What about you? Will you and your dad get together? Do you have other family?"

He shook his head. "It's just the two of us. Some years Finn and I get together, most years he's out and about."

Tanzy noted that it wasn't the first time Riley was less than specific where his father was involved. She supposed that was one other thing they shared. Less than stellar relationships with their parents. She couldn't even call hers a relationship. At least he had that.

She realized he was looking at her, his expression a bit . . . she couldn't exactly say. "What?"

"I want to ask you something."

"So, go ahead and ask."

"It's not that simple." He heaved a sigh when she merely gave him a look. "Okay. Let me get the whole thing out before you answer, all right?"

Intrigued and a little bit nervous, though she couldn't say exactly why, she nodded. "Promise."

Now he gave her the look. "Just do your best."

She jabbed him with her elbow, but they were both smiling. "Get on with it, already."

"Seeing as we don't have any plans for the holiday, barring whatever Millicent might have up her floral-print, lace-hankied sleeve—"

Tanzy snickered at the description, then shut her mouth tight when he sighed. "I can't help it, you make me laugh," she said, or muffled, through closed lips.

"The truly scary thing is, I think I understood that," Riley said wryly. He shifted her on his lap and pulled her closer. "Okay, here it is: I'd like to spend Christmas with you. Not because of the threat out there, though I'll admit I'll feel better if I know where you are, that someone is keeping a close eye on you. Someone trained to keep a close eye."

"I don't know, Millicent is pretty formidable with nothing more than a monocle and cane."

Riley looked at her.

"It wasn't an answer," Tanzy said in her defense, fighting back the laughter. "It was a defense of my poor great-aunt's hand-to-hand combat skills."

Riley fought to keep a straight face, but lost the battle.

Tanzy patted him on the back. "Was it the visual that put you over the edge?"

Riley just nodded, having to wipe his eyes. "And if you tell her I laughed, I'll torture you."

Tanzy wiggled her eyebrows. "Define torture."

Riley kissed her. Suddenly, hard and fast. Then he

framed her face in his hands. "The hell with it. I didn't want you to feel obligated. Because of how we spent most of the past few hours. Or because I'm involved with this SoulM8 thing. Or even because I've bonded with your great-aunt over sports. And I don't want you to assign some huge meaning to this because it's the holiday, but—"

She couldn't wait another second. She kissed him. Only it wasn't hard and fast. It was slow, and gentle, and sweet. It was the kind of kiss she didn't give. Ever. Because slow, sweet kisses led to things, led to expectations. But it was too late to worry about that. Because she had expectations already. And spending Christmas with him was just the beginning of them. And no matter what he said about not assigning special meaning to this, the look in his eyes said otherwise.

"That was a yes. In case you were wondering." She laughed and allowed herself to soak up the moment. His eyes were shining, he was smiling, and she thought she might be falling in love. It was definitely a moment to remember. To tuck away for the future. When she might need it.

Refusing to allow any negative thoughts to creep in, she bussed him again, this time loudly and briefly. "Now I have to go downstairs to my great-aunt, aka Ol' Eagle Eye, looking like a woman who has been thoroughly kissed and, what's more, thoroughly enjoyed it."

Riley helped her slide off his lap. "I'm pretty sure, given my state of undress when she arrived, that she's figured out we've done a whole lot more than that."

Now Tanzy flushed, even as she grinned. "True. And then there's this silly grin I can't seem to wipe off my face."

Riley winked at her before turning back to the computer. "I know the feeling."

* * *

Tanzy swore she floated down the stairs. Why had she resisted this falling in love business for so long? Had her mother's foibles really jaded her so badly? Or was it her best friends' less than perfect marriages? She wasn't sure. And at the moment, she didn't care.

Maybe it was simply because she hadn't met Riley yet.

Which reminded her. She owed Millicent a hug for parking them both under the same roof. Tanzy hated to think it of herself, but it was probably true that had she not been forced to get to know him first, to live with him, deal with him, this never would have happened.

"In here, dear," Millicent called from the front room.

Tanzy slowed down so she wouldn't skip into the room, tried to tame her smile down to a reasonable glow.

"I wasn't sure where to put the tray. I hope you don't mind, I rearranged a few things on the coffee table."

"Not a problem," she said, entering the room to find Millicent staring at one of the employee-list pages J.B. had delivered.

Millicent didn't bother to look up, much less look remotely abashed for her snooping. "I take it these are the employment lists from the Internet provider you use?"

"Yes. All women, as you can see. Not as helpful as we'd hoped. We're going to cross-check them with the lists from the Crystal Ball anyway, see what we come up with."

Millicent lowered her monocle and slid the paper back with the rest of the stack. She started pouring the tea. "You haven't decorated for the holidays," she said, as if they hadn't just been discussing a stalker.

"Haven't had time," Tanzy lied. She wasn't much for holiday decorating, Christmas or otherwise. "You really outdid yourself this year, though."

"Thank you, dear," Millicent said, not distracted for one minute. "You know, a tree would look lovely in that corner right there. Perhaps when Riley's knee is better, you two should head out and get one."

"Great idea." Tanzy silently groaned, but reminded herself that Millicent rarely visited, so she'd never know if they followed through or not. She didn't bother telling her she had no ornaments to put on the thing even if they did get one. "So, what brings you here today?"

But Millicent wasn't ready to move on quite yet. "He's quite an interesting young man, your Riley."

Tanzy opened her mouth to automatically refute her implication, then closed it again.

"Well, well," Millicent said, adding sugar to Tanzy's cup before handing it to her. There was nary a wobble of china on china. Nor was there a wobble in Millicent's unwavering stare. "I'm glad to see you kept your mother's tea set," she mentioned as Tanzy took her cup and saucer. "It was her mother's, you know. Though I don't imagine it gets much use by this generation, either."

No point in lying her way out of this one. "Once or twice, when I've had guests, but mostly it just gives me a reason to keep that corner hutch in my kitchen."

"Any word from Penelope of late?"

"No," Tanzy said, taking a sip, wishing they were still talking about Christmas trees now. "I'm sure that's for the best."

Millicent sighed and stirred her own cup. "Yes, I imagine you're right."

That had Tanzy pausing midsip. "I always thought you hoped we'd mend fences. Or that I'd force more of a relationship between us."

"Years ago, perhaps. You've never said what went on when the two of you got together all those summers ago, but I suppose I can fill in the blanks well enough. It's why I've never brought it up since." She gave her tea a final stir and leaned over to pat Tanzy's knee. "Mostly I worried that you'd let her set a bad example for you. That her wanderlust and irresponsibility would keep you from finding your own happiness. And, until today, I believed she had."

"It goes a lot deeper than wanderlust, Aunt Millicent." Then the rest of what her great-aunt had said sunk in. "As for Riley, well, I won't deny that I've developed . . . feelings for him."

Millicent's smile lit her entire face. "Yes, dear. It's quite obvious. And wonderful, too. I didn't think I'd ever see that particular light brighten your lovely face."

Tanzy felt the slight sting at the backs of her eyes. *Again with the tears!* These wobbly emotions were sandbagging her out of nowhere. This part of falling in love she could do without, thanks. She went back to sipping her tea, but eventually she couldn't hide behind her cup any longer. She started to speak, stopped, then finally sighed.

"What is it, dear?" Millicent lowered her cup as well.

"I've been perfectly happy alone, Aunt Millicent. I mean, yes, I'm enjoying Riley's company. I might even . . . well, I might even feel more than joy. But I was okay before him. I'll be okay after." Even as she said it, she didn't want to think about it. The after part. "I enjoy being with him, more than I ever thought possible. But I don't need him to make me a whole, happy person. I figured you of all people would understand that and not worry about me. You're whole, happy, fulfilled, and you've never married."

Millicent surprised her by shaking her head. "That's not true, I'm afraid." Her smile faded on a wistful sigh and she absently stirred her tea. "I was married. Once. Far too briefly. Long before you were born."

Tanzy couldn't have been more floored. Her spoon clattered to her saucer.

Millicent looked fondly at her. "I guess it's a day for shattering old beliefs, hmm?" She shook her head. "I suppose I never told you because it happened so long ago." She lifted a shoulder in a slight shrug. "Or perhaps I simply didn't want to share what is still, surprisingly, a bittersweet memory." She sighed, looked away, and Tanzy thought there might have been a shine of tears in her eyes. "He was the love of my life."

"You don't have to talk about it now."

Millicent slid her lace hanky from her sleeve and dabbed at the corner of her eye. "No, it's all right. I know it's silly, but for all the years he's been gone, it still feels like yesterday when I let myself think about it." She sniffed, then smiled through watery eyes. "I sometimes have the fantastical notion that he'll come walking through the front door, so proud and tall in his uniform, and inform me it was all a big mistake, he hadn't been shot down after all." She dabbed her eyes again, then sighed and looked back to Tanzy. "I'm sorry, I feel as if I've helped to steer you down this path, and it was never my intention. I suppose I should have realized—"

Tanzy leaned forward, covered her great-aunt's hand with hers. "Please, don't. We all make our own choices. And I respect yours. I'm glad you told me, because I love you and it makes me feel good, knowing you had something that powerful in your life. Thank you for sharing with me now."

Millicent sniffed again, dabbed again. "Yes, well, perhaps we share things when it's time to share them. And I agree with you, it's good to be healthy and whole, to be your own person. I'm proud of you, of the life you've built for yourself." Now she covered Tanzy's hand with her own. "But, darling, sharing that life, the good moments and the bad, the triumphs and the defeats, with someone you love ..." She trailed off with a little sigh. "Well, you said it. It's quite powerful stuff. Magnifies the pleasures tenfold, and makes the lumps a bit easier to take."

Tanzy sniffed a little herself, wishing things had been different for Millicent. "And all this time, you never remarried," she murmured, then looked up. "But your last name—"

After a final dab, Millicent picked up her saucer again, composed once more. "In my heart, I'm still Mrs. Jack Bingham. But I reverted back to my maiden name after your grandfather died. I was the only one left to carry on the family foundations and such. And in those days, with the various laws and legalities, well, it was simply . . . easier."

But Tanzy saw that it had been anything but. Forsaking the name of the man she'd loved. Still loved. "I'm sure he'd be proud of all you've done."

Millicent smiled then, and her face glowed once again. "Thank you, dear. I'd like to think so. The odd thing is, I'd have likely walked away from it all, settled for some small house on a naval base somewhere, and raised a patch of babies, if he'd only come back to me."

Tanzy smiled, then dared a little laugh. "No, you wouldn't have. Even if Grandpapa had lived, he would have mismanaged things and that would have driven you crazy. You'd have been knee deep in the Harrington holdings long before he died, and you know it."

Millicent smiled herself. "I suppose you're right. Perhaps."

Since they'd come this far, Tanzy dared another question. "Do you regret not having children?"

Now her great-aunt's smile was wide and instantaneous. "Why no, dear. I had you, didn't I?"

Tanzy flushed instantly, with pleasure. "Why of course you did." And she wondered if Millicent knew what a godsend she'd been to a child set adrift by her only parent, despite her grandniece's outgoing personality. "But you only got me when I was home from boarding school."

"And enjoyed every moment of it."

Tanzy laughed again. "I seem to recall differently."

"That's the wonderful thing about memories, dear. You pick and choose the ones you want to keep."

Tanzy uncurled her legs and stood, then leaned over and kissed Millicent's feathery cheek. "Well, I have bunches of them," she said softly. "I don't know what I would have done without you. I don't tell you often enough, but I owe you a great deal. You kept me sane and made sure I was happy. I always knew I could count on you. It made the difference, you know. All the difference." Now her eyes were watering up again.

Millicent sniffed as well. "Well," she said, half smiling, half laughing. "Aren't we a pair?"

"Yes," Tanzy said with a broad grin, settling herself once again on the futon couch. "And a formidable one, at that. We're Harringtons, after all. Speaking of which, I've been meaning to talk to you. About the charity ball—"

"I'm still so dreadfully sorry to have put you in the public eye like that, make you so obvious a target—"

Tanzy waved a hand. "Please, Aunt Millicent. He'd have found another way, so please don't beat yourself up. What I wanted to talk about was, well, maybe I'd like to get involved. On a minor scale, that is. With the family foundations. If there is something I could do to help you. I ... enjoyed handing out those scholarships, felt proud to be a part of it, and I guess a little bit like a fraud, seeing as I haven't been directly involved." She let out a short laugh. "Involved, period."

Millicent's face lit up. "I'd be delighted to have some assistance, but only if you feel you truly want to be involved. I've never pushed you and I never will. I've made sure, as

I've gotten older, to put our many interests in as good hands as possible. You needn't worry about them, you know. Naturally, you'll be the one I leave it all to when I go, but you'll have little to do if that's how you choose to handle it. I know you have no need of the income, so I've had the bulk of it put directly back into the various foundations. You can change that, naturally. All I want is for a Harrington to maintain overall directorship."

Tanzy didn't know what to say. It was exactly what she'd wanted to hear, and settled a goodly amount of the concerns she'd managed to bury for lo these many years. "Thank you, Aunt Millicent," she said, never more sincere. "I won't let you down. And I would like to be more involved. Maybe not dive in headfirst, but rather wade in. Slowly," she warned when her great-aunt's eyes began to twinkle.

"Yes, dear," was all Millicent said.

Tanzy swallowed hard, silently wondering just how many foundations she'd be running a year from now.

"I suppose we should discuss the reason I came here today," Millicent said. "It's about the baby shower for your friend Mariel."

"If you'd really rather we don't have it at the house, it's not a problem." Although, seeing as it was two days from now, well, she didn't want to be the one to tell Sue.

Millicent waved a heavily ringed hand. "Nonsense. I'm more than happy to have them. It will do Big Harry good to have his walls ring with the laughter and joy surrounding the coming of a new life."

Tanzy had been sighing in relief, so she almost choked on her tea at that last part.

"What," Millicent said, lowering a look at Tanzy over the rim of her teacup. "Just because I didn't have any of my own—"

"Not that," Tanzy managed to choke out. "I—I wasn't aware you knew—"

"Oh!" Millicent laughed. "That. Surely you didn't think I was unaware of the moniker you bestowed on Harrington House." Then she smiled somewhat slyly. "I've rather liked it, have privately thought of it that way for years."

Well, well, Tanzy thought, *it was a day for revelations indeed.* "Thank you for letting us have the party there. Is there a problem, though?"

"Oh, not at all. I've been corresponding with Sue—"

"You have?"

"Oh yes. We've been faxing and scanning and emailing our little hearts out. She called one afternoon earlier this week, asking after you. I suppose she hadn't gotten the word that you'd moved back home. We got to talking about her decoration scheme, which is really quite inspired, and I offered a few ideas of my own."

"You did."

"Oh my yes. We've been like two bees in a bonnet ever since. Buzzing, buzzing."

Tanzy didn't doubt it. Like Millicent, Sue also had MSS. Martha Stewart Syndrome.

"I hope you don't mind. We've quite commandeered this entire party."

Tanzy waved a hand. "Please, by all means, commandeer away."

"Well, now that that's all settled, I'd also hoped to borrow Riley for a spell. This time of year, it's all but impossible to hire anyone at the last moment. Sue's dear husband, Paul, is coming by a bit later to help as well. We need to move some furniture before the decorators come in to redo the room."

Tanzy opened her mouth to ask why in the world she was having the entire room redone for a party that was only going to last several hours, but wisely stopped herself at the last second. "You'll have to ask Riley. With his knee—"

"Oh, yes, I'd forgotten about that. You see, I'd planned to discuss it with him when I arrived, but he wasn't in his vehicle, so I assumed he was in here with you and thought to take care of both little tasks at the same time." She set her saucer down and stood, smoothing her skirt. "I'm really glad I did," she said sincerely. "I've enjoyed our little talk immensely."

Tanzy stood and stepped around the coffee table to give Millicent a hug. Her great-aunt felt both sturdy and frail, and Tanzy felt tears gather behind her eyes again at the thought that she really wouldn't be here for her forever. She supposed she'd never quite believed it possible. "Thank you," she whispered. "For sharing with me, for . . . well, for all of it."

Millicent patted her back as they stepped apart. "Thank you, too," she said, her eyes a bit overly bright as well. "For everything." She sniffed and turned, walking to the hall and glancing up the stairs. "I don't suppose he's coming down anytime soon."

Tanzy followed her out into the hall. "I can run up and get him. He might be asleep." Or still at the computer, most likely. But she really didn't want to take the conversation back in that direction.

"Don't bother. Just have him ring me up when he can. If he's up to it, we'd love to have another pair of strong hands." She lifted her monocle and looked at Tanzy. "Though I suspect his powers of recovery will be swift."

Tanzy blushed, but was glad to have Millicent ornery and at her most intimidating once again. "I'll have him call you."

"Wainwright is out front, so no need to see me out."

But when Millicent turned for the front door, Tanzy put her hand on her great-aunt's arm.

"Wait. Riley's Rules, remember?" Tanzy sighed and raced up the stairs.

"Yes, dear," Millicent said, looking up the stairs after her. "I was just wondering if you did." With a satisfied little smile, she patiently waited for them to come back down.

Sharing.

Being independent is fine. More than fine, really. I've long realized it's a good thing, knowing you can be good company all by yourself. Healthy even. But I've recently been made aware of how surprisingly fulfilling it can be to share your own good company with someone you care about. It really does magnify all the wonderful things. And the bad things? Well, as it turns out, a little comfort never hurt anybody. And if there's big, strong arms involved, all the better.

20

Don't you think that one looks fine?" Riley sighed and trudged on to yet another pine tree. Frankly, he could give a rat's ass about long needle versus short needle. "You know, for someone who's never had a tree, you're being awfully picky."

The rain had ended and there was a brisk wind now. Tanzy brushed her hair back and tried to keep it out of her eyes. "Which is why this one has to be perfect."

The color in her cheeks and the light in her eyes made him feel like the class A jerk he knew he was bordering on being. He didn't want to be a wet blanket and normally would have jumped into this whole venture wholeheartedly. After all, he was the one who'd asked her to spend the holiday with him. The least he could do was get into the spirit and buy a damn tree. And he wanted to.

But he was worried about the note and hadn't yet been able to look at it, much less tell her about it. He'd almost had a heart attack when he'd seen that the photo book had been moved and the stack of papers shifted. But neither of them had said a word, so he'd kept quiet about it, intending to deal with it immediately after seeing Millicent to her car.

Only somehow they'd ended up changing clothes and leaving when she did. Millicent had all but herded them into his truck as she left, wishing them well on their tree hunt. A hunt he hadn't even known they were going on. Tanzy had explained how she'd been railroaded into it, which he had no trouble believing whatsoever, seeing as he'd somehow ended up promising to head over to Big Harry that very evening to move some furniture around.

To look at Tanzy now, you'd never guess she was doing this little chore under duress. She was all but glowing. Riley, on the other hand, was too busy watching everyone else wandering through the trees to pay much attention to her selections, much less offer his opinion. This had to be the worst place they could have come, with no clear sight paths and a possibly unrecognizable SoulM8 out there somewhere, having taken his stalking up close and personal.

She'd grabbed his hand more than once to drag him to this tree or that, and he'd carefully disengaged his hand each time, hoping she didn't notice. Not that he didn't want the contact. In fact, he rather liked how quickly it was becoming second nature to her to touch him, reach for him. But he didn't want to incite SoulM8 to taking any additional action by making him think he had competition. Of course, just being with any man might do that, but he couldn't do anything about that.

"Let's take that one," he said, pointing to the one she was holding. "It looks perfect." *And will get us the hell out of here.* If he'd had any idea she was going to make this an epic journey, he'd have turned the truck around as soon as Millicent's car was out of sight. The back of his neck was crawling and he wanted to get her home and behind locked doors. He was going to have another conversation with her about upgrading her security. It was a good idea anyway, regardless of the current threat. He didn't expect he'd get much of an argument this time, after he showed her the most recent note.

"It's got a huge gap in the back," she was saying as she turned it around. "See? Riley, you're not even looking."

He shifted his gaze back to hers, shifting his body behind her as well. "I know, and I'm sorry." He kept a running scan as he spoke. "Listen, I hate to ruin this, but I really think we need to get out of here. Now."

"What's—" She took one look at his face, then immediately followed his gaze. The color in her cheeks faded instantly. "Here? You think he's here? But—"

He took hold of her arm from the back, where no one could see, and gave her a reassuring squeeze. "Just humor me, I'll explain when we're in the truck."

Thankfully she didn't argue, and they made a beeline for the parking lot. Riley felt a lot better when they were on the road and he only had the cars behind him to scan. No one had pulled out from the lot after him, as far as he could see, but there was no use in taking chances. SoulM8 could have stayed in his vehicle, parked out along the main road, whatever. Or Riley could be completely overreacting. And he hoped to hell he was. Either way, he was going to err on the side of caution.

Tanzy folded her arms. "What's going on? What's happened? Something happened, didn't it? Before we left the house. Did Ernie tell you something? Did you guys make a match or something?"

"First of all, I want to say I'm sorry. For ruining your tree hunt."

She snorted. "Don't. I was only doing it to humor Millicent."

Riley kept his gaze split between the road and the rearview mirror. "It might have started that way, but you wanted a tree." He spared her a glance. "And as soon as I think it's safe, we're going to go back out and pick the best damn tree there is. That's a promise."

She started to argue. He merely sent her a warning glance. She made a face, which made him smile. He caught her satisfied smile from the corner of his eye. They made a good team. He wondered how long that would last.

This all seemed so easy, so natural, when neither had ever been the case in the past for him. Maybe it was because they were a lot alike, the two of them. Both valuing their independence above all else, both struggling to put family issues in perspective, neither looking for someone else to make them happy.

How they'd ended up like this, he had no idea. And yet he had no plans on walking away from it. Scary, yes. But scarier still to run from it and wonder what it could have been like if he'd had the balls to stick it out. So he was sticking it out. He had no clue what he was doing, but staying was the obvious first step.

Apparently buying a Christmas tree was going to be the second. He smiled, feeling ridiculously happy, despite the threat they were dealing with. He'd been a kid the last time he'd really celebrated Christmas. He'd figured he'd merely outgrown the hoopla. Apparently he was wrong about that.

"Okay, you're right. I guess I want a tree." She pointed a finger. "But you have to be fully involved in the selection process. If we're going to celebrate Christmas together, it's going to be an equal-opportunity holiday. Meaning we both suffer the good with the bad. Now tell me what's going on. This is the thing you wanted to talk to me about, isn't it? About SoulM8."

"I was planning to tell you when you first came downstairs. But then Millicent showed up and I wasn't about to get into it in front of her."

Tanzy dropped the defensive posture. "But that was before you got online, right after we—"

Riley slowed and pulled into the next public parking lot.

He parked facing the street and the only lot entrance so he could monitor any comings and goings. He didn't want to tell her this while trying to pay attention to the road and the rearview mirror. He looked over at her, held her gaze. "While we were in bed, or in the shower, someone put a note through your slot."

She sucked in a breath, then swore. "Into my house? He put something *in my house?*"

He was glad her anger equaled her shock and fear. It would keep her focused. He didn't bother with the I told you so's. There was no point beating her up about the security measures she'd refused to take. The look on her face was punishment enough for them both. "I haven't opened it yet, but the handwriting on the outside was consistent with that on the note we got at the dance. Ernie did email the employment lists from the charity ball, so we have those now, too. We have the guest list from Millicent, so we can compare them both with the FishNet lists. I need to run prints on the new note." He looked at her. "And the figurine. It would help tremendously if we could also get a writing sample from Martin. We have enough now to do a good comparison."

But Tanzy was only half listening to him. She was rubbing her arms, and although it was a chilly day in the city, with the wind and the damp from the rain still in the air, Riley didn't think this had anything to do with her being cold.

"Come here." He didn't give a damn who might be watching. He tugged her close, silently cursing the huge console between the seats for keeping them too far apart. He smoothed a palm over her cheek. "We're going to go by your place and pick up the lists and the card. You're going to pack a few things, get your laptop. Then you can choose. We can go back to Big Harry. Or we can go to my place.

Either/or. Both have the security systems I require in place."

Tanzy merely stared at him, nonplussed. "I, uh—"

"Don't argue with me about this, Tanzy."

She looked into his eyes, and finally nodded. "Okay. We need to go to Millicent's tonight anyway. Besides, I don't want to put you out."

"You wouldn't." Not ever. Besides, now that he'd said it, he couldn't stop picturing her in his bed. "And I know you don't want to worry your aunt. Why don't we go to my place first, deal with the card and the figurine, let me make some calls. Then we'll go to Big Harry, help Millicent with the furniture, and if you want to stay there, fine. With everything going on getting ready for the shower, we can make some excuse about staying there without getting into details about why you don't want to be at home for the time being."

Tanzy shook her head. "I don't want to lie to her." She sighed. "But you're right. I don't want to worry her." She drew her fingertips over his cheek and along his chin. They were a bit shaky, as was her voice, and he hated that anything had ever made her feel that way. "And if you don't mind too much, I'd really rather not sleep alone tonight."

Something fierce and primal uncoiled inside of him. There was no denying the power she'd conferred on him by turning to him in her time of need. But there was more at stake here than her safety. And he discovered he wanted her turning to him for . . . everything. He shifted his head, just slightly, and pulled two of her fingers into his mouth. Her eyes widened and she gasped, both in surprise and in pleasure. He let them slide out, then claimed her mouth. Slowly, with the intent to seduce, to claim, so that she wanted him in her bed every night.

Not as a big watchdog, but because she couldn't imagine him anywhere else.

"Come home with me, Tanzy," he murmured, rubbing his lips over hers.

She merely nodded, then deepened the kiss again.

Riley had to force himself to pull away, to not let his need for her cloud every last ounce of judgment he possessed. "We should move on," he said.

"Yeah." She pressed one last lingering kiss to his lips, then another one on the curve of his chin, before settling back into her seat. She sighed and when he looked at her as he backed out, he was happy to see the edge of fear in her eyes was gone. Replaced by need. For him.

"We're getting pretty good at this necking in the car thing," she said finally, "but I have to tell you, I'm feeling sort of old, because I'd really prefer a nice soft bed somewhere."

Riley grinned and pulled back out on the street. "Yeah, I know what you mean. It's hell being a grown-up, isn't it?"

He pulled into the alleyway behind her row house and tucked his SUV in behind her little sports car. "I want you to stay with me, but let me go in first."

To her credit, she didn't shudder or hesitate to follow him. She'd gotten herself together on the short ride home and Riley knew he could count on her to keep a cool head. "Okay. Let's roll."

They moved swiftly. Thankfully there were no new notes, or any other surprises, waiting for them inside. Tanzy packed with surprising speed and Riley collected the papers and envelope—the figurine was already in the truck—and slid them in a big padded mailer that Tanzy got from her office. They were back in his truck and pulling out in under twenty minutes.

He checked the dash clock. "I'm about twenty-five, thirty minutes south of here. We'll still have plenty of time to make it back to Millicent's by eight." He glanced over at

Tanzy, who'd gotten very quiet. "You hungry? Want to stop and pick something up on the way in?"

She shook her head.

With an eye on the road, he reached over and took her hand. "It's going to be okay. It will end at some point. Maybe even today, depending on what we get from the note and figurine. I know you don't want to hear that, but we can't ignore that Martin has access to your email, he was at the dance, and he has your home address. I know you're feeling hunted and I'm not ruling out the FishNet angle. But I wouldn't uproot you if—"

"Actually, I'm pissed," she said, her voice all but vibrating. "I hate giving him even this much power, to run me out of my own house." She turned her hand palm up, wove her fingers through his, and squeezed. "But I won't feel comfortable sleeping here, knowing he was right on my front porch." She swore. "Whoever the hell he is."

It was the closest she'd come to admitting her own mentor might be stalking her. Riley said nothing more. She was dealing with enough at the moment. He decided maybe he'd take the scenic route down the coast and cut across town. Then, just on the outskirts, he saw the small hand-painted sign and smiled. He slowed the truck and turned off the main road.

"I thought you said you lived south of the city."

"I do. We have one stop to make first."

She merely nodded and stared out the window, but he knew her thoughts were focused inward. On SoulM8. On Martin. On what impact it might have on her entire future. He hoped to change all that. At least for a little while.

He went a few hundred yards, then saw another hand-painted sign. He turned off just past it into a small, makeshift lot. A lot dotted with rows of fir trees.

Tanzy turned to him, and the light in her eyes went a

long way toward assuaging a bit of the guilt he felt for putting her through all this.

"You didn't have to do this."

Oh, if she could see her face, she'd know that he absolutely had to do this. "Come on. Let's go find a tree."

"Where are we going to put it? Don't you already have a tree at your place?"

He shook his head.

"God, we're a pair, aren't we?"

He smiled. "I've been thinking about that, and you might have a point." He came around to her side of the truck, but she'd already slid out. This time when she grabbed his hand, he didn't slide his back out again.

One hour later and leaving no Christmas tree unexamined, they pulled back out of the lot, a nice Douglas fir tied to the top of Riley's SUV.

"I don't suppose you have a stand," she mentioned. "And I guess I shouldn't mention that we have absolutely nothing to decorate it with."

"I don't have a stand. But . . . I do have some decorations."

Something in the tone of his voice must have alerted her; she glanced over at him. "Aha," she teased. "So you have put up a tree before. You're not as pathetic about the holidays as I am after all."

"In my own defense, I've been known to carve a pumpkin or two. But no, I haven't put up a tree in years."

"Then . . . ?"

He sighed, but instead of feeling embarrassed or, worse, emotional and sad at the memories he was dredging up, he smiled, warmed by them, by sharing them with her. It was a pleasant surprise, a welcome one at that. "When my mother died, my dad stopped putting up trees. Claimed it was silly since we were both grown men. I was still in high school, but I know he stopped because it was her favorite time of the year and he simply couldn't bring himself to deal with it. He sold the house right after I went to college, but he let me put into storage whatever I wanted for after graduation. So I . . . I kept them. The decorations."

All of them. Boxes full of memories. All good, he realized now, wondering why he'd let his father's grief, his own grief, keep him from enjoying something he could still share with his mother. It seemed almost silly now, all these years later. And yet, maybe it was the fact that he wouldn't be sharing them alone that had finally made it okay. "They're packed away in a storage shed." He grinned, that ridiculous sense of happiness filling him again. "Somewhere."

"Are you sure you want to go digging them out?"

He glanced at her. "Yeah, positive."

Tanzy didn't know what she'd been expecting. Some small bachelor pad or something. A few rooms over a storefront that housed their business, whatever. Nothing would have surprised her. Or so she thought.

It was an admitted shock when they wound their way up a semiprivate road above Pacifica, into the hills, to a small house perched at an angle on the side of a mountain. It wasn't anything fancy; in fact, it was a sort of odd patchwork of rooms sticking up and out at various angles, with a long deck jutting off around the back. She didn't know that much about real estate down this way, but she did know that, regardless of its rather remote location and less than spacious size, the view of the valley and ocean alone would put a pretty price tag on the place.

He glanced over at her, must have seen something in her expression. "It was a good investment from my playing days. It's the one thing I kept. For the equity. And the view."

She looked out over the treetops as he swung into the short gravel drive and parked in front of the garage and a small outbuilding that was probably the shed he'd referred to earlier. Then she looked back at him and found him looking out past the trees, too, to the valley and ocean beyond. This place was a whole lot more than an investment. It radiated from his eyes, from his expression, even his body language. "You kept it because it's home." She smiled. "You love it up here."

He smiled at her. "That, too."

He turned off the ignition, but didn't get out right away.

"Does your father live out here with you?"

Riley laughed. "Not hardly. He hates it out here. Doesn't understand why I don't sell the place and buy us a condo on some golf course somewhere."

"You play golf?"

Riley shook his head. "My father's addiction. I still play some pickup basketball with the guys after practice. That's hell enough on the knee." He tapped the steering wheel with his palms, then took a breath and slid out of the truck. "Come on, I'll give you the nickel tour."

Tanzy smiled as she slid out of her side of the truck. She realized he was nervous about her reaction to his place. She could have told him she didn't care if he lived in the potting shed, but she merely smiled and looped her arm through his, wanting to see his home through his eyes.

"There's not much to see," he warned.

"You know what strikes me about this place, right off?" she said, ignoring the fact that he thought she needed big and fancy to be impressed. He didn't know everything. "It's peaceful. Quiet. You sort of feel the city noise and buzz just seep right out of your bones." She laughed a little.

"Actually, you pegged it pretty well. Magnify the city sounds by thousands of people cheering in the stands and you can see why I liked coming out here during the off-season."

She slid her hand down to his as they climbed onto the long, narrow deck that started at the side door and disappeared around the back corner of the house. Part of it was screened in and she spied a huge, wide hammock dominating almost the whole front corner. "And now that the cheering crowds are gone for good?"

He shrugged and propped the screen door open with his hip. "I still need the peace and quiet." He didn't need a key, he just opened the front door. "I'll warn you, it's decorated in Early Bachelor. And the maid hasn't been here in, oh, about six years."

Tanzy laughed and stepped in behind him. Her immediate impression was warmth. The room was long, narrow, with a high beamed ceiling, part of which had been replaced with a skylight. It was a cocoon of soft, overstuffed furniture, warm golden walls, polished wooden floors, and throw rugs everywhere. "All it needs is a big dog with a sloppy tongue lolling out of his mouth." She smiled up at him. "It's wonderful."

Riley surprised her by pulling her tight up against him and taking her in a kiss quite unlike any they'd shared before. There was something distinctly possessive about it. And Tanzy discovered that was quite all right with her.

When he let her toes reach the floor again, he half laughed as he lifted his head. "Sorry."

"What for? That was the best welcome a girl could ever want. Besides the drooling dog, I mean," she teased.

"I've always wanted one," he admitted. "But I was traveling too much when I first moved here, and now, with some jobs being unpredictable, I never know when I'll be back, so . . ." He shrugged.

"Yeah, I know what you mean. I thought about getting a cat once." She laughed. "But I'm not a cat person, so that never happened. I don't know why I didn't get a dog. I guess after growing up without a pet, the responsibility just seemed too huge."

Riley led her into the small kitchen at the rear of the house. "Like I said, we're a pair."

"Yeah. Oh, how beautiful," she said, looking out the back of the house, which was almost entirely glass. The treetops dropped away to provide a stunning view of valley and ocean. "How much of it is yours?"

"Not much. Just down the hill. But the land below me is undeveloped, as is the rest on the other sides. So I get to pretend I'm king of the mountain, even if I'm not."

She laughed. "It's good to be the king." Turning back to him, she said, "It's really stunning. I can see why you hung on to it."

There was a flash then of ... something in his eyes. "What?" She walked closer, put her hands on his arms. It was so natural, touching him, going to him. It amazed her when she let herself think about it. "Come on, tell me."

"It's nothing really. I just—" He laughed, shook his head, but there was no amusement in his eyes when he looked past her to the trees beyond the window. It was more like ... resignation.

She wished she knew what to say, surprised by how much even his mild discontent bothered her. She supposed this was part of it, too. This falling in love stuff. Even though she was perfectly aware that he was a grown man who was responsible for making his own happiness. And, if asked, she wouldn't have had it any other way. She knew, because she felt exactly the same about her own happiness. And yet she found she wanted to do something, anything, to make him smile, make him happy. It was shocking, really.

"What is it?"

He sighed. "Nothing, really. I've been wrestling lately with that whole condo on the golf course thing. With the idea of selling this place."

Surprised, she asked, "Would he really be happier, knowing you had to give this up?"

"He doesn't get all that sentimental about stuff. If I sold this place, he could retire, spend his days chasing a white ball around perfectly manicured turf. He gave up a lot for me, so I could go to college, chase my dreams of chasing a football around a different kind of turf. My promise to him, if I made it, was to make that dream of his come true. We've been trying, through the business, or I have anyway, but—" He stopped, shrugged. "I shouldn't have mentioned it. I guess it's the whole holiday thing."

She rubbed his arm. "Certainly he understands that more than his dreams were crushed when your knee was mangled."

He looked down at her then, a half smile curving his lips. She knew, in that moment, that she was no longer falling. She was there.

"It sounds so rational when you say it," he said with a wry smile. "But I could have made it happen. I guess that's the hard part to swallow, even now. I'd invested wisely. I didn't need much anyway, just for me. But Finn, well, he's got an eye for the ladies, but not much of one for business. The managing of it, anyway. He's good enough at what he does, very good actually, but—" He shrugged. "It took most of what I had to bail him out. But we still had the business, so what else was I supposed to do? I figured if I could get it up and solid, maybe we'd both eventually have something to retire on."

"But your dad isn't interested in the long-term payoff, I take it."

Riley nodded. "I guess he thought waiting all through school, college, then me finally making it through the draft into the pros was long-term enough."

"What about what you wanted to do? You said something about being a coach, at the college level."

"I figured there would be time for that later, after he retired. If I still wanted it. Only it looks like I'm going to have to think a bit long-term myself."

She slid her arms around his waist and hugged him. "What you did for your dad was—is—wonderful, but surely, sentimental or not, he wouldn't want you to give up this place, too. Doesn't it already bother him that you're working the business with him, instead of what you'd really rather be doing? Isn't that sacrifice enough?"

Riley shook his head. "It's more complicated than that. We're all we have. And I guess I wanted to share something with him, for all that he did for me, with sports. He was never into it himself. I thought this was a way for us to, I don't know, bond or something."

She looked up at him, waited for him to shift his gaze to hers. "Is it working?"

Riley laughed, this time the amusement reaching his eyes. "I'm not sure. We're making a run at it. And the business is steady enough. Accepting the job working for your aunt was a definite move in the right direction."

"Hoping for recommendations, are you?"

"That's how the business works. But Finn's still more interested in play than work. He gets the job done, for the most part, but there's no fire in his belly to really make something of it. He's past that, I guess. I think he's hoping I'll do it, the next generation and all that. He's trained me well enough. I'm good at the job. Though you wouldn't know it by how I've handled things with you, I guess."

She grinned, sliding her hands down to his quite fine

derriere. "Oh, you've handled things well enough, let me assure you."

"Have I, now?" He dipped his head, nipped at her lower lip, teased her with a few kisses, until she sighed and leaned into him, cupping him to her hips and moaning in appreciation at what she discovered when she did.

"Does the nickel tour include the bedroom?" she murmured, more than willing to let the subject change. This was his refuge and she felt bad that she'd dredged up old feelings probably better left undredged. "Actually, a tour of that couch would be perfectly fine." She shot him a fast grin. "As long as there's no console in the middle of it."

He kissed her in response, and she forgot all about aborted careers and parental expectations. Thoughts of stalkers and danger seemed far away.

"I think we can find our way to bed," he murmured against her mouth.

He did sweep her up in his arms this time, muffling her protest with another kiss. A short hallway later, the wide bed met his back with a soft thump. She bounced against his chest, and was quickly rolled beneath him. She reached for his shirt, but he pinned her wandering hands to the bed.

"Uh-uh. We've got hours. I'm taking this slow." To prove his intent, he began a lazy trail with his tongue. He unbuttoned the shirt she'd put on to hunt for trees when they'd left with Millicent, what seemed like a century ago now. He nudged aside her bra, and spent an inordinate amount of time making her moan as he toyed with her nipples.

His mouth moved tantalizingly lower. She arched her back. Hours of this? She should be so lucky. She almost giggled. Oh yeah. She *was* that lucky.

Then it would be his turn. Oh yes. She'd make him forget all about the pain in his knee. And, if she was really good, the one in his heart as well.

She hadn't forgotten about the note that hadn't been opened, the lists that needed comparing. The figurine. But at the moment, she simply couldn't think of anything more important than spending the afternoon making love with Riley.

Take that, SoulM8.

Holidays.

I always thought they were for kids. I guess that was my way, being single and all, of avoiding assigning them too much importance. No use borrowing sorrow, I always say.

As it happens, I've come to the conclusion that I was right. Holidays are for kids. The trick, I've discovered—or should I say someone helped me discover—is to find the kid inside of you. Even if you never knew you had one. It's trickier, but I'm here to tell you it can be done. Then celebrate. With that same sense of deliberate joy.

Before you know it, you'll even believe Santa really does exist. (And, as it happens, he has nothing to do with nooners at the Four Seasons.)

21

They didn't get the tree put up until the next day. Tanzy watched him struggle with several boxes of ornaments before she'd remanded him to the couch and taken over the entire decorating operation.

His knee still had to be screaming from the furniture they'd moved out of Millicent's parlor the night before. Not to mention the things they'd done when they'd gotten back last night in the wee hours.

And then she'd woken up at five A.M. to an empty bed. It was Riley's bed, though, so she hadn't felt all that alone. She'd scuffed around and found him tucked in a small office up a short staircase at the other end of the house, comparing lists and scanning fingerprints he'd lifted from the second note. To her great disappointment, Wile E. Coyote had provided no usable prints. She hadn't realized how far Riley had compromised her absolute belief in Martin's innocence until she'd felt that teensy shred of relief that the surface of the figurine had been too deeply grooved to offer up even a partial. Not that she didn't want this to end. Martin or no Martin. But everything was going to change if it was him. And she hated that she'd begun to doubt her own mind where he was concerned.

She'd left Riley at the computer and had gone back to

the kitchen and made a fresh pot of coffee. Even better, he'd had cold soda in the fridge. *Yep, they were going to cohabitate just fine.* She'd nudged some coffee at his elbow, then curled up in the recliner with her soda and the remainder of the lists.

The note inside the envelope had been short and to the point.

I am yours. You will be mine. Eternally.

Tanzy shuddered every time she thought about it. *Eternally.* Not "for the rest of my life." Eternally. As in, even after she was no longer part of this world. Again, the note could be interpreted as merely obsessed . . . or potentially homicidal. The only thing that kept her from losing it altogether was the anger she experienced every time she thought about the cowardly sicko creeping around on her front porch.

She'd already apologized to Riley for not taking his security suggestions more seriously. The prints on both notes matched. And Riley had made her promise to set up a face-to-face meeting with Martin so they could obtain a print. And a handwriting sample if she could swing it. She'd agreed it was the best course of action. All the while hating that it had come to this.

And then, after such a disappointing morning, they were rewarded by the discovery of a matching name right around noon. One Margaret Swingler. She'd been part of the wait staff at the Crystal Ball, a temp hired to handle the extra demands such a large shindig put on the catering service the foundation usually hired to oversee their functions. She had also been employed by FishNet since their inception, two years before.

Riley had rousted Ernie via phone and the two of them

had started digging, but as yet, no connection to the notes or the fingerprints had been made. If Margaret was a relative or a friend of SoulM8's, they were going to have a hard time proving it without her help. Which was exactly why Riley planned to be at FishNet headquarters this afternoon when Margaret got off work. If they couldn't talk to her there, he planned to do whatever it took to get Lori Sack to free up more personal information about her. Like the home phone and address they'd thought would be easy to obtain, but Ernie was, so far, having no luck digging up. She'd done the impossible, according to him. She'd managed to keep her personal info off the Internet.

But the confrontation with Ms. Swingler wasn't happening for another five hours or so. Plenty of time to get a tree decorated, right? Tanzy looked at the stack of bedraggled boxes piled in front of their slightly listing tree. Her euphoria over having a suspect other than Martin was waning in the face of her current project. "I'm feeling a bit like Charlie Brown here."

Riley shifted the ice pack on his knee so he could lean over and reach the top box. He hauled it into his lap before she could stop him. "I'll unwrap and pass, you make all placement decisions."

"Shouldn't we put lights on it or something?"

"There's probably a bunch in one of these boxes, but the chances of any of them working are about nil. Christmas lights seem to have a limited life span, in my memory."

"I wouldn't have a clue how to put them on anyway. It's going to be amateurish enough." She laughed. "Thank God the chances of Millicent seeing our creation are about as great as those lights working."

Riley smiled and flipped off the lid of the first box. His smile faltered, then turned a bit wistful as he pulled out a half-wrapped ornament, letting the crumple of tissue paper fall away to the floor, instantly forgotten as he turned the crudely made football over in his hands. "Bulldogs," he murmured, then rolled it over. "R.P. '85."

Tanzy watched him in silence, wishing like hell she had a clue what to say, what to do. "You sure you're up for this?" she asked quietly.

He nodded, then handed her the heavy lump of fired clay. "Yeah. I made this for my mom in art class. I think this was the last year we put up a tree. Before she got too sick to help." He laughed. "I'm sure she loved getting a football. Not very sentimental, I guess. Except when it came to sports."

"I'm guessing she loved it." Tanzy turned so he wouldn't see the sheen in her eyes. He was more sentimental than he thought he was. She very carefully hung it from one of the bigger branches.

Riley continued to uncover treasures from his past. Some ornaments had stories, some didn't. He made her laugh, and more than a few times he brought tears to her eyes.

"And you call me sentimental," he said as she sniffed suspiciously while hanging a baby ornament of his.

"If I am, it's all your fault." She stepped back. "I think we've crammed as much of your past on here as we possibly can." She wandered around the tree, trying to look at it objectively. From a purely aesthetic standpoint, it was godawful. But from a heart and soul standpoint, she'd never seen anything more beautiful.

Riley came to stand behind her. She hadn't heard him get off the couch. He leaned down and pressed a kiss to her neck. "Thank you," he whispered. And there was more emotion in those two words than she'd heard in her entire life.

She turned in his arms, a teasing smile on her face. "As

therapy goes, this has got to be cheaper, not to mention more fun. Maybe I should ring my mom up, see if she's got any ornaments stashed about from her childhood."

Riley's eyes were swimming with emotions. Too many for her to name. He cupped her face, kissed her so gently, so sweetly, it made her eyes water all over again. "I'm sorry," he said.

"What on earth for? Because I've suddenly got faucets for eyes?"

"Did you ever have a tree?"

"Sure. Dozens. Every year, in fact, at Millicent's."

"I meant one of your own." He nodded at the stuff hanging somewhat drunkenly from every branch. "With all the goofy detritus the public school system foists off on our poor, unsuspecting parents."

"I didn't go to public school. And my parents weren't around, remember?"

"What about Millicent?"

"I love her dearly, she was my savior, but she's not exactly in touch with her inner five-year-old." She laughed a little, even as she sniffed and pulled out of his arms. "Enough of this. I've got a tree now, don't I? And at this rate I'm going to look like I've been sobbing for hours at Sloan's opening tonight."

Riley frowned. "What opening?"

"Oh, didn't I mention it last night?"

He snagged her arm as she danced around the empty cartons, and spun her easily back against him. "No, as a matter of fact, you didn't."

"I could have sworn you were standing there while Sue and I were talking about it."

"I was numb from shoving around furniture that weighs more than the average Japanese import."

"Ah," Tanzy said, then kissed him fast and hard, before

ducking out of his arms. "Well, the plan is that Sue is going to keep Wolfgang preoccupied so I can corner Sloan for a few minutes alone and get the lowdown on what's going on with her. Call it a friendly intervention. Besides, we need to clear the tension before the shower tomorrow."

"What time? And how do I dress?"

Tanzy looked up at him, surprised. "You don't have to go. I'll be well looked after and Sloan always has tight security at these things. It's invitation only. I can give her Margaret Swingler's name and photo if that will make you feel any better. And she knows Martin," she added grudgingly. "He's not on the list for this thing anyway."

Riley just looked at her. "What do I wear?"

Tanzy started to argue, but she really wanted him with her. And not just for security purposes. "Casual nice."

"I can manage that. Do we need to go by your place to get something?"

She shook her head. "Just run me by Big Harry first. I've got enough stuff there. In fact, do you want to just drop me there while you and Ernie corner Ms. Swingler? I promise to stay barricaded behind Harry's massive and very heavily alarmed doors."

"I'll think about it. But first we've got something else to do."

She snugged up behind him. "We do, do we?"

He grabbed her hands before they could travel any lower than the waistband of his sweats. "Not that."

She tried not to pout. "What, then? Are you hungry? Because Sloan will have tons of food. Of course, it's all haute cuisine and horrible."

"Remind me to stop for a burger or a taco or something, then. But that's not it, either." He tugged her hand and headed to the kitchen. He wasn't limping, so the ice and Advil must have kicked in.

"I owe you, you know."

He glanced over his shoulder. "For what?"

"You're willingly attending an art gallery show, exposing yourself to dreadfully pretentious people, talking about whacko-looking paintings as if they have some deeper meaning, and eating snails stuffed with pâté or something equally disgusting. The champagne will be top-notch, though. Maybe we can snag a bottle and come home early."

He turned, smiling. "And watch the game."

She was already nodding, happy he was getting in the spirit. "Sure, and watch the—What game?"

"Basketball. Lakers are playing the Nets. Kobe and Kidd. We can begin your education."

She wanted to pout, to come up with any excuse. She had a column to write. She knew from this morning that he had other jobs he had to do billing for, and two proposals to work on that Finn hadn't gotten around to doing yet. But none of that mattered. "I guess this is the compromise part of having a relationship."

He nodded, quite satisfied. "If it makes you feel any better, while we watch I'll pop some of the best popcorn you've ever tasted. You'll be the first woman to learn the game sipping champagne and eating snack food."

"I suppose I can live with that." She nodded behind him. "So, what are we doing in here if we're not cooking?"

He walked over to the cabinet and pulled out a canister of flour, then got down a few other ingredients. "We're going to make some Christmas ornaments. I don't have any paint, so we'll have to use the Magic Markers I use for drawing up game plans for the guys, but—"

"Whoa-ho-ho. The tree is about to collapse under the weight of four hundred ornaments as it is. Three hundred and ninety-nine of which are football related. That's enough, don't you think?"

He merely shook his head and got out a bowl. "I'm not sure exactly what goes into this, but how hard can it be, right? As long as it's hard as a rock when we're done baking it is all that matters."

She grudgingly pulled out a stool at his small breakfast bar. "We're wasting time that could be spent making other, far more pleasurable things rock hard, but whatever."

He turned to her and planted his palms on the counter. She began to see why J.B. listened when Coach Parrish talked.

"You said this was your tree," he stated. "Well, until you have something of yours on it, you're really just borrowing my tree. Not the same thing at all."

"Can't we just go buy an ornament?"

He looked horrified. "Do you see any store-bought ornaments on that tree?"

"Do you really want me to answer that?"

He grinned. "It will make the other ornaments feel bad if you show them up with some glitzy designer ornament. Besides, it will mean more if you make it."

She groaned, but it was only halfhearted. He was cute when he was committed. "I've created a Kris Kringle-monster. How is it you've managed to have no tree for all these years, feeling as strongly as you do about all of this?"

He just shrugged, grinning unrepentantly.

And she had to admit, making him happy made her happy, too. "Okay. I know when I'm beaten. But does it have to be a football? Can it be something that means something to me?"

"Whatever your heart desires. And your fingers can create."

"I think you know how creative my fingers can be."

He gave her a warning glance. "No funny stuff. And when they're done and baking, I'll let you wash us both off in my shower."

Tanzy sighed, quite contentedly. Riley's home was modest by any standards, but the one upgrade he'd made was tearing out a walk-in closet next to the bathroom and turning the whole thing into a state-of-the-art sauna and whirlpool. For him it meant continued mobility. For her, it was just heaven. "Deal."

An hour and much flour coverage later, she had a perfectly hideous pair of high-heeled shoes baking in Riley's oven. "Jimmy Choo would roll over in his grave, if he were dead. If he saw these, it just might do the trick."

Riley peered through the glass window. "They'll look a lot better when you color them in."

She laughed and pulled him up and around so she could circle his waist with her arms. "Liar." Then she reached up and kissed his floured face, leaving wet lip prints on his cheek and chin. "Thank you anyway."

"For?" he asked dubiously.

"Well, not for proving that I missed out on the dreaded MSS gene. I have no regrets there."

"I'm not even going to ask."

"Smart man. But I guess it is nice to know I'm going to contribute in some way to Big Scary in there."

He laughed and kept her laughing all the way to the steam room. It didn't take long for their laughter to fade to sighs . . . and a few screams and growls for good measure.

By the time they showed up at Sloan's gallery, Riley's afternoon of wild sauna sex with Tanzy was a forgotten pleasure. Margaret Swingler had phoned in sick. And no amount of charm or blackmail was going to get Lori Sack to cough up more personal information. If the police came asking, she might consider it. Emphasis on *might*.

Riley had actually considered going to the locals. But

all he had at the moment were untraceable prints and a coincidence. And for all he knew, the fact that Swingler had been linked to FishNet and the charity ball was just that, a coincidence. Stranger things happened all the time. But his gut told him otherwise. Or maybe he was just really hoping that it would be anyone other than Martin Stanton.

Regardless, he maintained a steady presence at the front door of the gallery, standing between Sloan's hired muscle and the small office that Tanzy had dragged Sloan into moments earlier. At least there was only one entrance being used tonight, and one door to the office. He was still restless. All his instincts told him SoulM8 was gearing up for another pattern change. A major one. Once he'd crossed the boundary into Tanzy's personal space by coming onto her property, all bets were off as far as Riley was concerned.

On the one hand, he wanted to drag her out of there, back to his place, where his property was fully monitored. Even if SoulM8 got lucky and tracked them down, he'd never get within a hundred yards of the house without Riley and half the universe knowing about it.

On the other hand, he wanted to coax the sick bastard out into the open, where he could nail his ass down and put a stop to this harassment. Permanently.

One of Tanzy's friends chose that moment to sidle over. And she sidled quite smoothly. "Riley, right? I'm glad you and Tanzy could make it." Tall, sleek, and beautiful, she lifted a slender, heavily ornamented hand out to him. "I'm Rina."

"Yes, I know. Tanzy's spoken of you," he said when she raised an elegantly arched brow.

"All good, I hope."

Riley dredged up his social smile. "Naturally."

"Aren't you the smooth one." She laughed and the honest

warmth eased a bit of Riley's discomfort. "I take it this isn't your usual stomping ground."

Now his smile came more easily. "That obvious?"

"Only to someone who's been to more than her share and would be anywhere else at the moment if it weren't her best friend's livelihood at stake."

"It looks like Sloan is doing well."

Rina looked around, obviously proud of her friend's success. "She sure has. Have you met her? And Wolf?"

"Yes, earlier. Quite a pair." He knew from Tanzy's play-by-play of her friends and their abbreviated histories on the ride down that Rina wouldn't take offense at the characterization.

"Yes, they are. I know you met Sue and Paul last night. Mariel was supposed to be here, too, but she wasn't feeling up to it. It's getting close to her due date and she tires pretty easily. Of course, that's no surprise considering it looks like she's carrying three. Or one with lots of matching luggage," she added with a cheeky grin.

Riley laughed, understanding more why Tanzy liked Rina so much.

"I get tired just watching her get out of a chair," she said. "It's a good thing we decided to have this party for her before the holidays. I'm not so sure she's going to make it much past. Will you be there, too? At the shower, I mean?"

Riley nodded, careful to continue to monitor the front door. Normally chatty women, especially when he was working, could be irritating in the extreme. Rina was an exception. The cadence of Rina's voice was well modulated, almost musical, very soothing.

"Any news on the email-stalker front?" she asked. "I'm sorry, I couldn't help but notice you were 'on duty,' so to speak. I know Tanzy wasn't happy that Millicent interfered, but the rest of us are much more at ease knowing she's got you watching out for her."

Riley's attention turned more fully back to her. He'd gotten Tanzy to agree not to tell them any more details of the investigation. Or anything about Martin being a suspect. If it ended up that he was innocent, the fewer people that knew he'd ever been suspected, the better. Especially where Tanzy's career was concerned. And as much as she trusted her friends, even Tanzy knew the wrong thing could be said at the worst time.

What he didn't know was whether Rina and Company were aware of the change in their relationship in the past twenty-four or so hours. He hadn't thought to embargo that bit of information. Wasn't sure if he would even if he had thought about it. But he wasn't going to be the one to enlighten her, either. It was enough, for the moment, that he'd been accepted into Tanzy's inner circle with relative ease.

Of course, they all thought he was the hired help, but it was a start.

"We're monitoring several things," he said noncommittally.

Rina rubbed her arms despite the growing warmth in the place as the bodies began to fill up the space. "I can't imagine dealing with that kind of thing. I worry about her. I just hope you end it soon."

"So do I," Riley said, knowing she couldn't possibly understand just how sincerely he meant it.

"Well," she said, "I won't keep you. My husband is around here somewhere, buying God knows what." She squeezed his arm. "It was nice to meet you finally." Then she leaned in, a rather wicked grin on her face. "And no matter what, don't let her independent streak scare you away. You're the best thing that has ever happened to her."

Riley studied Rina's face, saw the knowing look in her eyes. "I'm not going anywhere," he said, and meant it. He knew that despite what Tanzy felt for him, or was coming to feel for him, what her friends thought would carry a lot of weight. "As for the rest, I'm thinking the same thing could be said about her."

Rina's face lit up and she clapped her hands before scooting off. Probably to alert the masses.

Riley frowned. A tactical slip, but what the hell. He was a goner and he might as well admit it.

And just to discombobulate him further, he looked to the door just in time to see another wealthy socialite, dripping in fur and jewels, step through the door. What made this particular woman stand out was the man on her arm.

"Dad?"

Finn turned, then grinned widely and scooted immediately over to his son, half dragging the beautiful redhead behind him. To Finn's credit, Riley noted, she was at least within a decade of his father's age. In fact, she was actually a member of Finn's peer group. He also realized that Finn was not all that surprised to see him. Meaning he finagled his way in here on purpose. He had no idea how Finn had known where he was this evening, but as he'd told Tanzy, his father was very good at his job, when he wanted to be.

He wondered what he wanted. He really wasn't prepared to introduce him to Tanzy. Yet. Or more specifically, Tanzy to him. He'd been thinking, oh, maybe six or seven years from now, when they decided to have kids, would have suited him much better.

He returned his father's hearty handshake and just as hearty backslapping hug. It had been almost a month since they'd laid eyes on each other, but he knew Finn would greet him just the same if they'd seen each other yesterday. It was part of his charm. And, Riley had to admit, he enjoyed knowing it was sincere where his son was concerned.

Finn was much shorter than Riley, though otherwise

they looked a great deal alike, except Finn's hair was a bright shock of white these days.

"Son, I'd like to introduce you to someone very important to me. Riley, this is Jacqueline Assante."

Riley was only mildly surprised. He'd assumed the woman was Patsy Shackelford, but it was no surprise that Finn had already moved on. He pasted on an attentive smile anyway, privately thinking this made Important Person No. 126,546. "A pleasure, I'm sure."

"I hope you think so," she said, with a fair bit more flair than Riley had expected. He glanced from his father's face back to Ms. Assante's and received a little shock. He knew that expression. He might not have a month ago, but he certainly did now. Because it was the same one that stared back at him from the mirror these days.

"Your father and I met years ago," Jacqueline was saying. She sent Finn a brief, very private smile, then turned back to Riley. "We ran into each other again just recently, and well, I must admit, he's charmed his way right back into my life, and into my heart."

Riley noticed Finn was beaming. He'd never really seen that particular look on his father's face. Like he'd won the lottery and hit a hole in one, all at the same time. It was a little bit of a shock.

"I realize this is neither the place nor the time to be getting into all this," she went on, "so we'd very much like it if you would agree to have dinner with us. Perhaps for Christmas? If you don't have other plans, that is."

Riley looked from Jacqueline to his father, at a loss for words. His father had the grace to look a little abashed for having ambushed him. Although, from even this brief an association with Jacqueline, he doubted his father had any real control over her. And it was that thought, and the corresponding reaction that she might, in fact, be exactly what his father needed, that brought the real smile to his face and unstuck his tongue. "I'd be honored. But I'll have to get back to you on the exact time, if you don't mind."

Finn stepped in, took his son's hand in another exuberant pump, and quietly said, "I'm sorry to spring this on you so sudden, boyo."

Riley grinned. "No, no, that's okay." And he meant it. He'd said he wanted to do something to bond with his father. And it appeared the Parrish men might just accomplish that after all. Only instead of it being a business affair, it looked to be an affair of the heart. Their hearts.

Jacqueline tugged Finn back. "We've bothered him enough. Can't you see the man's working? Come on, I promised to amaze you with my total lack of art education."

Finn merely smiled and shrugged and let himself be tugged away. He shot a wink at his son over his shoulder. Riley couldn't help it. He laughed. His father actually looked . . . well, happy. The kind of happy he hadn't been in years. Riley thought there might be something to the idea that it all came down to the power of the love of a good woman. They'd both just gone about finding it in an entirely different way.

Just then Tanzy popped out of the office. Sloan didn't follow. Riley wondered if she was hiding out from an ambush by the rest of the gang. "How did it go?" he asked.

Tanzy half shrugged, half shook her head, as if she was still trying to make sense of it all. She blew out a short breath and said, "Well, apparently Sloan and Wolf are getting a divorce."

"Oh no. I'm really sorry. I suppose that explains why he only made a brief appearance tonight."

"Yeah. And, I have to admit that while I wish it had worked out better for them, after talking to Sloan, I'm glad for her. She's, uh, well, found someone else."

"Oh? I thought Wolfgang was the infamous philanderer." Their rocky marriage had been section three of the play-by-play.

"He was. Is, in fact. Sloan was fed up and had already told Wolf he either went to counseling with her or it was over."

"I take it he opted out?"

"Actually, no. He took their marriage counselor to bed. Sloan's bed."

"Ouch."

"Yes, well, Wolf will have to hang his art in someone else's home. And gallery, I suppose. And the marriage counselor is facing a board inquiry and will likely lose her license."

"Sounds fair. But where did Sloan's extracurricular activity come into play?"

"Well, seems she started getting Swedish massages at the gym."

"Wait a minute, she slams hubby for fooling around with a paid professional, then she—"

"Hold on to your male indignation. She ran into him socially, outside the gym, at some business function. I have no idea how. And they went out for drinks. She switched to a new masseur at the gym, and well, the next time she met with Lars it was for more than after-party drinks."

"Lars?"

Tanzy snickered. "I know. And he's about six years younger than she is, too. But I swear, I've never seen her happier. She looked . . . free. I guess I never realized just how much of her stress wasn't work related. Which is another thing. Lars has already talked her into taking some kind of dance class thing with him. And next weekend, they're heading out of town to go snowboarding." She laughed. "Sloan. On a snowboard. I still can't bring up that visual."

"Sounds like maybe it has worked out for the best."

"Yeah. Now we just have to talk her into bringing him around so we can all meet him, then dish about him later."

Riley wanted to ask her if they'd done that to him yet, but managed to take the wiser course.

"When I came out, you were grinning. Who were you talking to?"

"Oh, uh." No point in even trying to get around it. "Finn showed up. With a date."

"Your father's here?" She looked around, eyes wide with surprise. "Can I meet him?"

"We're going to meet them for Christmas. If you're up for it." Maybe Finn wouldn't be the only one dropping bombshells that night. And despite all the hearts and flowers in the air, Riley wasn't looking forward to that little revelation. Finn would have a field day with it. "But right now, I'd love to get out of here. I feel like I've been sharing you for hours and I'm getting a bit greedy."

Tanzy smiled up at him. "Funny, I was thinking the same thing. Did you meet any of my other friends? I told them to come make nice with you."

"Rina. I didn't meet her husband, though. And I'm guessing you did more than tell her to make nice."

Tanzy shrugged, her smile turning a bit winsome. She didn't pull that off all that well. "You don't mind, do you?"

He shook his head. He could have told her just how accurately he understood her need to tell someone. He wanted to shout it to the world. To everyone but Finn, anyway. "If you're through with your intervention, let's blow this pop stand."

"Yes, my work here is done." She tugged on his hand, stopping him just inside the door. "I almost forgot. I had a brainstorm. About the whole fingerprint and handwriting-sample thing. I left a message on Martin's pager inviting him to Big Harry tomorrow. I said I needed to go over the column and I was having some other concerns I needed to discuss. I made it pretty ambiguous, but serious-sounding enough that I think he'll make the date."

"During the shower?"

"I figured that was the best way. With all those people around, and you there monitoring, plus Big Harry's security, it would really be the best place for a showdown."

"Does he know about the shower? Men traditionally like to be far away, preferably courtside, during those types of functions."

Tanzy grinned. "Nope. He just thinks it's a business meeting. I didn't mention why we were meeting at Millicent's. He'll probably assume I'm there for the holidays."

"And do you actually have something planned to talk about?"

"I'm still working on that part."

Riley smiled, then squeezed her hand. "Thank you. For doing this. I know this isn't easy on you. I know he's been a very important person to you." He leaned down and kissed her, in front of Rina, Finn, and artwork that defied description, though likely no one was paying the slightest bit of attention.

Riley held Tanzy's hand all the way home. The silence between them was easy and his thoughts wandered. To all the memories that had rushed to the surface earlier, to the things he'd told her about Finn, her reactions to it all. He thought about his father's expression tonight and what this new wrinkle might mean to their joint business venture. Which led him to think a great deal about personal happiness and what he owed himself, and Finn. And, maybe, Tanzy, too.

And somewhere between San Francisco and Pacifica, he realized he'd be dropping another bombshell at dinner with Finn and the woman he had a strong suspicion was about to become his stepmother. If Finn didn't drop it first.

Baby showers.

Does one tiny human being really need all that stuff? And here I thought we didn't get to be that high maintenance until we fit into our first pair of high heels.

22

Tanzy's mouth dropped open as she stepped into what had been Millicent's formal parlor. She supposed she should have paid more attention to Sue's excited ramblings the night they'd come to move furniture around. Then the eight-foot Mother Goose and the close-to-life-size Old Woman in a Shoe, complete with shoe, wouldn't have been such a shock.

Sue linked her arms through Tanzy's and Riley's, her eyes sparkling. "Isn't it amazing?"

"That's one word for it," Tanzy murmured, taking in the rest of the details. Three stuffed mice, each with black sunglasses, each about three feet tall, danced on the hearth in front of the stone fireplace. "Let me guess—"

"Three Blind Mice," Sue finished excitedly. "I had thought the Mother Goose theme would be fun since that's how Mariel is decorating the nursery. But your great-aunt just took my ideas and ran with them. I've told her a hundred times already that this was far more than necessary, but she kept telling me—"

"It's my pleasure, dear," Millicent finished herself, as she stepped into the room. "Riley," she said, greeting him with a smile and pat on the arm. "Brave man, stepping into the world of babies and expectant mothers and the like."

Riley grinned, darting Tanzy a quick look when her great-aunt presented her cheek.

Tanzy just winked at him, and Riley bestowed the expected kiss, then gracefully and somewhat abashedly accepted a buss on his cheek in return. "Actually," he said, after clearing his throat, "I'd hoped to use Tanzy's office for a while." He patted the carrying case he had over one shoulder. "I've brought some work."

Tanzy knew he'd brought surveillance equipment as well, or whatever he needed to tap into the stuff Millicent already had set up. He wanted to keep an eye on Big Harry's grounds and the comings and goings of the guests. Tanzy had drawn the line at making this some high-security, supersecret event. It was Mariel's day and she wasn't going to let this other mess interfere. Any more than necessary anyway. Big Harry was well secured and Riley would certainly spot anyone out of the ordinary on his monitors. He had the guest list. And his was the only male name on it other than Martin's, so it shouldn't be all that hard.

In the meantime, Ernie was putting in some overtime trying to track down Margaret Swingler's home address. Riley had sworn to Tanzy in bed that morning that he'd have this dealt with and over before the new year. Tanzy was all for that. She wished she felt better about her upcoming faux meeting with Martin, though. Her stomach wouldn't stop clenching. She kept telling herself the setup was a good thing, that by the time they left here today, Martin would be in the clear and they could focus all their attention on the Swingler woman.

"I'm going up," Riley whispered in her ear.

"Okay," she said, suddenly wishing he wasn't leaving, even just to go upstairs. She felt more than a little uneasy, and who wouldn't with an eight-foot goose breathing down their neck? But beyond the meeting with Martin, she also knew she'd been thinking about what happened when the case was wrapped up. Her future. Their future. He'd asked her to accompany him to dinner to meet his father and his father's woman friend, so that was some indication he saw this—them—sticking around together for a bit longer. She stretched up on her toes and kissed him. "I'll sneak up later, after Martin comes and goes. I'll bring you whatever I can get him to touch. And if I'm really good, a handwriting sample."

"Oh, you're really good," he said, investing just enough velvet into his tone to make her momentarily forget about everything else. "I can personally vouch for that."

She grinned, wishing she could do more than kiss him for the confidence his easy tone and grin instilled in her. "Thanks." She looked over his shoulder at the women beginning to crowd into the foyer, all bearing gifts wrapped in miles of pastel and ribbon. "I'll probably need a sanity check within the hour anyway," she murmured.

Riley grinned down at her, kissed her back. "Be brave, grasshopper."

She stuck her tongue out at him. He was chuckling as he left the room. Tanzy turned back, to find Sue grinning from ear to ear, arms folded as she waited expectantly.

"What?"

"This." She motioned between Tanzy and the spot where Riley had been standing. "You're impossibly cute with him. And that's so unlike you."

She stuck her tongue out at Sue. It seemed wrong to flip her the bird in front of Mother Goose. "Ha, ha. We're . . ." She tried to think of some throwaway line, but it was Riley. And Sue was one of her best friends. And she just couldn't. She blew out a breath. "This isn't the time or the place. You've got women bearing baby gifts descending on this place any second. But I gotta tell you, Sue, this whole relationship thing is a hell of a lot scarier than I thought."

"I don't know, you two seem to have fallen right into it like old hats."

"That's just it. We have. Is that normal? I mean, what if just when I start to get used to this, something happens, or he changes his mind, or—" She made a disgusted sound. "Listen to me. I sound like a silly teenager in the bathroom at the high school dance, wondering if Johnny really likes me." She looked back at Sue with big eyes. "But honestly, do you think he does, Susie, huh? Do you? Will he ask me to the prom?"

Sue cracked up laughing, then tugged Tanzy into a hug. "I'm so glad you've joined the herd. We're all going to enjoy this immensely."

Tanzy scowled, even as she appreciated the hug. "Yeah, I can hardly wait."

"Maybe before too long we'll hear wedding bells." Sue clapped her hands together. "Just think what Millicent and I can do with that shower!"

"Over my dead body," Tanzy warned. "And if it does ever get that far—and I'm not saying I've even thought about it—we're eloping. I've just decided."

"And deprive the world of watching Tanzy Harrington, perennial lone wolf, tie the knot? Join the herd? Accept what the rest of us have known forever?"

"Which is?"

Sue threw an arm around her shoulders and hugged her. "That love is a wonderful thing, baby."

Tanzy shook her head. "Thank you, Michael Bolton."

Sue laughed, but she went on. "All joking aside, it is a wonderful thing. In all its incarnations. It's easy to say it's not for you when you're not in it, until one day you wake up, and wham! Then there it is, staring you in the face. Daring you to say you don't want it." She grinned. "And you thought dating was an adventure. Honey, you don't even know."

"Well, don't get ahead of yourself here."

Sue merely winked at her as, mercifully, the guests began to logjam the foyer. Tanzy helped herself to a glass of punch, wishing like hell they'd planned this thing for a bit later than two in the afternoon. Then the punch could have been spiked.

Rina showed up next, looking almost as uncomfortable as Tanzy. She stuck close, armed with a cookie in one hand and a punch glass in the other. "Did you talk to Sloan?" she asked Rina, as Sue continued to welcome friends and members of Mariel's family the rest of them had never met. Thank God for Mariel's mother, or the guest list would have been very small.

"She'll be here." Rina sent Tanzy a look. "We talked. At the gallery. After you left." She shook her head. "I'm still sort of amazed by it all, but power to her, I say."

Tanzy raised her punch glass. "To getting rubbed the right way."

Rina gave her a look, then both of them snickered and clinked glasses.

"Get a load of that one," Rina said with a nod. She pointed her glass in the general direction of a woman who'd just entered the room wearing a wide-brimmed, rose-adorned hat. "That's almost as hideous as those mice."

Tanzy swallowed a laugh. "Now, now. I'm sure she thinks she's the height of fashion."

"Circa 1932 maybe. I wonder which side of the family she's from. Hopefully not Mariel's."

"Well, we can't pick our relatives." Tanzy made a face. "I should know."

Sue came in just then and clapped her hands. "Okay, everyone, places. Her car just pulled up."

Rina and Tanzy exchanged looks. "She missed her calling."

"Broadway?" Rina murmured.

"No," Tanzy interjected as they joined the rest of the group. "Dictator of Disney World."

"Shhh," Rina said, giggling, as Sue shushed them all, sending a fierce glance their way.

Tanzy and Rina made a silent show of locking up their lips and throwing away the key.

Sue merely rolled her eyes and went back to the foyer.

"Where's Tanzy? Are Rina and Sloan coming?" they heard Mariel ask as she came in. "I'm sorry I couldn't make it to the gallery last night. The baby's taken up Tae Bo or something and my ribs feel like a well-used set of bongo drums."

"Millicent set up tea in the formal parlor," Sue was saying.

"It was really nice of you guys to do this for me. You didn't have to, you know. I appreciate it. I really didn't want any fuss, so it's nice knowing it's just going to be the four of—"

"SURPRISE!"

Everyone stepped forward as one when Sue and Mariel came into the room. Mariel squealed, then grabbed her belly, and Tanzy was certain they'd shocked her right into labor. She ran forward, put her arm around her, with Sue on the other side. "We wanted it to be a surprise, but I swear if you have the baby right here in front of me, I won't be held responsible for my actions," Tanzy told her.

Mariel just looked up, tears of joy in her eyes. "Oh my God. I can't believe you guys did this!"

Tanzy exchanged looks with Sue. She'd said all along that with as much as Mariel loved being the center of attention, there was no such thing as overkill. "You da man," Tanzy whispered to Sue, who smiled smugly. To Mariel, she said, "You owe this all to Sue."

"And Tanzy's aunt Millicent," Sue interjected. "She took my ideas, and well—" They stepped back so Mariel could enter Mother Goose Land.

Mariel gasped, then cried, "It's . . . it's just wonderful."

After Rina hugged her, the two of them retreated to their place by the mice and watched Sue lead Mariel through the throng so she could accept hugs and cry more tears as she greeted her other friends and family.

Sloan scooted in, unnoticed, and took Tanzy's punch glass by way of hello. After downing the contents, she smiled and said, "Did I miss much?" Only then did she notice the décor. "Oh. My. God."

"Pretty much sums it up," Tanzy agreed. "Memo to self: Never underestimate the combined power of Sue and Millicent. It could get scary if they joined forces on a regular basis."

Sloan's still wide-eyed gaze wandered the room. "Yeah," she breathed. "They might rule the world."

"But at least it would be color coordinated and have a theme," Rina put in.

"Maybe we should send them to the Middle East," Sloan added.

Laughing, Tanzy nudged Sloan in the ribs. "You're looking pretty perky. Cheeks flushed, eyes sparkling. Let me guess, it wasn't some big account that made you late."

"Let's just say it was some big thing and leave it at that."

Tanzy would have choked on her punch, had Sloan not already downed it. "Hey, those are my lines."

"Yeah, well, one of us has to be a last bridesmaid, apparently." She grinned and scanned Tanzy from head to toe. "And, judging from your flushed cheeks and sparkling eyes, I'm guessing it's my turn."

Rina and Tanzy hugged her. Despite how happy she seemed, divorce was never easy. "We're all here for you, you know."

Rina was watching as Sue seated Mariel beneath a beach-size frilly umbrella that hung from the vaulted ceiling and said, "Maybe we can get Millicent and Sue to throw you a happily divorced party."

Tanzy shot her a look, but Sloan actually laughed. "Do you think if I mention I want strippers, they'll be this inventive?"

Rina and Tanzy both laughed with her. "That could be worth the risk," Tanzy said.

Then someone cleared his throat behind her. She turned to find Martin standing there, eyes still a bit glazed in shock as he took in the room.

Rina and Sloan looked at her questioningly, but Tanzy mouthed, "I'll explain later," and quickly escorted Martin to the front parlor, which she and Riley had agreed would be the meeting location.

"I'm so sorry to drag you out here on a weekend." She tried hard not to sound nervous, and yet she had to clasp her hands together to keep them from shaking. It was ridiculous really. He was her boss. Her friend. And it took every bit of willpower she possessed to keep from blurting out, "Are you obsessively in love with me?" Just the fact that she'd thought it should make her want to laugh hysterically. Instead she felt like she was going to puke.

"I had no idea," he was saying, smiling at her, also looking somewhat nervous. "About the party, I mean. I feel like I'm intruding."

Were those the words of a man who'd been stalking her? She didn't think so. Or didn't want to think so.

"Trust me, with all the hoopla going on in there, I'll never be missed." Probably *not* the thing to mention to a potential stalker.

"Wow," he said upon entering the parlor. "I see your aunt believes in leaving no room undecorated." He wandered into the room, looking at the various ornaments, pausing beneath the giant chandelier.

Tanzy thought about the first time she'd stood there, the

moment she'd first met Riley. She knew he was watching them, right this very second. She cleared her throat. She and Riley had agreed on this course of action, but putting it into motion was a lot harder than she'd thought it would be. "I, uh, I have some papers I want you to look at." The plan was to show him the SoulM8 emails, explain her concerns, without necessarily coming right out and asking him directly if he was behind the emails. She—and Riley—would monitor his reaction. And, at the very least, get his fingerprints on the documents.

"Oh?" He glanced at her, must have seen something in her expression, because his shoulders slumped and he let out a long sigh. "Oh," he repeated, this time with great resignation. "I knew it."

Tanzy's heart plummeted. *Dear God, could it really be?* He'd probably suspected the jig was up when she invited him here. That explained his nervousness. She should have been freaked out by the quasi-admission, but looking at the bleak expression on his face, all she could feel was sad. Immeasurably sad. For both of them. "Martin, really, you had to know that I'd—"

"Yeah, yeah," he interrupted, still not looking at her. "I saw it coming. I—I just didn't want to believe it." He scrubbed a hand over his face. "It sounds crazy, because I know this is business, not personal. But . . . well, I guess I always felt like we were more than merely business associates. That we'd be together for the long haul."

"Oh, Martin." Tanzy wanted to cry. *How had this happened? When had this happened?* But he looked so forlorn, she couldn't bring herself to torture him with a barrage of questions. Yes, she'd been victimized by him, but it was clear now that, from his perspective, they'd been harmless love letters. *Oh, Martin.* If only she'd confronted him sooner they could have both saved themselves a great deal of anguish.

"Listen, I know this is hard—"

He laughed, though there was no humor in it. "So what else is new?" He sighed again. "When your column took off, I admit I got a little excited. I guess I needed to feel ... needed. My life has been—well, you don't need to hear about that. The thing is, I let my own selfish needs blind me."

"You're going through a rough time," Tanzy told him. "We all have them."

Just then Rina poked her head in. "I'm really, really sorry to interrupt, but the punch bowl is empty, the food is disappearing, and Sue is hip deep in diaper pails and baby blankets. You said no caterer, so can you direct me to where the rest of the stuff is?"

Tanzy looked at Rina, then at Martin, who waved his hand. "Go, go. Please. I feel guilty enough as it is. We can finish all this up later."

"Are you sure?" She glanced at Rina, who was looking more than a little overwhelmed, and said, "I'll be out in a minute, just go hold the fort down." She looked back at Martin, who nodded.

"Please," he said.

"Okay." She sighed then, unable to believe it was all over. And so simply. She looked at Martin, who looked miserable. Okay, not so simply. Not for him. "Why don't you at least stay long enough to grab a bite to eat, maybe look around a little. I know you've mentioned before you always wanted to see Big Harry. I wish I had time for a guided tour—"

He shook his head. "No, I understand. And ... well, I want to thank you. For being strong enough to do this face-to-face. You're a class act. Always have been."

Tanzy smiled, felt like she was going to cry. "Thanks. So have you." She pointed him in the direction of the party. "Go. Have quiche. It sounds like it's winding down.

Millicent is here. She loves to show off the place, especially at Christmas."

She foisted him off on Rina, then ducked down the hall, pushing the punch-bowl cart laden with empty food platters to the kitchens for a refill. The reality that it was truly and finally over began to sink in, leaving her feeling almost light-headed, giddy. Mariel, she noted, seemed thrilled with all her booty. Rina had mentioned that Mariel'd been particularly touched by the baby-milestones journaling book Sue had helped Tanzy pick out. Appropriate from a writer, she'd thought. She'd noticed Sue looking over the mountain of baby gifts, cooing and ahhing, as she'd left the room.

"Oh, she's definitely next," she murmured, trundling down the hall. Anyone who looked that rapturous over some contraption that cleaned diapers was a total goner. At least it looked like Mariel would have someone to gab baby with, mercifully leaving the rest of them out of it.

God, the kitchen looked like a war zone. Millicent had offered to have the entire event catered and they'd eventually agreed to have the food brought in, but no wait staff. Tanzy hated having to insist on that, but after the charity ball, both she and Riley felt better knowing there was no hired help on the premises, no matter how vetted the caterer was ahead of time. Looking at the kitchens now, with the stalker crisis over and done with, she really wished she'd lightened up on the catering embargo.

"Need a hand?"

Tanzy squealed and jumped about a foot. Hand to her chest, she turned to find Riley lounging in the doorway. "God, you scared ten years off of me."

"I'm sorry, I thought you heard me." He took the bowl from her hands and put it on the counter, then drew her into his arms. "You okay?"

"Yeah. I guess you saw and heard everything?"

"Yeah." He didn't say anything else, just pulled her against his chest and rubbed her back. "I'm sorry."

She hadn't known what to expect from Riley. She should have known it would be compassion. For her, and for Martin. "It's so sad, really. I think he was just lonely. And one thing led to another and he built up this whole other fantasy in his head. I just wish I'd brought it all out in the open sooner."

"We didn't know. And I still think it was better to be cautious."

She smiled up at him. "Yeah, easy to say now that being cautious ended up landing us in bed together."

"Well, there is that." He grinned, then leaned down and kissed her. "I was really proud of how you handled the whole thing."

She hugged him. "Thanks. I—" She shook her head. "It's going to be a little weird for a while, but I think we nipped it off in a way that will allow us to salvage our working relationship okay. I just hope he gets some help."

"Yeah." Riley looked beyond her to the disaster area that was the kitchen. "You'll be happy to know I gave Millicent the go-ahead to bring in a cleaning crew when this is over."

"Does she know? About Martin?"

"I didn't think this was the right time. Who knows what she'd say to him."

Tanzy shuddered, glad they'd never included her great-aunt in their little plan. She'd have never been able to pull it off if she thought Millicent was out in the foyer, eavesdropping on the whole thing. Which she assuredly would have been, one way or the other. "True. What did you tell her?"

"I just whispered that the crisis was over and that we'd discuss it later, after the party. She's off giving Martin the grand tour."

"Oh, good." She took a breath, then let it out. "I can't

believe it's really over." She looked at the punch cart. "I guess I'd better get out there with more stuff before they start gnawing on the diapers. Who knew a bunch of women could eat and drink so much. Must be all the baby talk. Nesting hormones and eating for two, and all that rot."

Riley laughed. "It's not contagious, you know."

"Tell that to Sue." Tanzy began arranging food on the empty platters. "Sloan showed up."

"Yeah, I saw."

"Right. I forgot. You were upstairs playing Rocket Powers, International Man of Mystery."

"You're so amusing."

She gave him a cheeky grin. "I certainly try."

He kissed her, and what started out as a brief kiss turned into another, then another. "You sure you don't want to leave a bit early? I think wrapping this up deserves a celebration. I had something for two in mind."

"I can't leave until this is done. Sue would never forgive me. As it is, she'll want a full explanation of where I was during the gift oohing and ahhing portion of her program. I figure we have another hour at least." She smacked at his arm when he went to pull her back into his arms. "Stop flirting with the help."

"Wait till I show off my big muscles and manhandle that full punch bowl onto the cart for you. Gets 'em every time."

"If you really want to prove your manhood, you'll roll the cart into the parlor so I can carry these last trays of food out there."

He didn't even blink. "Sure thing."

"I don't think you understand. A roomful of women? Playing with baby things? Nesting? Cooing? It's the estrogen ocean in there."

He just winked. "I'm Rocket Powers, remember? If you get bored or you just need a break from bassinettes and strollers, you know where to find me." He rolled the cart to the door.

Tanzy pictured the women in the room enjoying watching Riley. She certainly did. He'd make an interesting contrast to all the pinks and blues, geese and mice. "Be brave," she called after him.

"I've managed to face the best defense the NFL can throw at me. I can handle this."

"Ah, but you underestimate us, grasshopper. Women have a sixth sense about weak spots. And you with that bum knee." She *tsk*ed. "You'll never stand a chance."

"You'll rescue me if necessary?"

She grinned and patted her hip. "I've got my estrogen laser gun already set to stun." She heard him chuckling as he rolled the cart down the hall. Still grinning, she turned back to the trays of food, suddenly feeling a whole lot more settled about the entire thing.

She was actually humming a tune to Jack and Jill, as she arranged the similarly themed salt and pepper shakers on one of the trays, when she heard him come back in.

"If you're coming back in here to lure me upstairs," she began, a wicked smile curving her lips, "you just might succeed. Because I was thinking that I could save some of these cherries and—"

"Finally, we're alone. I've waited such a long time for this moment."

Tanzy started in surprise. It wasn't Riley behind her. It was just one of the guests. What had she said? *Waited such a long time for this—?* Oh, she realized a second later. One of the ladies must have recognized her, had probably been waiting for a private moment to ask for an autograph.

She pasted a smile on her face and spun around. And felt her heart stutter. It was the woman with the floppy flower hat. Mariel's unfortunately frumpy relative. Only looking at her straight on, Tanzy now realized she'd seen her before. And not in Mariel's family photo album. She'd been thrown off by the dead-brown shade of hair. It had been blond in the employee photo.

"Margaret? Margaret Swingler?"

Her eyes, hidden behind thick-lensed glasses that made even Riley's sheep frames look stylish, widened slightly. "You've known? Known it was me?" She clasped her hands together, a look of almost maniacal rapture lighting her face.

It was the maniacal part Tanzy keyed in on. *Oh. My. God.*

Well, it appears I have an apology to make.

Someone, who shall remain nameless, pointed out to me that by categorizing men into sheep and wolves, I was really shortchanging both groups. I wasn't sure I agreed at the time. But now that I'm spending serious quality time with a man who could rightfully claim a space in both the herd and the pack, I suppose I have to admit that he might have had a point.

23

Martin wasn't her stalker after all!

But then, what in the hell had they just been talking about in the front parlor?

Tanzy would have to worry about that later. Right now, SoulM8's sister, or cousin, or whoever, was definitely commanding all of her attention.

And if this was indeed SoulM8's sister, it was apparent the whack-job gene ran rampant in the family.

"I hadn't dreamed—" the woman began, obviously flustered now. "I thought—When I saw you with—" She stopped, and actually pulled a hanky from the sleeve of her poorly designed suit. She shifted her glasses so she could dab at the corners of her eyes. "But I see now. It all makes sense. It was just a cover, wasn't it? If I'd only known you were waiting for me, I'd have come sooner."

Tanzy scrambled mentally, trying to figure out what in the world she was talking about. But coming on the heels of her supposed revelation from Martin, she was beyond comprehending what in the hell was going on. Margaret was obviously SoulM8's messenger, no doubt about it, but now that her words were sinking in, it sounded a hell of lot like *she* was the one with the fixation. Oh God. "It was you all along," Tanzy whispered. "The emails, the notes." A woman. They'd never even suspected, always assumed—

And it all came together then, making some bizarre sort of twisted sense. *You don't need any man. You have me.*

Mentally reviewing the emails in her head, all of them could have been written by a woman. Why hadn't either of them seen that? They'd simply leaped to the assumption that if someone had developed this fanatical passion for her, it had to be a man. She actually had to bite back the sudden, hysterical urge to laugh. Tanzy Harrington, notorious man-eater, was being stalked by a lesbian!

Margaret's smile began to falter. "But I thought you just said—"

"I—I did," Tanzy said quickly, trying like hell to stay focused, to think on her feet. "It's just—I can't believe it's you. That we're finally meeting. For real."

Margaret seemed to calm down a bit, though it was hard to tell. Tanzy couldn't stop staring at the overly bright light in the woman's eyes. Was she hopped up on some kind of drug? Or just completely nuts?

"Then I was right. He was for show," Margaret said. "Just for show. That man. I should have known." She was almost muttering, as if angry with herself. She clenched and unclenched her fists. "I should have come to you sooner. Just a decoy. I should have seen."

"Yes, he's just a bodyguard," Tanzy said, hoping to spin her along long enough so said bodyguard could come and find them both.

Margaret swung her wild-eyed gaze to Tanzy. "Why didn't you tell me! We could have been together. All this time."

The sudden shift in anger toward her made Tanzy jump. "My—my manager has this policy about providing protection when I do events. So—so I couldn't let them know. A-about us. For my safety. And yours." She had to force the bile back down her throat. "I sent you my schedule. Didn't you get it? I thought you'd come, then maybe I'd be able to slip away from my bodyguard and—"

"Liar!" Margaret suddenly screamed, her voice cracking oddly. "I saw you with him! On the dance floor. He—he put his hands on you." She shuddered almost violently. "You allowed it!"

"It was an act," Tanzy said quickly, backing up as Margaret took a step toward her.

She was grappling with her oversize, god-awful ugly purse. And Tanzy had a sick sense that there was a god-awful weapon tucked right inside of it, too.

"I had to pretend, to keep the others away," she improvised. "But I thought you, of all people, would see that." She sidled a bit to the left, hoping for a good angle to the door in case she could somehow make a run for it.

But Margaret saw her movement at the same instant she finally undid the clasp of her purse.

Tanzy had been right about the god-awful weapon. And though one part of her brain very rationally decided that the tiny silver derringer Margaret pulled out wasn't all that big, the other part of her brain decided, when the barrel was pointed right at her, that it might as well be a Howitzer.

They were equally deadly.

"Please, let me explain," Tanzy said, hoping she sounded confident. And not like a woman about to have a hole blasted into her. Margaret's hand was shaking, which didn't help much, since she might accidentally pull the trigger. But it was proof that she wasn't any cooler with this than Tanzy was.

Tanzy took a deep, steadying breath and slowly reached out with her left hand. Her right hand crept behind her back, searching the counter for anything she might use as a weapon. "Please, Margaret. Give me the gun. We don't need it." It took every bit of her willpower to utter the next words. "I want to be with you."

And if she ever had any doubts that she wanted to spend the rest of her life with Riley, they vanished right then. Because she'd have no trouble whatsoever saying those words to him. She loved him.

Tanzy Harrington was in love.

Great. It figured she'd only realize it moments before her tragic death.

She kept her gaze directly on Margaret's. "Don't you want to be with me, too?"

Margaret's entire body began to tremble. "You don't know how I've dreamed about you," she said, her voice strangely hoarse. "About us."

Tanzy tried not to shudder. "Well, now your dreams can come true, can't they? But we need to get rid of that." She nodded to the gun, as if it were merely some insignificant nuisance. She wiggled her fingers. "Just hand it to me. Then we can begin making our plans."

Margaret stared at the gun, then into Tanzy's eyes. "I wanted to wait until all the changes were final," she rasped out. "I—but then you wrote about the wolves at your door. And I couldn't wait. You needed me."

Tanzy had no idea what she was rambling about now. But her wrist had gone limp and the gun was drooping. Just as she stepped in to take it away from her, Riley came into the room.

"I survived, but just bare—" He paused, obviously surprised to find her with a guest, but just as obviously unable to see the gun being pointed at her, what with Margaret and her big honking hat blocking the way.

Margaret jumped at the sound of his voice and spun around just as Tanzy made a lunge for the gun.

"You!" she shrieked.

Riley's eyes went wide and he immediately lowered his shoulder and charged forward.

"No!" Tanzy shouted. Milliseconds of time passed, but it

was plenty long enough for her to imagine a bullet ripping through his chest.

"Stop!" Margaret commanded, suddenly lunging and dragging Tanzy up against her side.

As it turned out, the barrel seemed even bigger when it was jammed into her temple. And Margaret was not only a big woman, she was a strong woman. But it wasn't until she pulled Tanzy around in front of her that Tanzy got the biggest surprise of all.

Margaret wasn't a lesbian.

Not technically. At least not until she/he had that "last step" performed anyway.

"He's ruining everything," Margaret—or whatever his/her name really was—whispered viciously. "Tell him," he commanded Tanzy. "Tell him how you feel about men. You call them wolves, but we both know they're really dogs. Taking their pleasure, rutting on us like animals, then walking away." His grip tightened at her throat, cutting off her air. "It sickens me and I've hated the curse I've been saddled with all these years." He leaned down, pressing his mouth closer to her ear. "But not for long. It won't be like that for us. Don't you see? I'm the perfect one for you. I've known it for a long time." He jerked Tanzy's head back with a forearm across her throat and stared, crazed, at Riley. "All. Mine."

Riley stood motionless just inside the door. He looked directly into Tanzy's eyes. Spots were dancing around the edges of her vision, but she focused on Riley's face, his gaze.

Trust me.

She couldn't have heard him any more clearly if he'd actually spoken the words aloud.

She clenched her fists, fighting for air, only then realizing she had reflexively grabbed something from the counter when Margaret/whoever lunged for her. It was one of the Jack and Jill salt and pepper shakers.

Wonderful, she thought blindly. *I can season him to death.*

She couldn't even move enough to give Riley the barest of nods. She could only hope he'd read the same message in her eyes. He was focused exclusively on Margaret now. Since she—he—was the one holding the deadly weapon, Tanzy was perfectly fine with that. She wished there was some way to signal to Riley that Margaret was really a Mike, but since there was a gun involved, it probably didn't really matter the gender of the person holding it.

Bullets. The great equalizers.

She had a fleeting thought to expand on that in one of her columns. She could title it "Gender Equality: Guns at Work & at Play," which was proof right there that she was close to passing out.

"I just wanted to make sure she was in good hands," Riley said, slowly straightening, visibly relaxing his six-foot frame and once again adopting the ultimate neutral sheep voice he'd employed what seemed like a lifetime ago. "I can see you're quite capable of handling her."

He lifted his hands slowly, palms out, and stepped carefully away, so his back was actually just outside the door.

Man Margaret mercifully eased up on Tanzy's throat, but then slowly stroked the gun barrel down the side of her face. It took the last remaining shreds of Tanzy's willpower not to throw up, or pass out, at the look Margaret beamed down at her. "Yes. Yes, I can."

"Put the gun down."

Margaret and Tanzy looked back at him at the same time.

He had crossed the room and was now pointing a gun that made Man Margaret's look like a toy.

Tanzy decided right then and there that she was perfectly happy with Sheep Riley for the rest of her life.

Because she could go an awfully long time without ever seeing him handle a gun again. Or, more to the point, in a situation where handling a gun was his only option.

"You don't want to do that," Margaret warned.

Then he made the mistake of pointing the gun at Riley.

And Tanzy acted. She didn't even think it through. If she had, she'd have realized they all could have died in a hail of bullets. But seeing that gun aimed point-blank at Riley's heart was the last straw.

Up came the hand with the pepper, which she tossed in Margaret's eyes at the same instant that she brought the spike heel of her four-hundred-dollar Manolo Blahniks directly up into his soon-to-be-removed balls. "Let me help you out with that," Tanzy grunted.

Margaret howled, a gun went off. Tanzy went flying as Margaret flung her off and crumpled to the ground, cupping his unwanted family jewels. She took a hit in the ribs from the counter, and found her balance just in time to see Riley kick the gun from Margaret's hand and pin him facedown on the inlaid Italian marble floor.

"You okay?" he shouted.

"Yeah," she panted, holding her side. "You?"

"Yeah. Dial 911."

"Already done." Millicent, white-faced and looking every one of her eighty-two years, stood at the door with her hand pressed to her chest. Martin stood just behind her.

"Dear Lord," she said, voice shaking. But a moment later she miraculously pulled herself together, then turned to face the gathering crowd in the hall behind her. "Everyone return to the parlor. Everything is fine."

Martin still stood there, a shocked expression frozen on his face.

"Was that a gunshot?" someone asked from the hallway behind him.

Mercifully Millicent took Martin's arm and guided him

back to the rest of the group. "Champagne cork," she improvised. "We're going to toast the mother-to-be." She even managed a smile. "We have sparkling grape juice for those who can't imbibe." She motioned everyone into the formal parlor. "I'll be in momentarily with the glasses."

Tanzy didn't know which stunned her more, the events of the past fifteen minutes or Millicent's amazing performance. Millicent turned back to face them, and Tanzy realized her great-aunt wasn't as pulled together as she seemed. "Are you both truly all right?" She looked at Riley. "I—I thought you said it was over."

"We did," Tanzy managed. "I—I thought it was Martin."

"Martin? But I told Riley he'd never—"

"It's a long story," Tanzy said, stumbling her way over to Riley, who'd bound Margaret's hands with a cord he'd cut off the blender.

Margaret wasn't writhing or moaning. In fact, she seemed to be rather unconscious.

"I might have hit her head a bit too hard on the floor when I pinned her." Riley's expression wasn't exactly filled with remorse. "But she'll live." To Millicent he said, "I owe you a new appliance, Ms. Harrington." He rose unsteadily to his feet.

"Nonsense," she said, coming into the room and pulling both Tanzy and Riley close. "You just saved my girl here."

"Actually, she saved herself," Riley said, the first hint of a smile coming back to his face. "I was just the token male."

"Actually," Tanzy said, smiling for the first time as she looked at the unconscious form trussed up on the kitchen floor, "you might be surprised about that."

Hours later, Riley finally had Tanzy all to himself. The police had gone. The remaining guests had been released. Martin had gone home, but not until after a full explanation.

Tanzy and her girlfriends had huddled in the front parlor for the duration of the questioning. Mariel had thankfully managed to not give birth and had, despite it all, tearfully thanked them for a wonderful day.

But now they were all gone. And Riley had clearance to take Tanzy home. The only question remaining was which home she wanted to go to.

"I still can't believe Martin thought I'd called him here to tell him I was leaving *MainLine* for national newspaper syndication." She laughed. "I mean, when you think about what he said—" She shook her head. "I can't believe I thought—" She couldn't finish.

Martin had blushed fiercely when Tanzy had explained their suspicions. Thankfully, having witnessed Margaret's actions, he realized what kind of duress Tanzy had been under, and harbored no hard feelings that she'd suspected him. In fact, now that it was all said and done, he'd even admitted to being a bit flattered that she'd think him capable of a midlife affair. On another positive note, upon seeing how close Riley and Tanzy had come to not having a relationship to even begin, he'd vowed to go straight home and do whatever it took to convince Giselle to go into marriage counseling with him.

"I think saying this has been one hell of a day is the understatement of the century," Riley said. Now that all had been revealed, solved, and taken care of, at least until a trial date was set, it was slowly sinking into his rattled brain that his job here was over. Which meant his professional need to be around Tanzy twenty-four/seven had also come to an end.

So he just had to come up with another reason to stick close.

Millicent stepped into the upstairs office, where Riley was packing up the last of his gear. She reached out her hands and Tanzy climbed out of the recliner chair and went immediately into her arms.

"Thank God it's all over," Millicent said.

"I'm so sorry to have brought this here," Tanzy said, for what had to be the dozenth time.

And for the dozenth time, Millicent *tsk*ed her silent. After another hug, she held Tanzy back at arm's length. "Perhaps I have something else to be thankful for this holiday season. You know I've always believed in letting you chart your own course. And that hasn't changed. You've said, however, that you wanted to get a bit involved with the Harrington holdings. I would greatly enjoy that. But I have a similar request."

"You do?"

"I very much enjoyed being part of today's festivities. Well, all but that last bit of business anyway. I enjoy your friends and enjoy seeing you with them. I—I don't know how to say this without sounding like an old woman horning in where she isn't wanted, but . . . well, I'd like us to spend more time together. Perhaps I could attend one of your show tapings."

Tanzy grinned. "Really? I'd be delighted."

Millicent sighed, as if greatly relieved. As if she thought anyone could deny her anything, Riley thought privately.

"Well then," she said, uncustomarily at a loss for words. "That's lovely, then, isn't it?" Quite customarily, she regrouped quickly. "I think with all our talk of family and the past, I've realized that perhaps we've given each other a bit too much distance. I did it out of respect, not any lack of love, but—"

"Oh, Aunt Millie," Tanzy said, voice wavering as she pulled her great-aunt into her arms once again. "I love you, too."

Millicent was so pleased, she didn't even mention the dreaded use of the forbidden nickname. "Well then," she said, wiping some suspicious moisture from her own eyes. "I suppose I'll let you two finish packing up. Perhaps we can see one another over the holidays."

Riley chose that moment to step forward. Millicent had already cornered him and made certain he knew how profusely grateful she was for all he'd done. She'd made it clear Parrish Securities would be put forth for employment possibilities with everyone she knew. So Riley had been forced to tell her about his very recent decision to retire from the security business.

He hadn't even told Tanzy yet. But if Millicent's reaction to his newly decided career direction was any indication... Well, he just hoped Tanzy took the news half as well. He didn't want to think about how Finn was going to handle it. Of course, he had a sneaking suspicion that with Jacqueline in the picture, his father's working days were numbered anyway. And if he had to sell the house to make both their dreams come true, then he'd gladly do it.

A house was just a house. He looked at Tanzy and realized that home was simply wherever she was going to be.

"I'm supposed to have dinner Christmas night with my father and a friend of his," Riley told Millicent. "But I'd love it—" He took Tanzy's hand. "We'd love it, if you would come with us, also."

Tanzy's look of surprise changed swiftly to one of approval. "Please," she said.

Momentarily surprised by the invitation, Millicent also beamed. "Why, I'd be delighted. Do you have a place picked out already? Because I'd be more than delighted to host—"

Both Tanzy and Riley spoke at the same time. "No, that's okay." They shared a quick glance, then Tanzy said, "You've done so much already, what with this lavish bash for Mariel. We couldn't possibly impose."

The sage and sharp Millicent came back to the forefront as she stared them both down. She didn't even need the monocle. Finally she smiled and folded her hands together. "Fine, then. Just ring me with the details and I'll be there with bells on."

With a last kiss to Tanzy's cheek, as well as one on Riley's, she waltzed to the door. "I've got to see to the cleaning crew. It's quite the mess down there."

Once she was gone, Riley immediately pulled Tanzy into his arms. They simply stood like that, foreheads pressed together, for a long moment.

Finally, when he thought he could kiss her without consuming her whole, Riley leaned in and took his time with her mouth. She was smiling when he lifted his head.

"That's what I wanted to see." Color was starting to come back into her cheeks. "I—" He still couldn't put it into words, the emotions that had rocked him when he'd seen that gun at her temple. He pulled her tightly against his chest. "I don't want us to go through anything like that ever again."

"Me, either," Tanzy said, her words muffled against his chest. She leaned back, cupped his face and looked into his eyes. "I'm thinking I liked my Sheep Man better. He didn't pack heat."

He smiled then, bumped his hips against hers. "I don't know, I'm feeling a little hot."

Her lips twitched. "Imagine that."

Riley's smile faded. "I've got something to tell you."

Tanzy's smile faded, too. Along with what little color she'd recovered. "What is it?"

"Well, I haven't talked to Finn yet. Although, as it happens, I have told Millicent. But I had no choice."

"What are you talking about?"

"My job. I'm quitting it."

Tanzy fell against him, heaving a sigh of relief. "Oh, thank God."

"Did you hate it that much?" he said, half laughing at her response. "And do you even want to know what I will be doing?"

"It wasn't that, although I must say I could go the rest of my life being perfectly happy knowing you aren't carrying a gun, much less ever in a position to have to use it."

"The rest of your life, huh?"

She nodded, quite seriously.

"So, if it wasn't my job, why the relief?"

"It was just when you made that 'I have something to tell you' statement, you sounded so ominous. I've been racking my brain trying to come up with some reason to keep you around, now that you'll be moving on to another stakeout and all." She stopped, laughed. "Except I guess you won't have another stakeout, will you?"

He shook his head, doing everything he could to keep from pumping his fist and whooping for joy. So, she wanted to keep him around, huh? He might just be able to manage that.

"With everything going on, I haven't been able to think real clearly about anything. Except for one thing." She wrapped her arms around his waist. "I don't want this to be over. Not now. Not after Christmas. Just . . . not."

"Well, I do have a perfectly good reason to stick around."

"You do?"

"First you must pass one important test."

"Oh God, it's a sports question, isn't it? You told me there wouldn't be any quizzes after we watched that game together."

"You didn't watch the game, you watched a bunch of men in shorts and bulging biceps run up and down the court."

She grinned. "I was that obvious, huh?"

"Just a little."

She patted his butt. "Well, if I'd seen you in those tight football pants, I'd have hollered for you to shoot from the outside, too."

Riley just sighed. It was only the beginning of playoffs. He could get her up to speed by the Super Bowl. Okay, maybe by next year's Super Bowl.

"But it is a sports question. Sort of."

"The Lakers have cuter butts. But the Nets have bigger biceps."

He had to laugh. "No, that wasn't it."

"Damn," she said. "I just used up my entire font of sports trivia knowledge."

"What would you think, given your depth of love for the game, about hanging out with a guy who coaches college ball?"

Tanzy's eyes went wide. "Really? Where?"

"Here. At SFSU. It's not a done deal yet. But I'm meeting with them next week." He just held on as she jumped up and down, still holding his waist. "It doesn't pay all that well, but—"

She stopped instantly and looked at him. "Now it's your turn to answer a question. Do you honestly think that makes any difference to me? Did I ever—"

"No. But it means I might have to sell the house."

"Sell the house? Why?"

"I think Finn is about to ride off into the sunset. From a look at the glitter dripping off of Jacqueline's hand the other night, he might not need financial backing to do it, but if he does—"

"I don't want you to lose the house, Riley. And I'm not exactly broke."

"I don't want your money."

"It might just be a package deal."

They stared at each other stubbornly. "Why don't we

just wait until after dinner with them next week to discuss this," he said.

She sighed finally and relented. "I just don't want you to lose anything else," she said quietly, then reached up to stroke his face. "You've lost enough."

He kissed her then, and there was so much emotion in it, they were both a bit glassy-eyed when he finally let her go. "I've found you," he said hoarsely, "and that's more than I ever thought I'd have. I love you, Tanzanita Harrington. I want to have you in my life. For as long as you'll have me in yours." His lips curved in that sexy, boyish grin. "We can duke out who pays for what later, okay?"

She was staring at him. "Say that again?"

"I said I don't care who pays for what. Except maybe the shoes. I've seen your closet."

She laughed. "Oh, like those hefty basketball shoes don't go for a few bucks. I may not know Michael Jordan from Tiger Woods, but I do know how much his shoes go for." She squeezed him tight. "But that wasn't what I was referring to."

"I love you."

She sighed lustily and let her cheek rest on his chest. "Yeah. That. I don't think I'm ever going to get tired of that."

He tipped her chin up. "I probably wouldn't, either."

"You think?" she said, teasingly.

Now he sighed. "You're going to make me beg, aren't you?"

"Would I do that to the man I love?" Her eyes lit up then, and it wasn't a teasing light he saw there. "I do love you, Riley Parrish." She linked her arms around his neck. "And I might not know much about sports teams, but I do know we make a good team. I think I'm all done being a free agent. How about it? Will you take me as your first-round draft pick?"

He laughed. "Is that a proposition?"

She grinned. "No, that was a proposal." She tipped up on her toes and whispered in his ear.

He growled and scooped her up in his arms.

"That," she said with a satisfied grin, "was a proposition."

"Yes," he said. "To both."

Happily Ever After. A fairy tale? Perhaps. But we keep getting married, hunting for it. Maybe it's really just as simple as the species driven to propagate. Or maybe I'm a closet romantic coming out of the closet. I'll have to ponder that while I ride off into the sunset.

Oh, and by the way, does anyone have any handbooks on Football for Total Sports Losers? And while you're at it, if you've got any suggestions on how to keep a two-ton, three-year-old pound puppy from crawling into bed every night, I'm all ears. He's adorable, but hell on my sex life. One man in my bed for the rest of my life is all I need.

About the Author

Nationally bestselling author Donna Kauffman resides in northern Virginia, the alpha female living amongst her own personal pack of wolves (aka her teenage sons and husband). She has tried repeatedly, with little success, to instill at least a little sheep behavior in them. At this point, she'd be happy if they'd just put the seat down.

Did

The Big Bad Wolf Tells All

leave you howling for more?

Then turn the page to brush up on your

The Cinderella Rules . . .

available now

and let

Dear Prince Charming

on sale August 2004

sweep you off your feet!

Donna Kauffman

Author of *The Big Bad Wolf Tells All*

The Cinderella RULES

Rule #1:
Always try on more than one glass slipper.

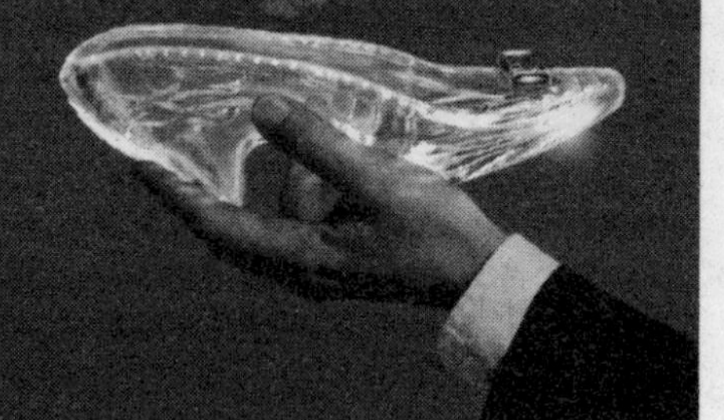

The Cinderella Rules
On Sale Now

Cinderella Rule # 1

While life occasionally makes it appear otherwise, no one has control over your life . . . but you. Make decisions with care, because in the end, you have only yourself to blame for the outcome.

—MERCEDES BROWNING, COFOUNDER
GLASS SLIPPER, INC.

"Do *not* tell me you had Tugger stop me in the middle of playing midwife to a first-time mother because you're stuck somewhere and need me to bail you out. Again."

Darby Landon didn't wait for a response, but tucked the cell phone under one arm so she could pull off her bicep-length rubber gloves, glaring at Tugger Jack, her ranch manager and all-around right hand. "I'll deal with you later," she told him as she squeezed by.

He shrugged and quickly ducked into the horse stall to take over where she'd left off. "Said it was a matter of life and death," she heard him mutter as the stall door clicked shut. "Don't pay me enough to listen to a woman cry."

"I don't pay *me* enough to have to put up with any of this," Darby grumbled. She wiped the phone off on the tail of her overalls and shifted it back to her ear, as her baby sister continued her latest version of Rescue Me. Baby being the key word. Despite the fact that Pepper had recently turned twenty-three.

Darby stalked out of the barn and across the back stretch of grass to the farmhouse situated on the rise about twenty yards away. Of course, anyone who was old enough to vote and still went by her childhood nickname had serious issues anyway. Not that her only sister did anything as important as vote, unless it was a *People* magazine poll on the world's sexiest bachelor.

Darby knocked her boots against the frame as her sister continued to whine in her ear, then pushed through the screen door to the back porch and went straight to the fridge she kept in the outside corner. That way she didn't have to track barn crud into the house more often than she managed to anyway. To be fair, of course, if she'd stayed back East, she'd likely be a thirty-year-old, politically conscious, *Town & Country* subscribing BiBi or Dinky herself by now.

She popped the top on a can of soda and took a long gulp, then rolled it across her sweaty forehead, ignoring the resulting smear of grime, and used her sleeve to wipe off the wet left from the can. "You can't keep doing stuff like this, Pepper," she said, finally interrupting the steady chatter she'd let flow in one ear and out the other.

"But I didn't *do* anything. I can't help it if I'm needed elsewhere. It's not like I'm asking you to come down here. I just need one teensy little favor. I'm sure Daddy won't mind, as long as one of us shows up."

Striving for a calm she definitely didn't feel, Darby spoke slowly, through clenched teeth. "When Dad hears you're not keeping your word—again—he's going to have a cat. And a cow." She broke off, swearing under her breath when she heard her sister's first little sniffle. "You know, he's *this* close to cutting you off permanently, and I don't blame him. After the last stunt you pulled at the regatta in Monaco, he—"

"I know," Pepper wailed. "But it wasn't my fault the ropes got all tangled. I had no idea they were important. You gotta help me out, DarDar."

"And half the reason you didn't worry about literally running a million-dollar sailboat aground in a coral reef is because you knew Dad or I would bail you out. Well, he finally wised up. Maybe it's time I did, too."

"But—"

"And if you value your trust fund, you'll never—ever—call me DarDar again. It makes me feel like an extra on *Star Wars*."

There was dead silence on the other end of the long-distance call, then a snuffle, a little hiccup. And, as always, Darby felt the burden of responsibility begin to creep in. Dammit. "You've got plenty of time to hightail it back home," she said firmly. She wouldn't cave. Not this time. "I'm sure there's an airport within spitting distance of wherever you are." Pepper wasn't much for roughing it.

"But, Dar ... there's something else. Or should I say someone."

"Isn't there always?"

"But it's different with Paolo, Dar, I swear—"

"Paolo?" Darby squeezed the bridge of her nose as the throbbing in her forehead increased. "Where the hell are you calling me from, anyway?"

In a tiny voice, her sister said, "Brazil."

"BRAZIL?" she shouted. No amount of nose-pinching was going to stave off this latest Pepper-induced migraine. Pinching her sister's head off at the neck, maybe. "You said you were out of town, not off the damn continent."

Pepper huffed. "You're being unfair. I wouldn't ask if it weren't important. I do everything for Daddy, and we both know how impossible he is. When was the last time you—"

"June fifteenth. Nineteen-ninety-nine. I showed up for your graduation. I'm due at least another decade or so before I have to descend into the snake pit of Washington power movers and shakers again."

"For Christ's sake, you make it sound like the Animal Kingdom or something."

"Exactly. Watching the food chain in action is a perfect analogy. The powerful feasting on the weak." Darby sighed as the silence spun out. "Listen, you know I've always wanted what was best for you. And I know it's partly my fault for not pushing you to deal with things—"

"And I've told you a million times that you don't have to play mommy to me anymore."

Well, then, grow up, Darby wanted to tell her. And it didn't matter how often Pepper told her she didn't need a mother figure. She did. Hell, they both probably did. Their real mother had died when Darby was eight and Pepper was barely out of the crib. Of course Darby felt responsible for her baby sister. It didn't help matters any that at the age of eleven, Darby had basically run away from home—or away from their father, to be exact. A man who measured a person's value by their net worth. In the case of his two daughters, that translated to parlaying the family name into brokering a decent merger—what other folks called marriage—to another, equally powerful family name.

On that scale, they'd both been dismal failures. Darby could care less, but Pepper had to deal with that reality—and him—on a daily basis.

"Even if I was willing—which I'm not—you really don't want to be counting on me to keep this guy happy until Dad shows up. I'm good with animals, not people."

"But I'm not relying solely on you. I mean, not entirely. I have help all lined up, in fact." She said that last part brightly. Too brightly.

Darby propped open the screen door with her boot and stared unseeingly at the Big Belt Mountains that pitched up just beyond the boundaries of her land, an ominous feeling gathering in the pit of her stomach. "Meaning what, exactly? What have you done now?"

There was a pause, then a slight clearing of throat, then, in a perky voice that would put even Reese Witherspoon to shame, she asked, "Did you see that feature article in *People* magazine? About that company that does makeovers? And I don't mean just beauty makeovers, but, like, entire life makeovers. Glass Slipper, Incorporated?"

"Tell me I am *not* hearing what I think I'm hearing. I like movies as much as the next guy, probably more, given the social life—or lack of one—in Big Bend, Montana. But I don't want to read about the people who act in them. You're the one who cares who Ben Affleck is screwing, not me."

"Now don't get your chaps in a knot," she said, dropping the perky persona. "Just hear me out. Besides, it certainly wouldn't hurt you any to do this. I'm actually doing you a favor when you think about it. In return for the one you're doing for me," she added hastily when Darby growled. "Think of it as a vacation."

"Very funny," Darby said darkly. "This is not about me. This is your harebrained idea. Your problem. And I refuse to be the solution, but thanks for calling. Please let me know when you've found the mind you obviously lost somewhere in the Brazilian jungle."

"Wait! Don't hang up on me, Dar, please?" Pepper resorted to her little-girl wheedling voice, which went a lot further with men—any age, any tax bracket, didn't matter—than it did with Darby. But it was effective enough to keep her from clicking the OFF button. "You know I wouldn't ask if this wasn't absolutely my last possible chance at happiness."

Darby snorted.

"Okay, okay. I know I've been a bit fickle with men." She sighed, deeply and with the kind of palpable emotion that could have made her a star on Broadway. "But he could be the one."

"Pressing the OFF button."

"It's only a week," Pepper cajoled. "And you get a spa vacation."

"Spa vacation. You mean, makeover hell. I've been out

here almost twenty years. It's going to take a lot more than a new hairdo and pair of heels to make me believable as a Washington socialite. This guy I'm supposed to drag all over town and impress for Dad will take one look at me and be on the first plane back to his homeland."

"Which is precisely why Glass Slipper is perfect. That's exactly what they do. They can help get a person past whatever obstacles are in her way to getting what she wants. Whether it's a new job, a new location, a new man, a new life—they'll help give you the tools you need to succeed. It's a week. And only three days of actual society stuff. There are only a few events scheduled that you have to schlep him to. Dad needs this deal to go through. It's important."

Aren't they all? Darby and her father had long ago agreed to disagree. Or, more realistically, she agreed to ignore him and he agreed to pretend he only had one daughter.

"All Dad needs is for someone to play hostess until he can fly in and take over. Stefan is flying into Reagan next Thursday at one. I booked you on a flight into Dulles, arriving Saturday afternoon. I know it's not as close to home as flying into D.C., but it was the only direct flight I could get out of Bozeman and I know how you are about—"

Darby groaned. "God, I hadn't even thought about—"

"There will be a car from Glass Slipper waiting at the main terminal," Pepper rushed on. "You'll be with them through Thursday morning. Then you can pick up Stefan and get settled in at the house. I've already alerted the staff, so everything will be ready."

"You've thought of everything," Darby murmured, still not quite believing she was actually going to go through with this. Twenty minutes ago she'd been shoulder-deep up a mare's birth canal. And perfectly content with her life. Now? She thought about what she was going to face and knew she'd feel a lot scuzzier after twenty minutes back in

Washington than she would later tonight, when her newest foal finally came into the world.

"There's a charity event Thursday night, then the rest of the weekend is easy. You're expected on Friday at the annual Belmont Stakes party at Four Stones. Daddy's supposed to fly in Sunday and meet you out there by midday before the race starts. You can cut out then. All in all, you'll only be gone a week. It's a breeze, really."

Darby sighed. "Who's funding this little Glass Slipper escapade?"

"Paolo," Pepper said. Then, with a little laugh, added, "He considers it an investment in his team's chances for the playoffs." Then she heard a man's deep voice in the background, sexy and cajoling. Then her sister's stifled squeal, the muffled sound of the phone being covered, then Pepper's breathless, "I have to go. Thanks, Darby!"

Darby shook her head, but couldn't help smiling. Pepper was very likely smiling, too, and would be for some time if that deep voice held the kind of promise Darby thought it did. She sighed in envy. "And they said sporting victories couldn't be bought."

Darby fought to maintain that smile as she headed back to the stables, to finish bringing that new foal into the world ... and to talk with Tugger about her upcoming absence.

Any ability to smile was long gone by the time she exited the plane, white-knuckled and pasty-faced, some three days and five hours later. She more than hated flying. She despised it. Had forgotten just how much she despised it until the plane had pulled away from the earth ... and her guts had pulled away from the rest of her insides and twisted into a knot. She had wished the worst South American disease known to mankind on her sister as she'd upchucked horrible airline food into a paper bag at thirty thousand feet. After all, it was only fair.

She collided with more people in the five minutes it took her to navigate her way to Baggage Claim than she'd bumped into in the past year and a half at home. If she hadn't already sworn to walk all the way back to Montana rather than ever set foot inside an airplane again, she'd have hopped on the next plane to Brazil and personally kicked her sister's sorry, soccer-humping ass all the way to Washington.

So the very last thing she needed to see, the capper on a very long day, and the one thing guaranteed to make her feel every yucky inch of herself . . . was the man wearing a crisp black-and-white driver's uniform, standing with a sign bearing her last name in one hand.

And a glass slipper in the other.

Donna Kauffman

Author of *The Cinderella Rules*

America's #1 advice author is about to give away his biggest secret....

Dear Prince Charming
On Sale August 2004

Truth

A key element in successful relationships is honesty. Namely, being able to detect when your significant other isn't practicing it.

—ERIC JERMAINE,
aka Dear Prince Charming

Chapter 1

At age thirty, Valerie Wagner had begun to fear that the fashion career she'd dreamed of since opening her first *Vogue* at age nine was actually a grand and cruel delusion, and perhaps medical intervention might be required in getting her over it.

Maybe her fourth grade teacher, Ms. Spagney, had been right all along. She'd sent *Vogue*-enhanced Valerie home from school the following day with strict instructions to never scare the other students like that again. Privately, Valerie had thought Ms. Spagney could use some heavy kohl eyeliner and spiky bangs herself. It would have done much to hide the deep grooves that came from too many years of frowning down at young, independent thinkers like herself.

However, she'd been objective enough to realize that maybe makeup artist and hairstylist weren't her strengths. So, she'd stared down at her flat chest and thought . . . hmm. Valerie had been the only girl in her sixth grade class secretly thrilled not to need a training bra. After all, she'd never walk the runways in Milan if she had boobies.

Unfortunately, she'd forgotten about the height clause. By sixteen, even in wobbly heels, with hair gelled to within an inch of it's life, she barely flirted with the five-eight mark. Much less the five-ten she knew from her by then slavish devotion to *W* was barest of industry standards.

Cruelly, the now-welcome boobies never had appeared.

Undeterred, she'd resolutely turned to design. If she wasn't made to model fashion, by damn, she'd create it. Which would have been great, except stick figures sporting Magic Marker-colored, triangle-shaped outfits weren't exactly going to win her any scholarships. And yet, she'd hung in there, convinced her calling was still within reach. She'd go for a degree in fashion merchandising and work for an upscale chain as a buyer. She envisioned trips to Paris, London. So what if she had as much chance of balancing her check book as she did of discovering the formula for cold fusion? It wasn't like she was going to be spending her own money, right?

Then had come the Big Breakthrough. In her senior year of high school, the brokerage firm her father worked for had transferred him to Chicago. She'd gotten a summer job with *Madame* magazine—for full figured gals, not call girl employers—though as switchboard operator she'd heard every hooker joke and pimp pun on the planet. She hadn't minded.

She'd found her people.

Obviously she'd just misinterpreted the gospel according to *Elle*. It wasn't the people populating those glossy pages that called to her. It was the glossy pages themselves. Fashion magazines, the force that drove the industry, deciding what was hip and what was hopelessly last year . . . that was her true calling, her primary function, her niche.

Ten years later she'd become a serial niche killer. There wasn't a job she hadn't held. Or gone on to abandon, feeling more unfulfilled and depressed with each failure. Fortunately, she'd stumbled upon her last hope before getting a prescription for Paxil.

When she'd heard that the owners of Glass Slipper, Incorporated, the company renowned for performing what they called "life makeovers," were looking for a publicist for their new endeavor, the glossy *Glass Slipper* magazine, she knew she'd found the career holy grail she'd been searching for. And it was do or die time.

She'd winged her way through what she privately thought was the best job pitch performance of her life. And by performance she meant audition, because it had been the acting job of the century. She had no specific qualifications for the job. But when had that stopped her? She might have been slow finding her own niche, but the upside was she knew a whole lot about everyone elses. So she talked a good game. In fact, talking people into doing things her way was the one special talent she knew she had. In spades.

So when Mercedes Browning contacted her to tell her she'd gotten the job as the publicist for their new endeavor, a bi-monthly glossy magazine, she hadn't been completely surprised.

The real shock was that she hadn't realized her true calling sooner.

And now, six months to the day later, she'd topped it all by scoring the biggest coup in magazine history. Not only had she landed Prince Charming, the mysterious and elusive best-selling self-help author, as *Glass Slipper*'s spokesperson and exclusive columnist . . . she'd gotten him to agree to show his face to the world for the very first time, on the cover of their launch issue!

Valerie wove her way through the crowded outdoor tables at Sonsi's, Potomac's newest swank spot, where Washington movers and shakers came to see and be seen. Because, honestly, despite Chef Andre's impeccable and well advertised qualifications, no one was here because they had an undying craving for venison stuffed pumpkin or Moulard duck wrapped in foie gras and fig.

At the moment, however, she didn't care about unnatural food combinations. She was too busy savoring her triumph and trying to refrain from conga-ing her way through the tables. So many years of trying, of wondering, of worrying if she'd ever get to this moment. Hell, wondering if this moment actually existed. And now, finally, it was here. And it was even better than she could have hoped for.

"Cinderella, eat your heart out," she whispered beneath her breath.

She had the Glass Slipper, she had Prince Charming, she even had her own fairy godmother—three of them in fact. All she needed now was the Bedazzler-encrusted pumpkin carriage and the fairy tale would be complete. Her smile spread to a grin. However, her brand-new, sporty little Beemer would definitely do in the meantime. Life was good.

She waved to the Godmother Collective as she spied their table. In order, Mercedes Browning, Aurora Favreaux, and Vivian dePalma—the founders of Glass Slipper, Inc., and now *Glass Slipper* magazine—nodded, fluttered, and lifted a drink in her general direction as she navigated the final handful of tables.

Flushed with her success and hoping she didn't look as smug as she felt—oh what the hell, how often did one reach a career pinnacle?—Valerie took her seat across from Mercedes, with Aurora and Vivian flanking her on either side. "Everything is set," she announced. "Nigel is onboard. We shoot the cover Monday morning."

"We never had a doubt," Vivian exclaimed, lifting a bottle of Cristal from the ice bucket next to the table. Her trademark flame red hair had been teased into a spiky pouf around her head, her makeup had been stenciled on with laser-like accuracy, and her outfit was as outrageous as always. Of course, most women couldn't make zebra prints work. Valerie had quickly learned that Vivian wasn't most women. The youngest of the three at sixty-eight, Vivian was also the most outspoken. "Let me pour you a glass or three, honey. Lord knows, you've earned it."

"A proper celebration is definitely in order," Aurora added after a quick frown at Vivian. Swathed in layers of gossamer silk, Aurora had that effortless, delicate southern charm that quite successfully hid the steel magnolia beneath.

"So, everything is in order then? You've spoken with Elaine, I assume? No other last-minute emergencies?" Mercedes' expression was serious as always. Valerie privately thought of her as the Eeyore of the group. It had come as no shock to learn that, prior to launching their life-makeover empire, Mercedes had been headmistress of a private New England girls' boarding school.

"For heaven's sake, Mercy, let the girl have some bubbly before you start interrogating her." Vivian handed Valerie her glass, then topped off the other three. "I'm sure everything is just fine. We're ever so grateful." She lifted her glass a bit higher as she turned her attention to them all. "Here's to our new venture, and the dynamite publicist who single-handedly assured us a smashing debut!"

"Here, here," Vivian agreed readily. "Here's to knocking those bitchy industry insiders on their collective jealous asses! And they said our plan to launch a magazine in this 'economic climate' was foolhardy. Ha!"

Mercedes' frown only deepened, but she tipped glasses with the rest of them, then spoke before they'd barely finished swallowing. "You've confirmed with Mr. Jermaine for the cover shoot for Monday?"

Valerie assured her she had, even as Vivian rolled her eyes.

"We're all looking so forward to finally meeting him in the flesh," Aurora said, leaning forward a bit, the multiple rings on her fingers sparkling as the sun reflected off the champagne glass.

"Flesh you've promised is cover model worthy," Vivian reminded her.

"Oh, you won't be disappointed, trust me," Valerie said, enjoying the feel of the fizz as it tickled her nose.

"Here, here," Aurora agreed, finishing off her glass, then covering her mouth when she hiccupped. "Best five hundred grand we've ever spent."

Mercedes just took a deep breath and downed the rest of her champagne.

Valerie knew come Monday, even Mercedes would be won over. Her greatest fear when she'd first met Eric was that he'd be a paunchy, balding guy who looked like he had a better shot at demystifying her taxes than her love life. She couldn't have been proven more spectacularly wrong. Cinderella rules! "Well, you'll all get the chance to see just how well your money has been spent on Monday at the photo shoot."

Just then her cell phone buzzed. "Excuse me," she said, and slipped it from her bag to check the read out. It was Eric. "Speak of the devil," she said with a smile, and flipped the phone open. "Hello, handsome, we were just—"

"Valerie?"

With just that one word, Valerie knew something was wrong. She just managed to keep the concern out of her voice, and hopefully off her face. "It sure is. What's up?"

"We need to talk. Right away. It's—it's important."

Tamping down any hint of alarm, she said, "Just a moment." Then covered the phone. "Why don't I just take this inside, it won't take a minute."

Her mind racing ahead, Valerie tried to fathom what

Eric's problem could possibly be, but nothing sprang to mind. Maybe he had a conflicting engagement with the shoot on Monday. Well, he was going to have to reschedule. Getting Nigel had been her second miracle and no way was she going to risk losing him on this project. They were so close.

As soon as she got a table or two away, she uncovered the phone. "Hi, Eric. I have some privacy now. I'm sure whatever it is, we can handle it. Is this about the shoot on Monday?"

"In a manner of speaking, yes."

She frowned. "I've spoken with Nigel's people and we're confirmed. This is really going to be a wonderful opportunity for us all, Eric. You couldn't be in better hands."

"I know."

He sounded quiet, almost ... remorseful. She was just inside the doorway and waiters were bustling past her with heavily laden trays. She shifted her back to the noise and cupped her hand over her ear, praying it was just the surroundings and that she'd misheard the tone in his voice. "So what is the problem?"

"I've—I need to talk with you. Before I—before we go any further with this."

No personal pep talk in the world would have prevented the alarm from creeping in then. "But we're all set, aren't we?" She wanted to add, "You signed a contract. With a lot of zeroes attached. We sent you a check," but managed not to. Just barely. She couldn't however, keep from glancing over her shoulder, back to the table. All three women were staring in her direction. She managed a brief smile and motioned she was almost done. She turned her back to them and edged further into the wait staff passageway. "Can't you just tell me now? I'm sure whatever it is, we can resolve—"

"Valerie, I'm gay."

He'd just blurted it out in a rush. So fast, she couldn't really absorb it. In fact, after she managed to close her mouth and put the phone back to her ear, she was certain she'd misheard him. "I'm sorry," she said, forcing a light laugh. "It sounded like you just said you're—"

"Gay. I did. And I am. Dammit, I didn't want to tell you this way!" There was a pause, which she had no earthly way of filling. She was as frozen as one of Andre's ice sculptures.

Prince Charming. The man who proved that a guy exists who sees women as human beings first, and sex objects second . . . was gay. She shook her head. *Like we shouldn't have seen that coming.*

She grabbed a glass of something alcoholic off a passing tray and downed it before the waiter even knew it was missing. She looked down, half expecting to see her blue Ann Taylor suit had turned into rags. And her red and white MINI out in the lot had probably turned into a pumpkin.

She hadn't even made it to midnight, dammit.